TEEN TITANS GO!

THEIR GREATEST HIJINKS

Sholly Fisch   Merrill Hagan
Amy Wolfram   Heather Nuhfer
P.C. Morrissey
Writers

Marcelo DiChiara   Dario Brizuela
Jorge Corona   Ben Bates   Jeremy Lawson
Artists

Ben Bates   Jeremy Lawson
Franco Riesco
Colorists

Wes Abbott
Letterer

Dan Hipp
Collection Cover Artist

ALEX ANTONE, KRISTY QUINN Editors - Original Series JESSICA CHEN Associate Editor - Original Series
BRITTANY HOLZHERR Assistant Editor - Original Series JEB WOODARD Group Editor - Collected Editions
ERIKA ROTHBERG Editor - Collected Edition STEVE COOK Design Director - Books LOUIS PRANDI Publication Design

BOB HARRAS Senior VP - Editor-in-Chief, DC Comics PAT McCALLUM Executive Editor, DC Comics

DIANE NELSON President DAN DiDIO Publisher JIM LEE Publisher GEOFF JOHNS President & Chief Creative Officer
AMIT DESAI Executive VP - Business & Marketing Strategy, Direct to Consumer & Global Franchise Management
SAM ADES Senior VP & General Manager, Digital Services BOBBIE CHASE VP & Executive Editor, Young Reader & Talent Development
MARK CHIARELLO Senior VP - Art, Design & Collected Editions JOHN CUNNINGHAM Senior VP - Sales & Trade Marketing
ANNE DePIES Senior VP - Business Strategy, Finance & Administration DON FALLETTI VP - Manufacturing Operations
LAWRENCE GANEM VP - Editorial Administration & Talent Relations ALISON GILL Senior VP - Manufacturing & Operations
HANK KANALZ Senior VP - Editorial Strategy & Administration JAY KOGAN VP - Legal Affairs JACK MAHAN VP - Business Affairs
NICK J. NAPOLITANO VP - Manufacturing Administration EDDIE SCANNELL VP - Consumer Marketing
COURTNEY SIMMONS Senior VP - Publicity & Communications JIM (SKI) SOKOLOWSKI VP - Comic Book Specialty Sales & Trade Marketing
NANCY SPEARS VP - Mass, Book, Digital Sales & Trade Marketing MICHELE R. WELLS VP - Content Strategy

TEEN TITANS GO!: THEIR GREATEST HIJINKS

DC Comics, 2900 West Alameda Ave., Burbank, CA 91505
Printed by LSC Communications, Owensville, MO, USA. 5/11/18. First Printing.
ISBN: 978-1-4012-8240-0

Library of Congress Cataloging-in-Publication Data is available.

MIX
Paper from responsible sources
FSC® C132124
www.fsc.org

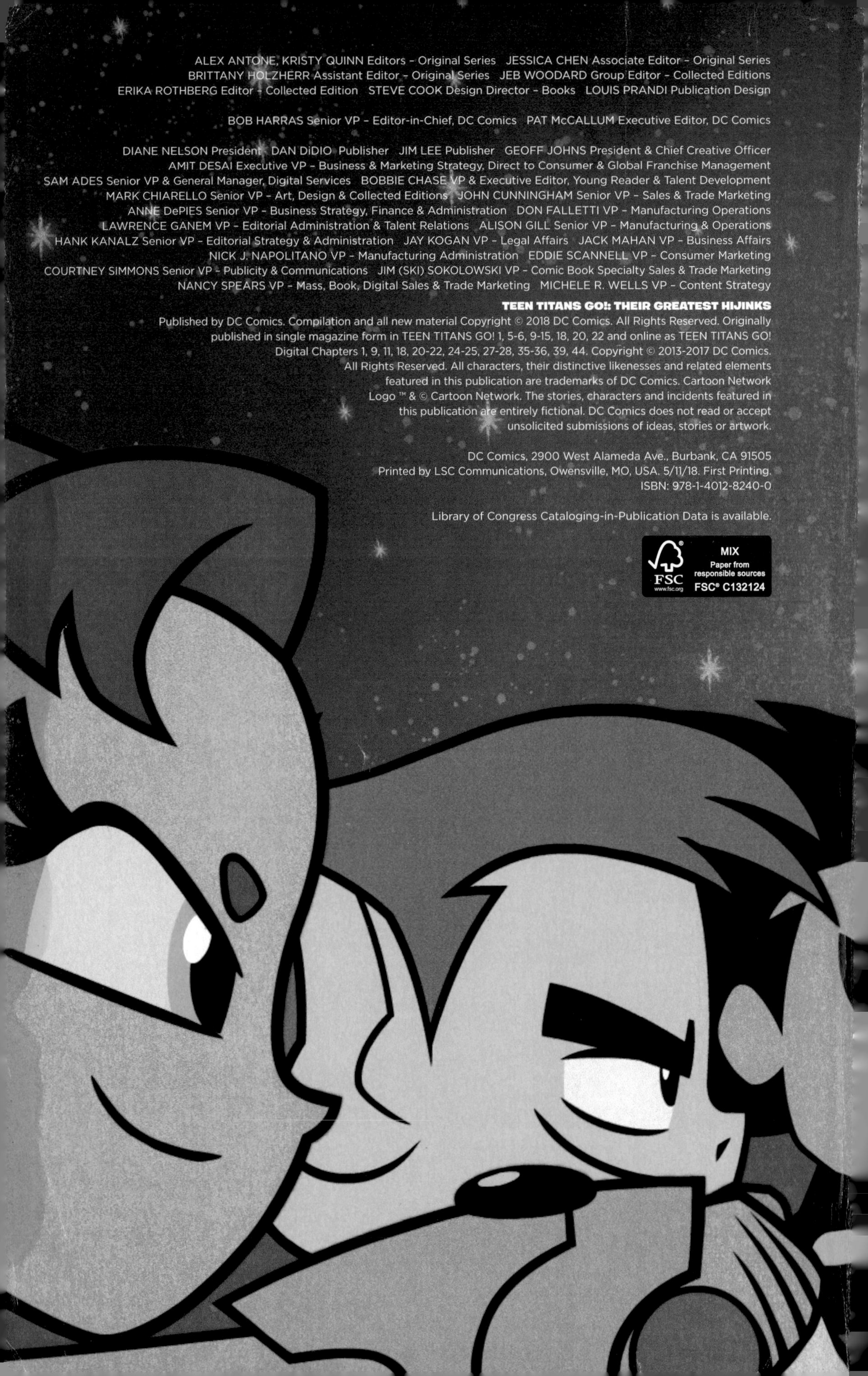

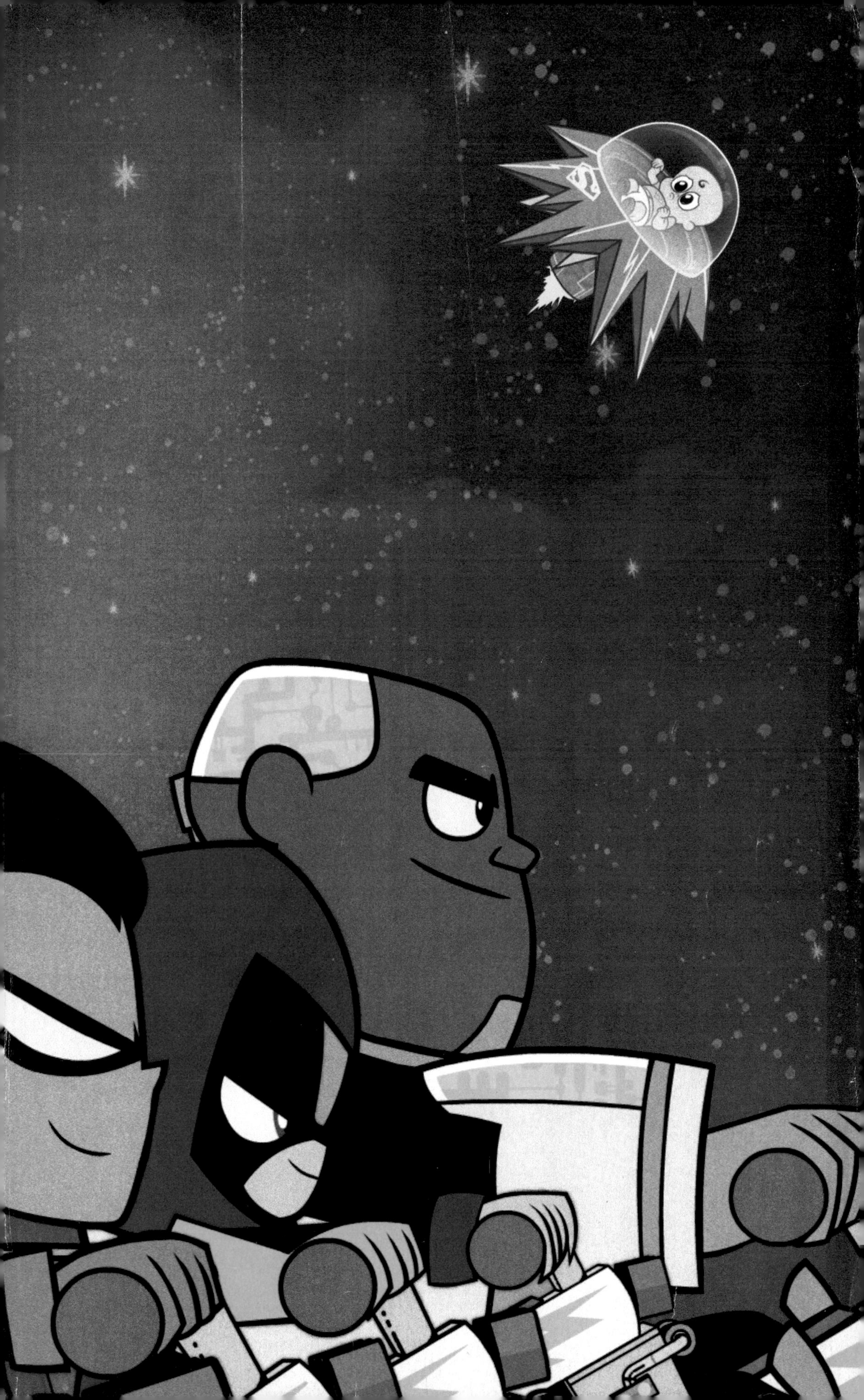

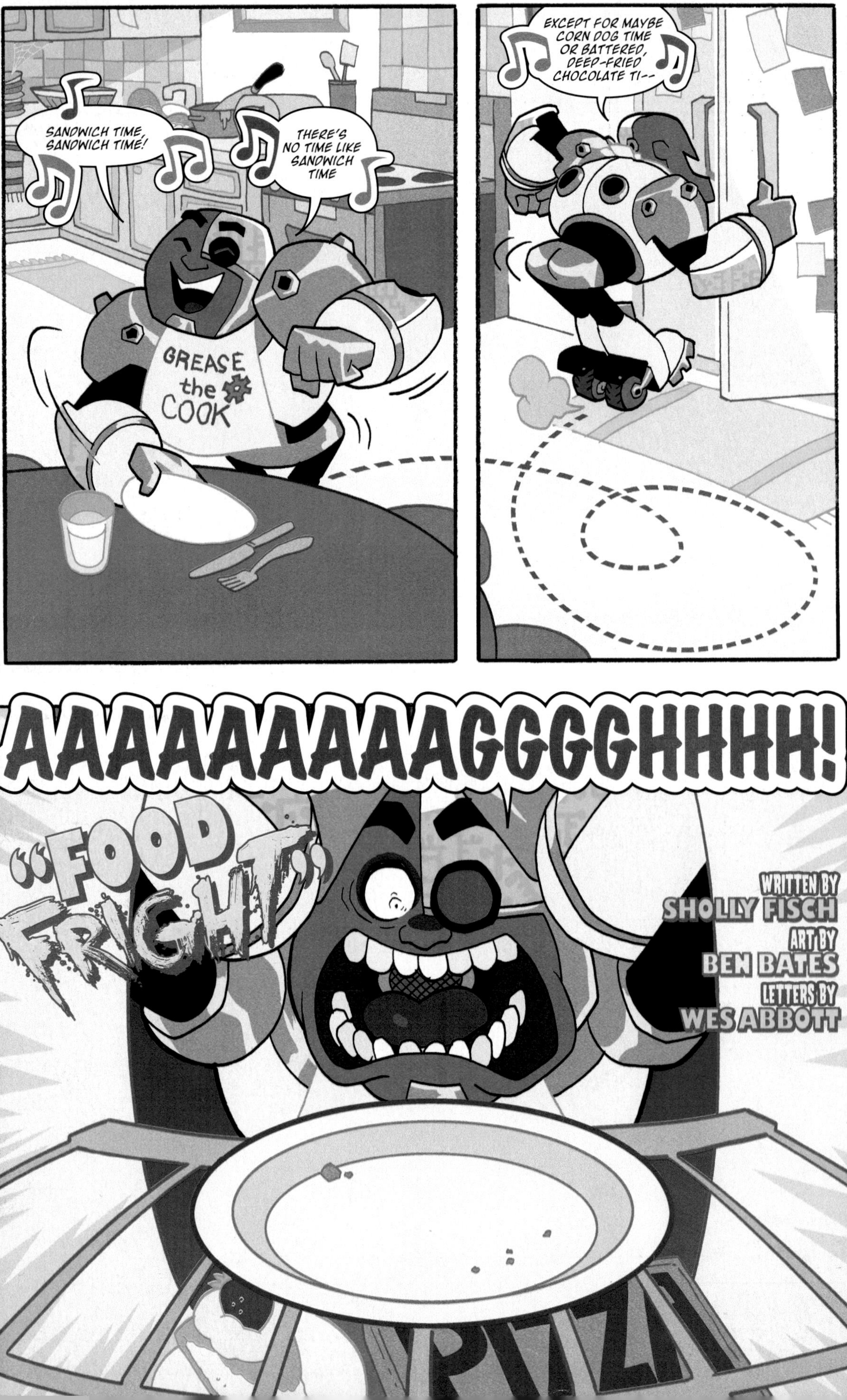
SANDWICH TIME, SANDWICH TIME!
THERE'S NO TIME LIKE SANDWICH TIME
GREASE the COOK
EXCEPT FOR MAYBE CORN DOG TIME OR BATTERED, DEEP-FRIED CHOCOLATE TI--
AAAAAAAAAAGGGGHHHH!
"FOOD FRIGHT"
WRITTEN BY SHOLLY FISCH
ART BY BEN BATES
LETTERS BY WES ABBOTT

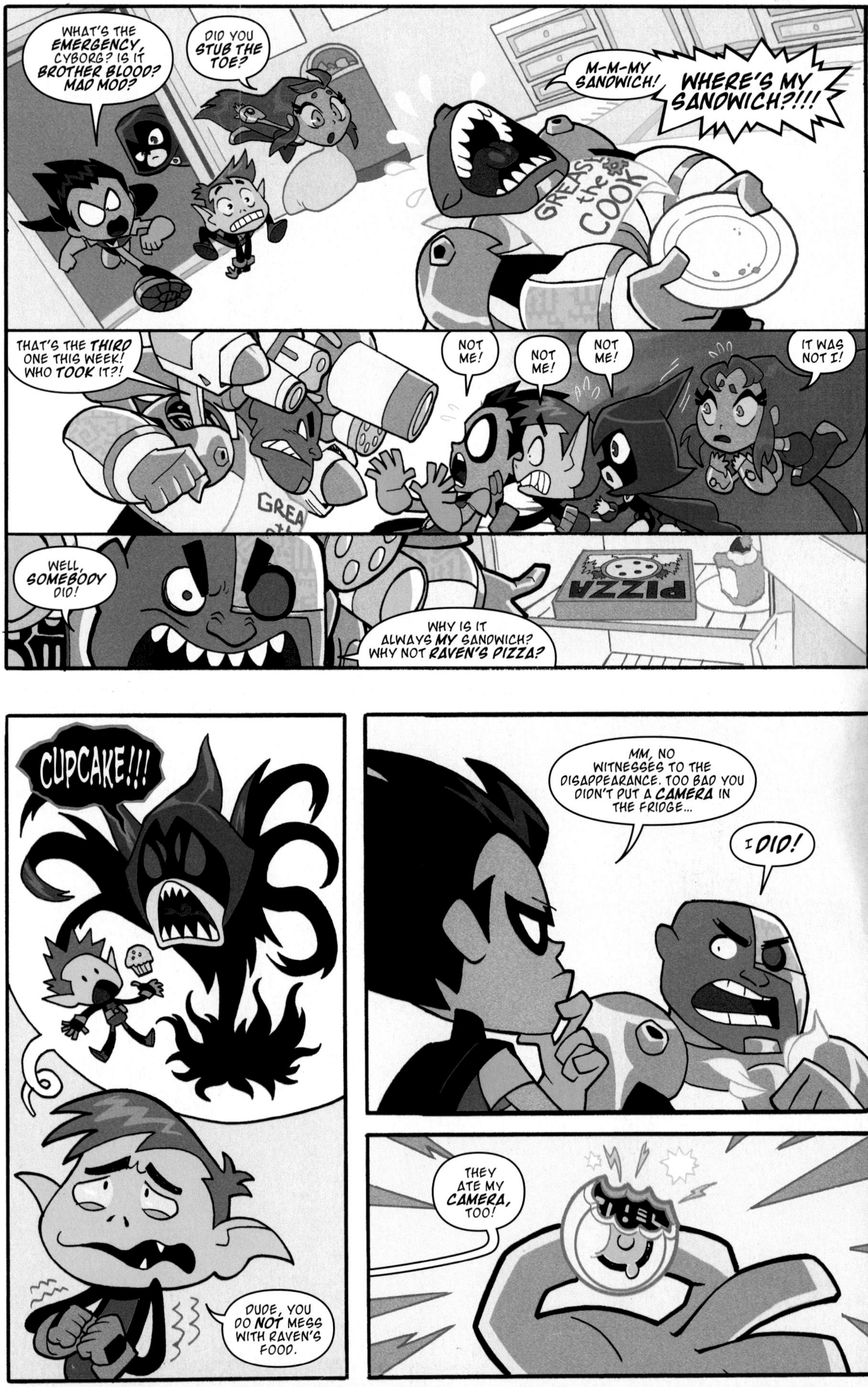

WHAT'S THE **EMERGENCY**, CYBORG? IS IT **BROTHER BLOOD? MAD MOD?**
DID YOU **STUB THE TOE?**
M-M-MY SANDWICH!
WHERE'S MY SANDWICH?!!!
THAT'S THE **THIRD** ONE THIS WEEK! WHO **TOOK** IT?!
NOT ME!
NOT ME!
NOT ME!
IT WAS NOT I!
WELL, **SOMEBODY** DID!
WHY IS IT ALWAYS **MY** SANDWICH? WHY NOT **RAVEN'S PIZZA?**
CUPCAKE!!!
DUDE, YOU DO **NOT** MESS WITH RAVEN'S FOOD.
MM, NO WITNESSES TO THE DISAPPEARANCE. TOO BAD YOU DIDN'T PUT A **CAMERA** IN THE FRIDGE...
I **DID!**
THEY ATE MY **CAMERA**, TOO!

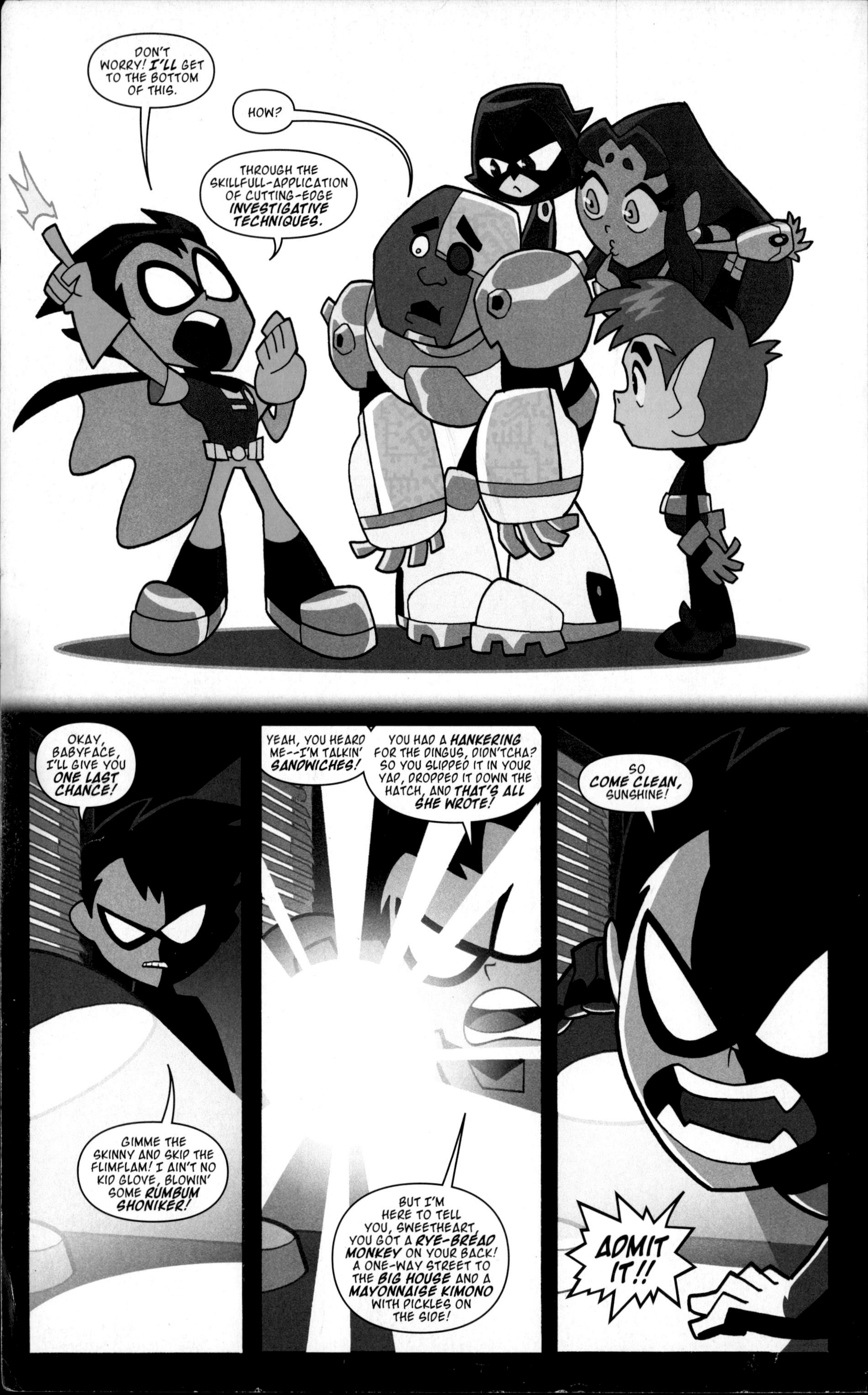
DON'T WORRY! I'LL GET TO THE BOTTOM OF THIS.
HOW?
THROUGH THE SKILLFULL-APPLICATION OF CUTTING-EDGE INVESTIGATIVE TECHNIQUES.
OKAY, BABYFACE, I'LL GIVE YOU ONE LAST CHANCE!
GIMME THE SKINNY AND SKIP THE FLIMFLAM! I AIN'T NO KID GLOVE, BLOWIN' SOME RUMBUM SHONIKER!
YEAH, YOU HEARD ME--I'M TALKIN' SANDWICHES!
YOU HAD A HANKERING FOR THE DINGUS, DIDN'TCHA? SO YOU SLIPPED IT IN YOUR YAP, DROPPED IT DOWN THE HATCH, AND THAT'S ALL SHE WROTE!
BUT I'M HERE TO TELL YOU, SWEETHEART, YOU GOT A RYE-BREAD MONKEY ON YOUR BACK! A ONE-WAY STREET TO THE BIG HOUSE AND A MAYONNAISE KIMONO WITH PICKLES ON THE SIDE!
SO COME CLEAN, SUNSHINE!
ADMIT IT!!

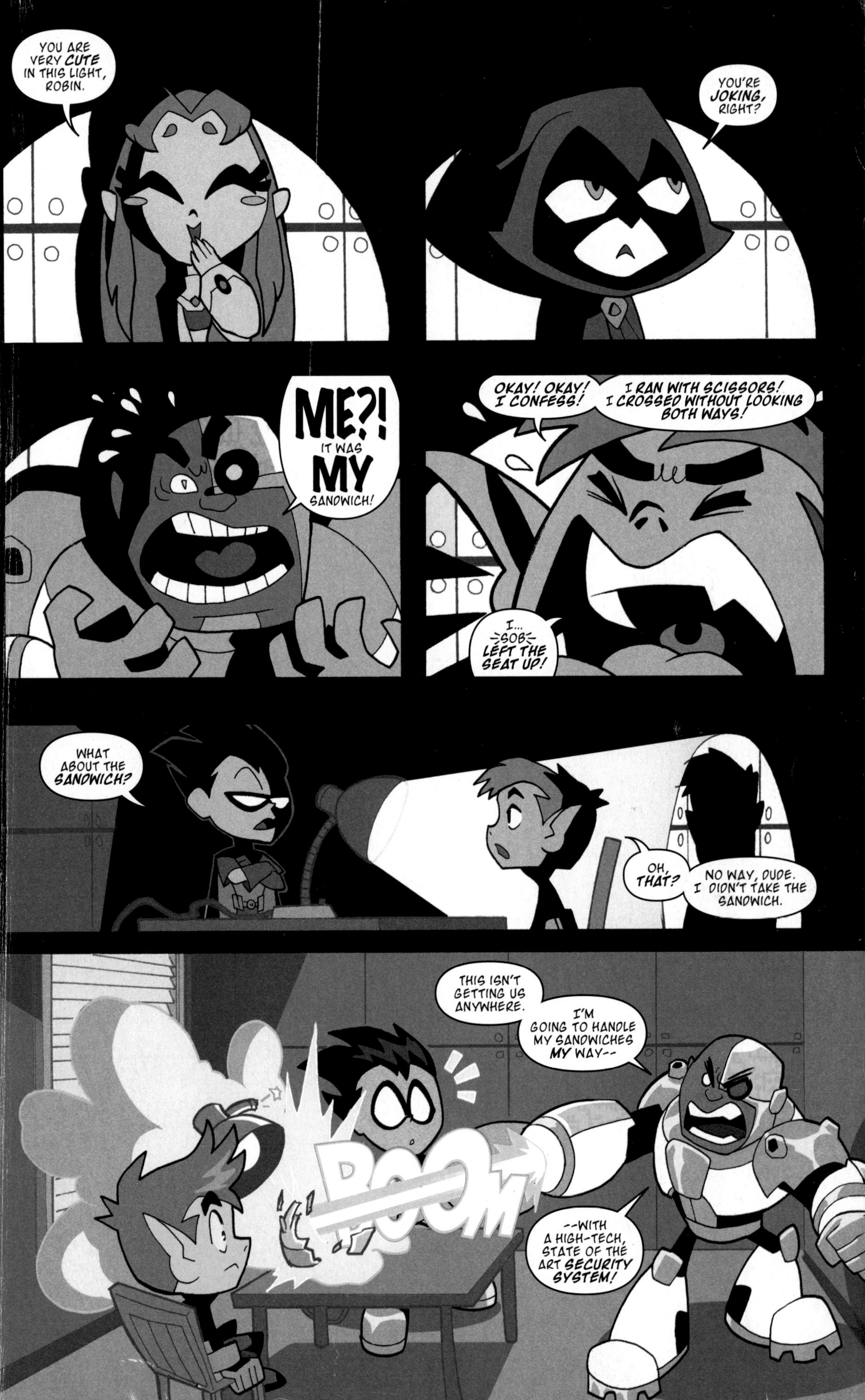
YOU ARE VERY CUTE IN THIS LIGHT, ROBIN.
YOU'RE JOKING, RIGHT?
ME?! IT WAS MY SANDWICH!
OKAY! OKAY! I CONFESS!
I RAN WITH SCISSORS! I CROSSED WITHOUT LOOKING BOTH WAYS!
I... -SOB- LEFT THE SEAT UP!
WHAT ABOUT THE SANDWICH?
OH, THAT?
NO WAY, DUDE. I DIDN'T TAKE THE SANDWICH.
THIS ISN'T GETTING US ANYWHERE.
I'M GOING TO HANDLE MY SANDWICHES MY WAY--
BOOM
--WITH A HIGH-TECH, STATE OF THE ART SECURITY SYSTEM!

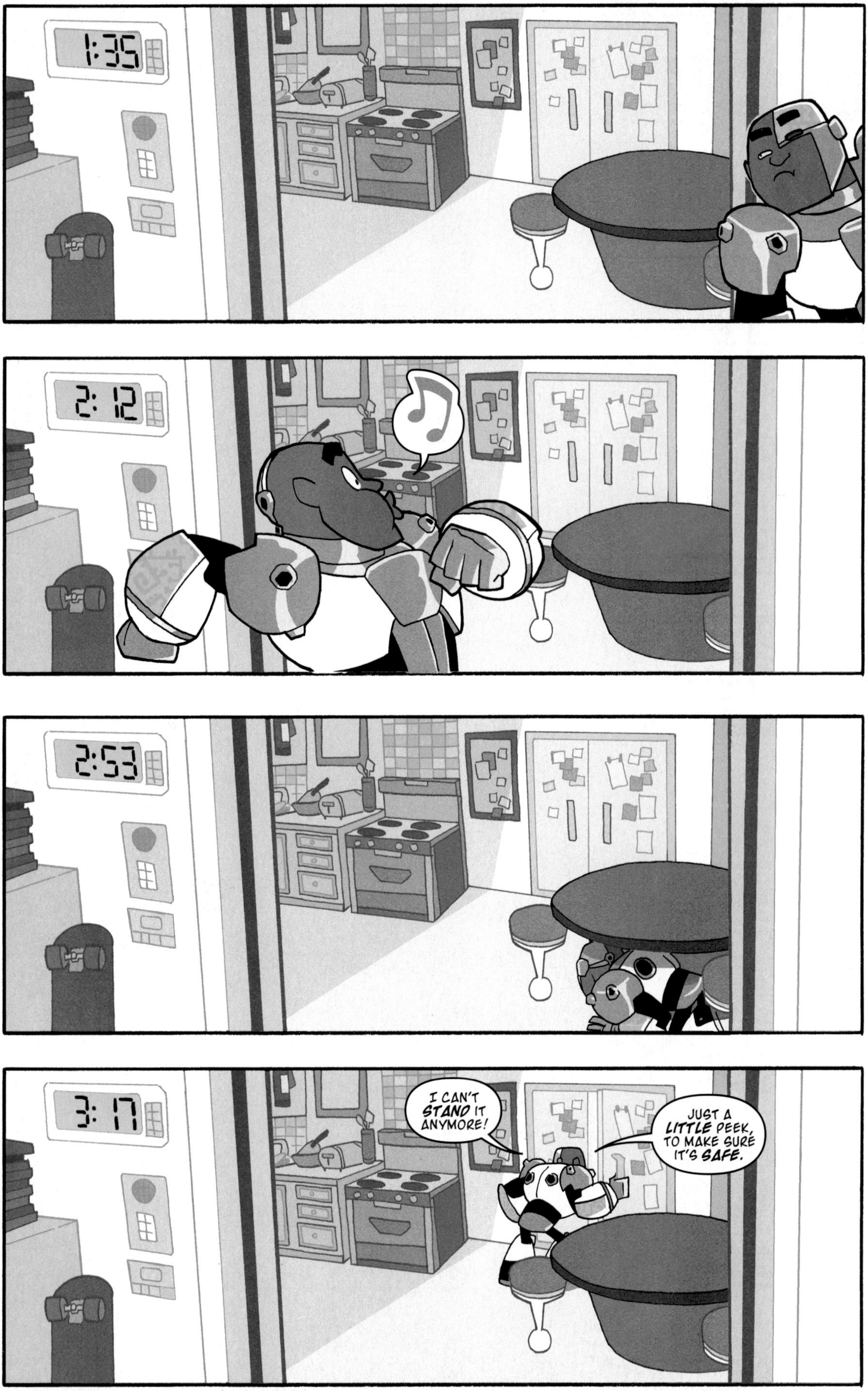
1:35
2:12
2:53
3:17
I CAN'T STAND IT ANYMORE!
JUST A LITTLE PEEK, TO MAKE SURE IT'S SAFE.

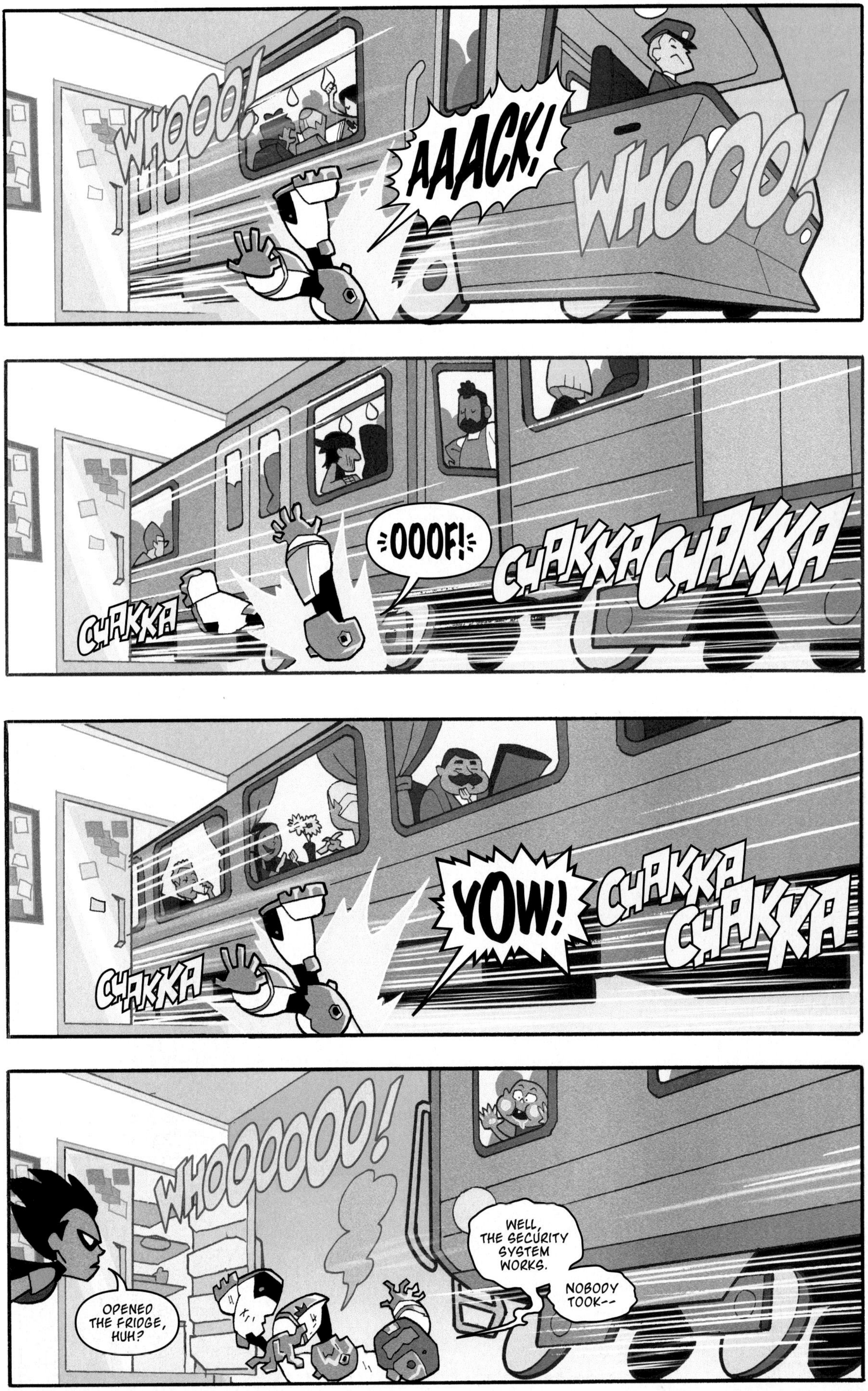
WHOOO!
AAACK!
WHOOOO!
CHAKKA
OOOF!
CHAKKACHAKKA
CHAKKA
YOW!
CHAKKA CHAKKA
WHOOOOOO!
OPENED THE FRIDGE, HUH?
WELL, THE SECURITY SYSTEM WORKS.
NOBODY TOOK--

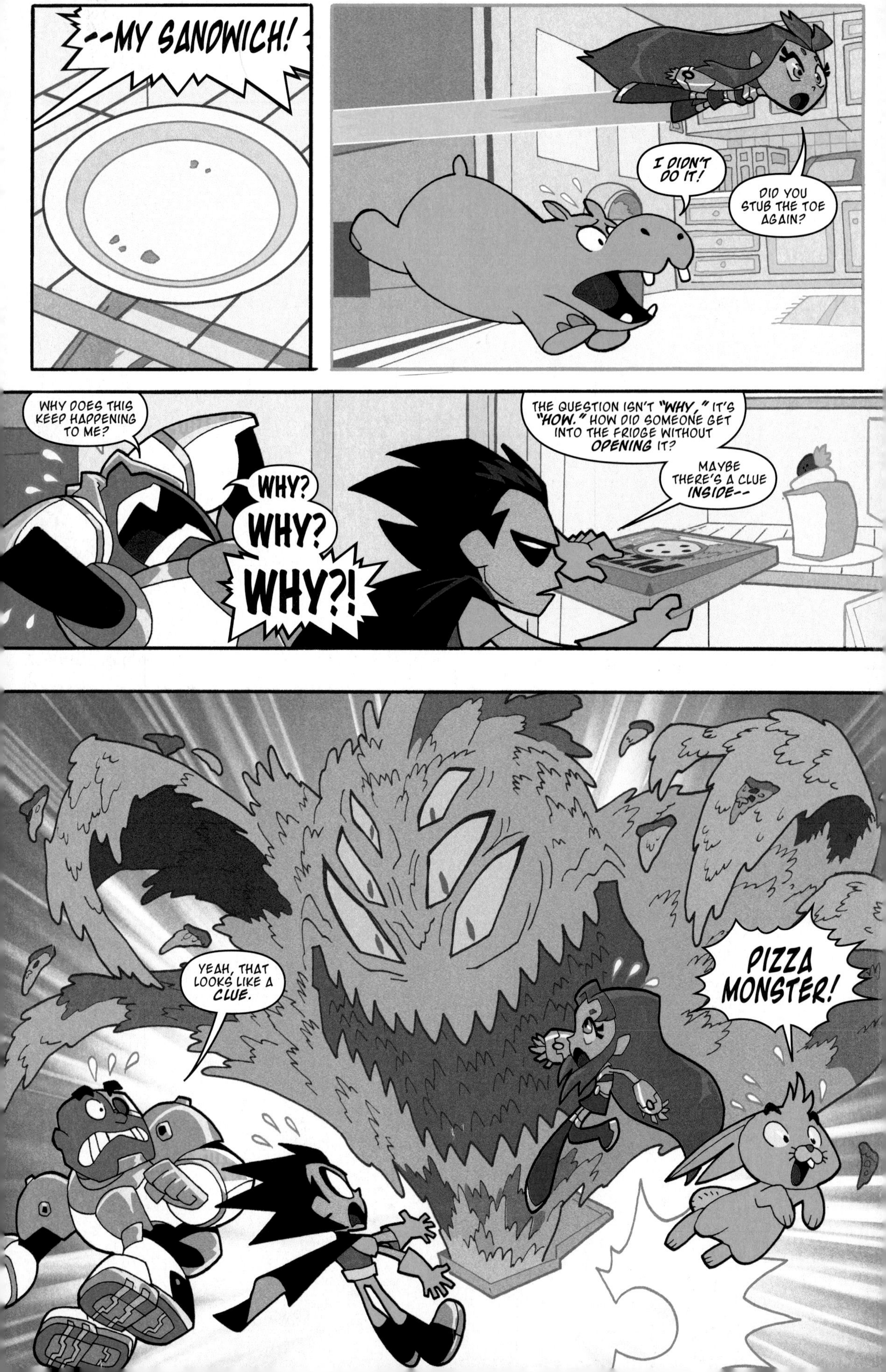
--MY SANDWICH!
I DIDN'T DO IT!
DID YOU STUB THE TOE AGAIN?
WHY DOES THIS KEEP HAPPENING TO ME?
WHY?
WHY?
WHY?!
THE QUESTION ISN'T "WHY," IT'S "HOW." HOW DID SOMEONE GET INTO THE FRIDGE WITHOUT OPENING IT?
MAYBE THERE'S A CLUE INSIDE--
YEAH, THAT LOOKS LIKE A CLUE.
PIZZA MONSTER!

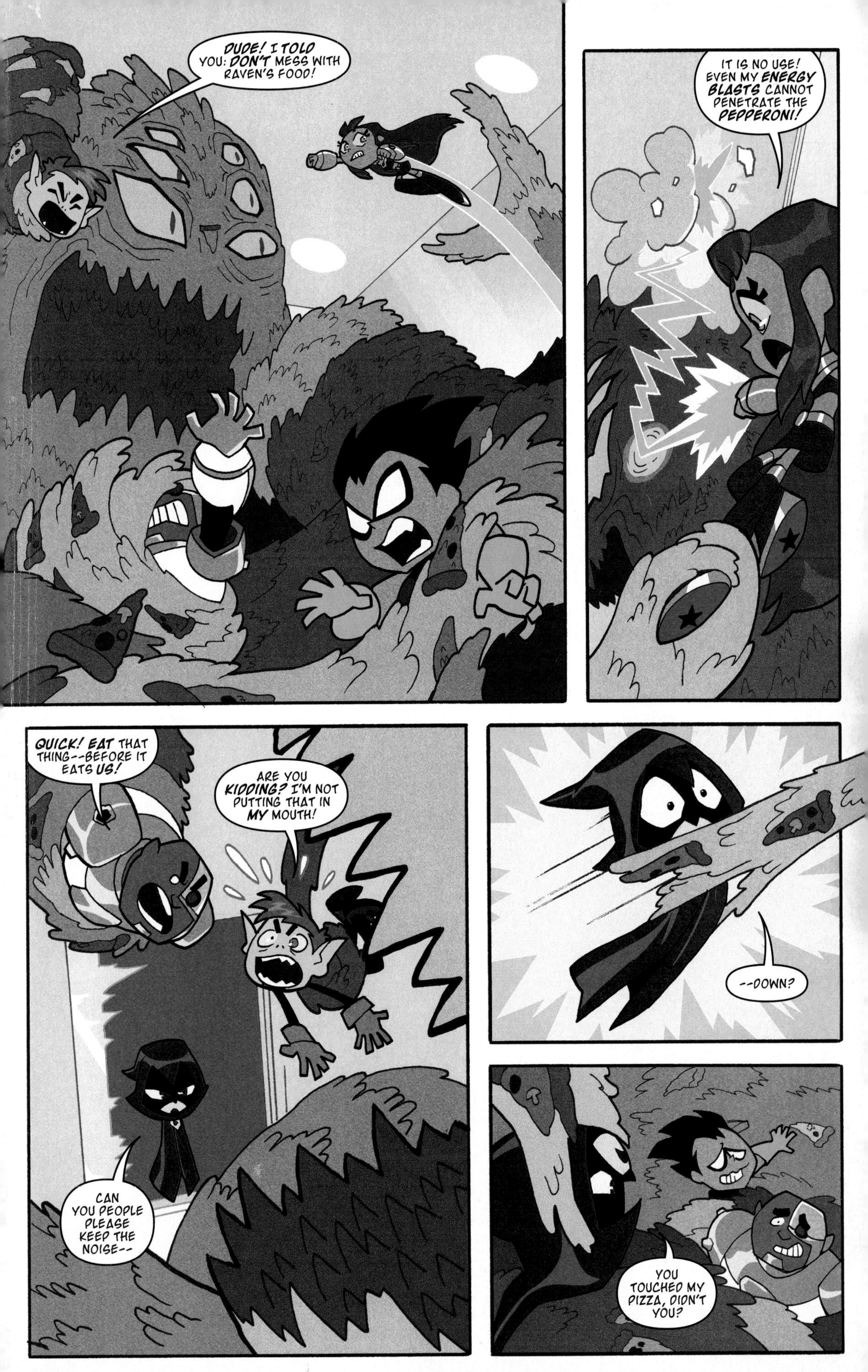
DUDE! I TOLD YOU: DON'T MESS WITH RAVEN'S FOOD!
IT IS NO USE! EVEN MY ENERGY BLASTS CANNOT PENETRATE THE PEPPERONI!
QUICK! EAT THAT THING--BEFORE IT EATS US!
ARE YOU KIDDING? I'M NOT PUTTING THAT IN MY MOUTH!
CAN YOU PEOPLE PLEASE KEEP THE NOISE--
--DOWN?
YOU TOUCHED MY PIZZA, DIDN'T YOU?

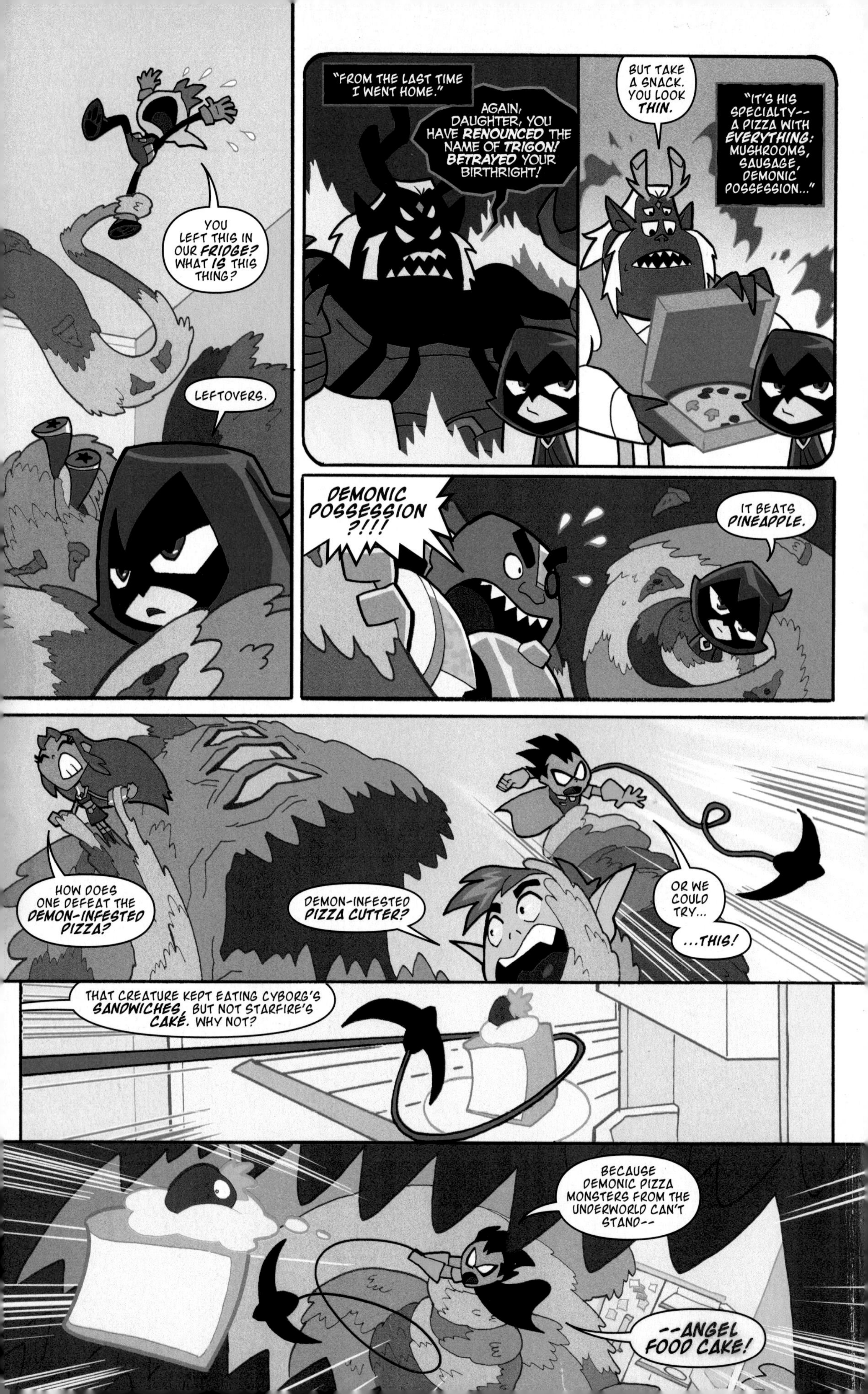
YOU LEFT THIS IN OUR FRIDGE? WHAT IS THIS THING?
LEFTOVERS.
"FROM THE LAST TIME I WENT HOME."
AGAIN, DAUGHTER, YOU HAVE RENOUNCED THE NAME OF TRIGON! BETRAYED YOUR BIRTHRIGHT!
BUT TAKE A SNACK. YOU LOOK THIN.
"IT'S HIS SPECIALTY--A PIZZA WITH EVERYTHING: MUSHROOMS, SAUSAGE, DEMONIC POSSESSION..."
DEMONIC POSSESSION?!!!
IT BEATS PINEAPPLE.
HOW DOES ONE DEFEAT THE DEMON-INFESTED PIZZA?
DEMON-INFESTED PIZZA CUTTER?
OR WE COULD TRY...
...THIS!
THAT CREATURE KEPT EATING CYBORG'S SANDWICHES, BUT NOT STARFIRE'S CAKE. WHY NOT?
BECAUSE DEMONIC PIZZA MONSTERS FROM THE UNDERWORLD CAN'T STAND--
--ANGEL FOOD CAKE!

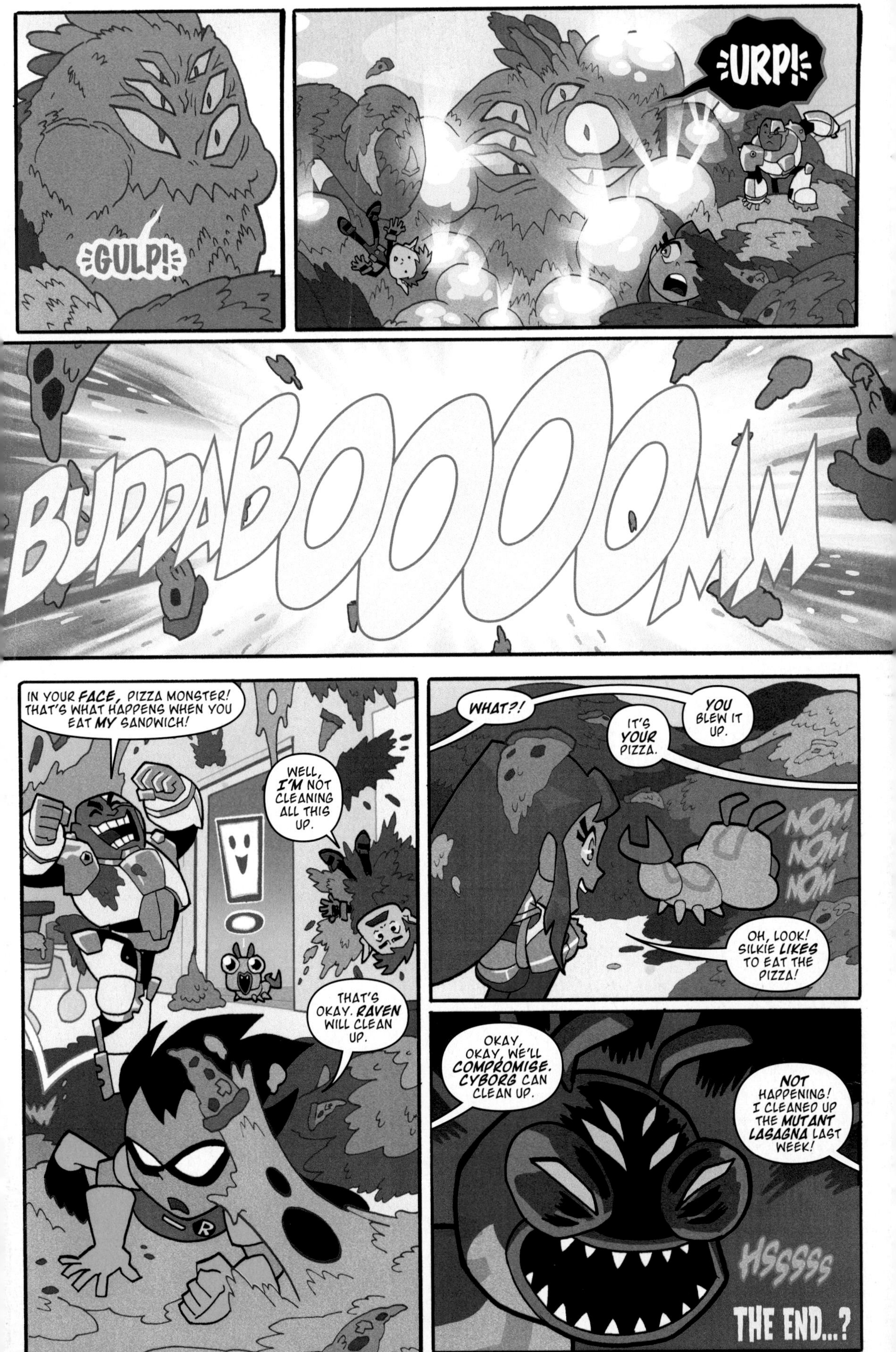
GULP!
URP!
BUDDABOOOOOMM
IN YOUR FACE, PIZZA MONSTER! THAT'S WHAT HAPPENS WHEN YOU EAT MY SANDWICH!
WELL, I'M NOT CLEANING ALL THIS UP.
THAT'S OKAY. RAVEN WILL CLEAN UP.
WHAT?!
IT'S YOUR PIZZA.
YOU BLEW IT UP.
NOM NOM NOM
OH, LOOK! SILKIE LIKES TO EAT THE PIZZA!
OKAY, OKAY, WE'LL COMPROMISE. CYBORG CAN CLEAN UP.
NOT HAPPENING! I CLEANED UP THE MUTANT LASAGNA LAST WEEK!
HSSSSS
THE END...?

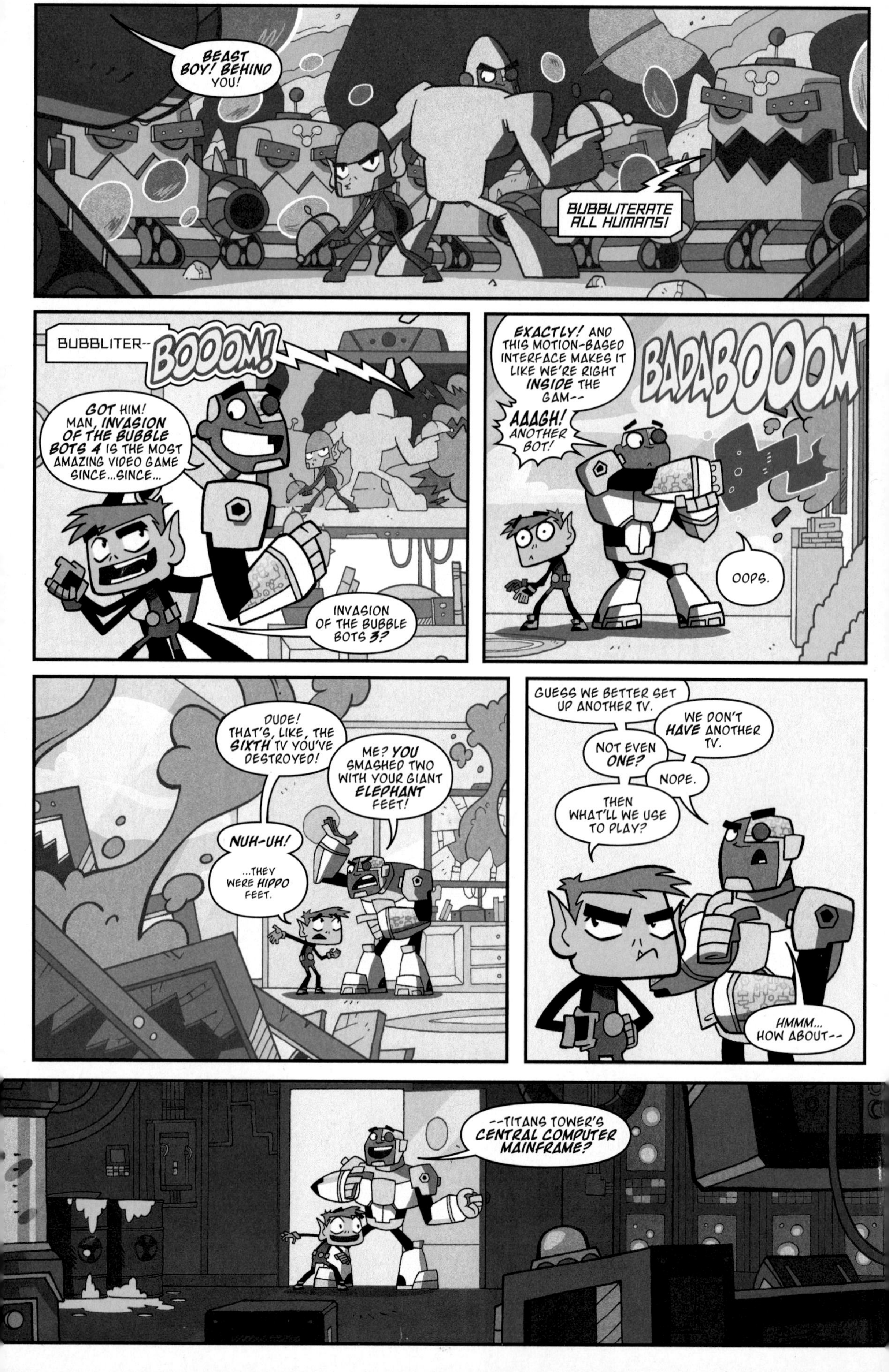
BEAST BOY! BEHIND YOU!
BUBBLITERATE ALL HUMANS!
BUBBLITER--
BOOOM!
GOT HIM! MAN, INVASION OF THE BUBBLE BOTS 4 IS THE MOST AMAZING VIDEO GAME SINCE...SINCE...
INVASION OF THE BUBBLE BOTS 3?
EXACTLY! AND THIS MOTION-BASED INTERFACE MAKES IT LIKE WE'RE RIGHT INSIDE THE GAM--
BADABOOOM
AAAGH! ANOTHER BOT!
OOPS.
DUDE! THAT'S, LIKE, THE SIXTH TV YOU'VE DESTROYED!
ME? YOU SMASHED TWO WITH YOUR GIANT ELEPHANT FEET!
NUH-UH!
...THEY WERE HIPPO FEET.
GUESS WE BETTER SET UP ANOTHER TV.
WE DON'T HAVE ANOTHER TV.
NOT EVEN ONE?
NOPE.
THEN WHAT'LL WE USE TO PLAY?
HMMM... HOW ABOUT--
--TITANS TOWER'S CENTRAL COMPUTER MAINFRAME?

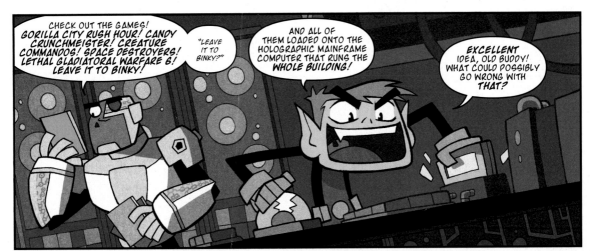

CHECK OUT THE GAMES! GORILLA CITY RUSH HOUR! CANDY CRUNCHMEISTER! CREATURE COMMANDOS! SPACE DESTROYERS! LETHAL GLADIATORAL WARFARE 6! LEAVE IT TO BINKY!

"LEAVE IT TO BINKY?"

AND ALL OF THEM LOADED ONTO THE HOLOGRAPHIC MAINFRAME COMPUTER THAT RUNS THE WHOLE BUILDING!

EXCELLENT IDEA, OLD BUDDY! WHAT COULD POSSIBLY GO WRONG WITH THAT?

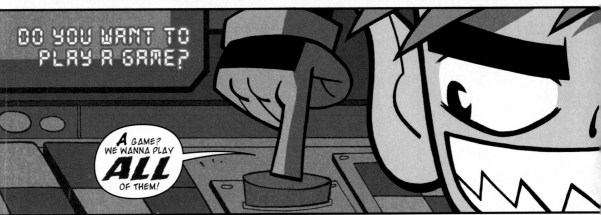

DO YOU WANT TO PLAY A GAME?

A GAME? WE WANNA PLAY ALL OF THEM!

INITIATING LEVEL 1

YOW! BUT NOT LIKE THIS!

THEY'RE-- THEY'RE ALIVE!

HUH. I DID NOT SEE THAT COMING.

"BUT GAMES CAN NEVER HURT ME"

WRITTEN BY **SHOLLY FISCH** ART BY **JORGE CORONA** COLOR BY **JEREMY LAWSON** LETTERS BY **WES ABBOTT**

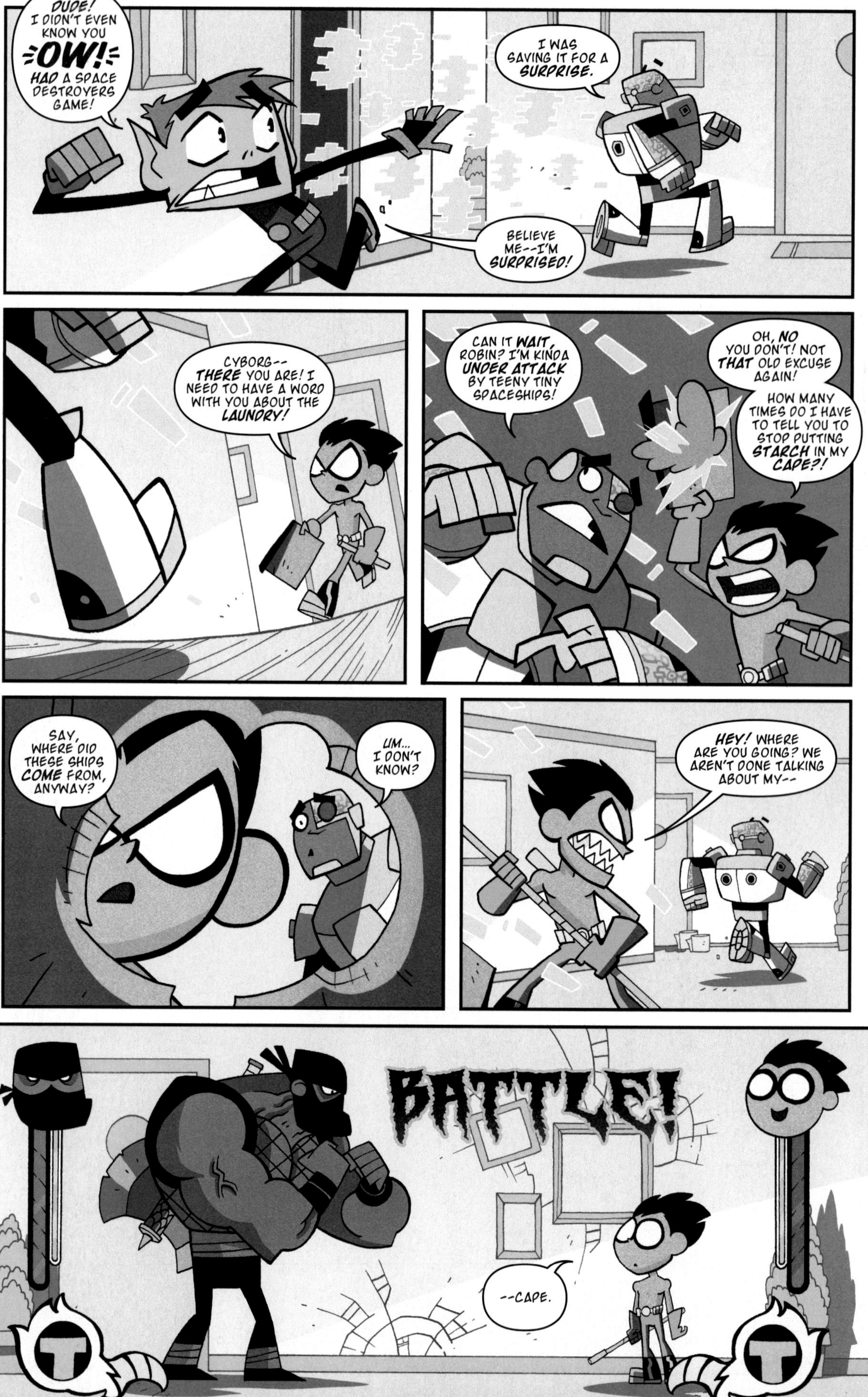
DUDE! I DIDN'T EVEN KNOW YOU OW! HAD A SPACE DESTROYERS GAME!
I WAS SAVING IT FOR A SURPRISE.
BELIEVE ME--I'M SURPRISED!
CYBORG--THERE YOU ARE! I NEED TO HAVE A WORD WITH YOU ABOUT THE LAUNDRY!
CAN IT WAIT, ROBIN? I'M KINDA UNDER ATTACK BY TEENY TINY SPACESHIPS!
OH, NO YOU DON'T! NOT THAT OLD EXCUSE AGAIN!
HOW MANY TIMES DO I HAVE TO TELL YOU TO STOP PUTTING STARCH IN MY CAPE?!
SAY, WHERE DID THESE SHIPS COME FROM, ANYWAY?
UM... I DON'T KNOW?
HEY! WHERE ARE YOU GOING? WE AREN'T DONE TALKING ABOUT MY--
BATTLE!
--CAPE.

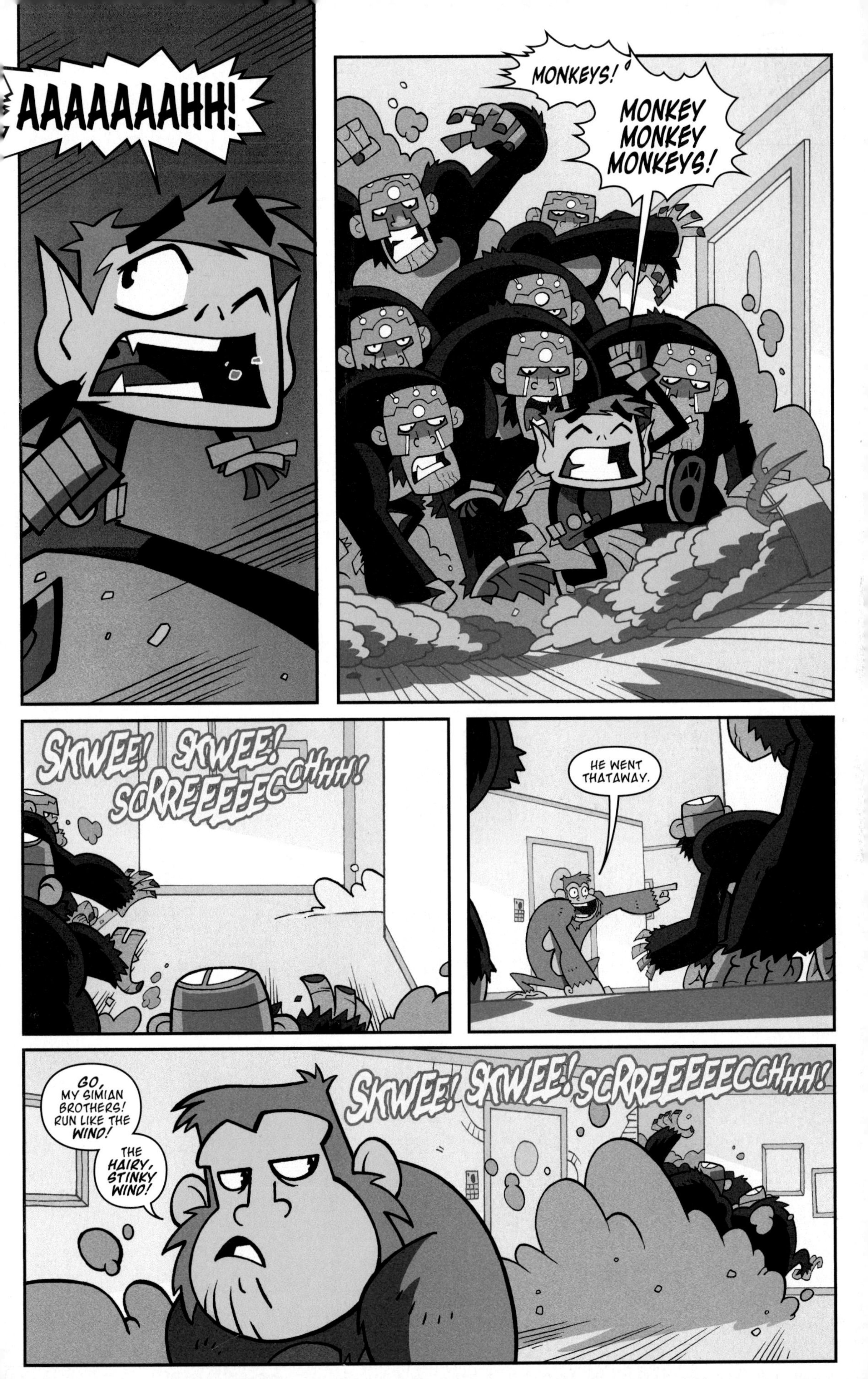
AAAAAAAHH!
MONKEYS!
MONKEY MONKEY MONKEYS!
SKWEE! SKWEE! SCRREEEEECCHHH!
HE WENT THATAWAY.
GO, MY SIMIAN BROTHERS! RUN LIKE THE WIND!
THE HAIRY, STINKY WIND!
SKWEE! SKWEE! SCRREEEEECCHHH!

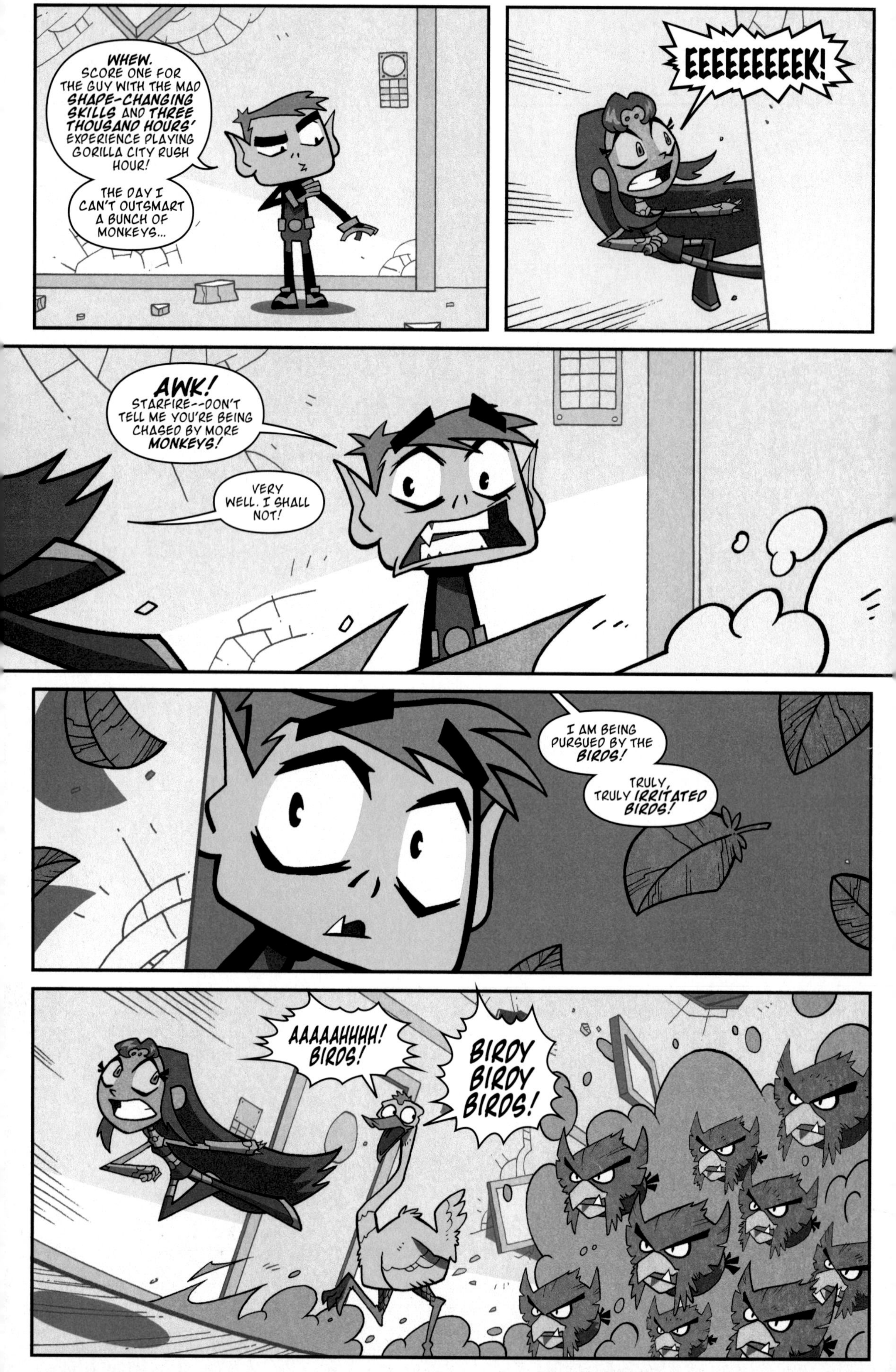
WHEW. SCORE ONE FOR THE GUY WITH THE MAD SHAPE-CHANGING SKILLS AND THREE THOUSAND HOURS' EXPERIENCE PLAYING GORILLA CITY RUSH HOUR!
THE DAY I CAN'T OUTSMART A BUNCH OF MONKEYS...
EEEEEEEEEEK!
AWK! STARFIRE--DON'T TELL ME YOU'RE BEING CHASED BY MORE MONKEYS!
VERY WELL. I SHALL NOT!
I AM BEING PURSUED BY THE BIRDS!
TRULY, TRULY IRRITATED BIRDS!
AAAAAHHHH! BIRDS!
BIRDY BIRDY BIRDS!

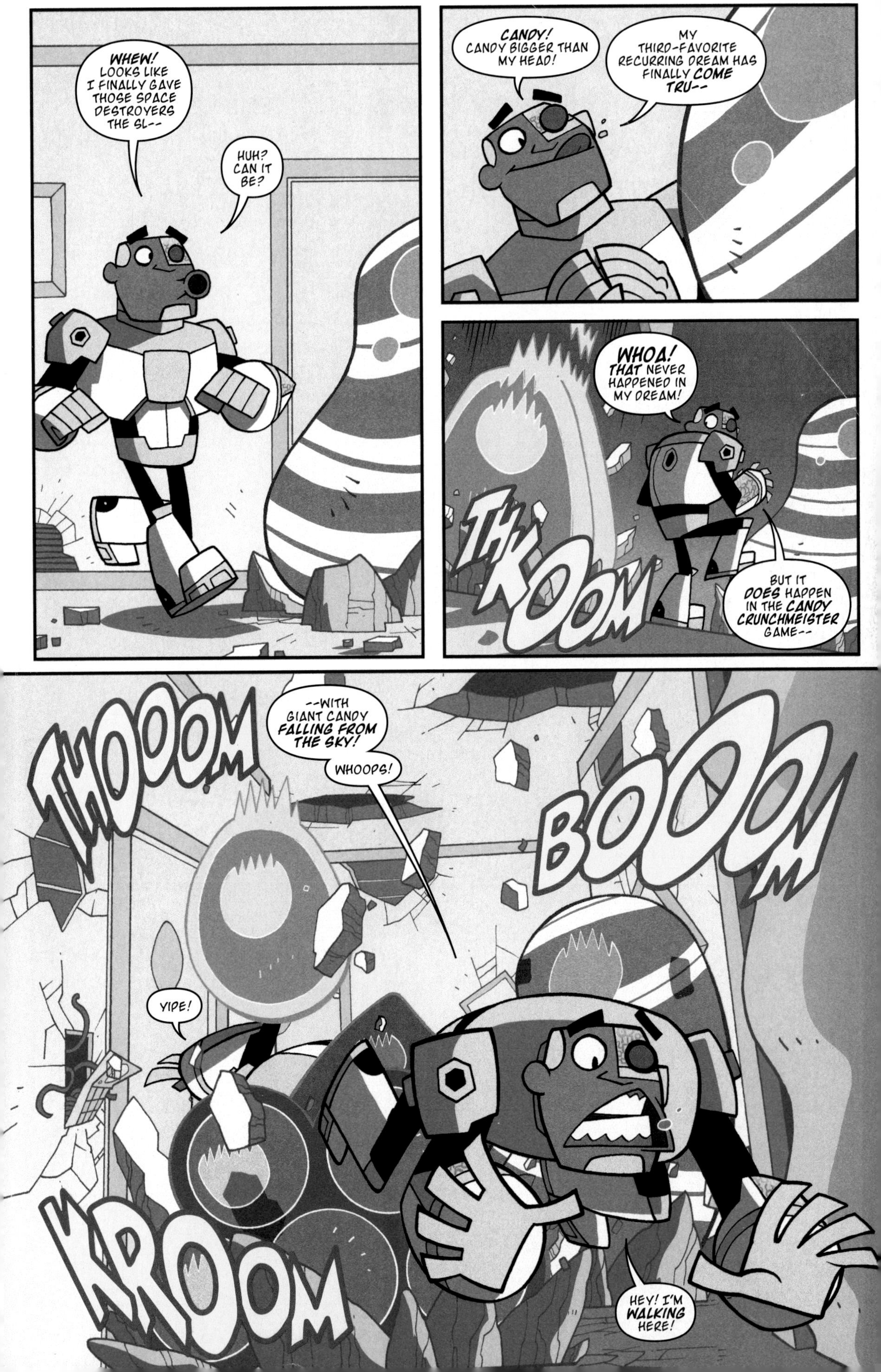
WHEW! LOOKS LIKE I FINALLY GAVE THOSE SPACE DESTROYERS THE SL--
HUH? CAN IT BE?
CANDY! CANDY BIGGER THAN MY HEAD!
MY THIRD-FAVORITE RECURRING DREAM HAS FINALLY COME TRU--
WHOA! THAT NEVER HAPPENED IN MY DREAM!
THKOOM
BUT IT DOES HAPPEN IN THE CANDY CRUNCHMEISTER GAME--
THOOOM
--WITH GIANT CANDY FALLING FROM THE SKY!
WHOOPS!
BOOOM
YIPE!
KROOM
HEY! I'M WALKING HERE!

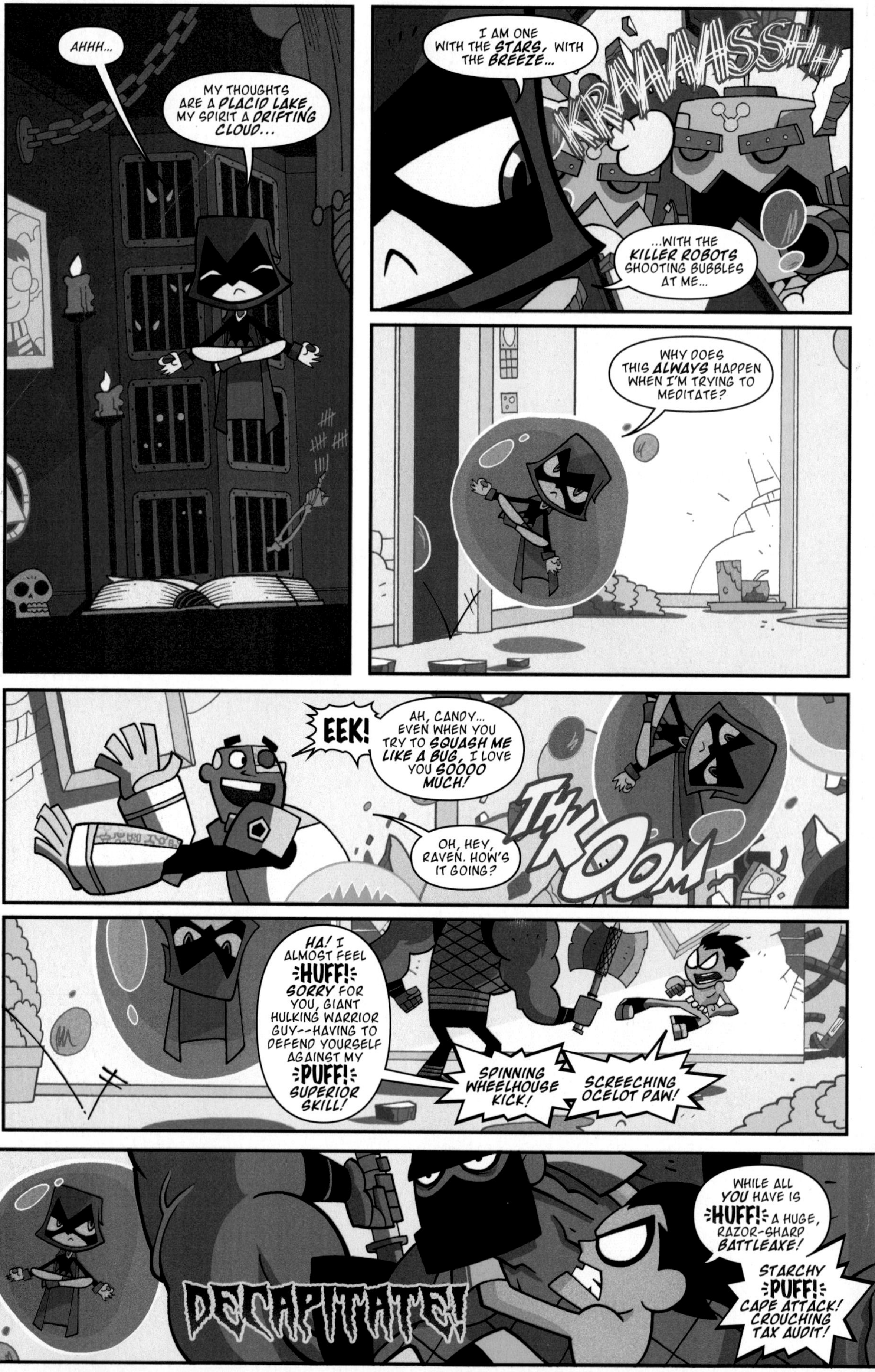
AHHH...
MY THOUGHTS ARE A PLACID LAKE, MY SPIRIT A DRIFTING CLOUD...
I AM ONE WITH THE STARS, WITH THE BREEZE...
KRAAAASSHH
...WITH THE KILLER ROBOTS SHOOTING BUBBLES AT ME...
WHY DOES THIS ALWAYS HAPPEN WHEN I'M TRYING TO MEDITATE?
EEK!
AH, CANDY... EVEN WHEN YOU TRY TO SQUASH ME LIKE A BUG, I LOVE YOU SOOOO MUCH!
OH, HEY, RAVEN. HOW'S IT GOING?
THOOM
HA! I ALMOST FEEL HUFF! SORRY FOR YOU, GIANT HULKING WARRIOR GUY--HAVING TO DEFEND YOURSELF AGAINST MY PUFF! SUPERIOR SKILL!
SPINNING WHEELHOUSE KICK!
SCREECHING OCELOT PAW!
WHILE ALL YOU HAVE IS HUFF! A HUGE, RAZOR-SHARP BATTLEAXE!
STARCHY PUFF! CAPE ATTACK! CROUCHING TAX AUDIT!
DECAPITATE!

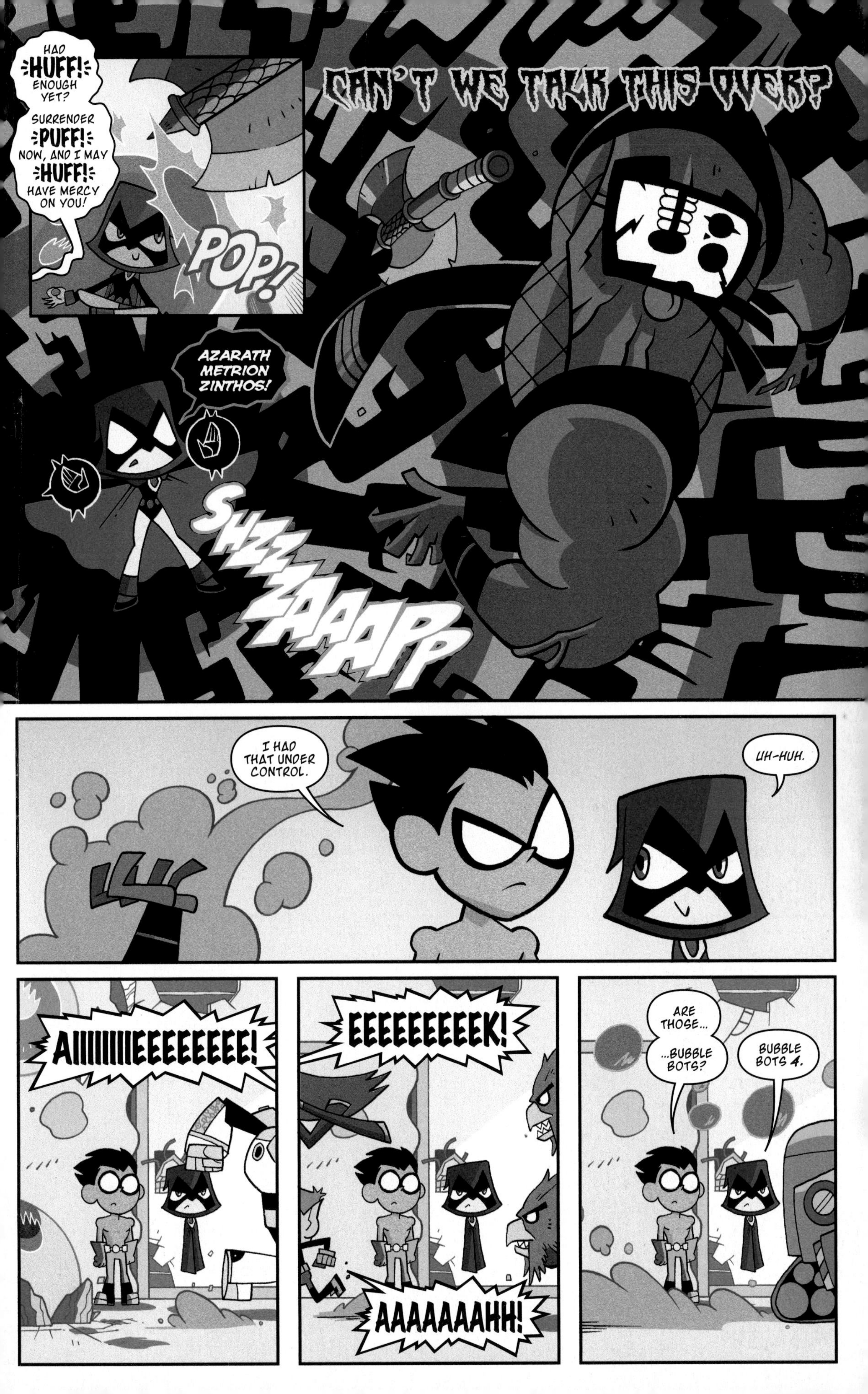
HAD HUFF! ENOUGH YET? SURRENDER PUFF! NOW, AND I MAY HUFF! HAVE MERCY ON YOU!
POP!
CAN'T WE TALK THIS OVER?
AZARATH METRION ZINTHOS!
SHZZZAAAPP
I HAD THAT UNDER CONTROL.
UH-HUH.
AIIIIIIIEEEEEEEE!
EEEEEEEEEK!
AAAAAAAHH!
ARE THOSE...
...BUBBLE BOTS?
BUBBLE BOTS 4.

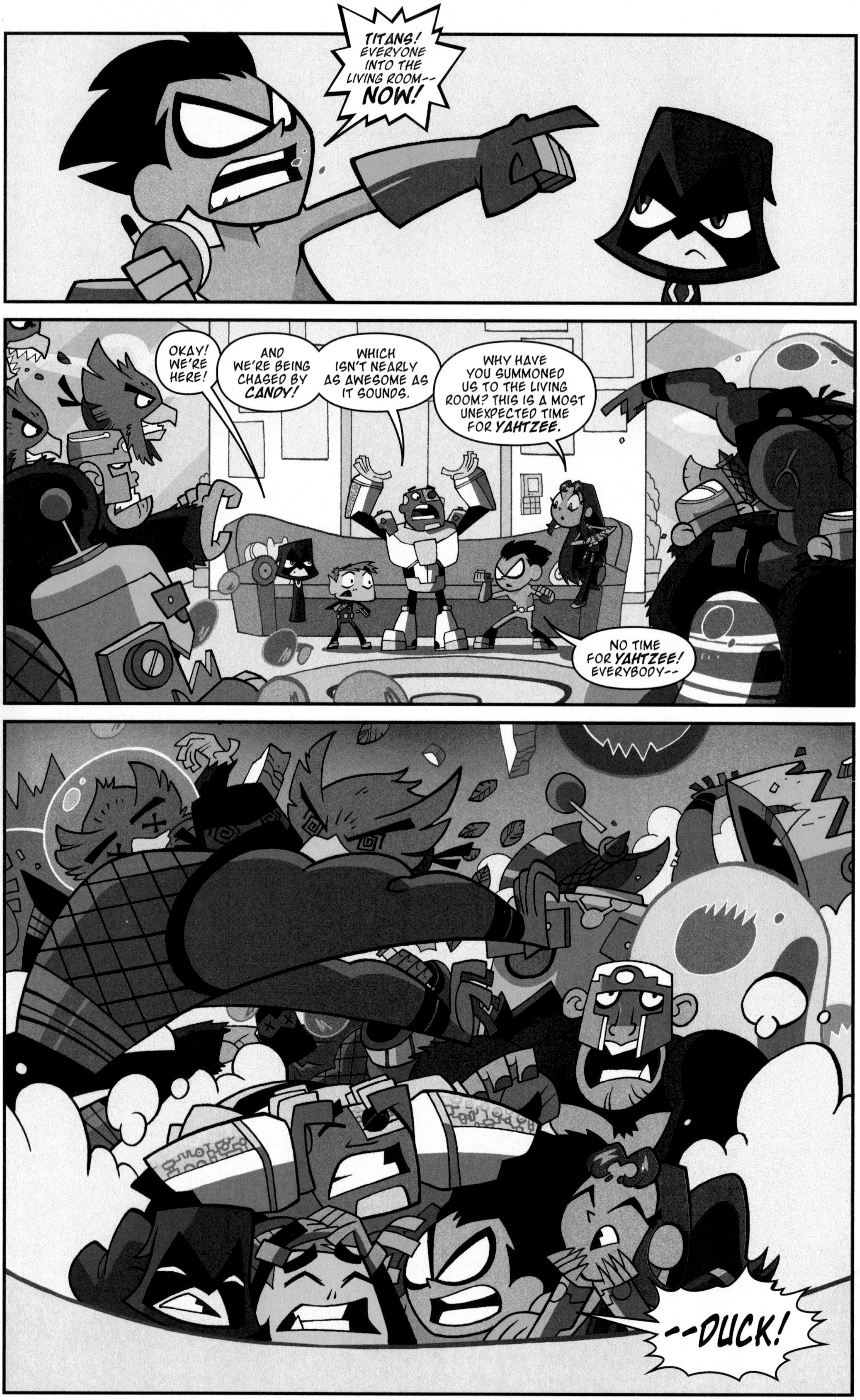

TITANS! EVERYONE INTO THE LIVING ROOM-- NOW!
OKAY! WE'RE HERE!
AND WE'RE BEING CHASED BY CANDY!
WHICH ISN'T NEARLY AS AWESOME AS IT SOUNDS.
WHY HAVE YOU SUMMONED US TO THE LIVING ROOM? THIS IS A MOST UNEXPECTED TIME FOR YAHTZEE.
NO TIME FOR YAHTZEE! EVERYBODY--
--DUCK!

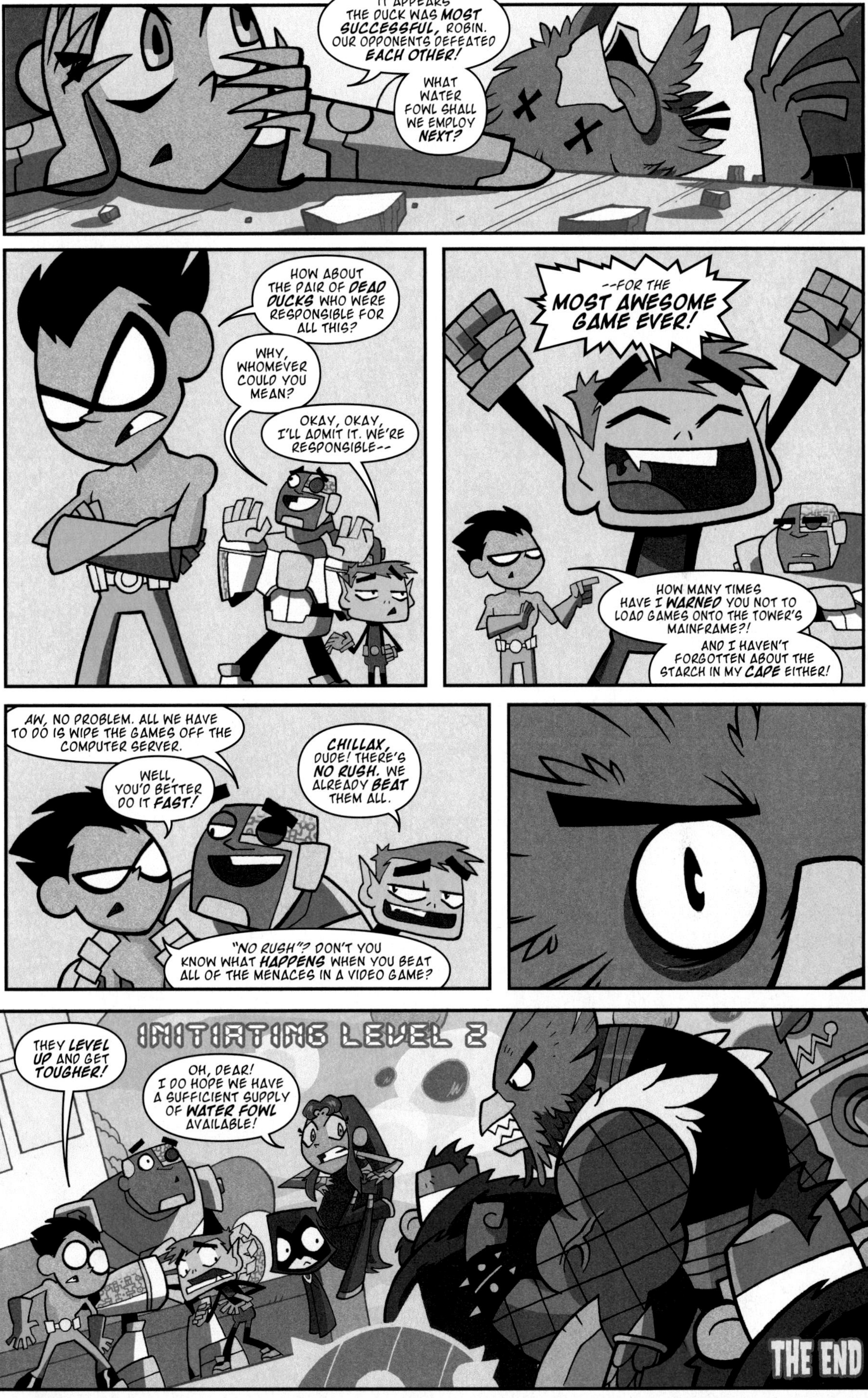
IT APPEARS THE DUCK WAS MOST SUCCESSFUL, ROBIN. OUR OPPONENTS DEFEATED EACH OTHER!
WHAT WATER FOWL SHALL WE EMPLOY NEXT?
HOW ABOUT THE PAIR OF DEAD DUCKS WHO WERE RESPONSIBLE FOR ALL THIS?
WHY, WHOMEVER COULD YOU MEAN?
OKAY, OKAY, I'LL ADMIT IT. WE'RE RESPONSIBLE--
--FOR THE MOST AWESOME GAME EVER!
HOW MANY TIMES HAVE I WARNED YOU NOT TO LOAD GAMES ONTO THE TOWER'S MAINFRAME?!
AND I HAVEN'T FORGOTTEN ABOUT THE STARCH IN MY CAPE EITHER!
AW, NO PROBLEM. ALL WE HAVE TO DO IS WIPE THE GAMES OFF THE COMPUTER SERVER.
WELL, YOU'D BETTER DO IT FAST!
CHILLAX, DUDE! THERE'S NO RUSH. WE ALREADY BEAT THEM ALL.
"NO RUSH"? DON'T YOU KNOW WHAT HAPPENS WHEN YOU BEAT ALL OF THE MENACES IN A VIDEO GAME?
INITIATING LEVEL 2
THEY LEVEL UP AND GET TOUGHER!
OH, DEAR! I DO HOPE WE HAVE A SUFFICIENT SUPPLY OF WATER FOWL AVAILABLE!
THE END

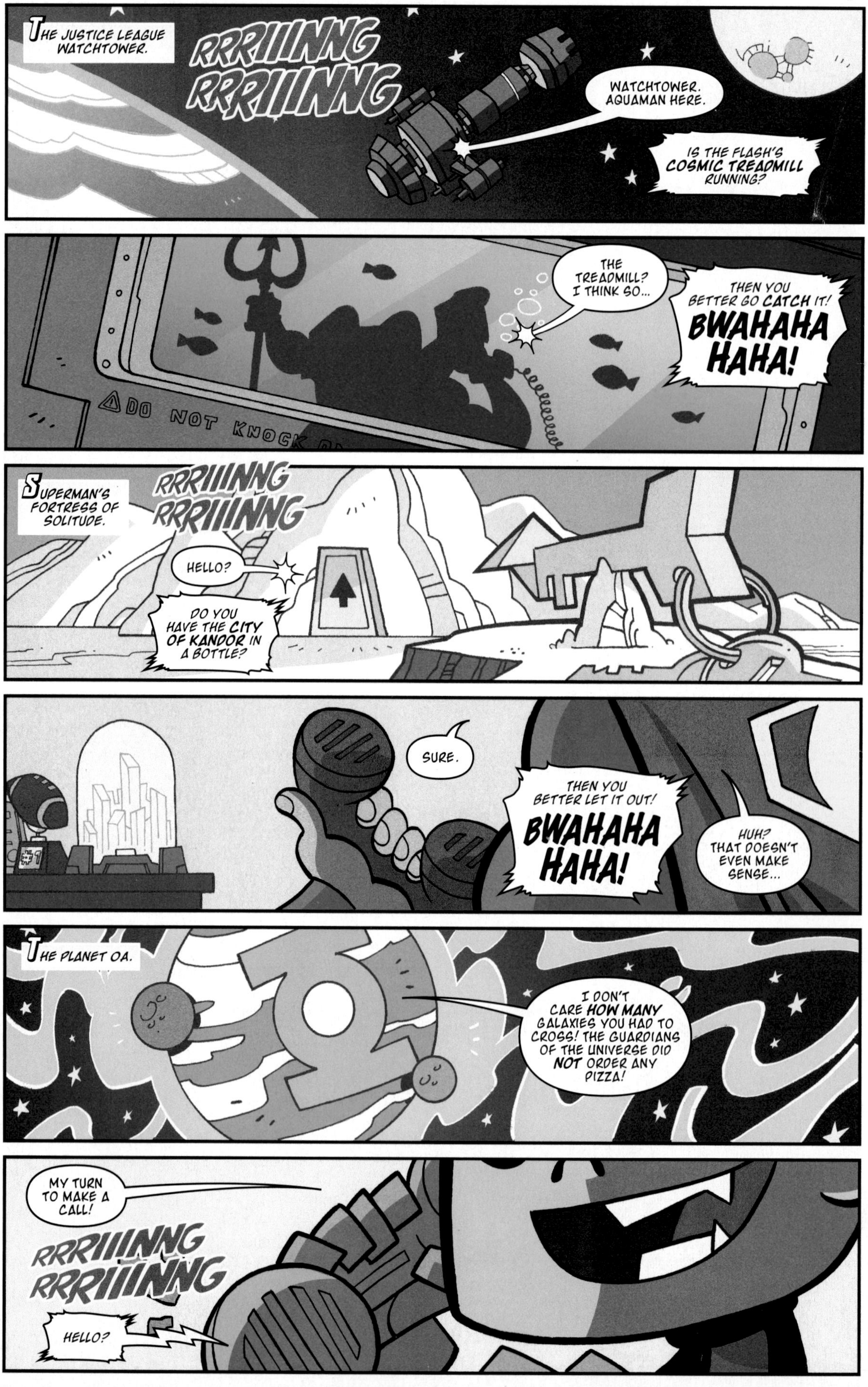
THE JUSTICE LEAGUE WATCHTOWER.
RRRIIINNG RRRIIINNG
WATCHTOWER. AQUAMAN HERE.
IS THE FLASH'S COSMIC TREADMILL RUNNING?
THE TREADMILL? I THINK SO...
THEN YOU BETTER GO CATCH IT! BWAHAHA HAHA!
DO NOT KNOCK
SUPERMAN'S FORTRESS OF SOLITUDE.
RRRIIINNG RRRIIINNG
HELLO?
DO YOU HAVE THE CITY OF KANDOR IN A BOTTLE?
SURE.
THEN YOU BETTER LET IT OUT! BWAHAHA HAHA!
HUH? THAT DOESN'T EVEN MAKE SENSE...
#1
THE PLANET OA.
I DON'T CARE HOW MANY GALAXIES YOU HAD TO CROSS! THE GUARDIANS OF THE UNIVERSE DID NOT ORDER ANY PIZZA!
MY TURN TO MAKE A CALL!
RRRIIINNG RRRIIINNG
HELLO?

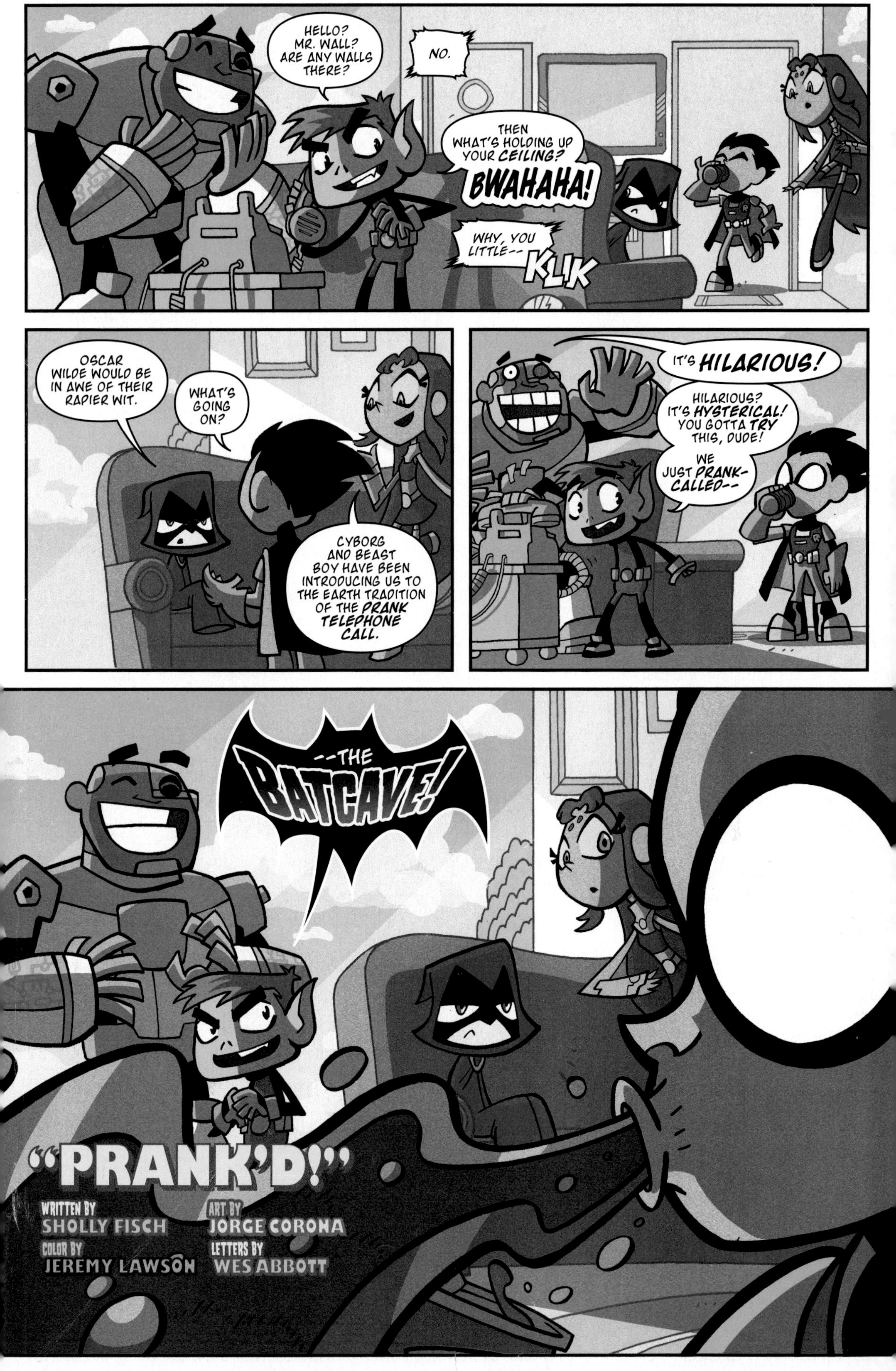
HELLO? MR. WALL? ARE ANY WALLS THERE?
NO.
THEN WHAT'S HOLDING UP YOUR CEILING? BWAHAHA!
WHY, YOU LITTLE--
KLIK
OSCAR WILDE WOULD BE IN AWE OF THEIR RAPIER WIT.
WHAT'S GOING ON?
CYBORG AND BEAST BOY HAVE BEEN INTRODUCING US TO THE EARTH TRADITION OF THE PRANK TELEPHONE CALL.
IT'S HILARIOUS!
HILARIOUS? IT'S HYSTERICAL! YOU GOTTA TRY THIS, DUDE!
WE JUST PRANK-CALLED--
--THE BATCAVE!
"PRANK'D!"
WRITTEN BY SHOLLY FISCH
ART BY JORGE CORONA
COLOR BY JEREMY LAWSON
LETTERS BY WES ABBOTT

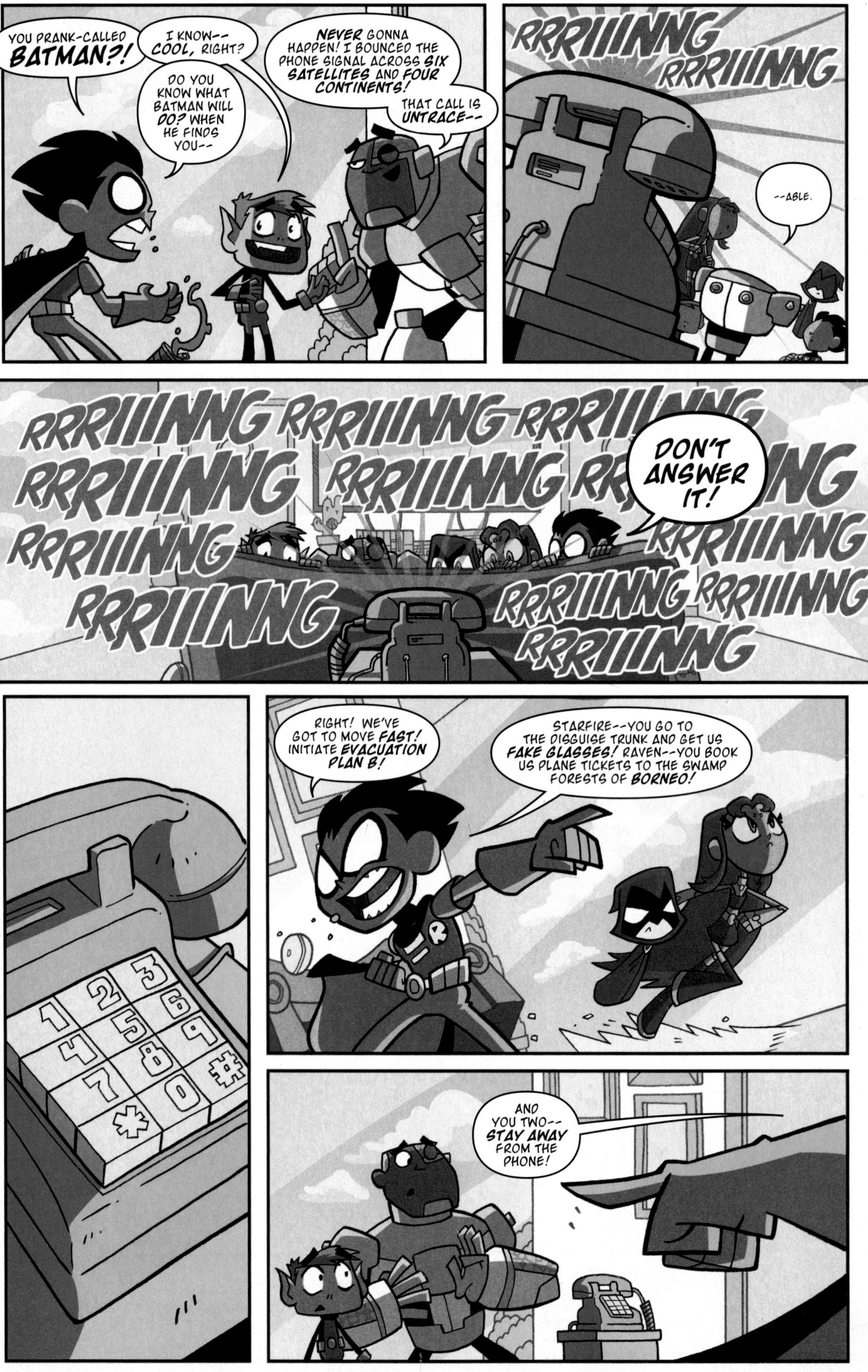
YOU PRANK-CALLED BATMAN?!
I KNOW--COOL, RIGHT?
DO YOU KNOW WHAT BATMAN WILL DO? WHEN HE FINDS YOU--
NEVER GONNA HAPPEN! I BOUNCED THE PHONE SIGNAL ACROSS SIX SATELLITES AND FOUR CONTINENTS!
THAT CALL IS UNTRACE--
RRRIIINNG
RRRIIINNG
--ABLE.
RRRIIINNG RRRIIINNG RRRIIINNG
RRRIIINNG RRRIIINNG
DON'T ANSWER IT!
RRRIIINNG
RRRIIINNG
RRRIIINNG RRRIIINNG
RRRIIINNG
RRRIIINNG
RIGHT! WE'VE GOT TO MOVE FAST! INITIATE EVACUATION PLAN B!
STARFIRE--YOU GO TO THE DISGUISE TRUNK AND GET US FAKE GLASSES! RAVEN--YOU BOOK US PLANE TICKETS TO THE SWAMP FORESTS OF BORNEO!
AND YOU TWO--STAY AWAY FROM THE PHONE!

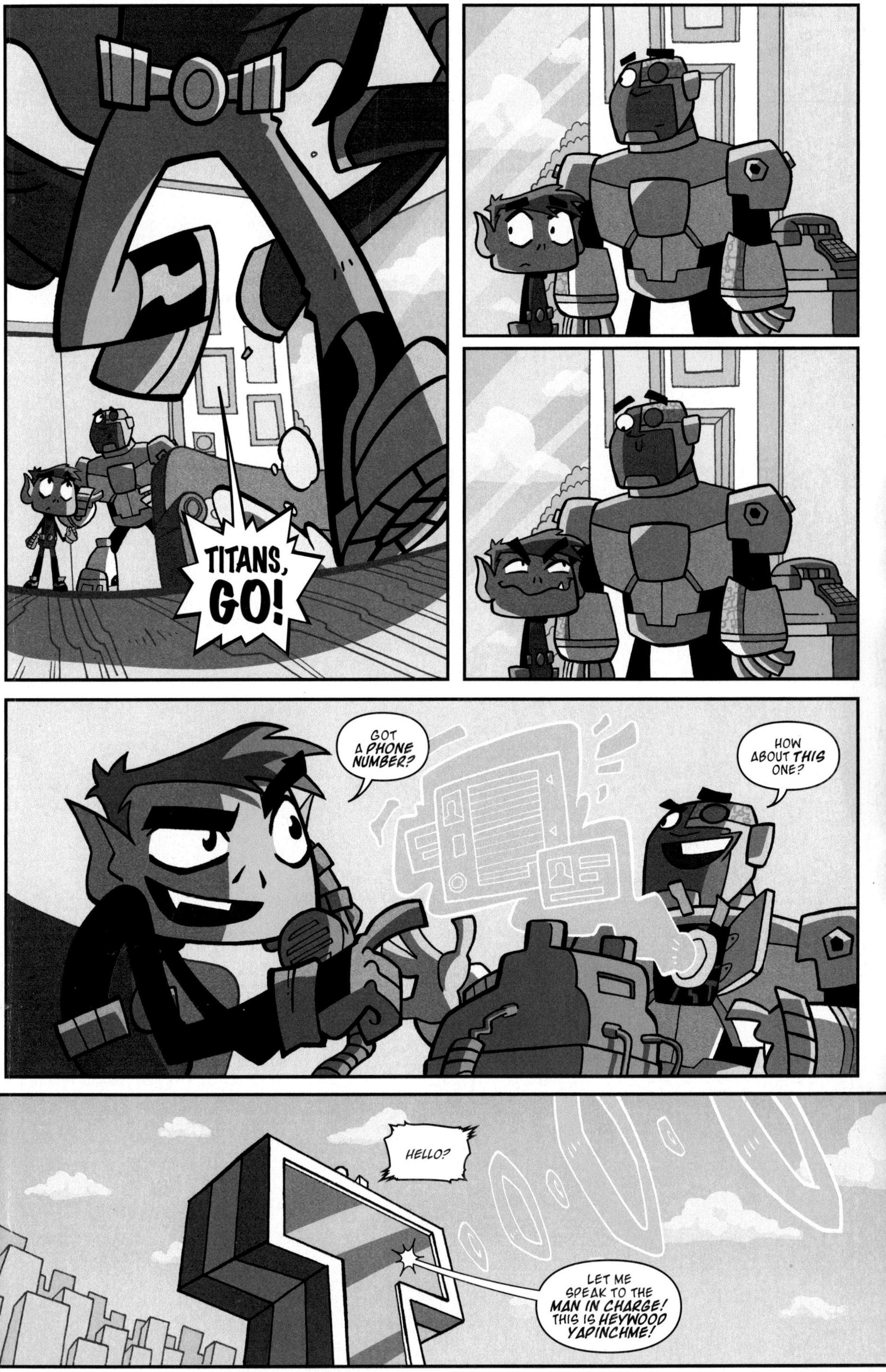

TITANS, GO!
GOT A PHONE NUMBER?
HOW ABOUT THIS ONE?
HELLO?
LET ME SPEAK TO THE MAN IN CHARGE! THIS IS HEYWOOD YAPINCHME!

"HEYWOOD YAPINCHME?"

OW!

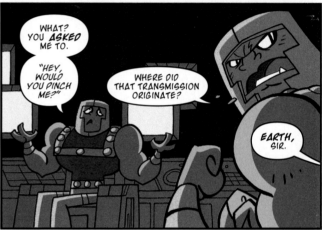

WHAT? YOU **ASKED** ME TO.

"HEY, WOULD YOU PINCH ME?"

WHERE DID THAT TRANSMISSION ORIGINATE?

EARTH, SIR.

CHANGE COURSE!

BUT, COMMANDER--

--WE HAVEN'T FINISHED **DESTROYING** THE PLANET **HNY'XX** YET!

THE HNY'XXIANS WILL JUST HAVE TO **WAIT THEIR TURN!**

THIS IS AN **INSULT** TO THE GORDANIAN HOMEWORLD! WE GO TO **EARTH!**

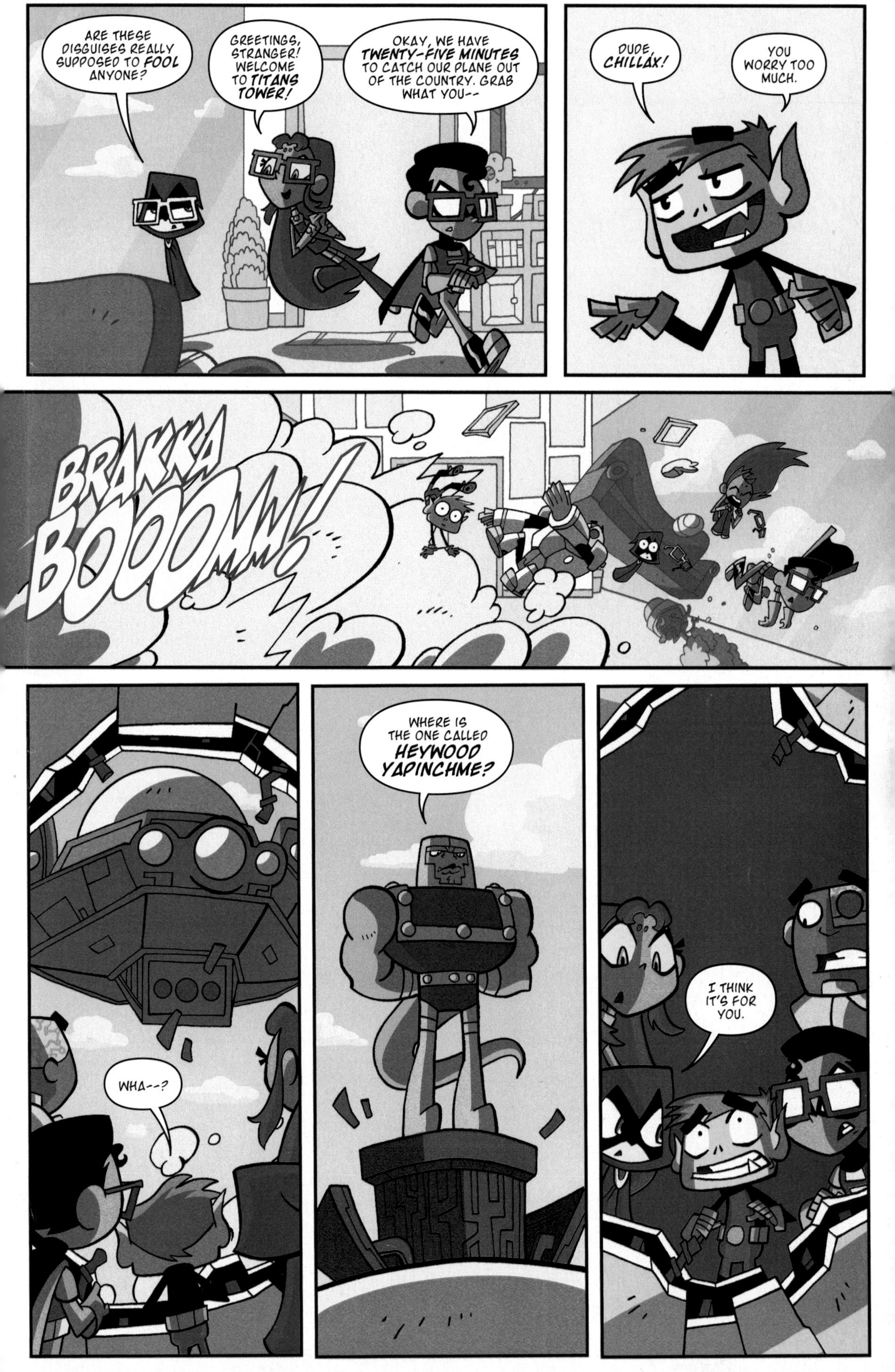

ARE THESE DISGUISES REALLY SUPPOSED TO FOOL ANYONE?
GREETINGS, STRANGER! WELCOME TO TITANS TOWER!
OKAY, WE HAVE TWENTY-FIVE MINUTES TO CATCH OUR PLANE OUT OF THE COUNTRY. GRAB WHAT YOU--
DUDE, CHILLAX!
YOU WORRY TOO MUCH.
BRAKKA BOOOOM!
WHA--?
WHERE IS THE ONE CALLED HEYWOOD YAPINCHME?
I THINK IT'S FOR YOU.

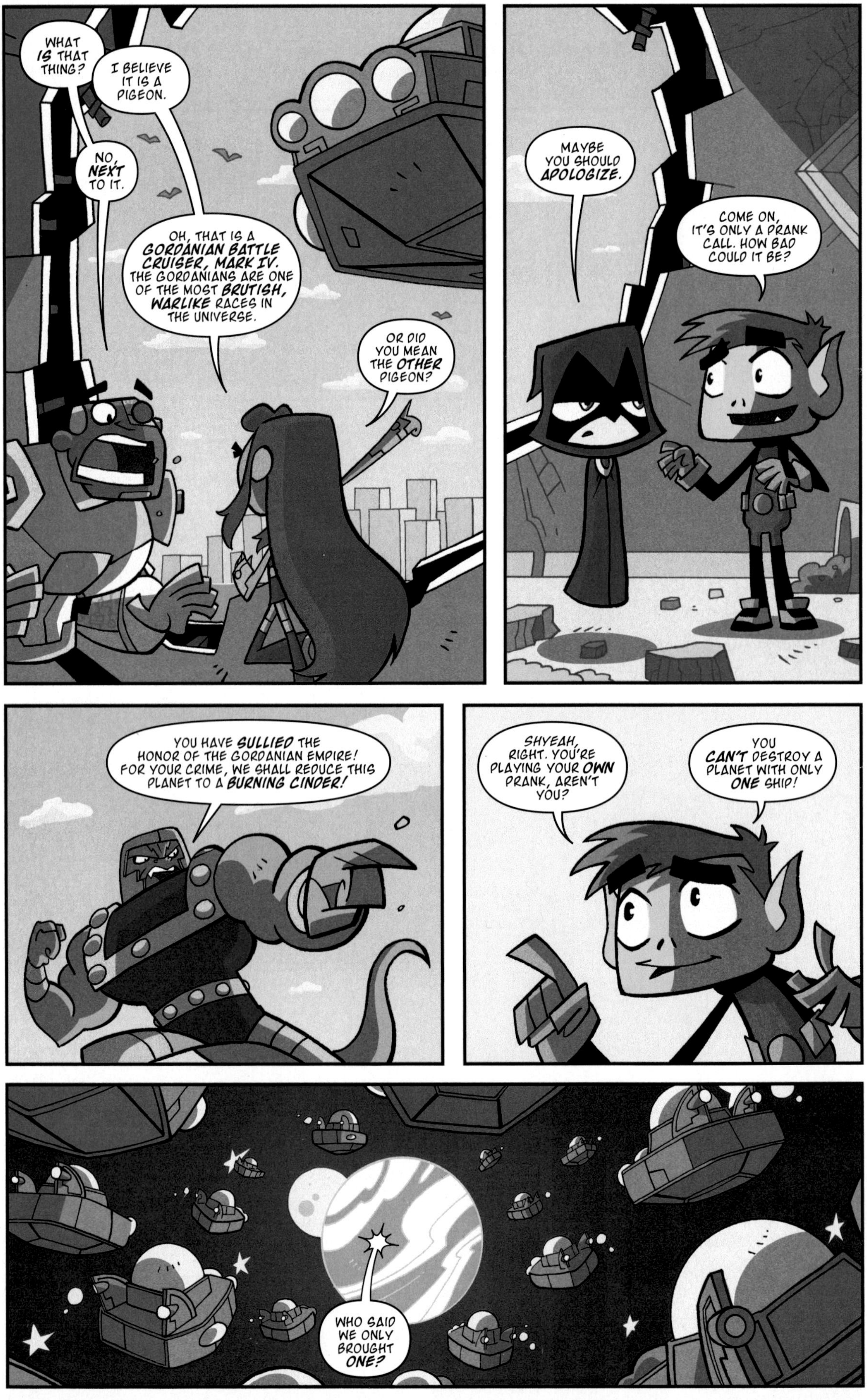
WHAT IS THAT THING?
I BELIEVE IT IS A PIGEON.
NO, NEXT TO IT.
OH, THAT IS A GORDANIAN BATTLE CRUISER, MARK IV. THE GORDANIANS ARE ONE OF THE MOST BRUTISH, WARLIKE RACES IN THE UNIVERSE.
OR DID YOU MEAN THE OTHER PIGEON?
MAYBE YOU SHOULD APOLOGIZE.
COME ON, IT'S ONLY A PRANK CALL. HOW BAD COULD IT BE?
YOU HAVE SULLIED THE HONOR OF THE GORDANIAN EMPIRE! FOR YOUR CRIME, WE SHALL REDUCE THIS PLANET TO A BURNING CINDER!
SHYEAH, RIGHT. YOU'RE PLAYING YOUR OWN PRANK, AREN'T YOU?
YOU CAN'T DESTROY A PLANET WITH ONLY ONE SHIP!
WHO SAID WE ONLY BROUGHT ONE?

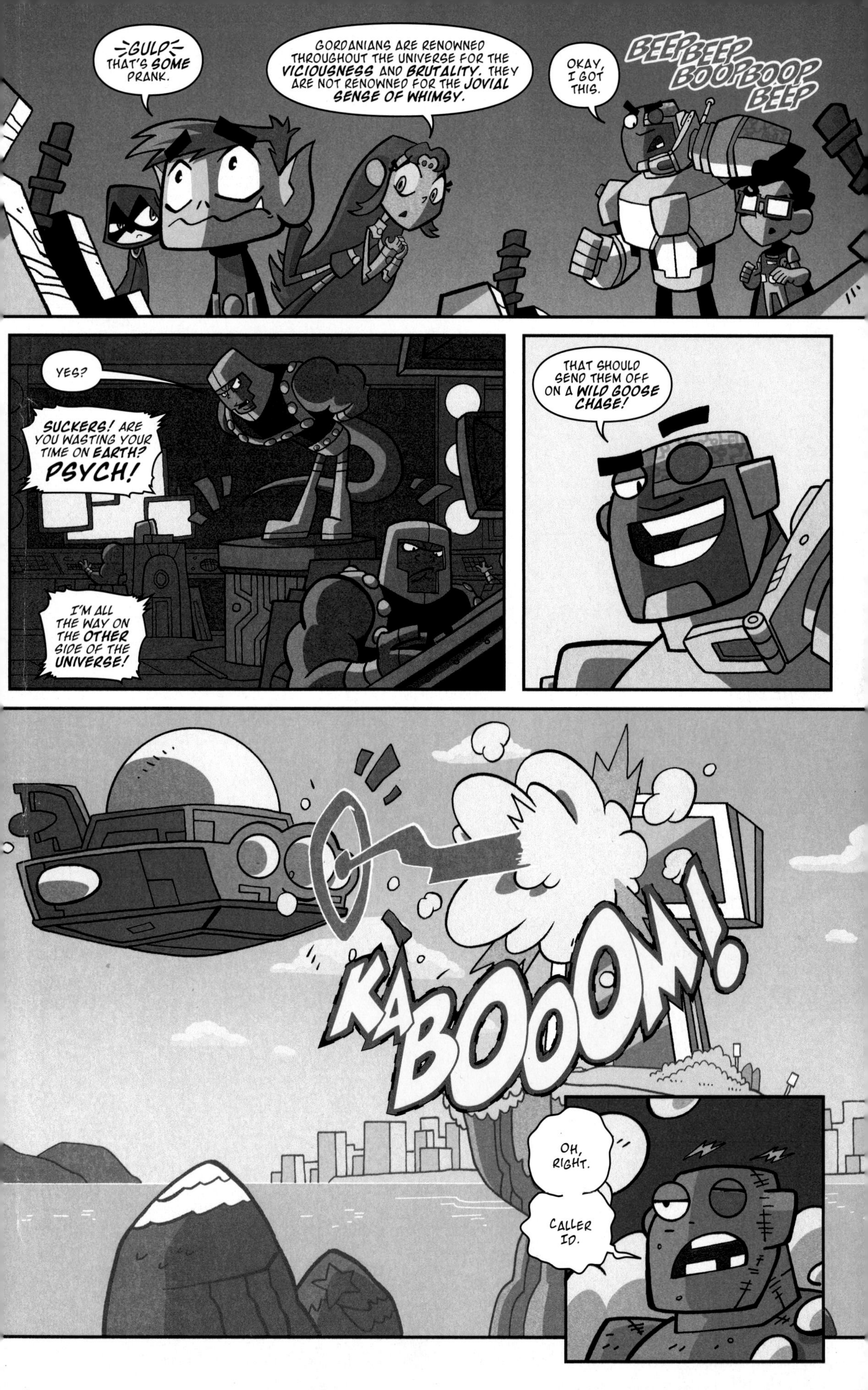

GULP
THAT'S SOME PRANK.
GORDANIANS ARE RENOWNED THROUGHOUT THE UNIVERSE FOR THE VICIOUSNESS AND BRUTALITY. THEY ARE NOT RENOWNED FOR THE JOVIAL SENSE OF WHIMSY.
OKAY, I GOT THIS.
BEEP BEEP BOOP BOOP BEEP
YES?
SUCKERS! ARE YOU WASTING YOUR TIME ON EARTH? PSYCH!
I'M ALL THE WAY ON THE OTHER SIDE OF THE UNIVERSE!
THAT SHOULD SEND THEM OFF ON A WILD GOOSE CHASE!
KA BOOOM!
OH, RIGHT.
CALLER ID.

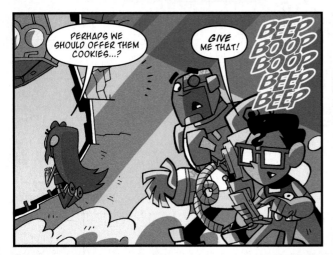

PERHAPS WE SHOULD OFFER THEM COOKIES...?

GIVE ME THAT!

BEEP BOOP BOOP BEEP BEEP

HELLO?

HELLO! I'M CALLING TO CONFIRM YOUR ORDER OF *STILTS*, *CALAMINE LOTION*, AND AN APRON MARKED *"KISS ME, I'M A WIMP!"*

ANOTHER PRANK CALL?! I'LL--

KLIK

IS IT REALLY A GOOD IDEA TO MAKE THE ALIENS *ANGRIER?*

I DIDN'T *CALL* THE ALIENS.

BUT I *DID* REDIRECT THE SIGNAL.

ON MY COMMAND...

...ALL BATTERIES FI--

I BELIEVE YOU HAVE AN *APRON* FOR ME.

EH?

YOU THINK MAKING PRANK PHONE CALLS IS *FUNNY?*

THEN YOU SHOULD WATCH OUT FOR *CALLER ID!*

B-B-B-BATMAN!

BATMAN?!

RUN!!

DO THEY NOT WANT THE *COOKIES?*

SO...YOU PRANK-CALLED THE *BATCAVE*, BUT REDIRECTED THE CALL...?

...SO THAT IT *LOOKED* LIKE THE CALL CAME FROM THE *GORDANIAN FLAGSHIP!*

WOW. YOU'RE AN *EVIL GENIUS.*

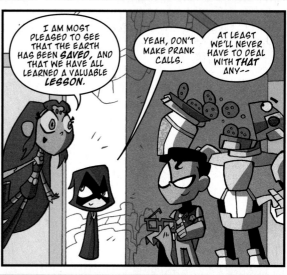

I AM MOST PLEASED TO SEE THAT THE EARTH HAS BEEN *SAVED*, AND THAT WE HAVE ALL LEARNED A VALUABLE *LESSON.*

YEAH, DON'T MAKE PRANK CALLS.

AT LEAST WE'LL NEVER HAVE TO DEAL WITH *THAT* ANY--

--MORE?

HELLO, DARKSEID?

THE END

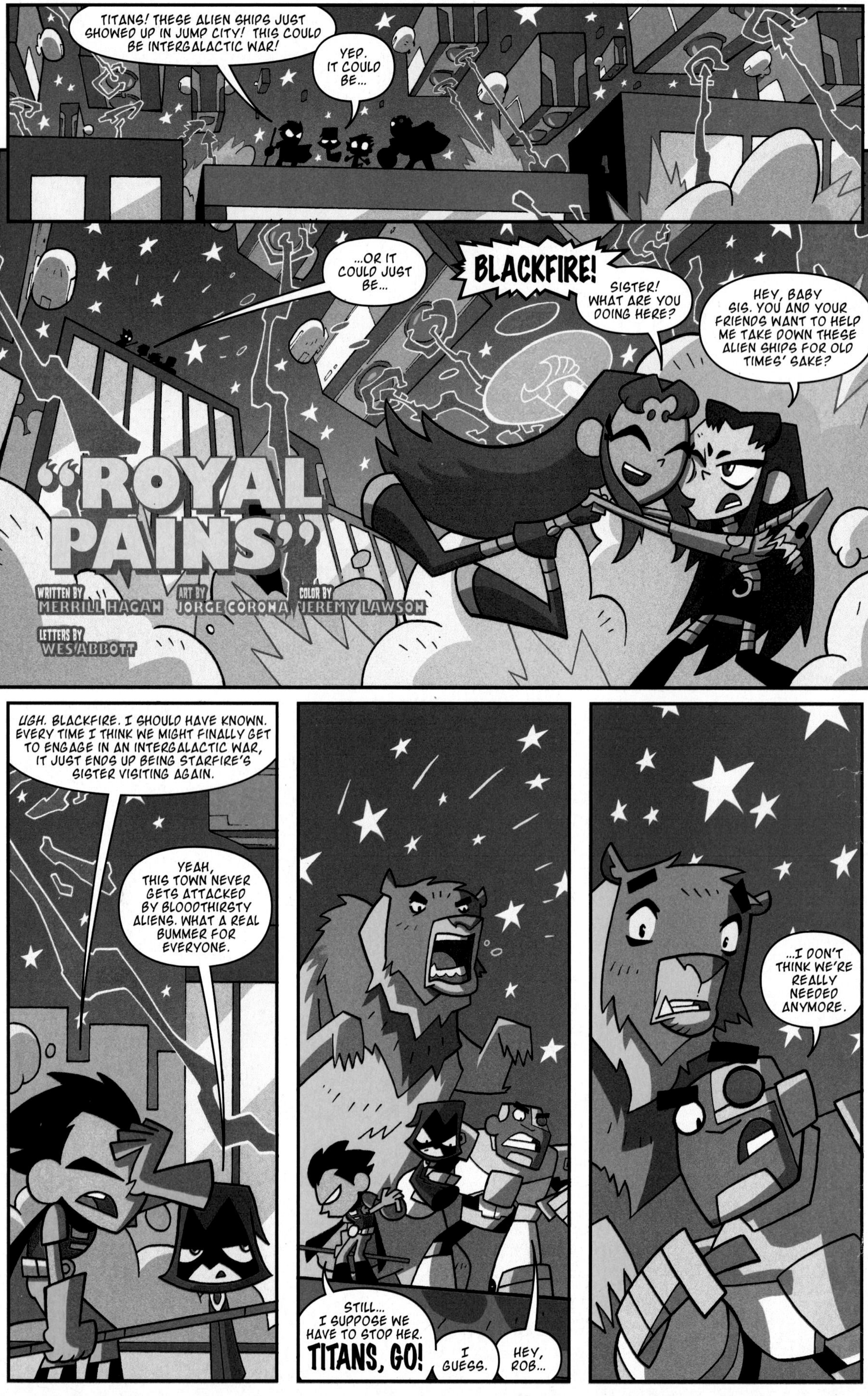
TITANS! THESE ALIEN SHIPS JUST SHOWED UP IN JUMP CITY! THIS COULD BE INTERGALACTIC WAR!
YEP. IT COULD BE...
...OR IT COULD JUST BE...
BLACKFIRE!
SISTER! WHAT ARE YOU DOING HERE?
HEY, BABY SIS. YOU AND YOUR FRIENDS WANT TO HELP ME TAKE DOWN THESE ALIEN SHIPS FOR OLD TIMES' SAKE?
"ROYAL PAINS"
WRITTEN BY MERRILL HAGAN
ART BY JORGE CORONA
COLOR BY JEREMY LAWSON
LETTERS BY WES ABBOTT
UGH. BLACKFIRE. I SHOULD HAVE KNOWN. EVERY TIME I THINK WE MIGHT FINALLY GET TO ENGAGE IN AN INTERGALACTIC WAR, IT JUST ENDS UP BEING STARFIRE'S SISTER VISITING AGAIN.
YEAH, THIS TOWN NEVER GETS ATTACKED BY BLOODTHIRSTY ALIENS. WHAT A REAL BUMMER FOR EVERYONE.
STILL... I SUPPOSE WE HAVE TO STOP HER. TITANS, GO!
I GUESS.
HEY, ROB...
...I DON'T THINK WE'RE REALLY NEEDED ANYMORE.

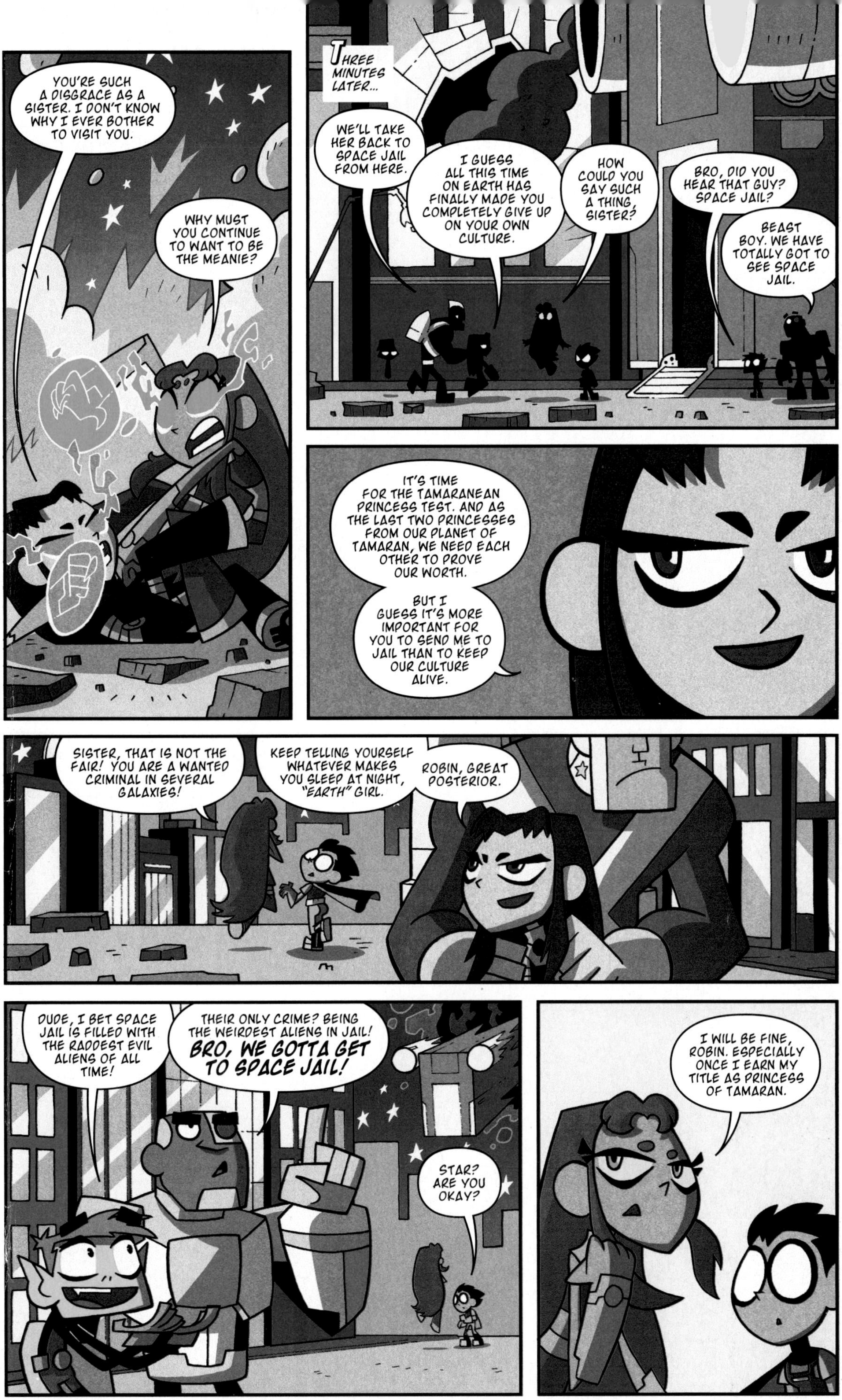
YOU'RE SUCH A DISGRACE AS A SISTER. I DON'T KNOW WHY I EVER BOTHER TO VISIT YOU.
WHY MUST YOU CONTINUE TO WANT TO BE THE MEANIE?
THREE MINUTES LATER...
WE'LL TAKE HER BACK TO SPACE JAIL FROM HERE.
I GUESS ALL THIS TIME ON EARTH HAS FINALLY MADE YOU COMPLETELY GIVE UP ON YOUR OWN CULTURE.
HOW COULD YOU SAY SUCH A THING, SISTER?
BRO, DID YOU HEAR THAT GUY? SPACE JAIL?
BEAST BOY. WE HAVE TOTALLY GOT TO SEE SPACE JAIL.
IT'S TIME FOR THE TAMARANEAN PRINCESS TEST. AND AS THE LAST TWO PRINCESSES FROM OUR PLANET OF TAMARAN, WE NEED EACH OTHER TO PROVE OUR WORTH.
BUT I GUESS IT'S MORE IMPORTANT FOR YOU TO SEND ME TO JAIL THAN TO KEEP OUR CULTURE ALIVE.
SISTER, THAT IS NOT THE FAIR! YOU ARE A WANTED CRIMINAL IN SEVERAL GALAXIES!
KEEP TELLING YOURSELF WHATEVER MAKES YOU SLEEP AT NIGHT, "EARTH" GIRL.
ROBIN, GREAT POSTERIOR.
DUDE, I BET SPACE JAIL IS FILLED WITH THE RADDEST EVIL ALIENS OF ALL TIME!
THEIR ONLY CRIME? BEING THE WEIRDEST ALIENS IN JAIL! BRO, WE GOTTA GET TO SPACE JAIL!
STAR? ARE YOU OKAY?
I WILL BE FINE, ROBIN. ESPECIALLY ONCE I EARN MY TITLE AS PRINCESS OF TAMARAN.

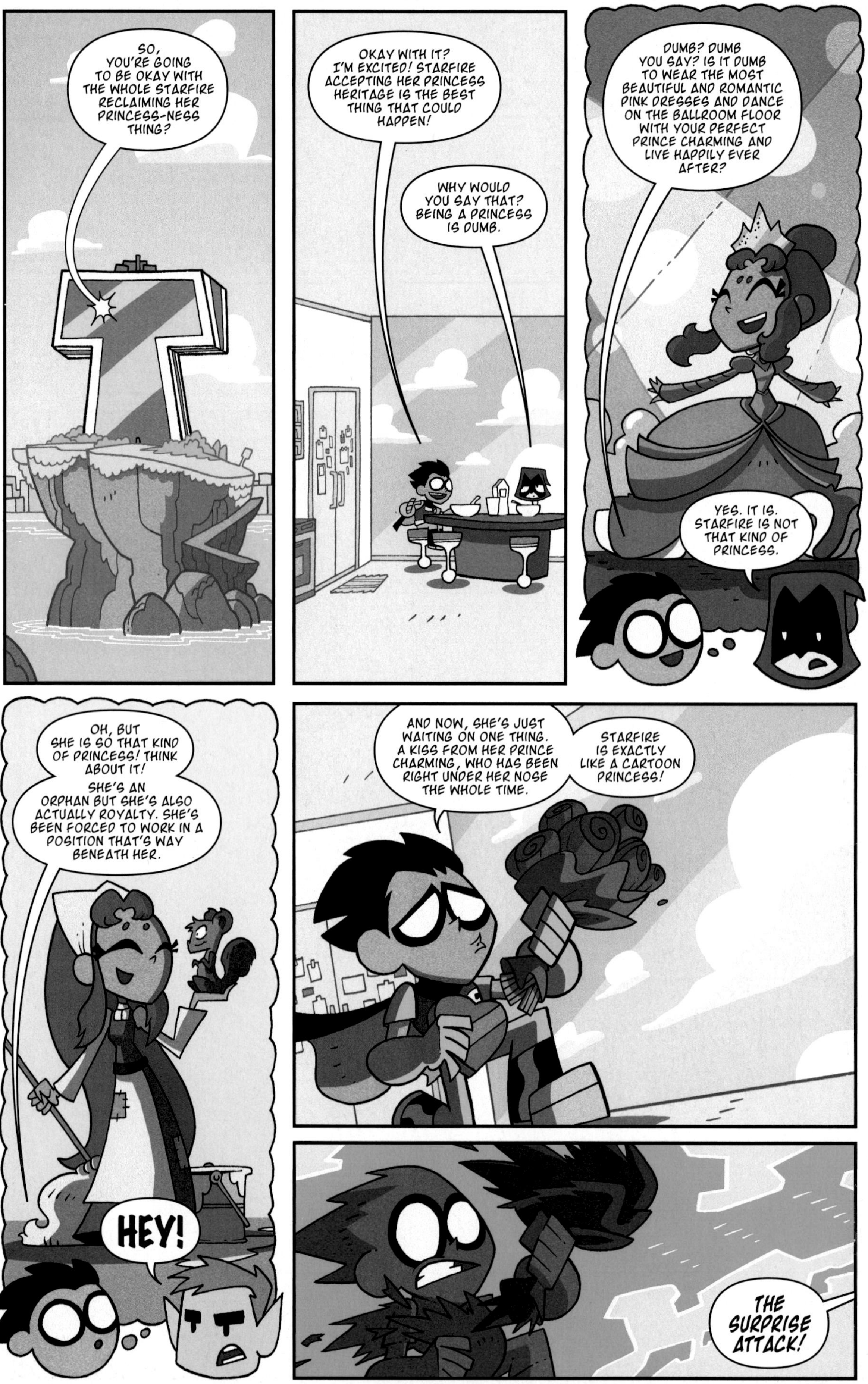
SO, YOU'RE GOING TO BE OKAY WITH THE WHOLE STARFIRE RECLAIMING HER PRINCESS-NESS THING?
OKAY WITH IT? I'M EXCITED! STARFIRE ACCEPTING HER PRINCESS HERITAGE IS THE BEST THING THAT COULD HAPPEN!
WHY WOULD YOU SAY THAT? BEING A PRINCESS IS DUMB.
DUMB? DUMB YOU SAY? IS IT DUMB TO WEAR THE MOST BEAUTIFUL AND ROMANTIC PINK DRESSES AND DANCE ON THE BALLROOM FLOOR WITH YOUR PERFECT PRINCE CHARMING AND LIVE HAPPILY EVER AFTER?
YES. IT IS. STARFIRE IS NOT THAT KIND OF PRINCESS.
OH, BUT SHE IS SO THAT KIND OF PRINCESS! THINK ABOUT IT!
SHE'S AN ORPHAN BUT SHE'S ALSO ACTUALLY ROYALTY. SHE'S BEEN FORCED TO WORK IN A POSITION THAT'S WAY BENEATH HER.
HEY!
AND NOW, SHE'S JUST WAITING ON ONE THING. A KISS FROM HER PRINCE CHARMING, WHO HAS BEEN RIGHT UNDER HER NOSE THE WHOLE TIME.
STARFIRE IS EXACTLY LIKE A CARTOON PRINCESS!
THE SURPRISE ATTACK!

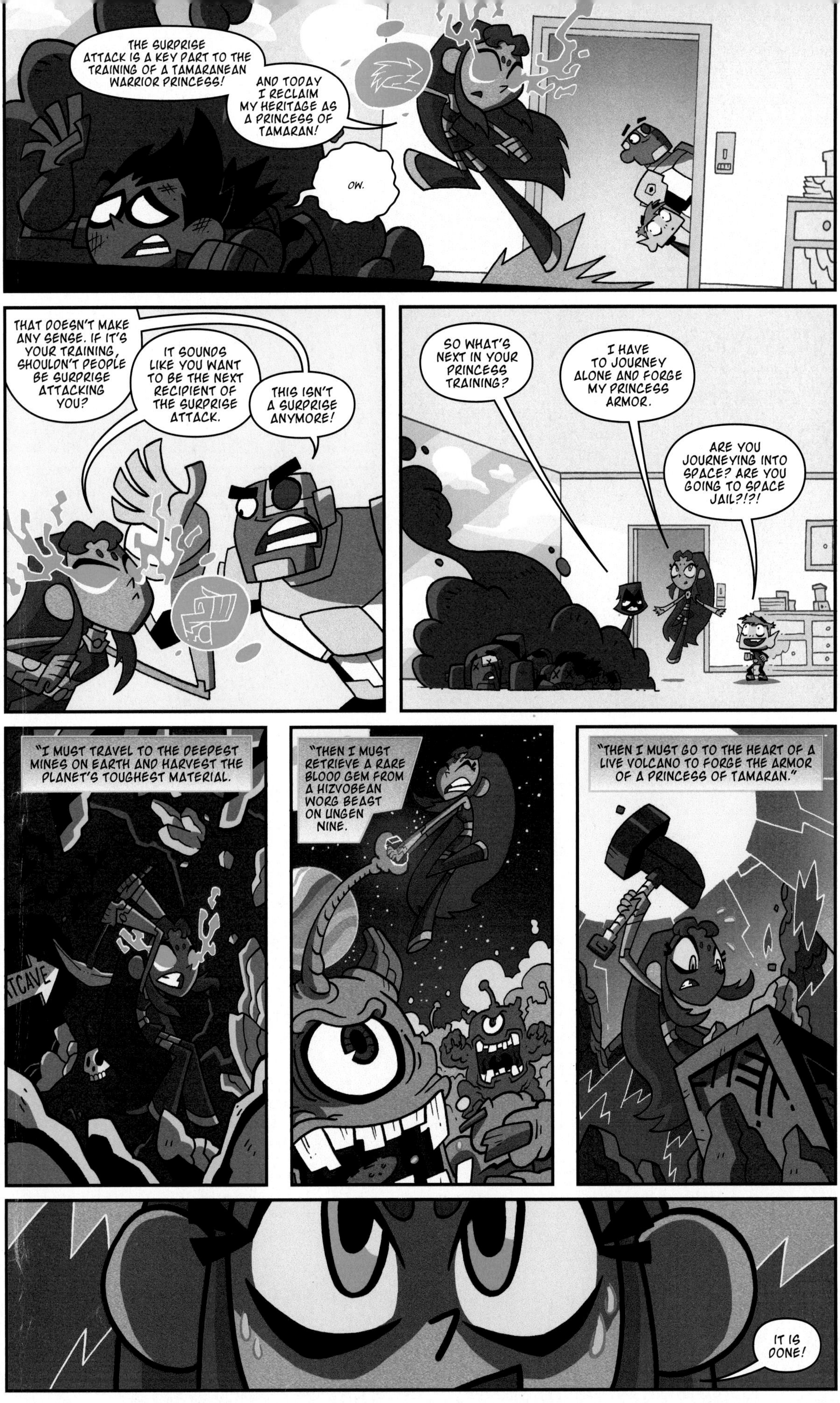
THE SURPRISE ATTACK IS A KEY PART TO THE TRAINING OF A TAMARANEAN WARRIOR PRINCESS!
AND TODAY I RECLAIM MY HERITAGE AS A PRINCESS OF TAMARAN!
OW.
THAT DOESN'T MAKE ANY SENSE. IF IT'S YOUR TRAINING, SHOULDN'T PEOPLE BE SURPRISE ATTACKING YOU?
IT SOUNDS LIKE YOU WANT TO BE THE NEXT RECIPIENT OF THE SURPRISE ATTACK.
THIS ISN'T A SURPRISE ANYMORE!
SO WHAT'S NEXT IN YOUR PRINCESS TRAINING?
I HAVE TO JOURNEY ALONE AND FORGE MY PRINCESS ARMOR.
ARE YOU JOURNEYING INTO SPACE? ARE YOU GOING TO SPACE JAIL?!?!
"I MUST TRAVEL TO THE DEEPEST MINES ON EARTH AND HARVEST THE PLANET'S TOUGHEST MATERIAL.
TCAVE
"THEN I MUST RETRIEVE A RARE BLOOD GEM FROM A HIZVOBEAN WORG BEAST ON UNGEN NINE.
"THEN I MUST GO TO THE HEART OF A LIVE VOLCANO TO FORGE THE ARMOR OF A PRINCESS OF TAMARAN."
IT IS DONE!

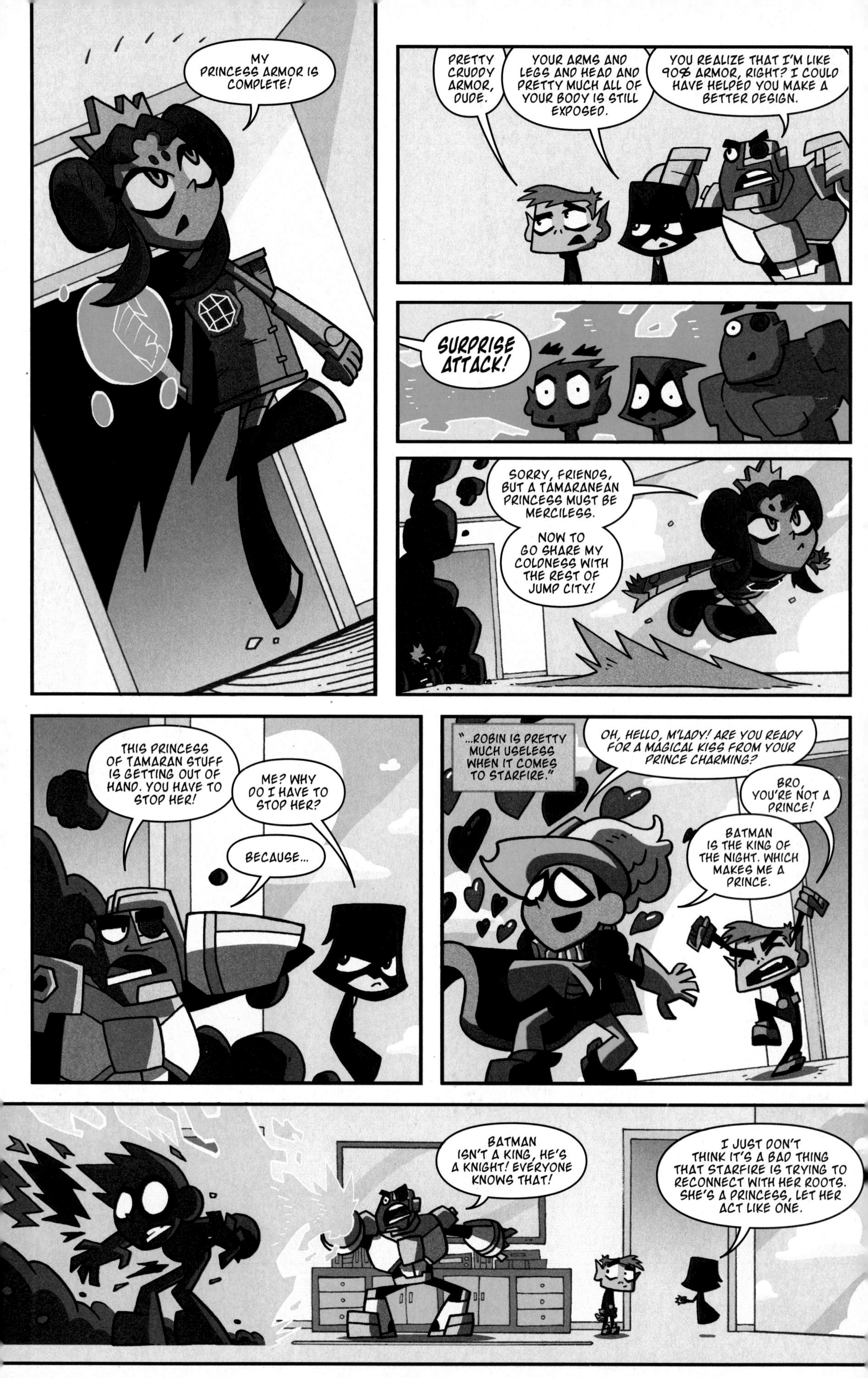
MY PRINCESS ARMOR IS COMPLETE!
PRETTY CRUDDY ARMOR, DUDE.
YOUR ARMS AND LEGS AND HEAD AND PRETTY MUCH ALL OF YOUR BODY IS STILL EXPOSED.
YOU REALIZE THAT I'M LIKE 90% ARMOR, RIGHT? I COULD HAVE HELPED YOU MAKE A BETTER DESIGN.
SURPRISE ATTACK!
SORRY, FRIENDS, BUT A TAMARANEAN PRINCESS MUST BE MERCILESS.
NOW TO GO SHARE MY COLDNESS WITH THE REST OF JUMP CITY!
THIS PRINCESS OF TAMARAN STUFF IS GETTING OUT OF HAND. YOU HAVE TO STOP HER!
ME? WHY DO I HAVE TO STOP HER?
BECAUSE...
"...ROBIN IS PRETTY MUCH USELESS WHEN IT COMES TO STARFIRE."
OH, HELLO, M'LADY! ARE YOU READY FOR A MAGICAL KISS FROM YOUR PRINCE CHARMING?
BRO, YOU'RE NOT A PRINCE!
BATMAN IS THE KING OF THE NIGHT. WHICH MAKES ME A PRINCE.
BATMAN ISN'T A KING, HE'S A KNIGHT! EVERYONE KNOWS THAT!
I JUST DON'T THINK IT'S A BAD THING THAT STARFIRE IS TRYING TO RECONNECT WITH HER ROOTS. SHE'S A PRINCESS, LET HER ACT LIKE ONE.

FRIENDS! I HAVE FINISHED ONE MORE PRINCESS CHALLENGE BY VANQUISHING OUR COMMON FOES AND SHOWING THEM THE NO MERCY!

MAD MOD! CONTROL FREAK! WHAT HAPPENED?

I USED AN EXPIRED COUPON AT THE PHARMACIST'S.

I WAS ILLEGALLY STREAMING CABLE TO WATCH HOUR-LONG DRAMAS.

WE HAVE TO STOP STARFIRE. SHE'S GONE TOO FAR. LOOK WHAT SHE'S DONE.

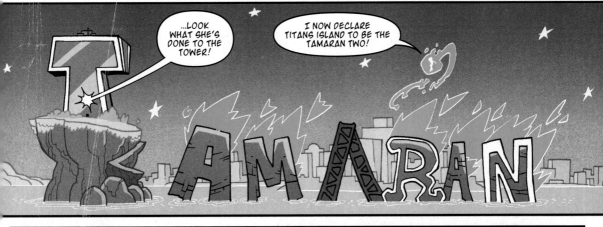

...LOOK WHAT SHE'S DONE TO THE TOWER!

I NOW DECLARE TITANS ISLAND TO BE THE TAMARAN TWO!

AND NOW, BEAST BOY, I NEED YOU TO BE THE ROYAL STEED FOR THE PRINCESS OF TAMARAN TWO!

I'M SPLITTING, DUDE!

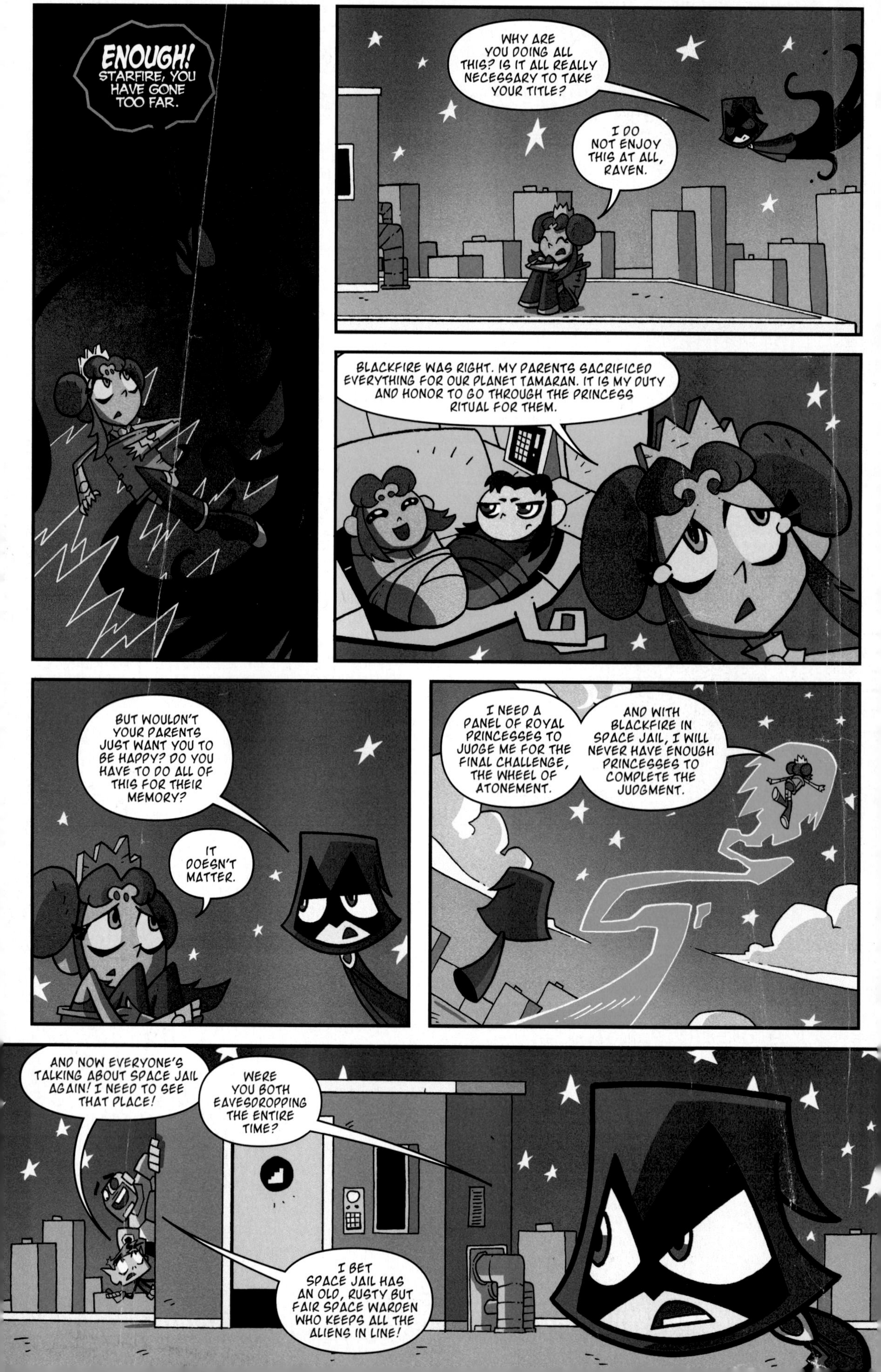
ENOUGH! STARFIRE, YOU HAVE GONE TOO FAR.
WHY ARE YOU DOING ALL THIS? IS IT ALL REALLY NECESSARY TO TAKE YOUR TITLE?
I DO NOT ENJOY THIS AT ALL, RAVEN.
BLACKFIRE WAS RIGHT. MY PARENTS SACRIFICED EVERYTHING FOR OUR PLANET TAMARAN. IT IS MY DUTY AND HONOR TO GO THROUGH THE PRINCESS RITUAL FOR THEM.
BUT WOULDN'T YOUR PARENTS JUST WANT YOU TO BE HAPPY? DO YOU HAVE TO DO ALL OF THIS FOR THEIR MEMORY?
IT DOESN'T MATTER.
I NEED A PANEL OF ROYAL PRINCESSES TO JUDGE ME FOR THE FINAL CHALLENGE, THE WHEEL OF ATONEMENT.
AND WITH BLACKFIRE IN SPACE JAIL, I WILL NEVER HAVE ENOUGH PRINCESSES TO COMPLETE THE JUDGMENT.
AND NOW EVERYONE'S TALKING ABOUT SPACE JAIL AGAIN! I NEED TO SEE THAT PLACE!
WERE YOU BOTH EAVESDROPPING THE ENTIRE TIME?
I BET SPACE JAIL HAS AN OLD, RUSTY BUT FAIR SPACE WARDEN WHO KEEPS ALL THE ALIENS IN LINE!

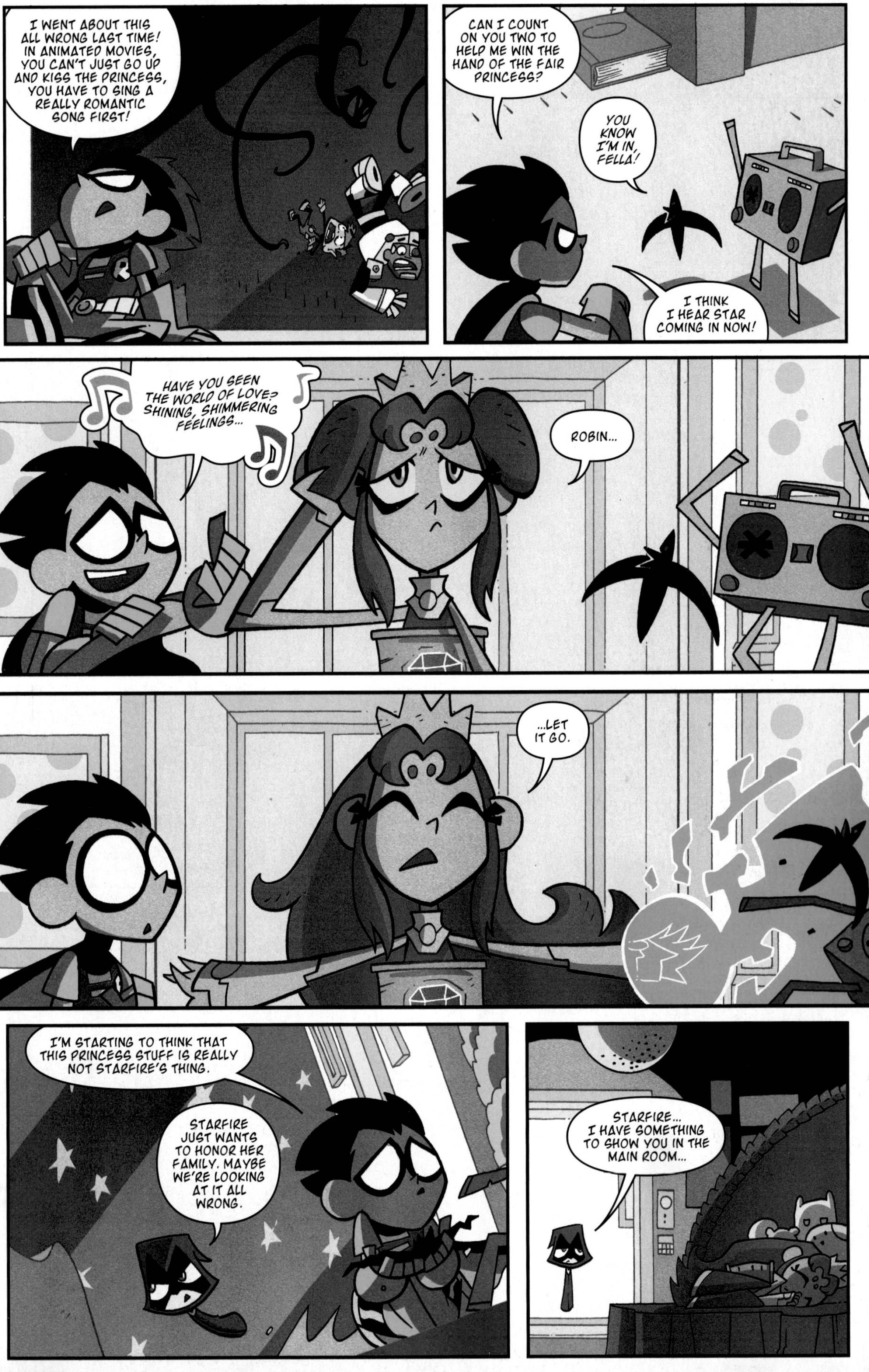
I WENT ABOUT THIS ALL WRONG LAST TIME! IN ANIMATED MOVIES, YOU CAN'T JUST GO UP AND KISS THE PRINCESS, YOU HAVE TO SING A REALLY ROMANTIC SONG FIRST!
CAN I COUNT ON YOU TWO TO HELP ME WIN THE HAND OF THE FAIR PRINCESS?
YOU KNOW I'M IN, FELLA!
I THINK I HEAR STAR COMING IN NOW!
HAVE YOU SEEN THE WORLD OF LOVE? SHINING, SHIMMERING FEELINGS...
ROBIN...
...LET IT GO.
I'M STARTING TO THINK THAT THIS PRINCESS STUFF IS REALLY NOT STARFIRE'S THING.
STARFIRE JUST WANTS TO HONOR HER FAMILY. MAYBE WE'RE LOOKING AT IT ALL WRONG.
STARFIRE... I HAVE SOMETHING TO SHOW YOU IN THE MAIN ROOM...

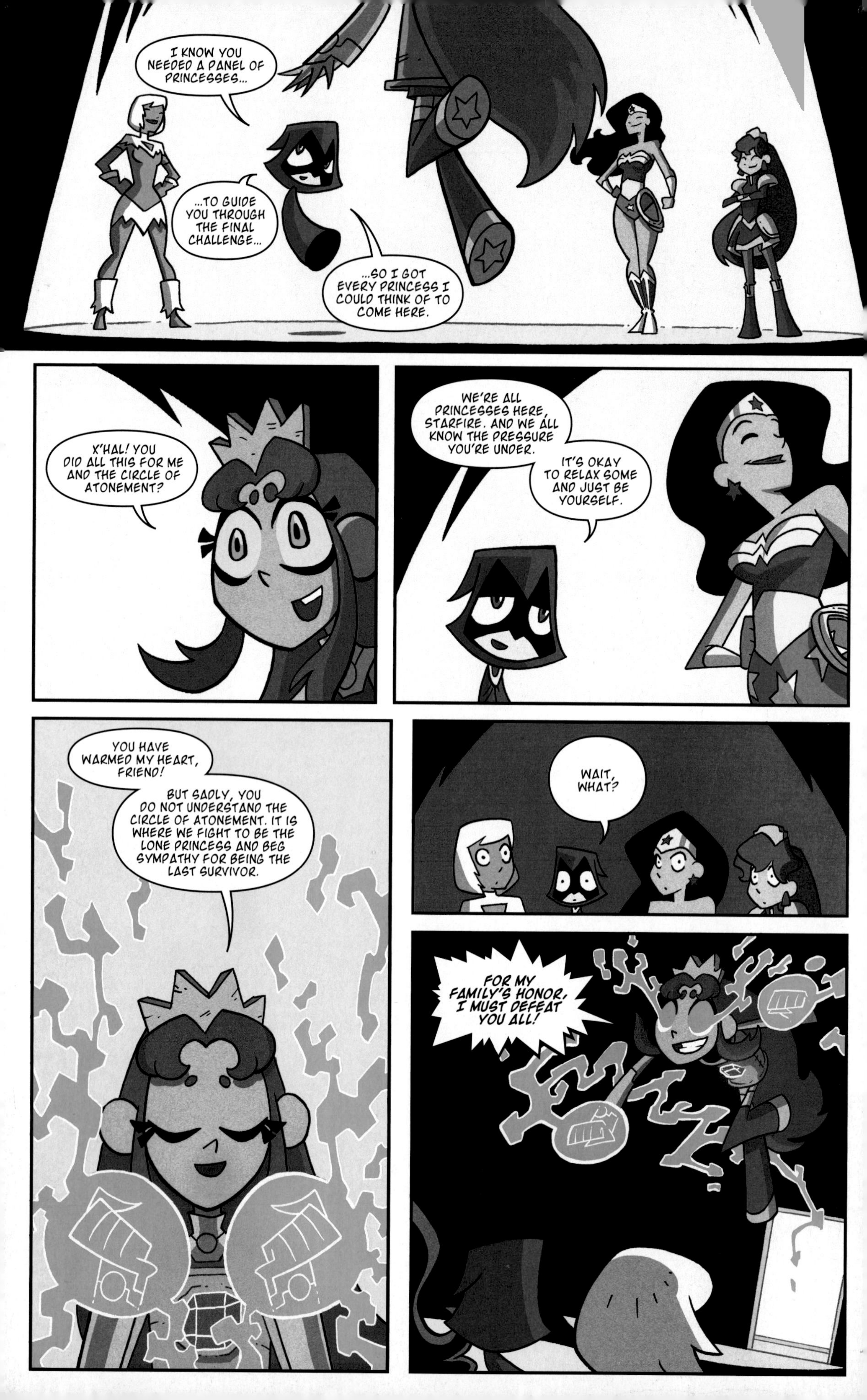
I KNOW YOU NEEDED A PANEL OF PRINCESSES...
...TO GUIDE YOU THROUGH THE FINAL CHALLENGE...
...SO I GOT EVERY PRINCESS I COULD THINK OF TO COME HERE.
X'HAL! YOU DID ALL THIS FOR ME AND THE CIRCLE OF ATONEMENT?
WE'RE ALL PRINCESSES HERE, STARFIRE. AND WE ALL KNOW THE PRESSURE YOU'RE UNDER.
IT'S OKAY TO RELAX SOME AND JUST BE YOURSELF.
YOU HAVE WARMED MY HEART, FRIEND!
BUT SADLY, YOU DO NOT UNDERSTAND THE CIRCLE OF ATONEMENT. IT IS WHERE WE FIGHT TO BE THE LONE PRINCESS AND BEG SYMPATHY FOR BEING THE LAST SURVIVOR.
WAIT, WHAT?
FOR MY FAMILY'S HONOR, I MUST DEFEAT YOU ALL!

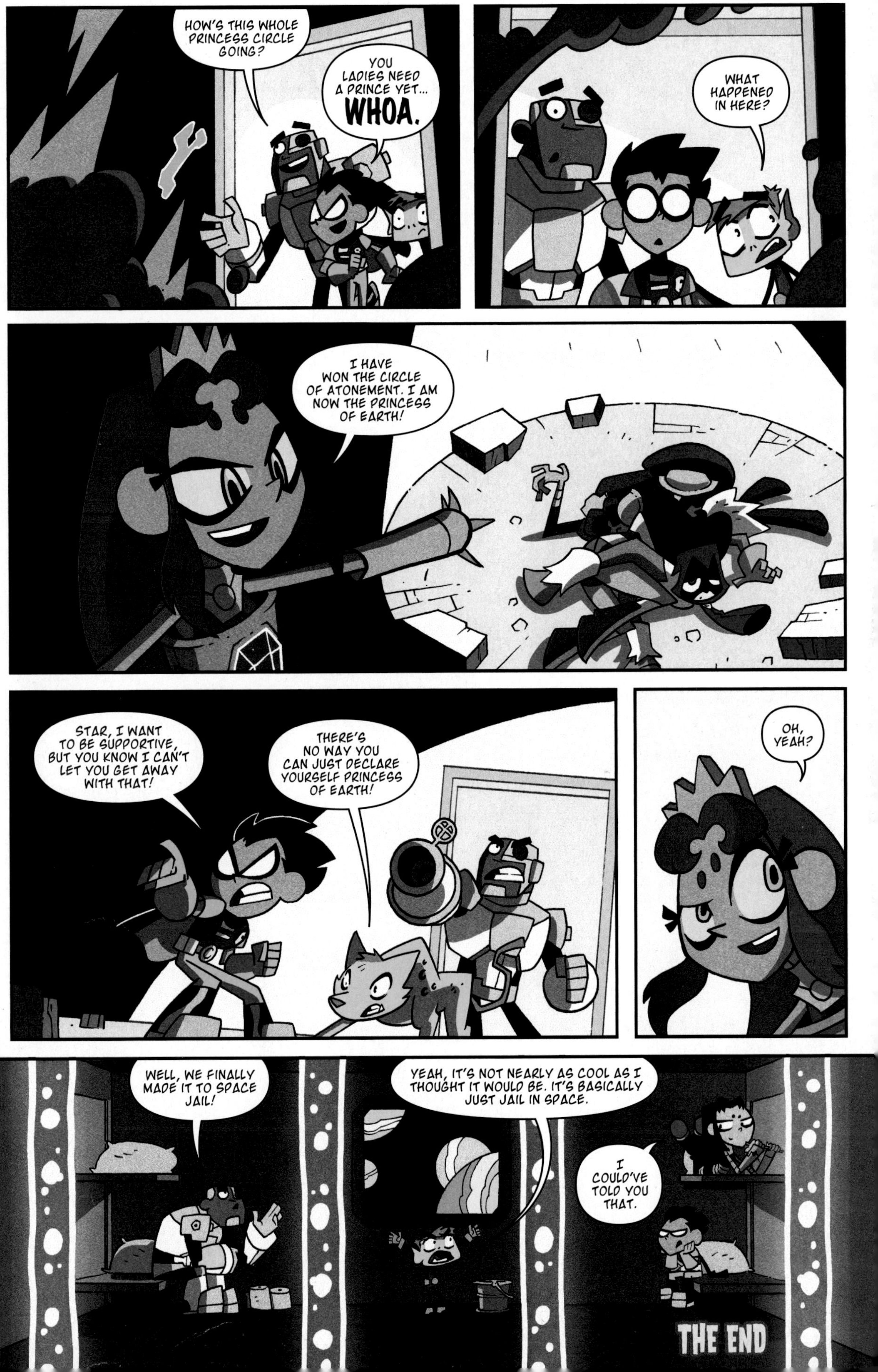
HOW'S THIS WHOLE PRINCESS CIRCLE GOING?
YOU LADIES NEED A PRINCE YET... WHOA.
WHAT HAPPENED IN HERE?
I HAVE WON THE CIRCLE OF ATONEMENT. I AM NOW THE PRINCESS OF EARTH!
STAR, I WANT TO BE SUPPORTIVE, BUT YOU KNOW I CAN'T LET YOU GET AWAY WITH THAT!
THERE'S NO WAY YOU CAN JUST DECLARE YOURSELF PRINCESS OF EARTH!
OH, YEAH?
WELL, WE FINALLY MADE IT TO SPACE JAIL!
YEAH, IT'S NOT NEARLY AS COOL AS I THOUGHT IT WOULD BE. IT'S BASICALLY JUST JAIL IN SPACE.
I COULD'VE TOLD YOU THAT.
THE END

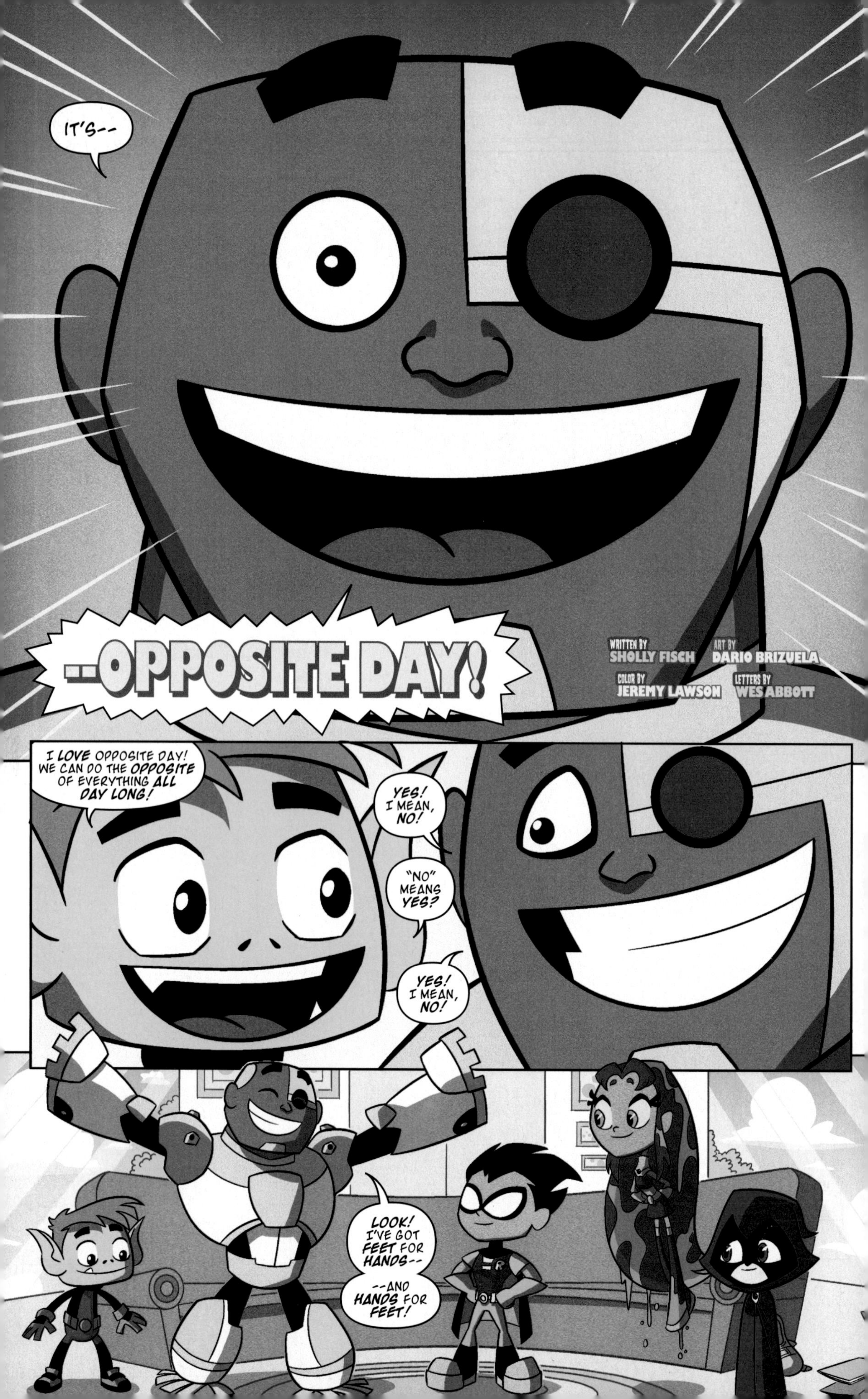
IT'S--
..OPPOSITE DAY!
WRITTEN BY SHOLLY FISCH
ART BY DARIO BRIZUELA
COLOR BY JEREMY LAWSON
LETTERS BY WES ABBOTT
I LOVE OPPOSITE DAY! WE CAN DO THE OPPOSITE OF EVERYTHING ALL DAY LONG!
YES! I MEAN, NO!
"NO" MEANS YES?
YES! I MEAN, NO!
LOOK! I'VE GOT FEET FOR HANDS--
--AND HANDS FOR FEET!

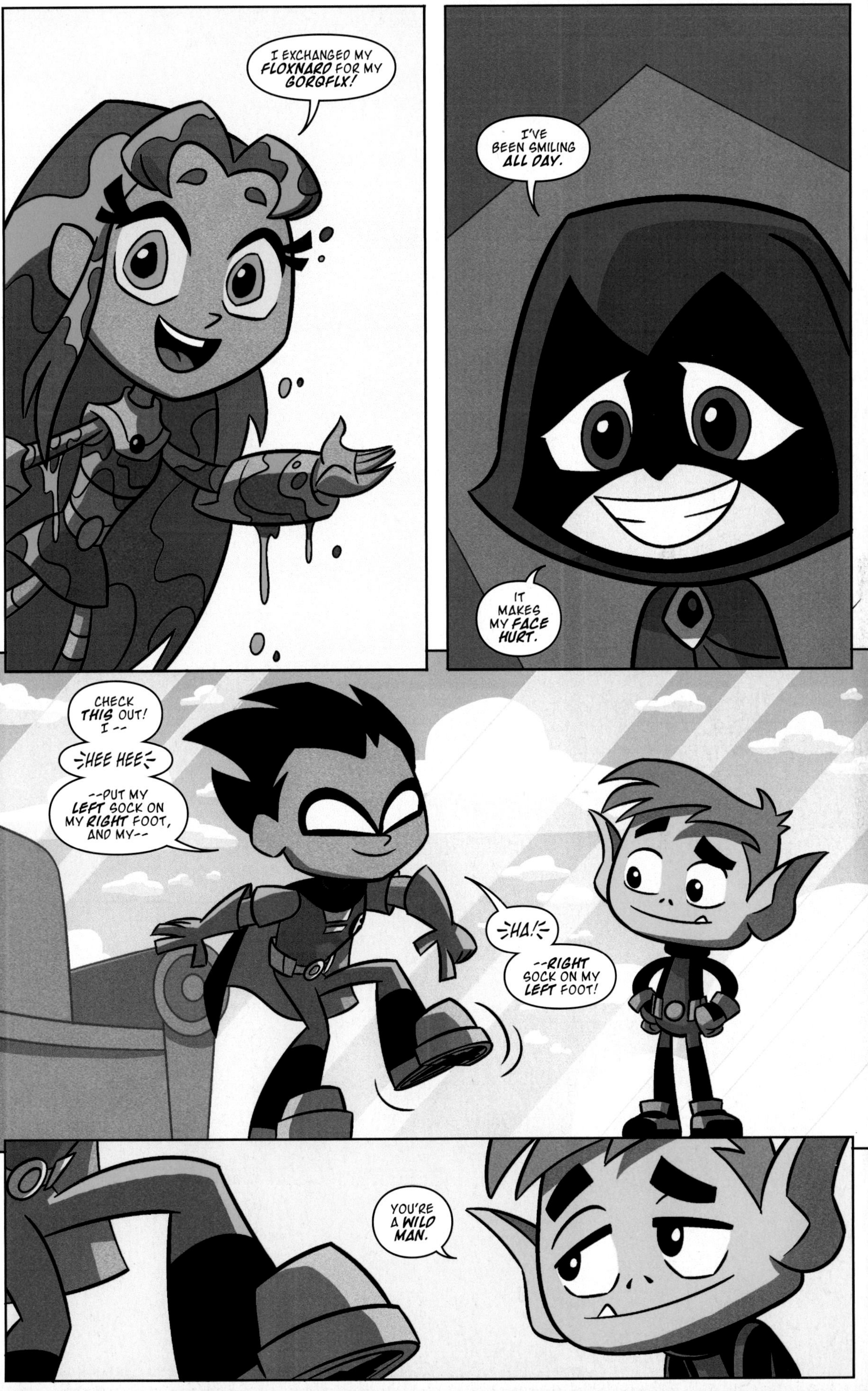
I EXCHANGED MY FLOXNARD FOR MY GORQFLX!
I'VE BEEN SMILING ALL DAY.
IT MAKES MY FACE HURT.
CHECK THIS OUT! I --
HEE HEE
--PUT MY LEFT SOCK ON MY RIGHT FOOT, AND MY--
HA!
--RIGHT SOCK ON MY LEFT FOOT!
YOU'RE A WILD MAN.

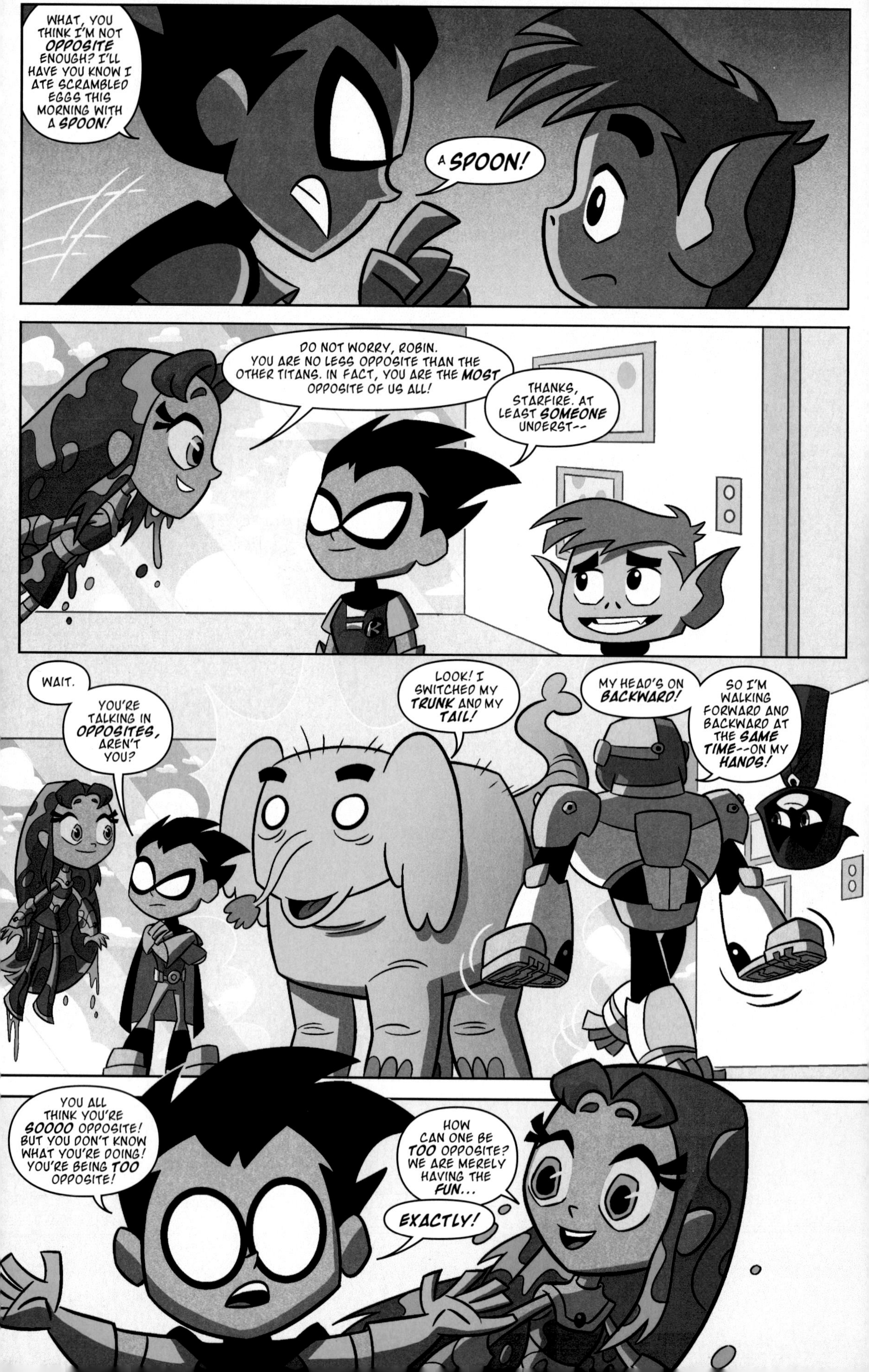
WHAT, YOU THINK I'M NOT OPPOSITE ENOUGH? I'LL HAVE YOU KNOW I ATE SCRAMBLED EGGS THIS MORNING WITH A SPOON!
A SPOON!
DO NOT WORRY, ROBIN. YOU ARE NO LESS OPPOSITE THAN THE OTHER TITANS. IN FACT, YOU ARE THE MOST OPPOSITE OF US ALL!
THANKS, STARFIRE. AT LEAST SOMEONE UNDERST--
WAIT.
YOU'RE TALKING IN OPPOSITES, AREN'T YOU?
LOOK! I SWITCHED MY TRUNK AND MY TAIL!
MY HEAD'S ON BACKWARD!
SO I'M WALKING FORWARD AND BACKWARD AT THE SAME TIME--ON MY HANDS!
YOU ALL THINK YOU'RE SOOOO OPPOSITE! BUT YOU DON'T KNOW WHAT YOU'RE DOING! YOU'RE BEING TOO OPPOSITE!
HOW CAN ONE BE TOO OPPOSITE? WE ARE MERELY HAVING THE FUN...
EXACTLY!

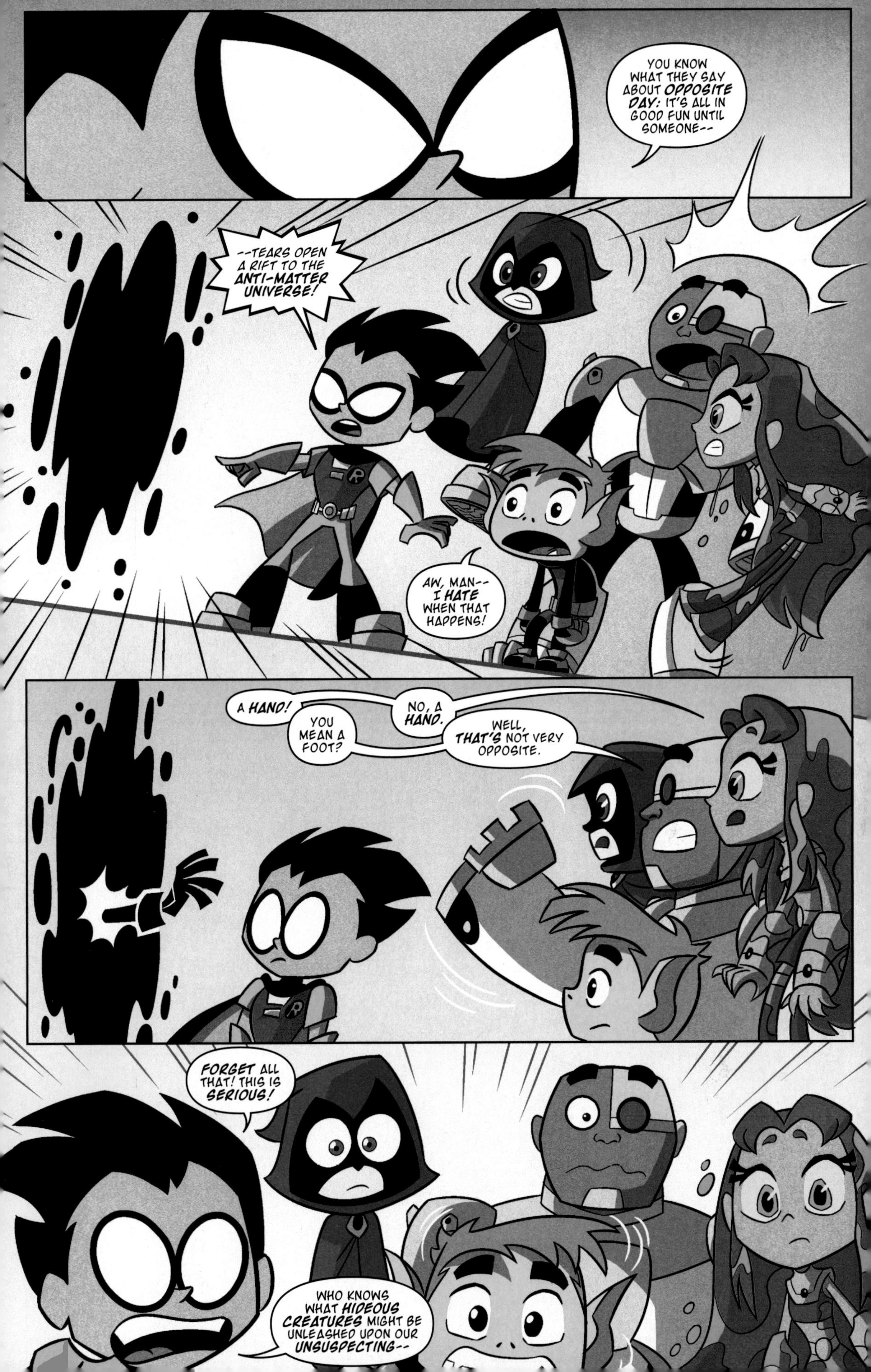
YOU KNOW WHAT THEY SAY ABOUT OPPOSITE DAY: IT'S ALL IN GOOD FUN UNTIL SOMEONE--
--TEARS OPEN A RIFT TO THE ANTI-MATTER UNIVERSE!
AW, MAN-- I HATE WHEN THAT HAPPENS!
A HAND!
YOU MEAN A FOOT?
NO, A HAND.
WELL, THAT'S NOT VERY OPPOSITE.
FORGET ALL THAT! THIS IS SERIOUS!
WHO KNOWS WHAT HIDEOUS CREATURES MIGHT BE UNLEASHED UPON OUR UNSUSPECTING--

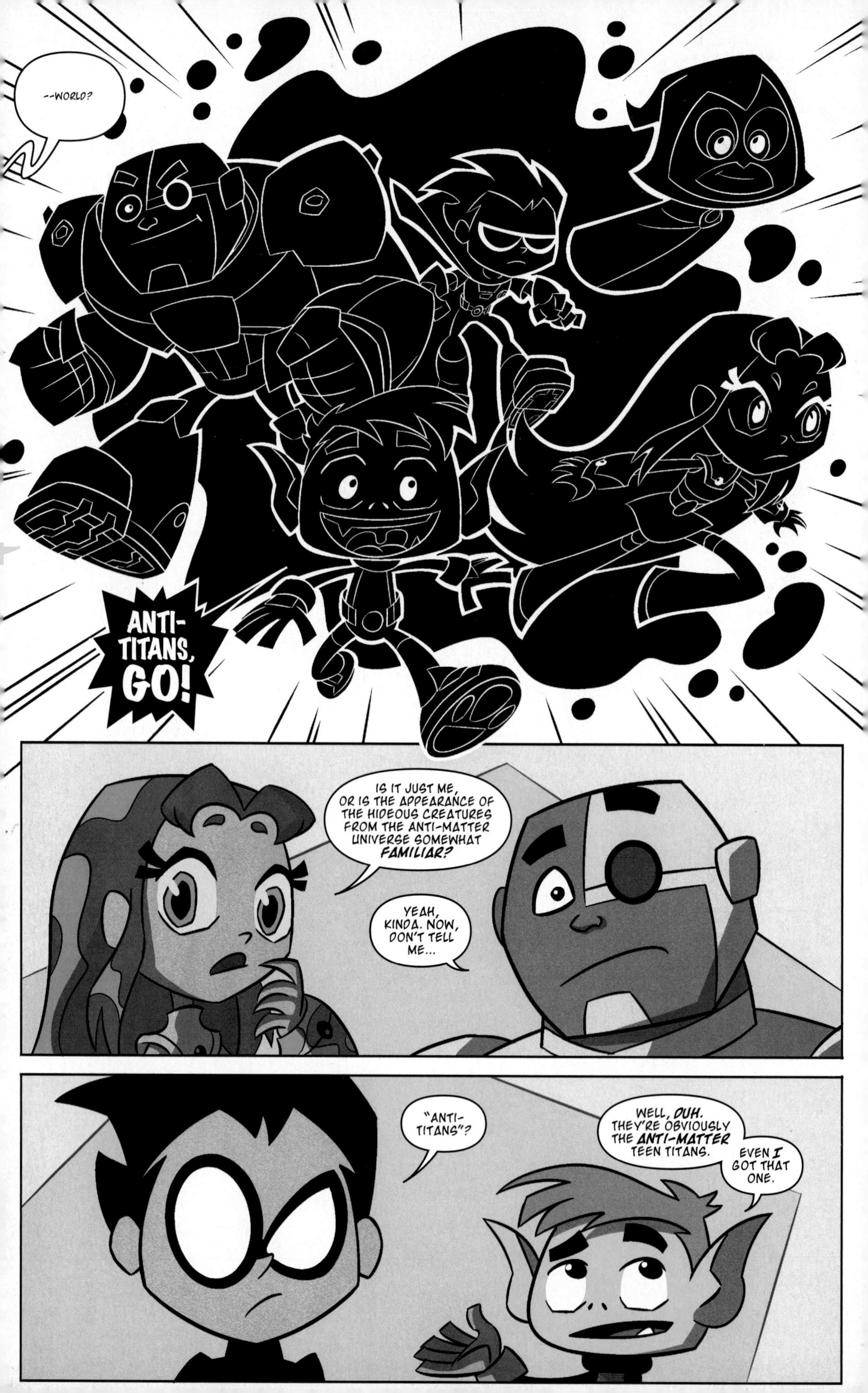
--WORLD?
ANTI-TITANS, GO!
IS IT JUST ME, OR IS THE APPEARANCE OF THE HIDEOUS CREATURES FROM THE ANTI-MATTER UNIVERSE SOMEWHAT FAMILIAR?
YEAH, KINDA. NOW, DON'T TELL ME...
"ANTI-TITANS"?
WELL, DUH. THEY'RE OBVIOUSLY THE ANTI-MATTER TEEN TITANS.
EVEN I GOT THAT ONE.

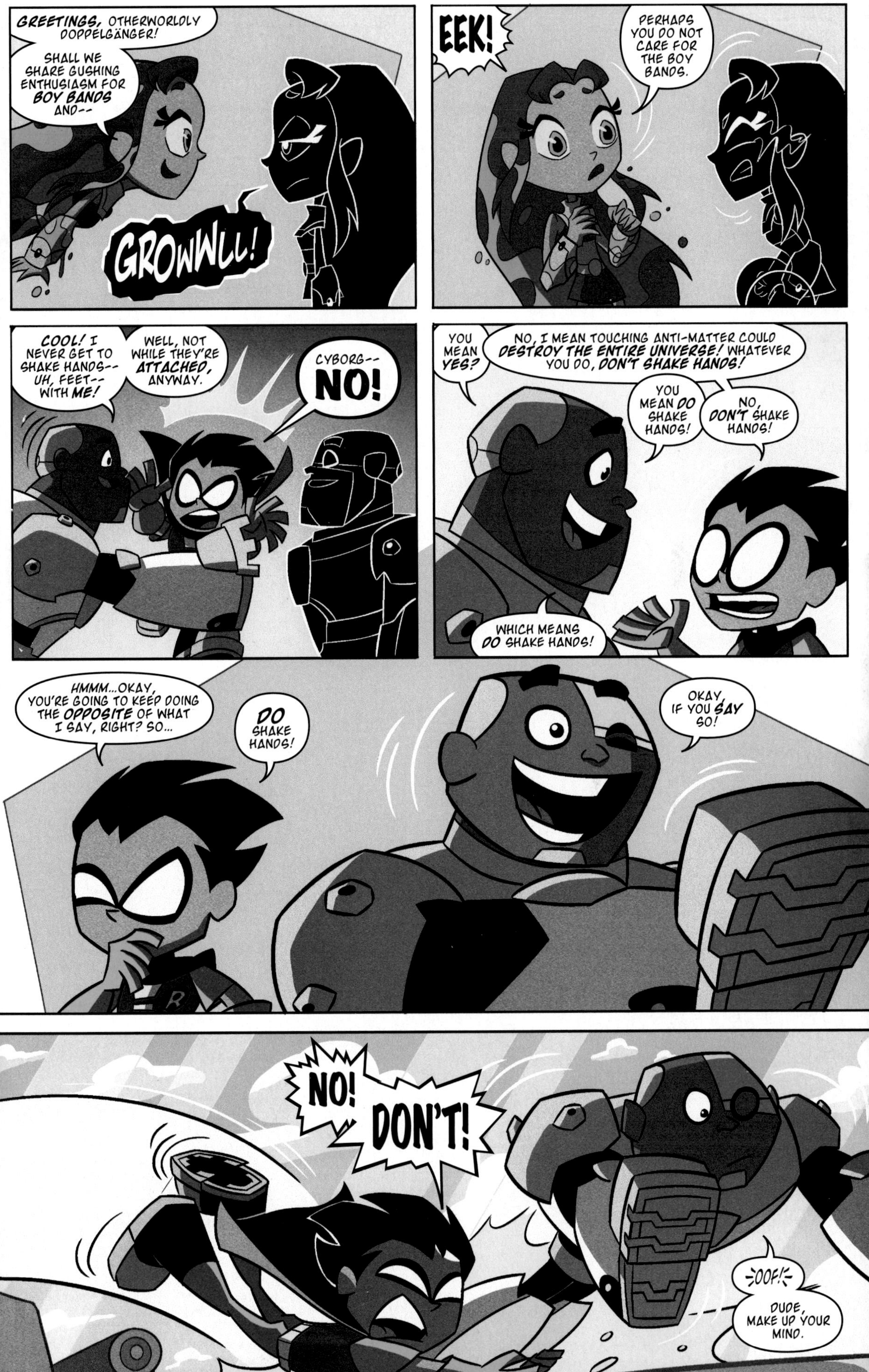
GREETINGS, OTHERWORLDLY DOPPELGÄNGER!
SHALL WE SHARE GUSHING ENTHUSIASM FOR BOY BANDS AND--
GROWWLL!
EEK!
PERHAPS YOU DO NOT CARE FOR THE BOY BANDS.
COOL! I NEVER GET TO SHAKE HANDS-- UH, FEET-- WITH ME!
WELL, NOT WHILE THEY'RE ATTACHED, ANYWAY.
CYBORG-- NO!
YOU MEAN YES?
NO, I MEAN TOUCHING ANTI-MATTER COULD DESTROY THE ENTIRE UNIVERSE! WHATEVER YOU DO, DON'T SHAKE HANDS!
YOU MEAN DO SHAKE HANDS!
NO, DON'T SHAKE HANDS!
WHICH MEANS DO SHAKE HANDS!
HMMM...OKAY, YOU'RE GOING TO KEEP DOING THE OPPOSITE OF WHAT I SAY, RIGHT? SO...
DO SHAKE HANDS!
OKAY, IF YOU SAY SO!
NO! DON'T!
OOF!
DUDE, MAKE UP YOUR MIND.

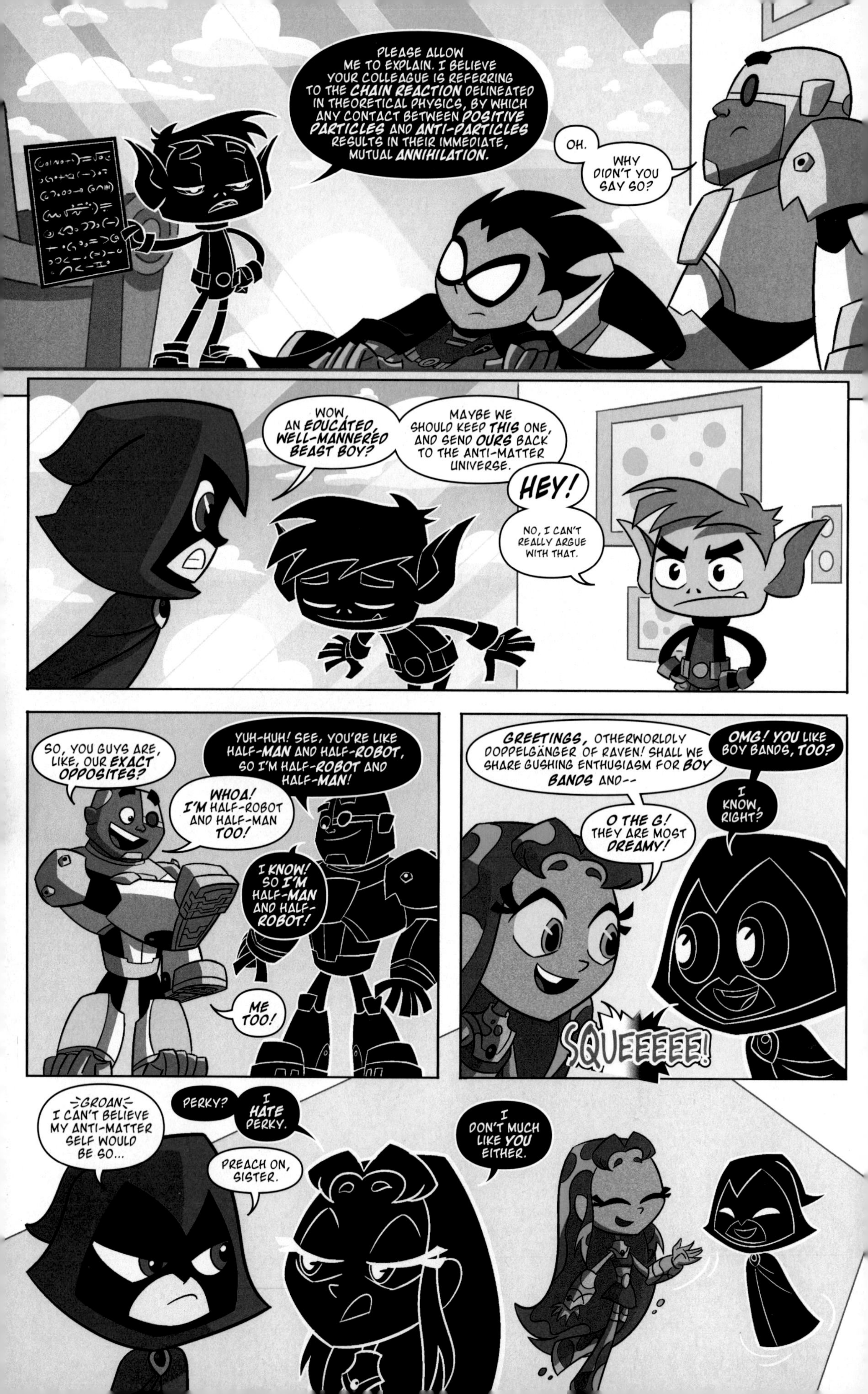
PLEASE ALLOW ME TO EXPLAIN. I BELIEVE YOUR COLLEAGUE IS REFERRING TO THE CHAIN REACTION DELINEATED IN THEORETICAL PHYSICS, BY WHICH ANY CONTACT BETWEEN POSITIVE PARTICLES AND ANTI-PARTICLES RESULTS IN THEIR IMMEDIATE, MUTUAL ANNIHILATION.
OH.
WHY DIDN'T YOU SAY SO?
WOW, AN EDUCATED, WELL-MANNERED BEAST BOY?
MAYBE WE SHOULD KEEP THIS ONE, AND SEND OURS BACK TO THE ANTI-MATTER UNIVERSE.
HEY!
NO, I CAN'T REALLY ARGUE WITH THAT.
SO, YOU GUYS ARE, LIKE, OUR EXACT OPPOSITES?
YUH-HUH! SEE, YOU'RE LIKE HALF-MAN AND HALF-ROBOT, SO I'M HALF-ROBOT AND HALF-MAN!
WHOA! I'M HALF-ROBOT AND HALF-MAN TOO!
I KNOW! SO I'M HALF-MAN AND HALF-ROBOT!
ME TOO!
GREETINGS, OTHERWORLDLY DOPPELGÄNGER OF RAVEN! SHALL WE SHARE GUSHING ENTHUSIASM FOR BOY BANDS AND--
OMG! YOU LIKE BOY BANDS, TOO?
O THE G! THEY ARE MOST DREAMY!
I KNOW, RIGHT?
SQUEEEEEE!
GROAN
I CAN'T BELIEVE MY ANTI-MATTER SELF WOULD BE SO...
PERKY?
I HATE PERKY.
PREACH ON, SISTER.
I DON'T MUCH LIKE YOU EITHER.

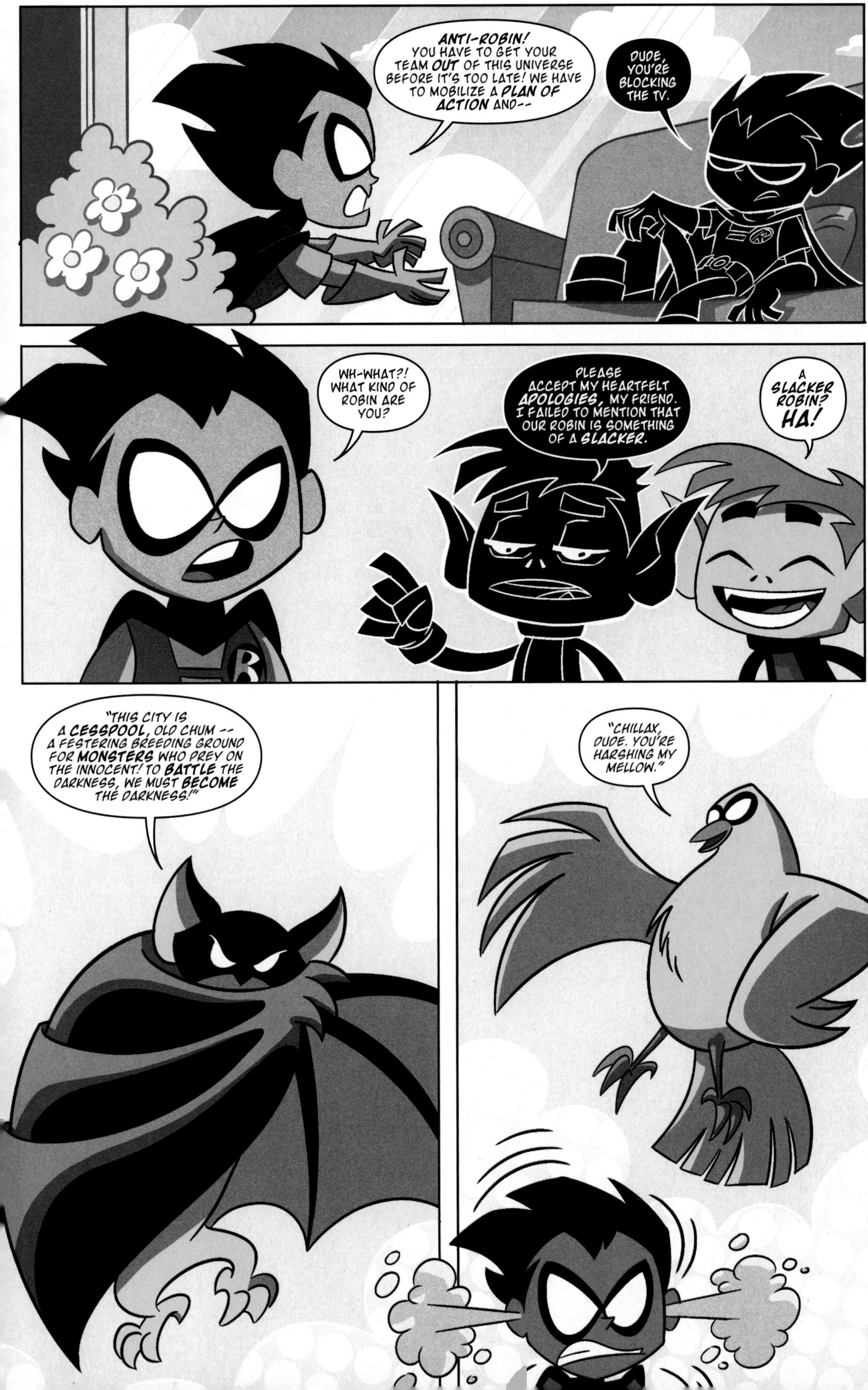
ANTI-ROBIN! YOU HAVE TO GET YOUR TEAM OUT OF THIS UNIVERSE BEFORE IT'S TOO LATE! WE HAVE TO MOBILIZE A PLAN OF ACTION AND--
DUDE, YOU'RE BLOCKING THE TV.
WH-WHAT?! WHAT KIND OF ROBIN ARE YOU?
PLEASE ACCEPT MY HEARTFELT APOLOGIES, MY FRIEND. I FAILED TO MENTION THAT OUR ROBIN IS SOMETHING OF A SLACKER.
A SLACKER ROBIN? HA!
"THIS CITY IS A CESSPOOL, OLD CHUM -- A FESTERING BREEDING GROUND FOR MONSTERS WHO PREY ON THE INNOCENT! TO BATTLE THE DARKNESS, WE MUST BECOME THE DARKNESS!"
"CHILLAX, DUDE. YOU'RE HARSHING MY MELLOW."

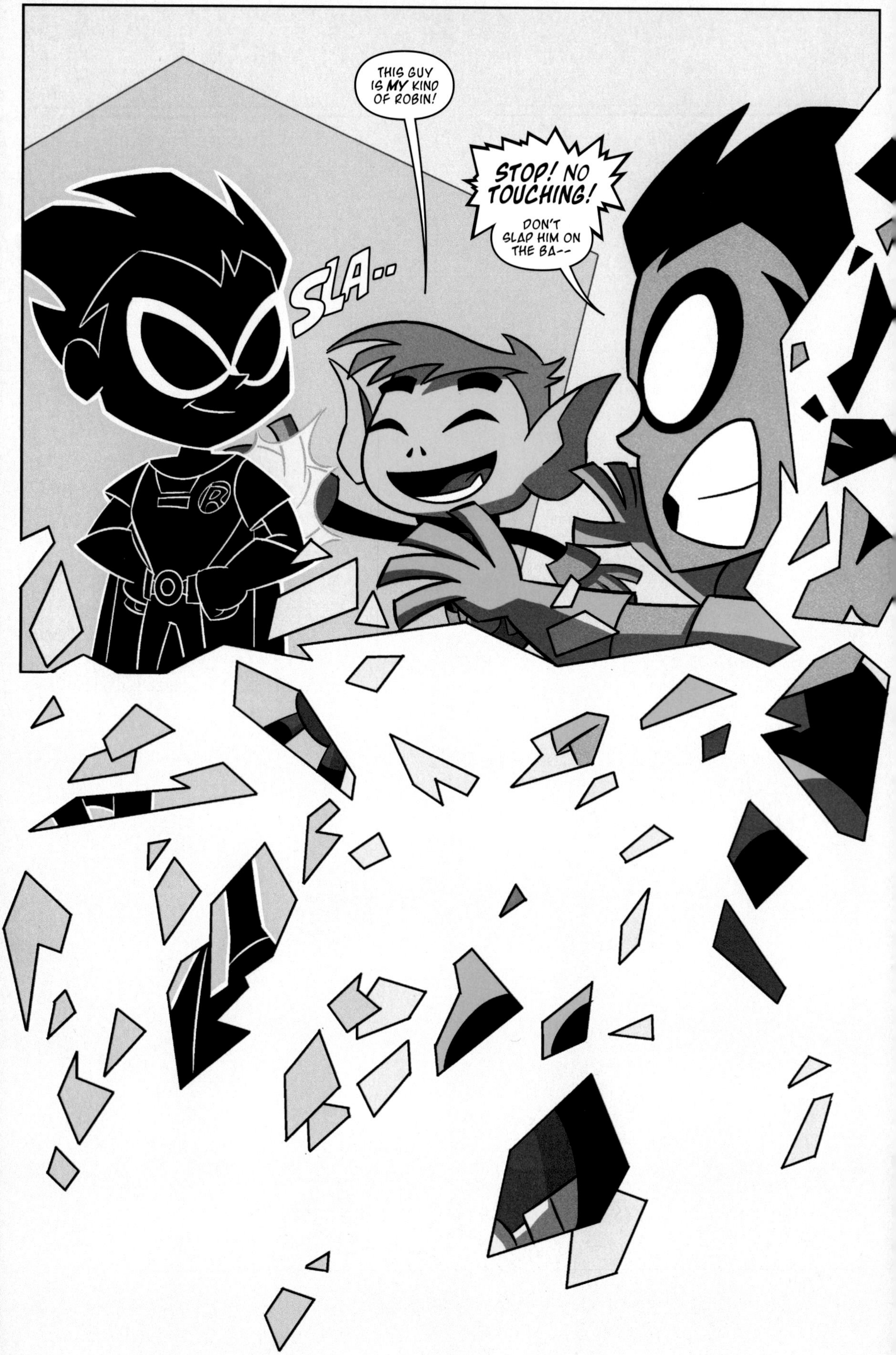
SLA..
THIS GUY IS MY KIND OF ROBIN!
STOP! NO TOUCHING!
DON'T SLAP HIM ON THE BA--

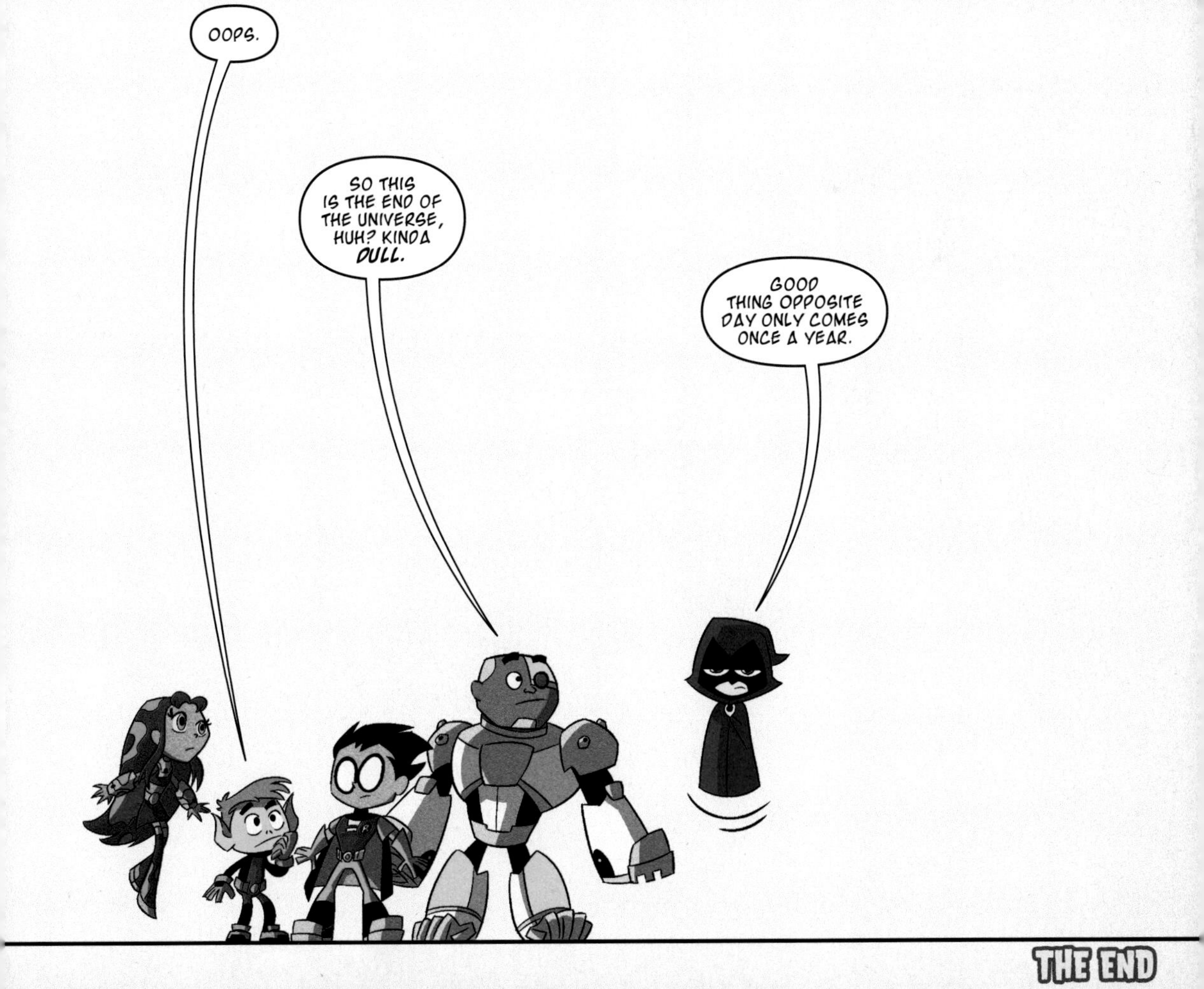
OOPS.
SO THIS IS THE END OF THE UNIVERSE, HUH? KINDA DULL.
GOOD THING OPPOSITE DAY ONLY COMES ONCE A YEAR.
THE END

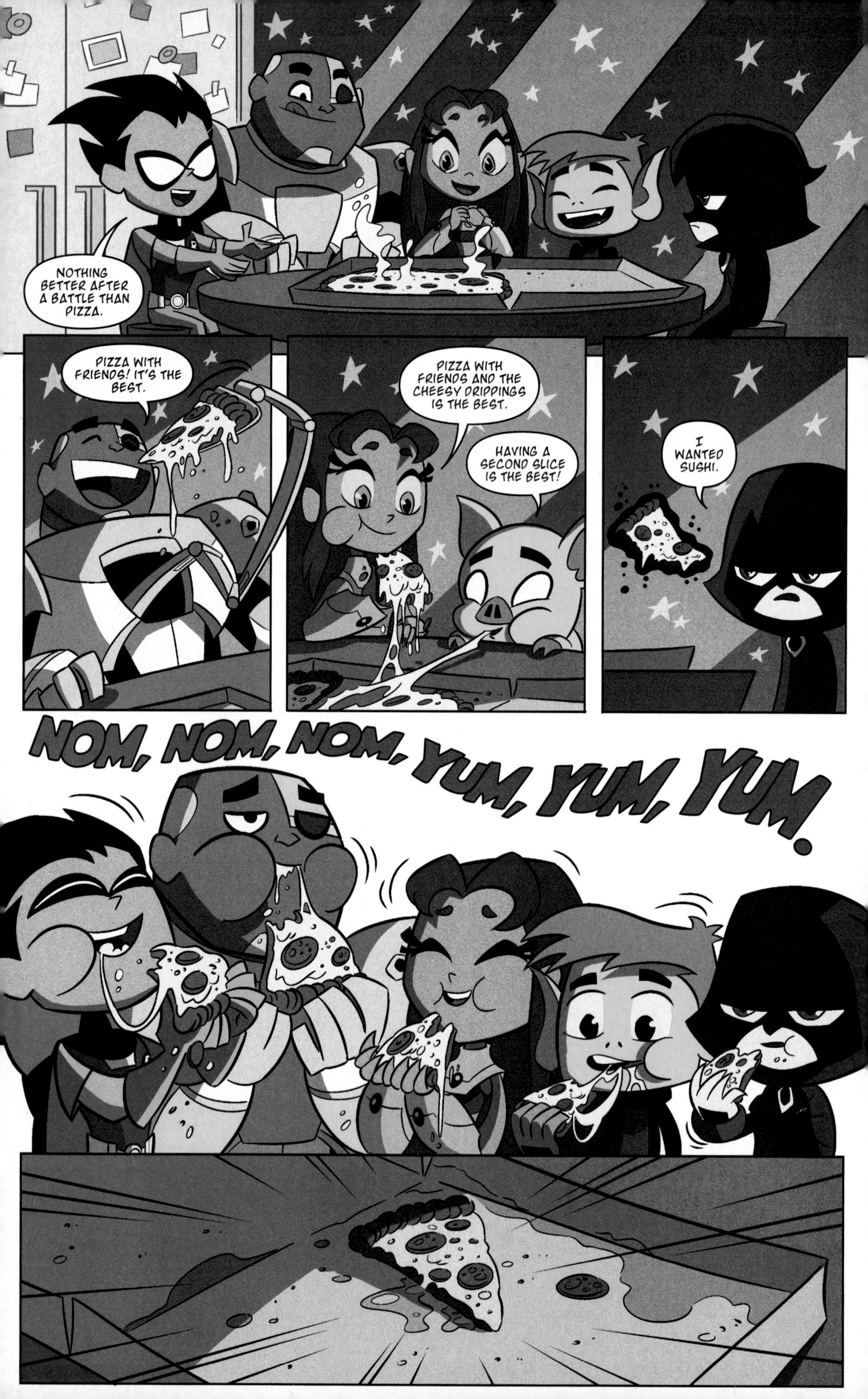

NOTHING BETTER AFTER A BATTLE THAN PIZZA.
PIZZA WITH FRIENDS! IT'S THE BEST.
PIZZA WITH FRIENDS AND THE CHEESY DRIPPINGS IS THE BEST.
HAVING A SECOND SLICE IS THE BEST!
I WANTED SUSHI.
NOM, NOM, NOM, YUM, YUM, YUM.

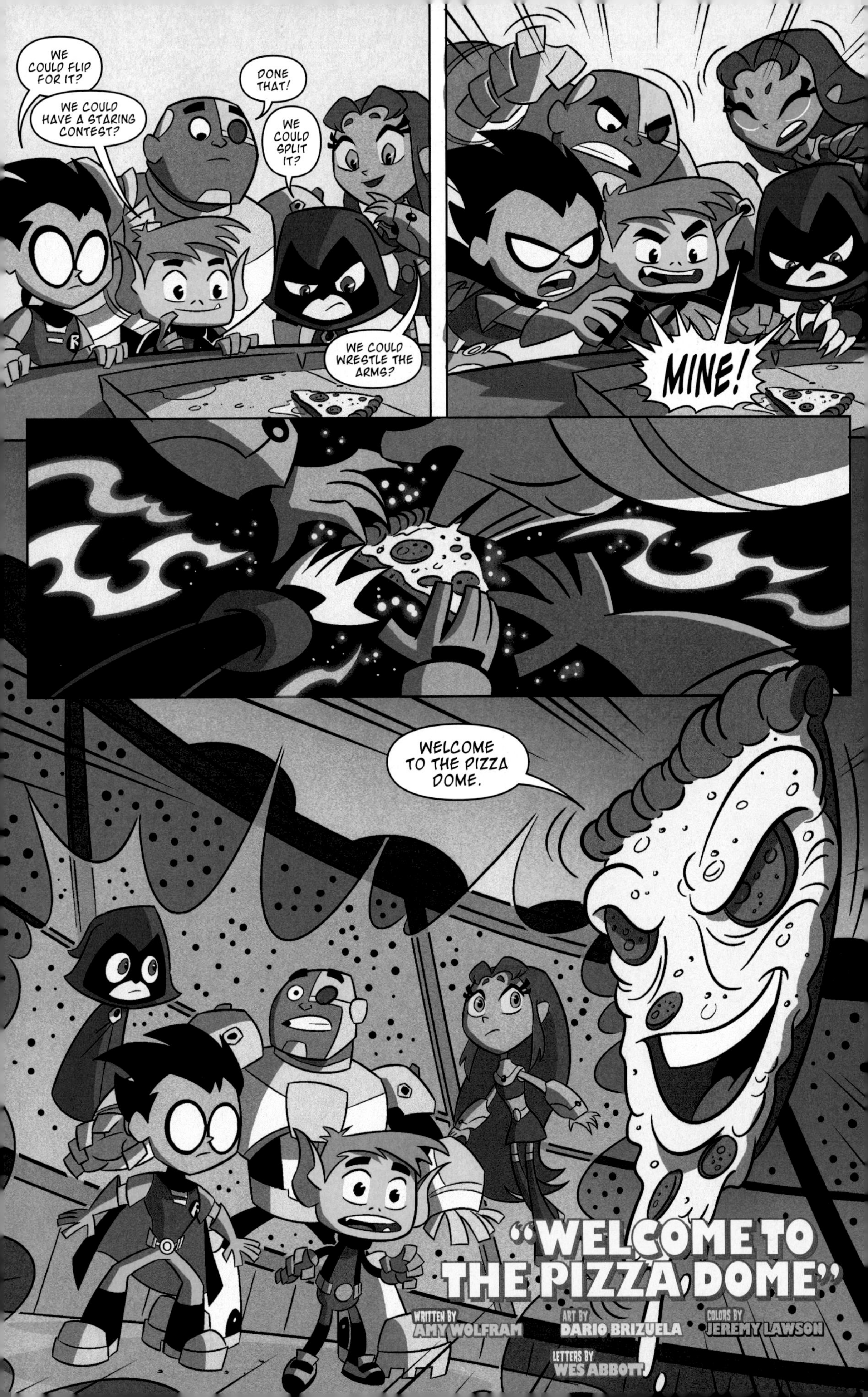
WE COULD FLIP FOR IT?
WE COULD HAVE A STARING CONTEST?
DONE THAT!
WE COULD SPLIT IT?
WE COULD WRESTLE THE ARMS?
MINE!
WELCOME TO THE PIZZA DOME.
"WELCOME TO THE PIZZA DOME"
WRITTEN BY AMY WOLFRAM
ART BY DARIO BRIZUELA
COLORS BY JEREMY LAWSON
LETTERS BY WES ABBOTT

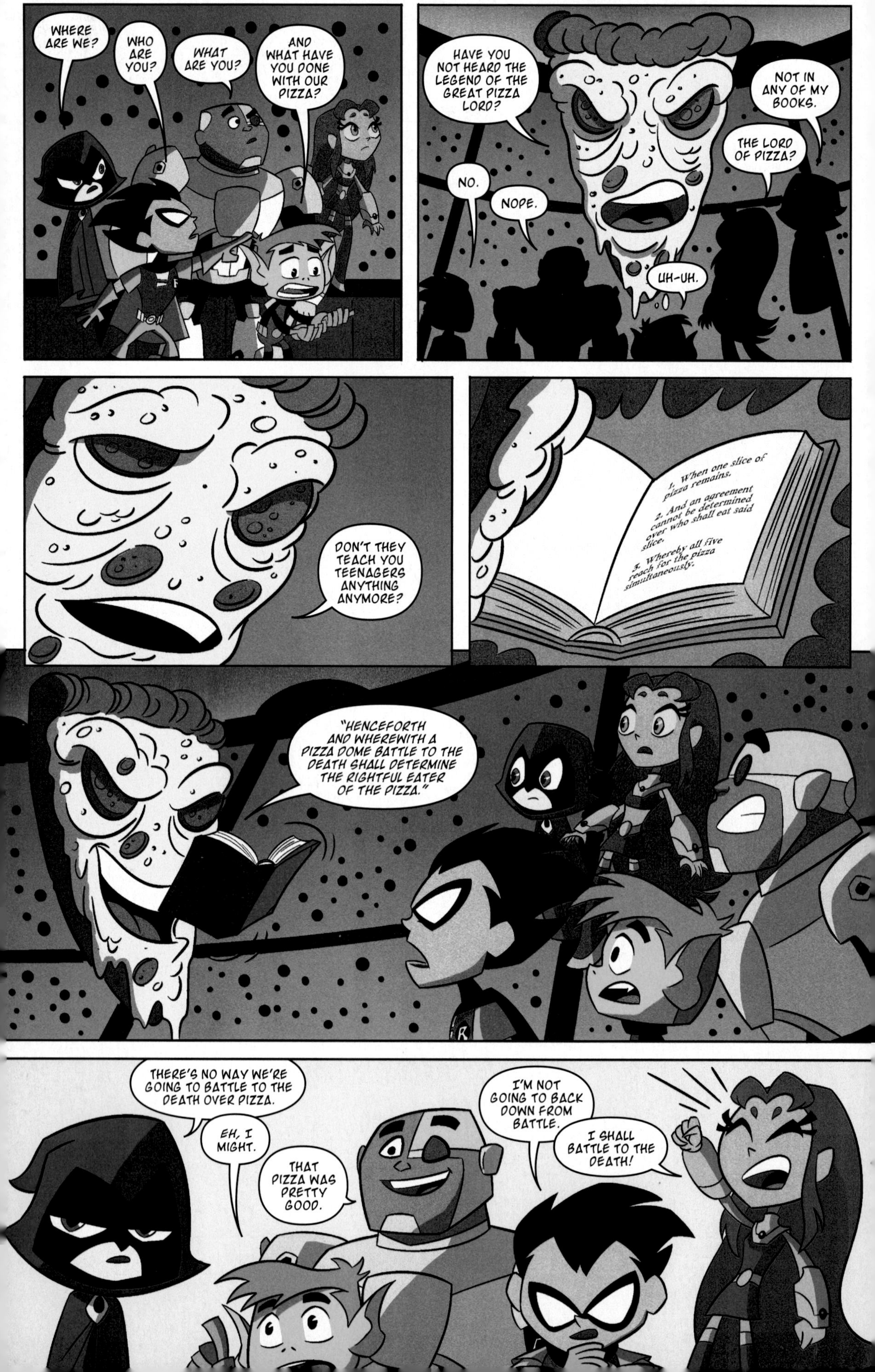
WHERE ARE WE?
WHO ARE YOU?
WHAT ARE YOU?
AND WHAT HAVE YOU DONE WITH OUR PIZZA?
HAVE YOU NOT HEARD THE LEGEND OF THE GREAT PIZZA LORD?
NOT IN ANY OF MY BOOKS.
THE LORD OF PIZZA?
NO.
NOPE.
UH-UH.
DON'T THEY TEACH YOU TEENAGERS ANYTHING ANYMORE?
1. When one slice of pizza remains.
2. And an agreement cannot be determined over who shall eat said slice.
3. Whereby all five reach for the pizza simultaneously.
"HENCEFORTH AND WHEREWITH A PIZZA DOME BATTLE TO THE DEATH SHALL DETERMINE THE RIGHTFUL EATER OF THE PIZZA."
THERE'S NO WAY WE'RE GOING TO BATTLE TO THE DEATH OVER PIZZA.
EH, I MIGHT.
THAT PIZZA WAS PRETTY GOOD.
I'M NOT GOING TO BACK DOWN FROM BATTLE.
I SHALL BATTLE TO THE DEATH!

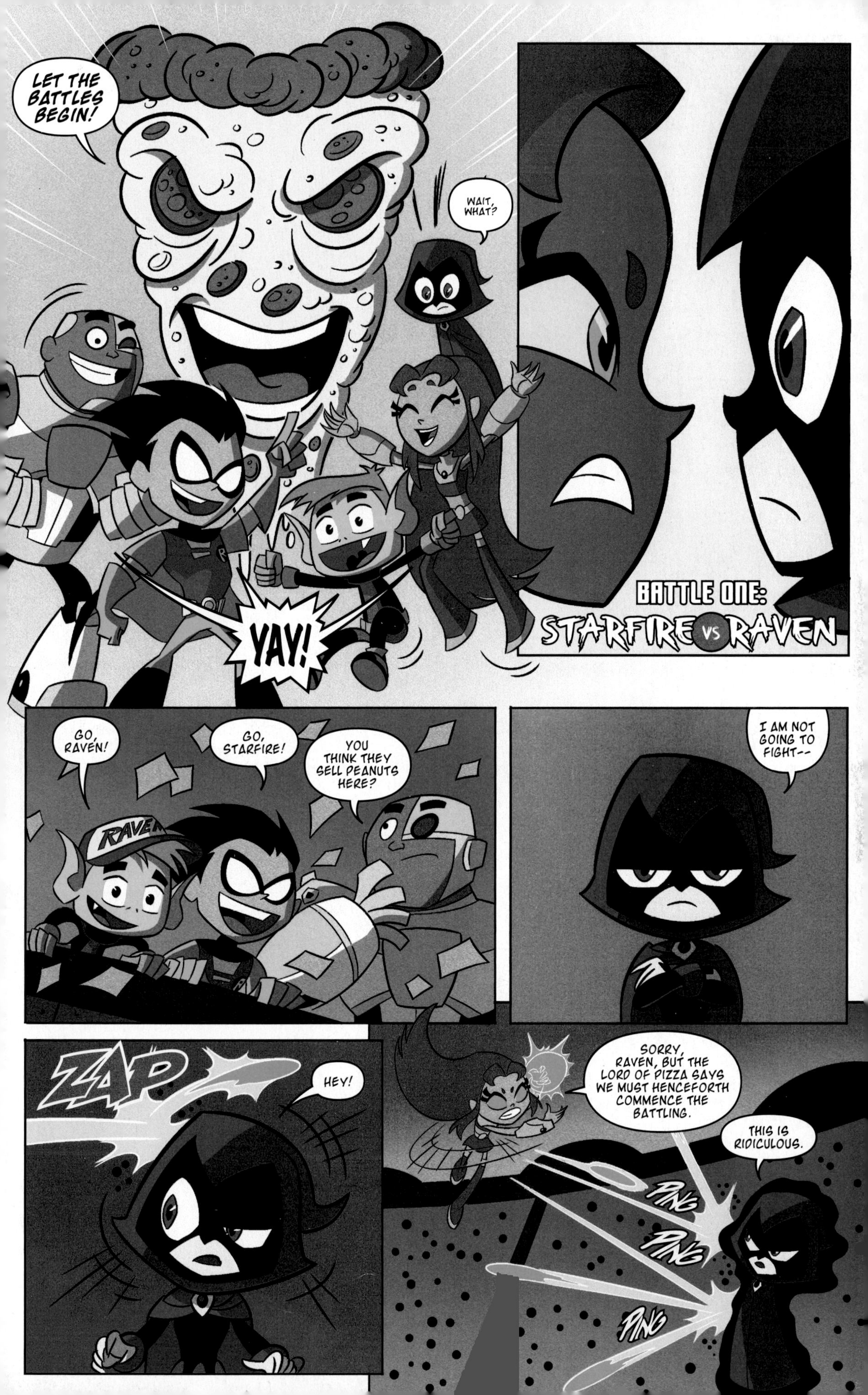
LET THE BATTLES BEGIN!
WAIT, WHAT?
YAY!
BATTLE ONE:
STARFIRE VS RAVEN
GO, RAVEN!
GO, STARFIRE!
YOU THINK THEY SELL PEANUTS HERE?
RAVEN
I AM NOT GOING TO FIGHT--
ZAP
HEY!
SORRY, RAVEN, BUT THE LORD OF PIZZA SAYS WE MUST HENCEFORTH COMMENCE THE BATTLING.
THIS IS RIDICULOUS.
PING
PING
PING

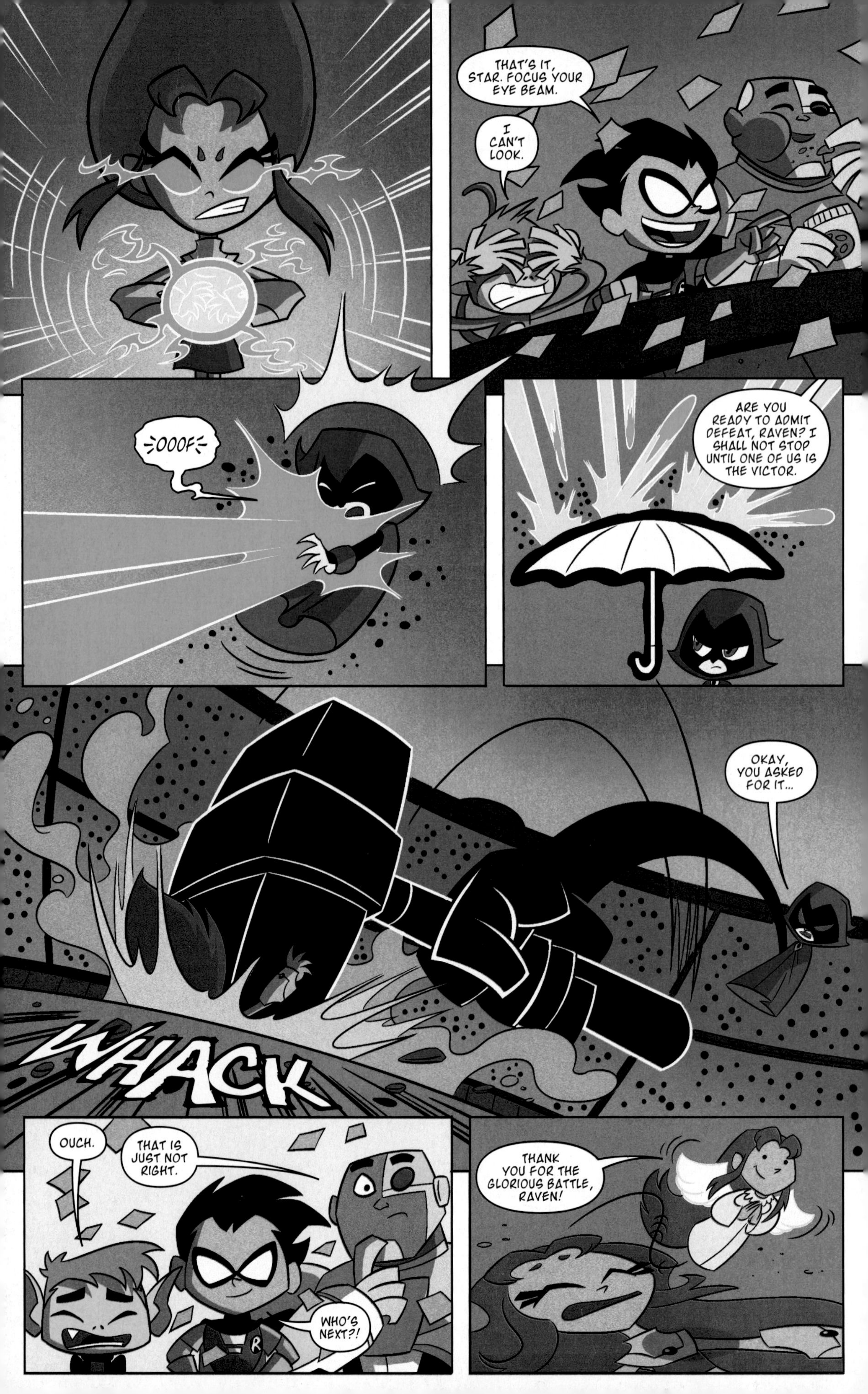
THAT'S IT, STAR. FOCUS YOUR EYE BEAM.
I CAN'T LOOK.
OOOF
ARE YOU READY TO ADMIT DEFEAT, RAVEN? I SHALL NOT STOP UNTIL ONE OF US IS THE VICTOR.
OKAY, YOU ASKED FOR IT...
WHACK
OUCH.
THAT IS JUST NOT RIGHT.
WHO'S NEXT?!
THANK YOU FOR THE GLORIOUS BATTLE, RAVEN!

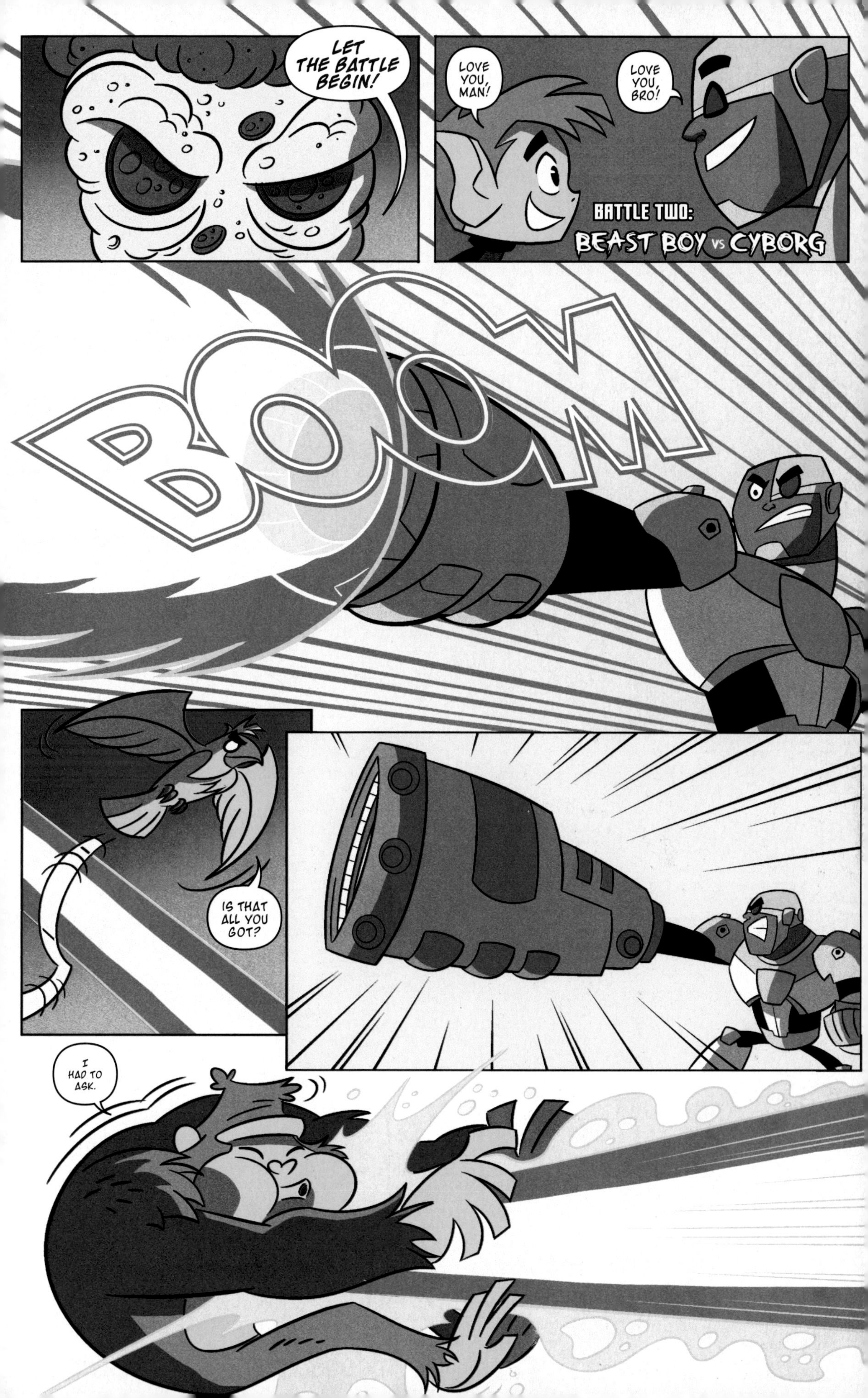
LET THE BATTLE BEGIN!
LOVE YOU, MAN!
LOVE YOU, BRO!
BATTLE TWO:
BEAST BOY VS CYBORG
BOOM
IS THAT ALL YOU GOT?
I HAD TO ASK.

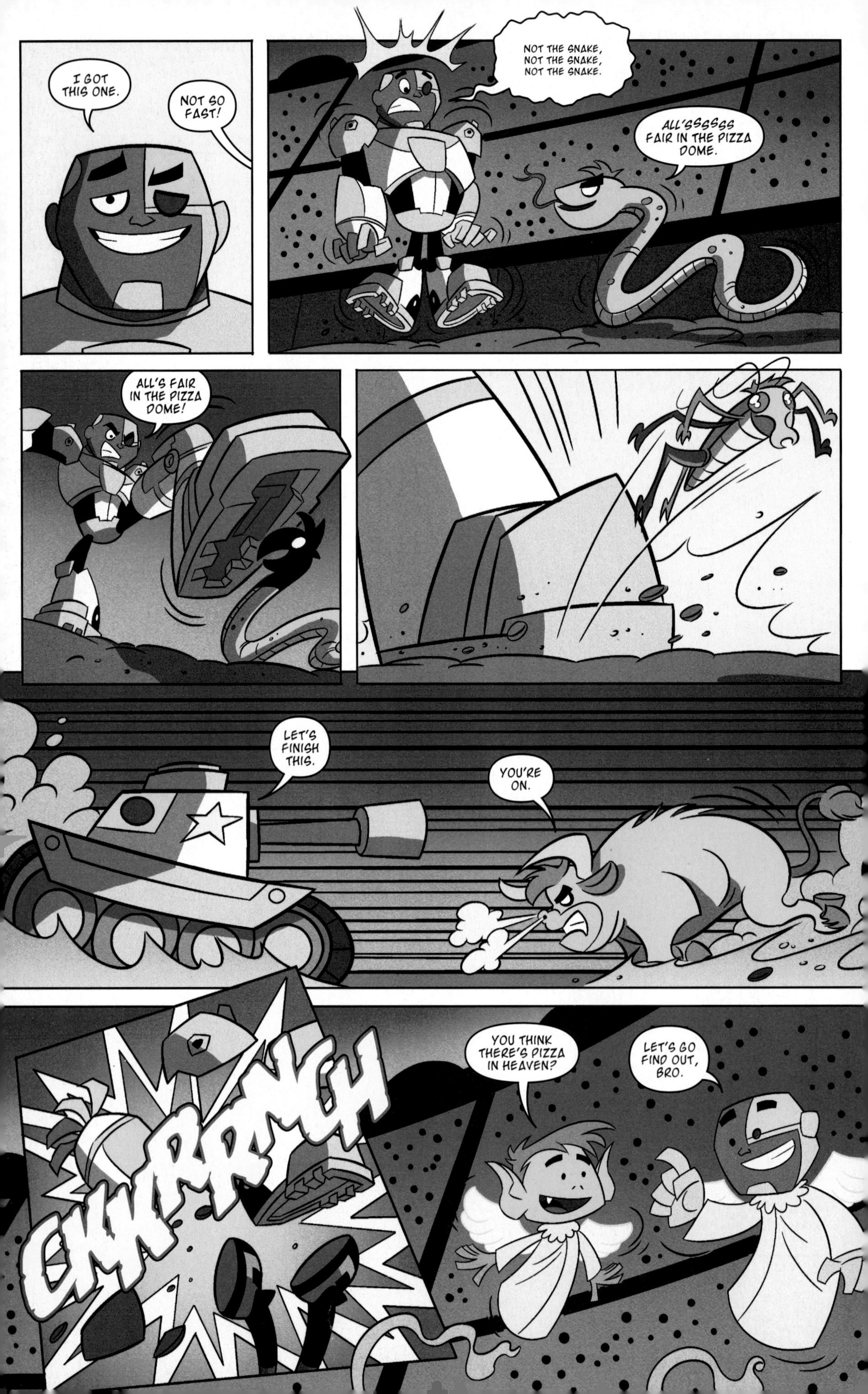
I GOT THIS ONE.
NOT SO FAST!
NOT THE SNAKE, NOT THE SNAKE, NOT THE SNAKE.
ALL'SSSSSS FAIR IN THE PIZZA DOME.
ALL'S FAIR IN THE PIZZA DOME!
LET'S FINISH THIS.
YOU'RE ON.
CKKRRNCH
YOU THINK THERE'S PIZZA IN HEAVEN?
LET'S GO FIND OUT, BRO.

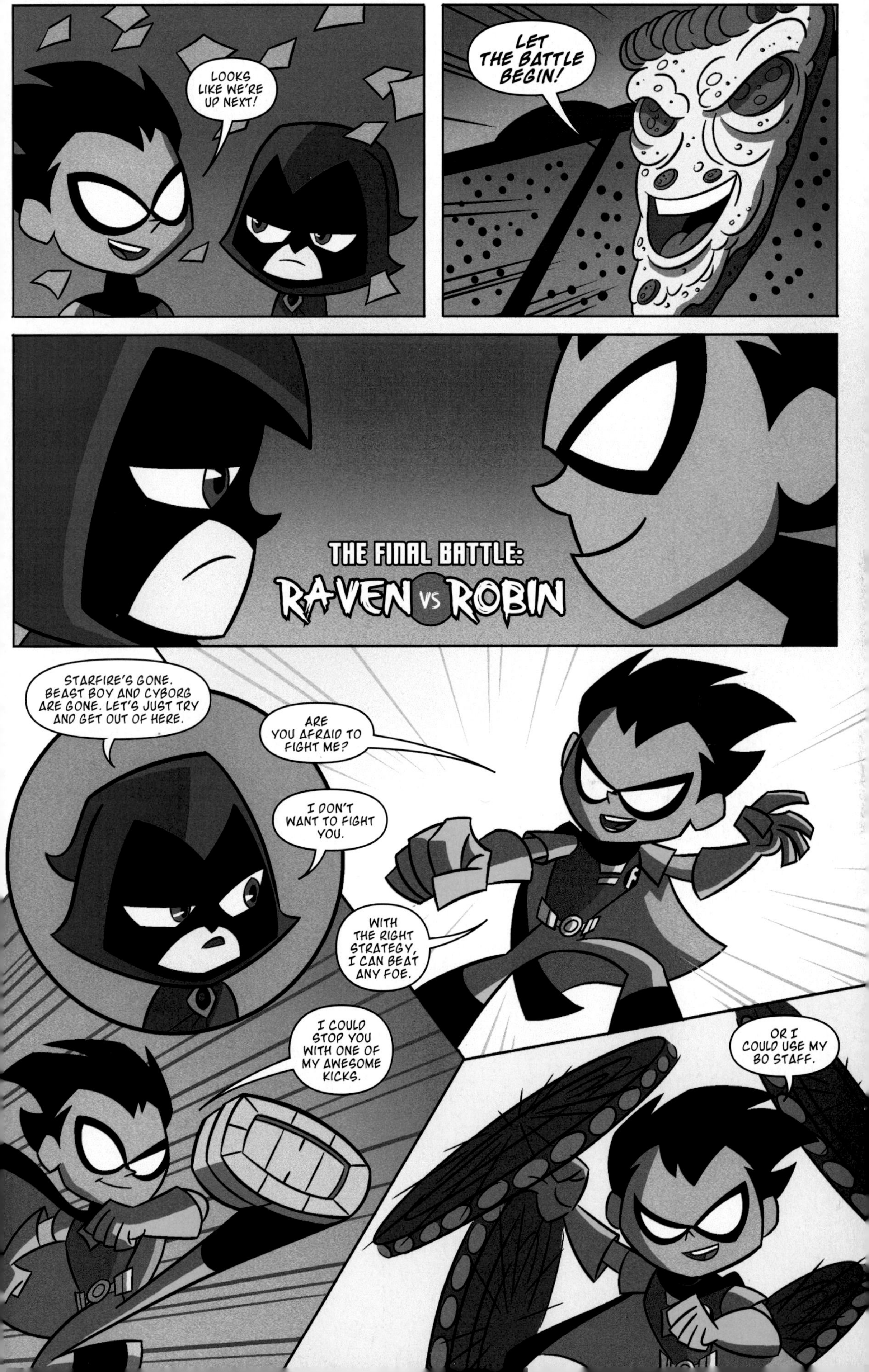
LOOKS LIKE WE'RE UP NEXT!
LET THE BATTLE BEGIN!
THE FINAL BATTLE:
RAVEN VS ROBIN
STARFIRE'S GONE. BEAST BOY AND CYBORG ARE GONE. LET'S JUST TRY AND GET OUT OF HERE.
ARE YOU AFRAID TO FIGHT ME?
I DON'T WANT TO FIGHT YOU.
WITH THE RIGHT STRATEGY, I CAN BEAT ANY FOE.
I COULD STOP YOU WITH ONE OF MY AWESOME KICKS.
OR I COULD USE MY BO STAFF.

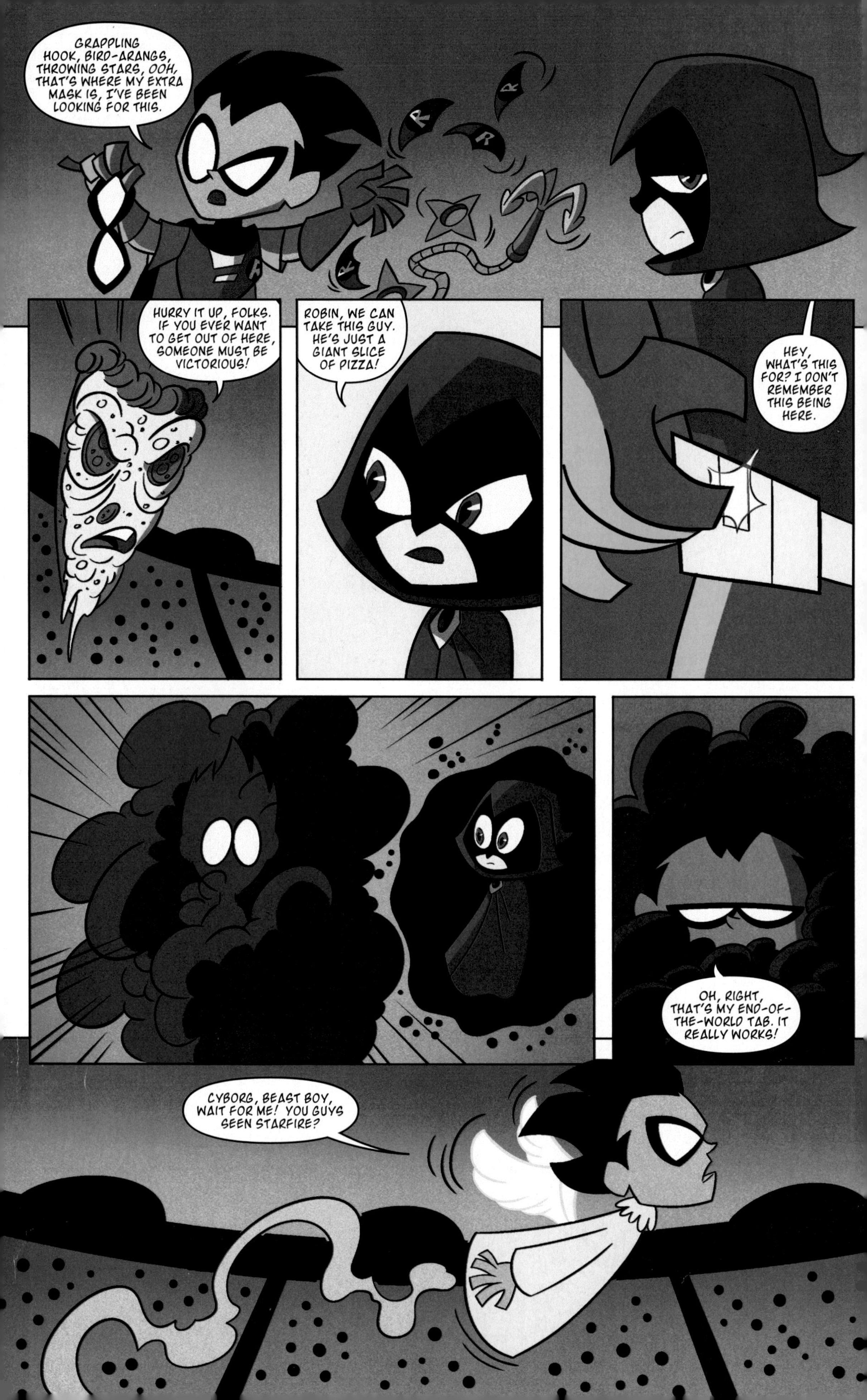
GRAPPLING HOOK, BIRD-ARANGS, THROWING STARS, OOH, THAT'S WHERE MY EXTRA MASK IS, I'VE BEEN LOOKING FOR THIS.
HURRY IT UP, FOLKS. IF YOU EVER WANT TO GET OUT OF HERE, SOMEONE MUST BE VICTORIOUS!
ROBIN, WE CAN TAKE THIS GUY. HE'S JUST A GIANT SLICE OF PIZZA!
HEY, WHAT'S THIS FOR? I DON'T REMEMBER THIS BEING HERE.
OH, RIGHT, THAT'S MY END-OF-THE-WORLD TAB. IT REALLY WORKS!
CYBORG, BEAST BOY, WAIT FOR ME! YOU GUYS SEEN STARFIRE?

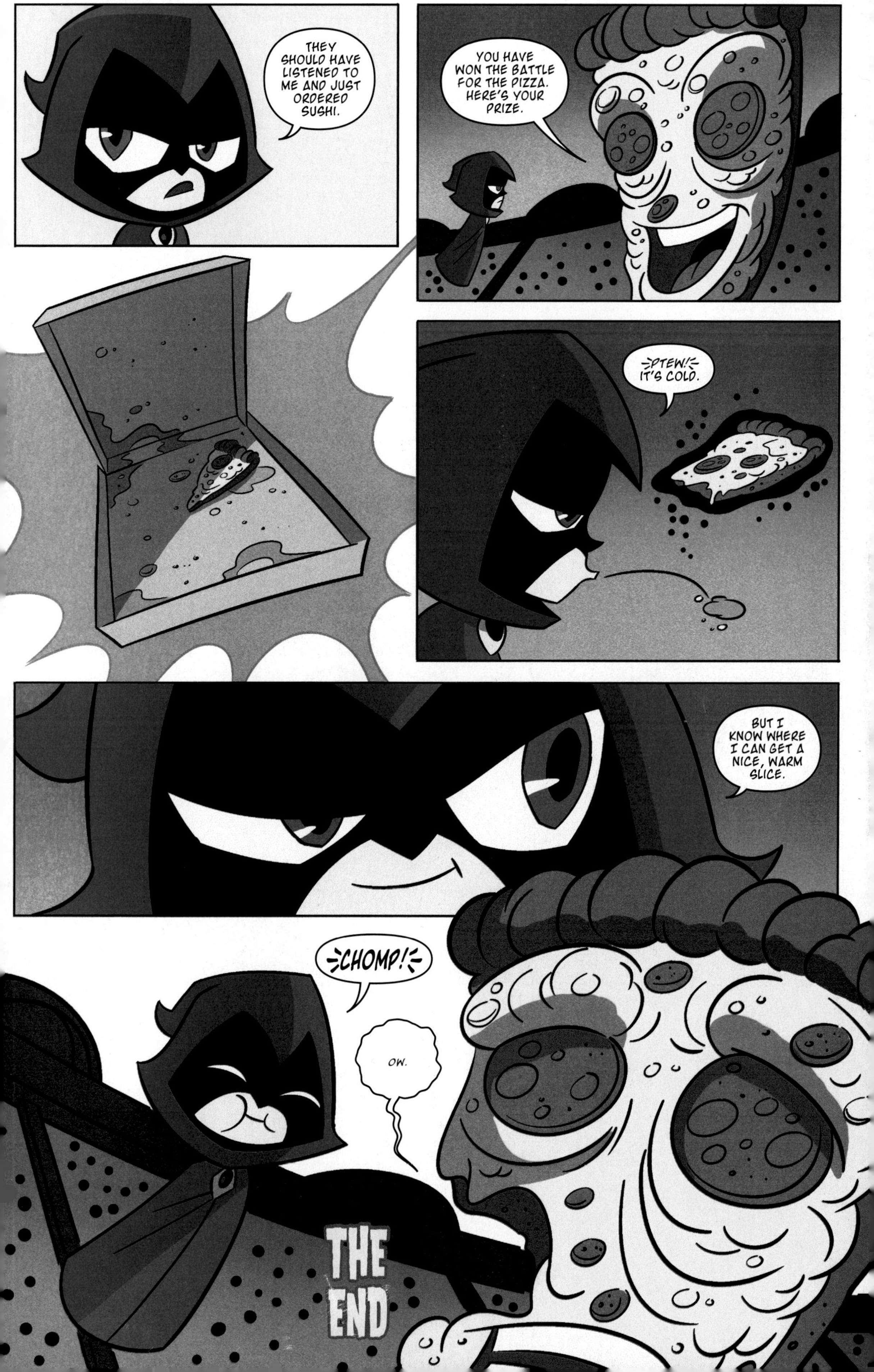
THEY SHOULD HAVE LISTENED TO ME AND JUST ORDERED SUSHI.
YOU HAVE WON THE BATTLE FOR THE PIZZA. HERE'S YOUR PRIZE.
PTEW! IT'S COLD.
BUT I KNOW WHERE I CAN GET A NICE, WARM SLICE.
CHOMP!
OW.
THE END

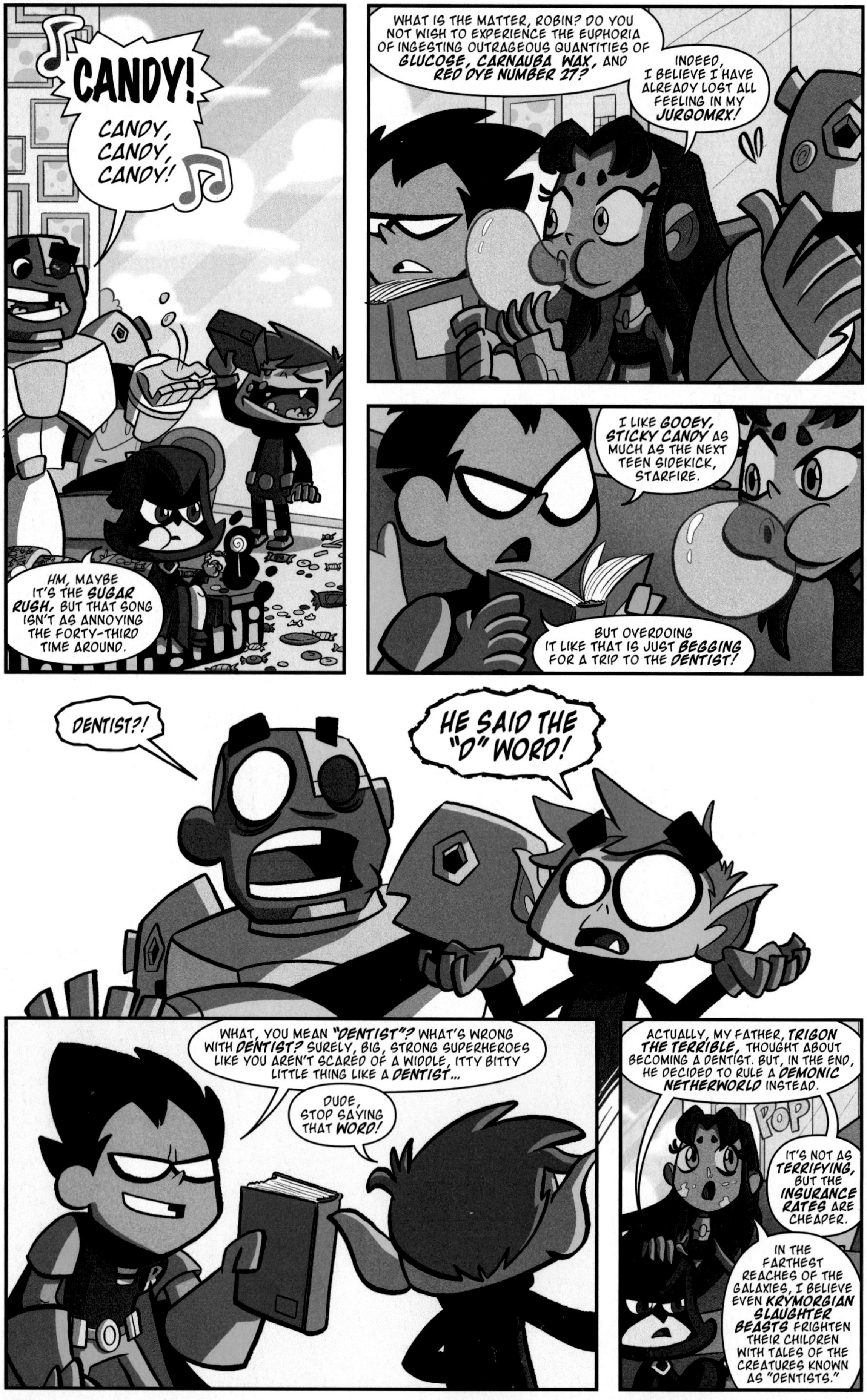
CANDY!
CANDY, CANDY, CANDY!
HM, MAYBE IT'S THE SUGAR RUSH, BUT THAT SONG ISN'T AS ANNOYING THE FORTY-THIRD TIME AROUND.
WHAT IS THE MATTER, ROBIN? DO YOU NOT WISH TO EXPERIENCE THE EUPHORIA OF INGESTING OUTRAGEOUS QUANTITIES OF GLUCOSE, CARNAUBA WAX, AND RED DYE NUMBER 27?
INDEED, I BELIEVE I HAVE ALREADY LOST ALL FEELING IN MY JURQOMRX!
I LIKE GOOEY, STICKY CANDY AS MUCH AS THE NEXT TEEN SIDEKICK, STARFIRE.
BUT OVERDOING IT LIKE THAT IS JUST BEGGING FOR A TRIP TO THE DENTIST!
DENTIST?!
HE SAID THE "D" WORD!
WHAT, YOU MEAN "DENTIST"? WHAT'S WRONG WITH DENTIST? SURELY, BIG, STRONG SUPERHEROES LIKE YOU AREN'T SCARED OF A WIDDLE, ITTY BITTY LITTLE THING LIKE A DENTIST...
DUDE, STOP SAYING THAT WORD!
ACTUALLY, MY FATHER, TRIGON THE TERRIBLE, THOUGHT ABOUT BECOMING A DENTIST. BUT, IN THE END, HE DECIDED TO RULE A DEMONIC NETHERWORLD INSTEAD.
POP
IT'S NOT AS TERRIFYING, BUT THE INSURANCE RATES ARE CHEAPER.
IN THE FARTHEST REACHES OF THE GALAXIES, I BELIEVE EVEN KRYMORGIAN SLAUGHTER BEASTS FRIGHTEN THEIR CHILDREN WITH TALES OF THE CREATURES KNOWN AS "DENTISTS."

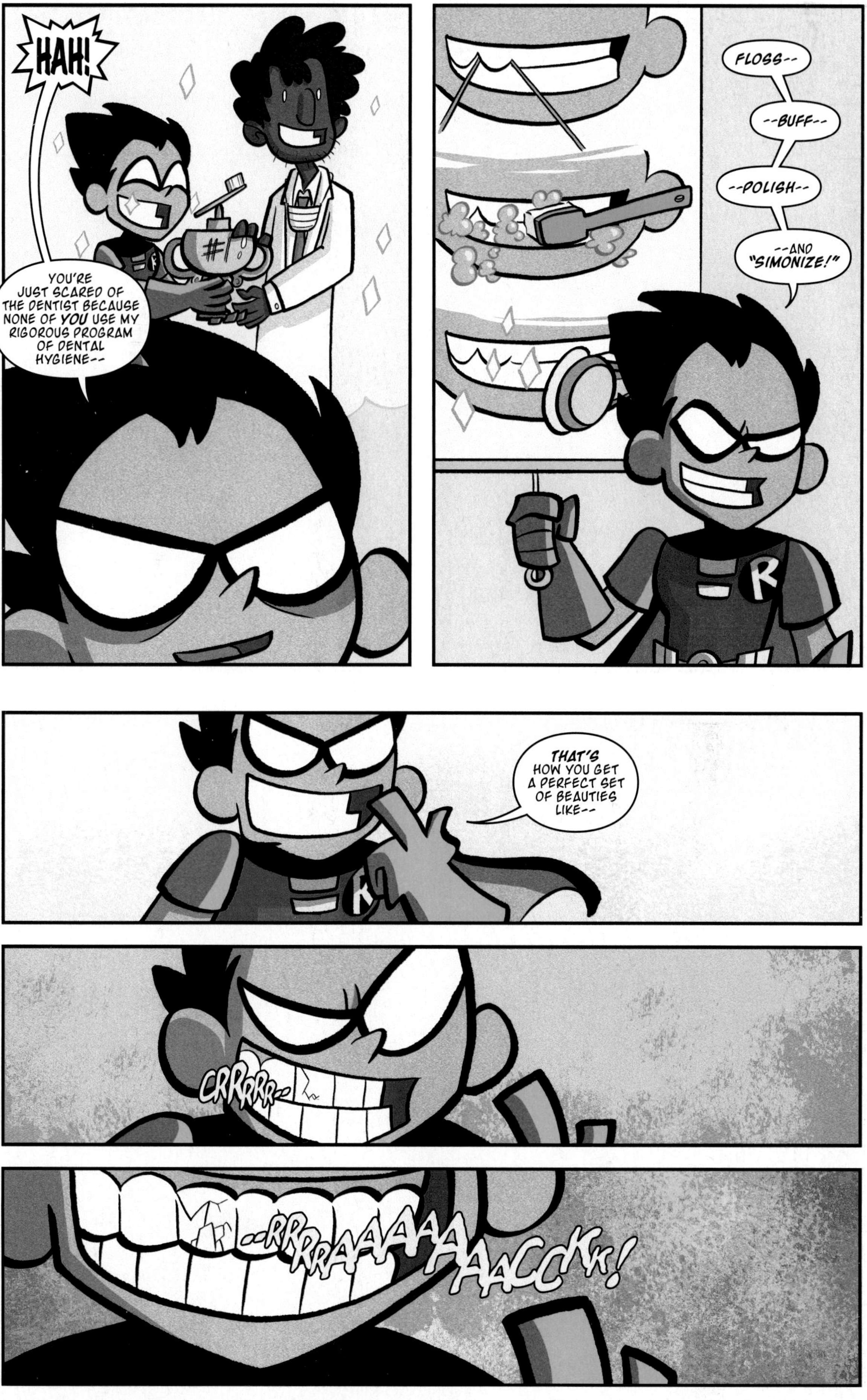
HAH!
YOU'RE JUST SCARED OF THE DENTIST BECAUSE NONE OF YOU USE MY RIGOROUS PROGRAM OF DENTAL HYGIENE--
FLOSS--
--BUFF--
--POLISH--
--AND "SIMONIZE!"
THAT'S HOW YOU GET A PERFECT SET OF BEAUTIES LIKE--
CRRRRR--
--RRRRAAAAAAAAACCKK!

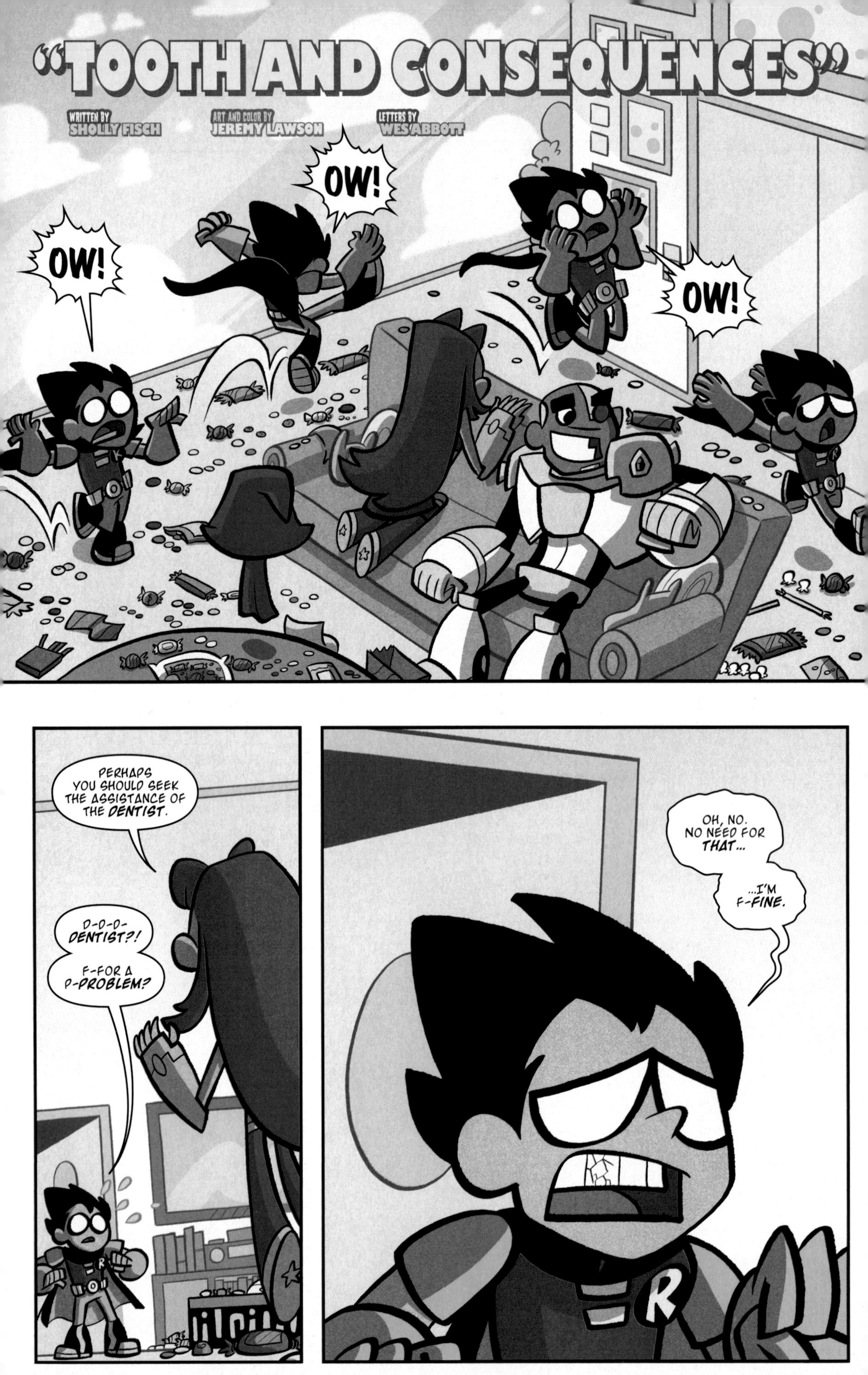
"TOOTH AND CONSEQUENCES"
WRITTEN BY SHOLLY FISCH
ART AND COLOR BY JEREMY LAWSON
LETTERS BY WES ABBOTT
OW!
OW!
OW!
PERHAPS YOU SHOULD SEEK THE ASSISTANCE OF THE DENTIST.
D-D-D- DENTIST?!
F-FOR A P-PROBLEM?
OH, NO. NO NEED FOR THAT...
...I'M F-FINE.

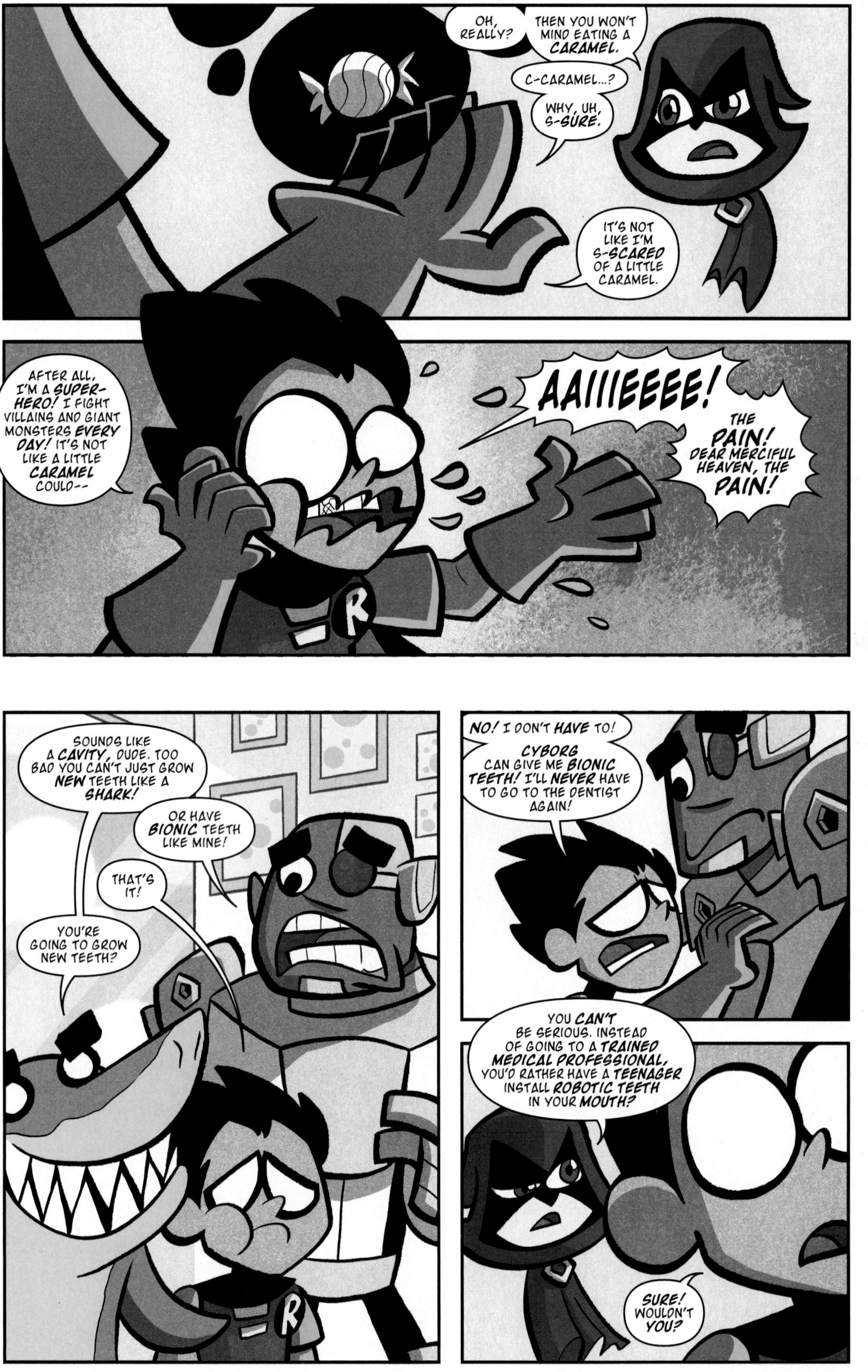
OH, REALLY?
THEN YOU WON'T MIND EATING A CARAMEL.
C-CARAMEL...?
WHY, UH, S-SURE.
IT'S NOT LIKE I'M S-SCARED OF A LITTLE CARAMEL.
AFTER ALL, I'M A SUPER-HERO! I FIGHT VILLAINS AND GIANT MONSTERS EVERY DAY! IT'S NOT LIKE A LITTLE CARAMEL COULD--
AAIIIEEEE!
THE PAIN! DEAR MERCIFUL HEAVEN, THE PAIN!
SOUNDS LIKE A CAVITY, DUDE. TOO BAD YOU CAN'T JUST GROW NEW TEETH LIKE A SHARK!
OR HAVE BIONIC TEETH LIKE MINE!
THAT'S IT!
YOU'RE GOING TO GROW NEW TEETH?
NO! I DON'T HAVE TO!
CYBORG CAN GIVE ME BIONIC TEETH! I'LL NEVER HAVE TO GO TO THE DENTIST AGAIN!
YOU CAN'T BE SERIOUS. INSTEAD OF GOING TO A TRAINED MEDICAL PROFESSIONAL, YOU'D RATHER HAVE A TEENAGER INSTALL ROBOTIC TEETH IN YOUR MOUTH?
SURE! WOULDN'T YOU?

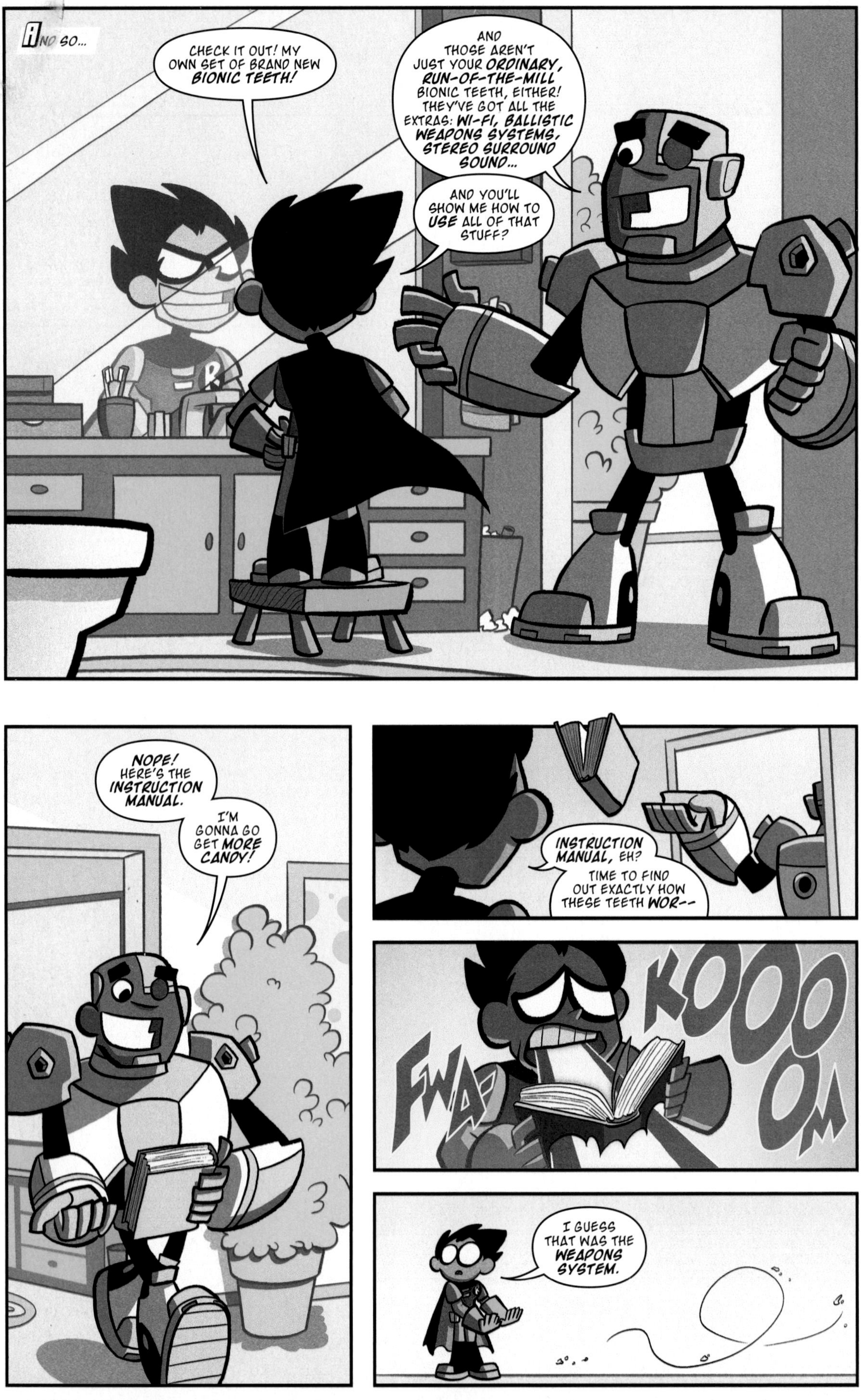
AND SO...
CHECK IT OUT! MY OWN SET OF BRAND NEW BIONIC TEETH!
AND THOSE AREN'T JUST YOUR ORDINARY, RUN-OF-THE-MILL BIONIC TEETH, EITHER! THEY'VE GOT ALL THE EXTRAS: WI-FI, BALLISTIC WEAPONS SYSTEMS, STEREO SURROUND SOUND...
AND YOU'LL SHOW ME HOW TO USE ALL OF THAT STUFF?
NOPE! HERE'S THE INSTRUCTION MANUAL.
I'M GONNA GO GET MORE CANDY!
INSTRUCTION MANUAL, EH?
TIME TO FIND OUT EXACTLY HOW THESE TEETH WOR--
FWA
KOOOOOM
I GUESS THAT WAS THE WEAPONS SYSTEM.

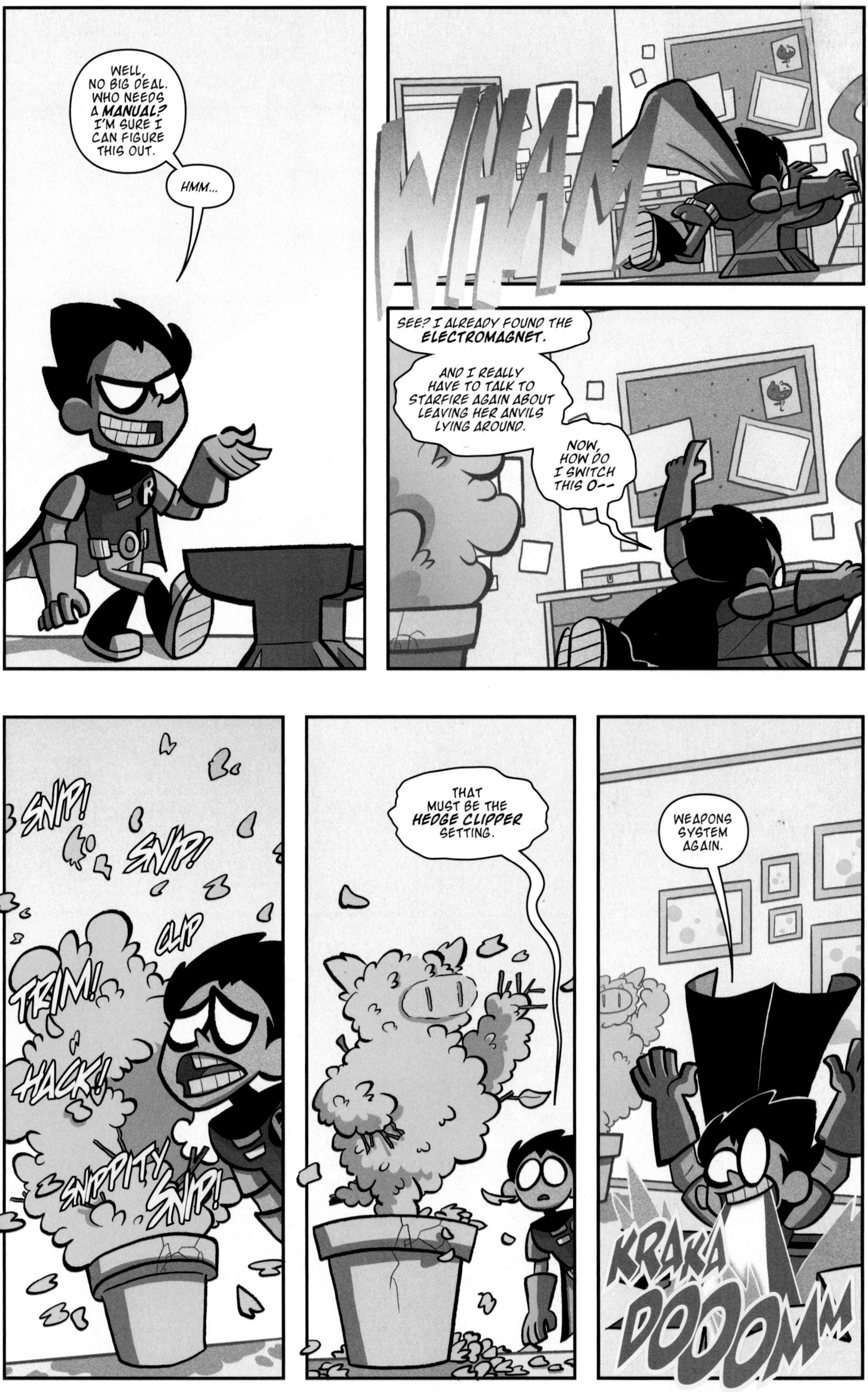
WELL, NO BIG DEAL. WHO NEEDS A MANUAL? I'M SURE I CAN FIGURE THIS OUT.
HMM...
WHAM
SEE? I ALREADY FOUND THE ELECTROMAGNET.
AND I REALLY HAVE TO TALK TO STARFIRE AGAIN ABOUT LEAVING HER ANVILS LYING AROUND.
NOW, HOW DO I SWITCH THIS O--
SNIP!
SNIP!
CLIP
TRIM!
HACK!
SNIPPITY SNIP!
THAT MUST BE THE HEDGE CLIPPER SETTING.
WEAPONS SYSTEM AGAIN.
KRAKA DOOOMM

MWAHA HAHAHAHA!

HEY, HOW ABOUT THAT? THESE TEETH EVEN LAUGH *AUTOMATICALLY* SO I DON'T HAVE TO GO THROUGH THE DRUDGERY OF LAUGHING MYSELF!

FOOL! I AM NO MERE *LAUGH TRACK!*

I AM *KILLG%RE,* A LIVING *ALIEN COMPUTER VIRUS* WHO HAS INVADED YOUR TEETH'S *ARTIFICIAL INTELLIGENCE!*

HUH?

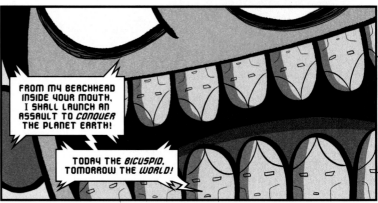

FROM MY BEACHHEAD INSIDE YOUR MOUTH, I SHALL LAUNCH AN ASSAULT TO *CONQUER* THE PLANET EARTH!

TODAY THE *BICUSPID,* TOMORROW THE *WORLD!*

DREAM ON, KILLG%RE! THE TITANS STAND READY TO *DEFEND THE EARTH!*

WE'LL FIGHT YOU *ANY TIME...*

...ANY...

...WHERE...

DON'T MAKE ME COME IN THERE!

ACTIVATING WEAPONS SYSTEMS.

YIKES!

CHOOM! CHOOM! CHOOM! CHOOM!

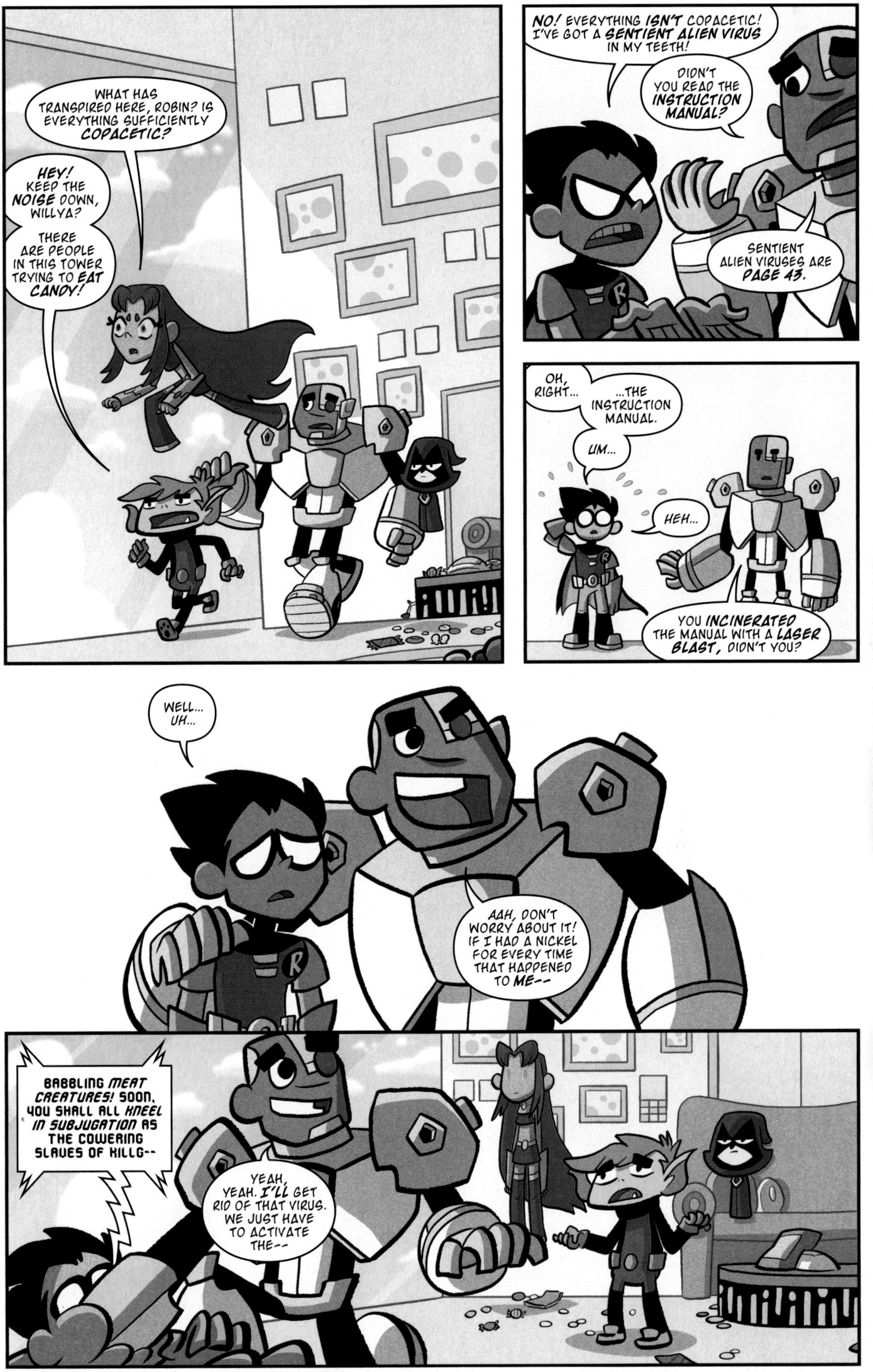
WHAT HAS TRANSPIRED HERE, ROBIN? IS EVERYTHING SUFFICIENTLY COPACETIC?
HEY! KEEP THE NOISE DOWN, WILLYA?
THERE ARE PEOPLE IN THIS TOWER TRYING TO EAT CANDY!
NO! EVERYTHING ISN'T COPACETIC! I'VE GOT A SENTIENT ALIEN VIRUS IN MY TEETH!
DIDN'T YOU READ THE INSTRUCTION MANUAL?
SENTIENT ALIEN VIRUSES ARE PAGE 43.
OH, RIGHT...
...THE INSTRUCTION MANUAL.
UM...
HEH...
YOU INCINERATED THE MANUAL WITH A LASER BLAST, DIDN'T YOU?
WELL... UH...
AAH, DON'T WORRY ABOUT IT! IF I HAD A NICKEL FOR EVERY TIME THAT HAPPENED TO ME--
BABBLING MEAT CREATURES! SOON, YOU SHALL ALL KNEEL IN SUBJUGATION AS THE COWERING SLAVES OF KILLG--
YEAH, YEAH. I'LL GET RID OF THAT VIRUS. WE JUST HAVE TO ACTIVATE THE--

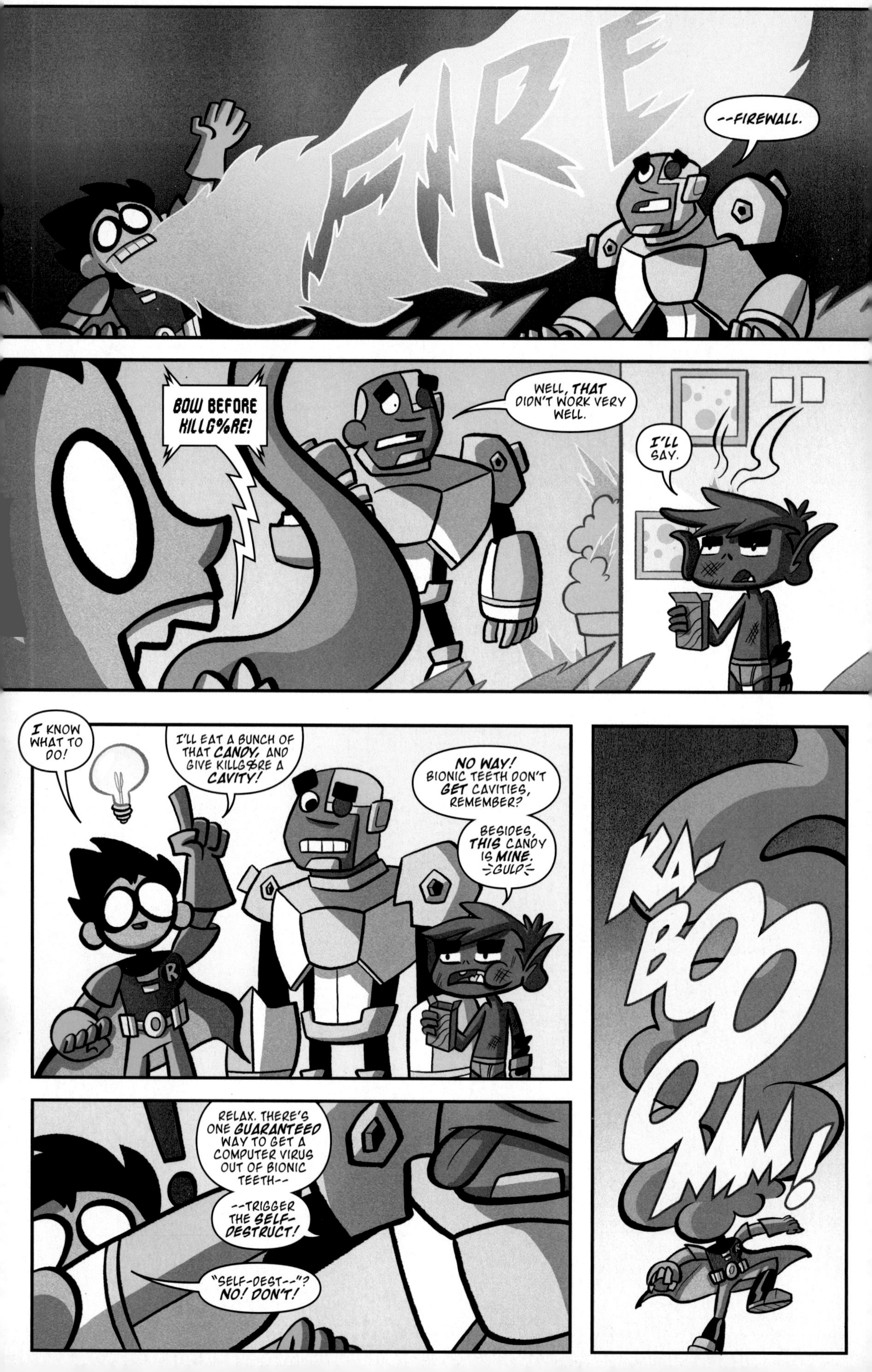
--FIREWALL.
BOW BEFORE KILLG%RE!
WELL, THAT DIDN'T WORK VERY WELL.
I'LL SAY.
I KNOW WHAT TO DO!
I'LL EAT A BUNCH OF THAT CANDY, AND GIVE KILLG%RE A CAVITY!
NO WAY! BIONIC TEETH DON'T GET CAVITIES, REMEMBER?
BESIDES, THIS CANDY IS MINE. GULP
RELAX. THERE'S ONE GUARANTEED WAY TO GET A COMPUTER VIRUS OUT OF BIONIC TEETH--
--TRIGGER THE SELF-DESTRUCT!
"SELF-DEST--"? NO! DON'T!
KA-BOOOM!

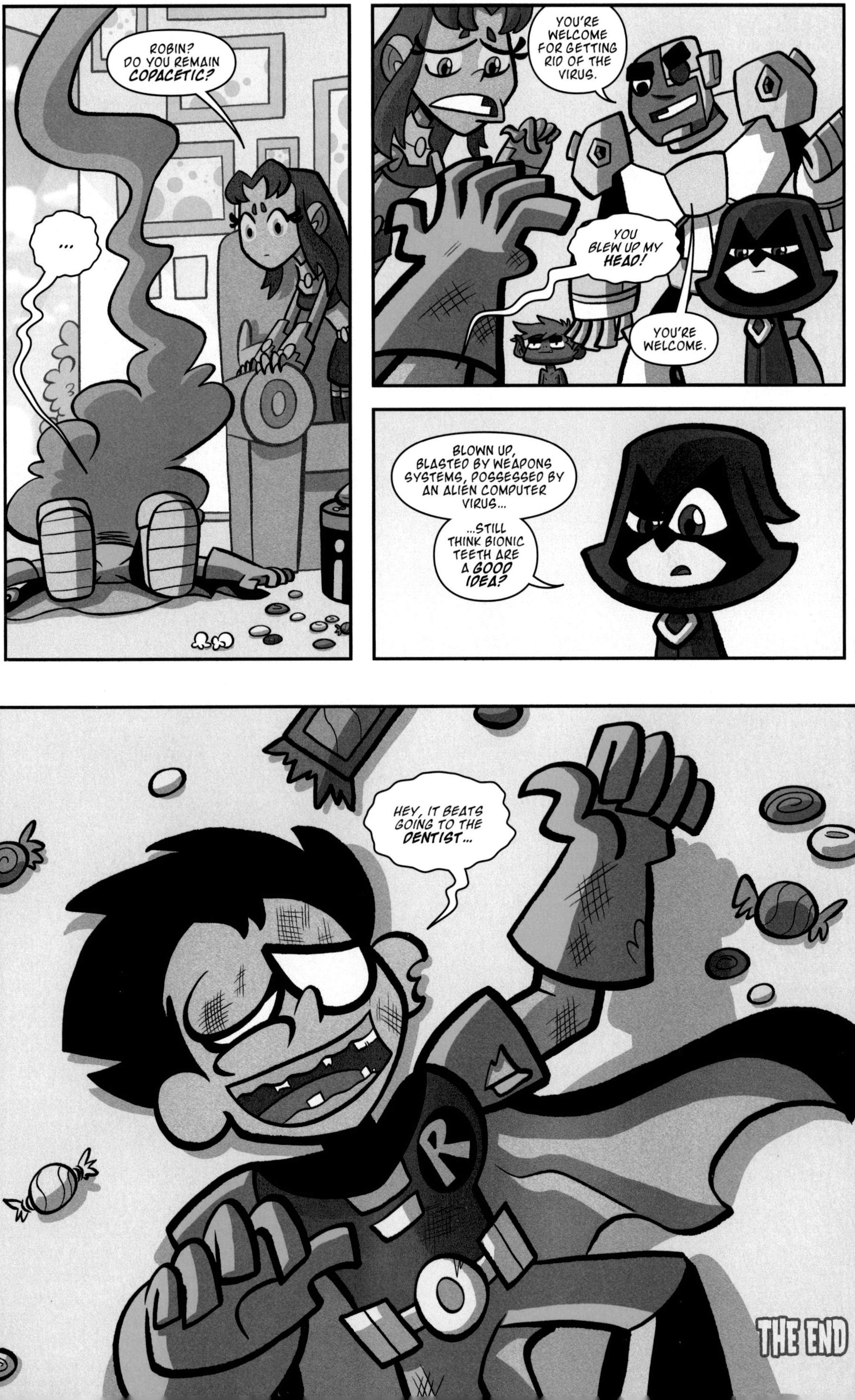
ROBIN? DO YOU REMAIN **COPACETIC?**
...
YOU'RE WELCOME FOR GETTING RID OF THE VIRUS.
YOU BLEW UP MY **HEAD!**
YOU'RE WELCOME.
BLOWN UP, BLASTED BY WEAPONS SYSTEMS, POSSESSED BY AN ALIEN COMPUTER VIRUS...
...STILL THINK BIONIC TEETH ARE A **GOOD IDEA?**
HEY, IT BEATS GOING TO THE **DENTIST**...
THE END

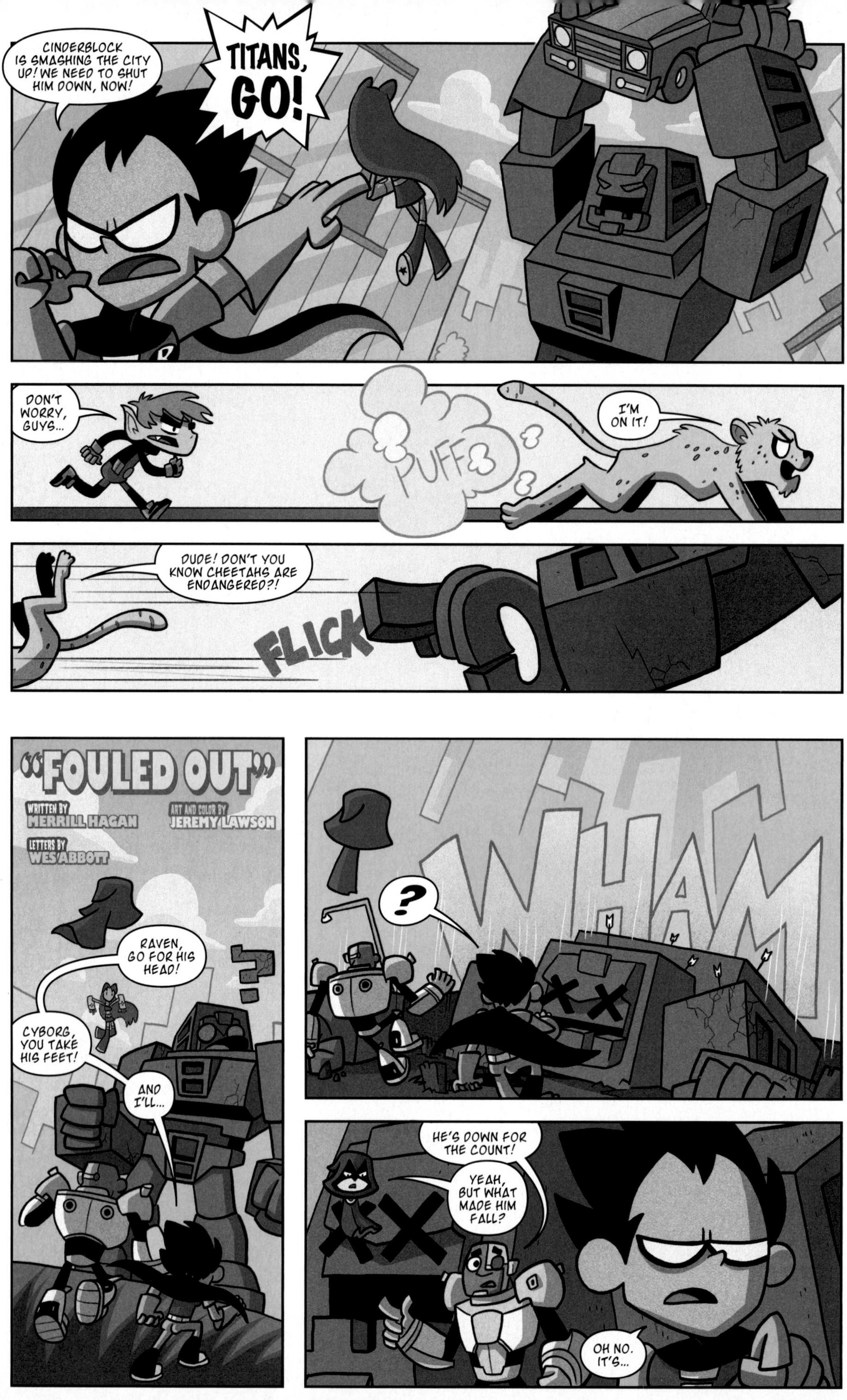
CINDERBLOCK IS SMASHING THE CITY UP! WE NEED TO SHUT HIM DOWN, NOW!
TITANS, GO!
DON'T WORRY, GUYS...
PUFF
I'M ON IT!
DUDE! DON'T YOU KNOW CHEETAHS ARE ENDANGERED?!
FLICK
"FOULED OUT"
WRITTEN BY MERRILL HAGAN
ART AND COLOR BY JEREMY LAWSON
LETTERS BY WES ABBOTT
RAVEN, GO FOR HIS HEAD!
CYBORG, YOU TAKE HIS FEET!
AND I'LL...
WHAM
?
HE'S DOWN FOR THE COUNT!
YEAH, BUT WHAT MADE HIM FALL?
OH NO. IT'S...

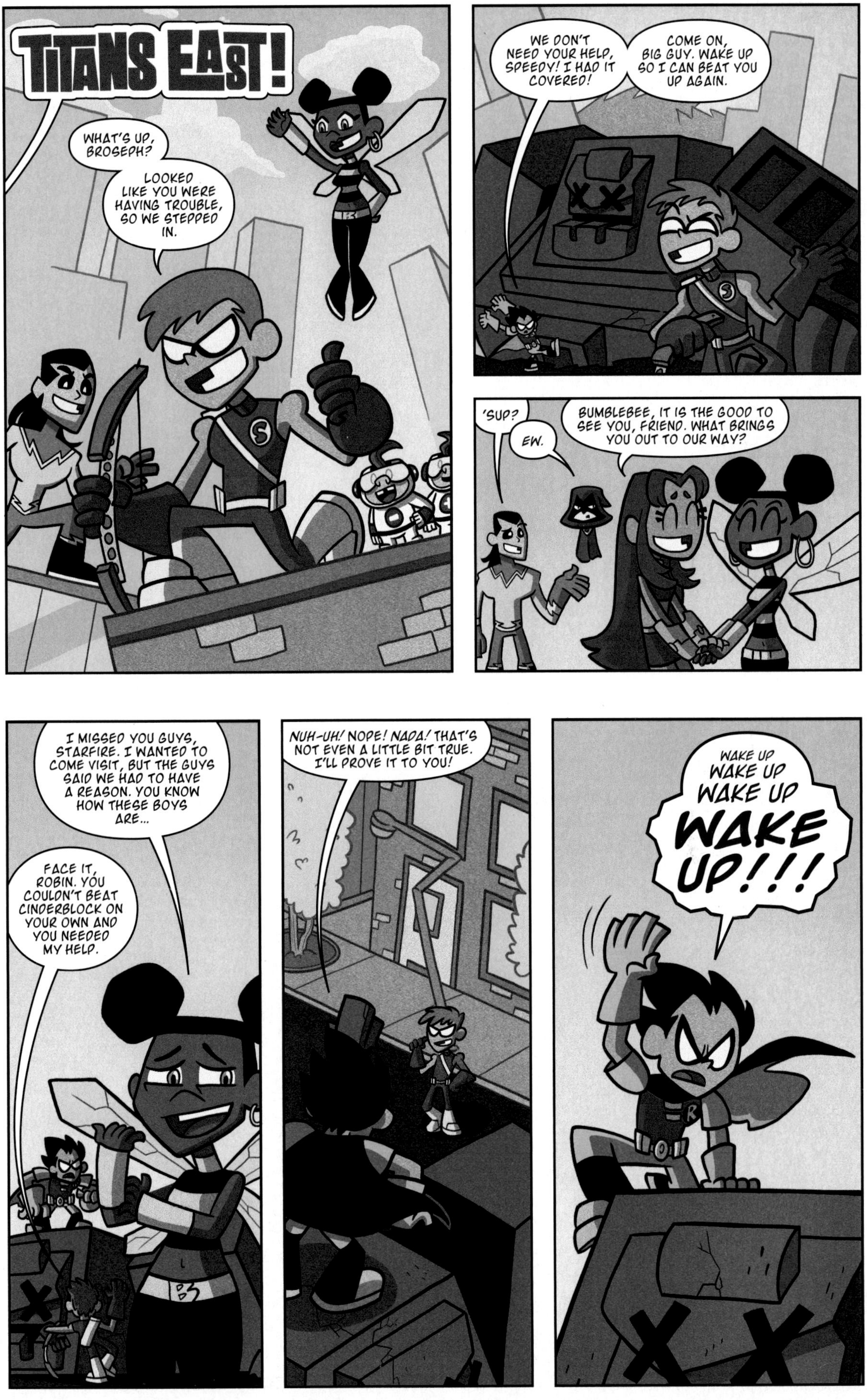
TITANS EAST!
WHAT'S UP, BROSEPH?
LOOKED LIKE YOU WERE HAVING TROUBLE, SO WE STEPPED IN.
WE DON'T NEED YOUR HELP, SPEEDY! I HAD IT COVERED!
COME ON, BIG GUY. WAKE UP SO I CAN BEAT YOU UP AGAIN.
'SUP?
EW.
BUMBLEBEE, IT IS THE GOOD TO SEE YOU, FRIEND. WHAT BRINGS YOU OUT TO OUR WAY?
I MISSED YOU GUYS, STARFIRE. I WANTED TO COME VISIT, BUT THE GUYS SAID WE HAD TO HAVE A REASON. YOU KNOW HOW THESE BOYS ARE...
FACE IT, ROBIN. YOU COULDN'T BEAT CINDERBLOCK ON YOUR OWN AND YOU NEEDED MY HELP.
NUH-UH! NOPE! NADA! THAT'S NOT EVEN A LITTLE BIT TRUE. I'LL PROVE IT TO YOU!
WAKE UP WAKE UP WAKE UP WAKE UP!!!

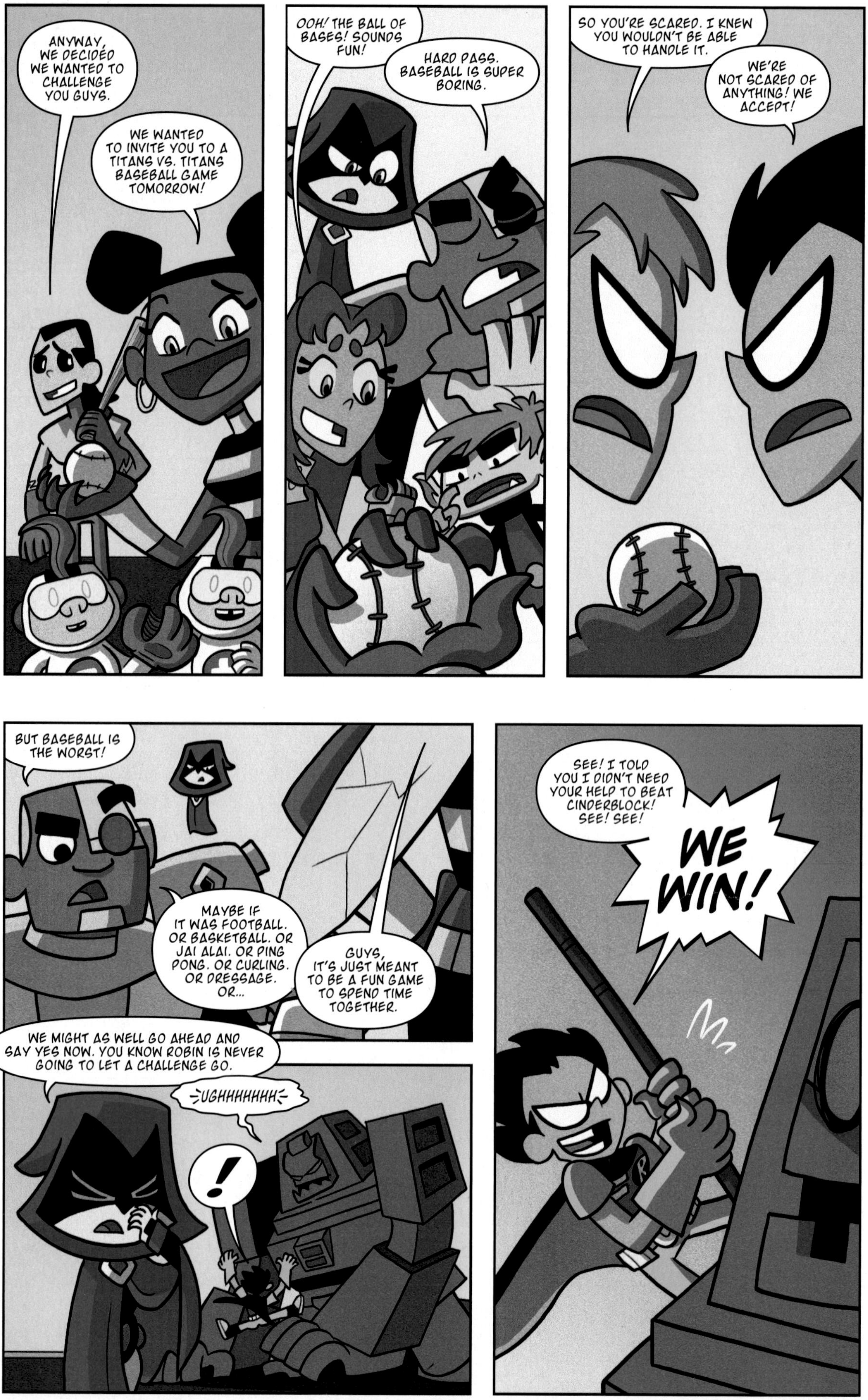
ANYWAY, WE DECIDED WE WANTED TO CHALLENGE YOU GUYS.
WE WANTED TO INVITE YOU TO A TITANS VS. TITANS BASEBALL GAME TOMORROW!
OOH! THE BALL OF BASES! SOUNDS FUN!
HARD PASS. BASEBALL IS SUPER BORING.
SO YOU'RE SCARED. I KNEW YOU WOULDN'T BE ABLE TO HANDLE IT.
WE'RE NOT SCARED OF ANYTHING! WE ACCEPT!
BUT BASEBALL IS THE WORST!
MAYBE IF IT WAS FOOTBALL. OR BASKETBALL. OR JAI ALAI. OR PING PONG. OR CURLING. OR DRESSAGE. OR...
GUYS, IT'S JUST MEANT TO BE A FUN GAME TO SPEND TIME TOGETHER.
WE MIGHT AS WELL GO AHEAD AND SAY YES NOW. YOU KNOW ROBIN IS NEVER GOING TO LET A CHALLENGE GO.
UGHHHHHHHH
!
SEE! I TOLD YOU I DIDN'T NEED YOUR HELP TO BEAT CINDERBLOCK! SEE! SEE!
WE WIN!

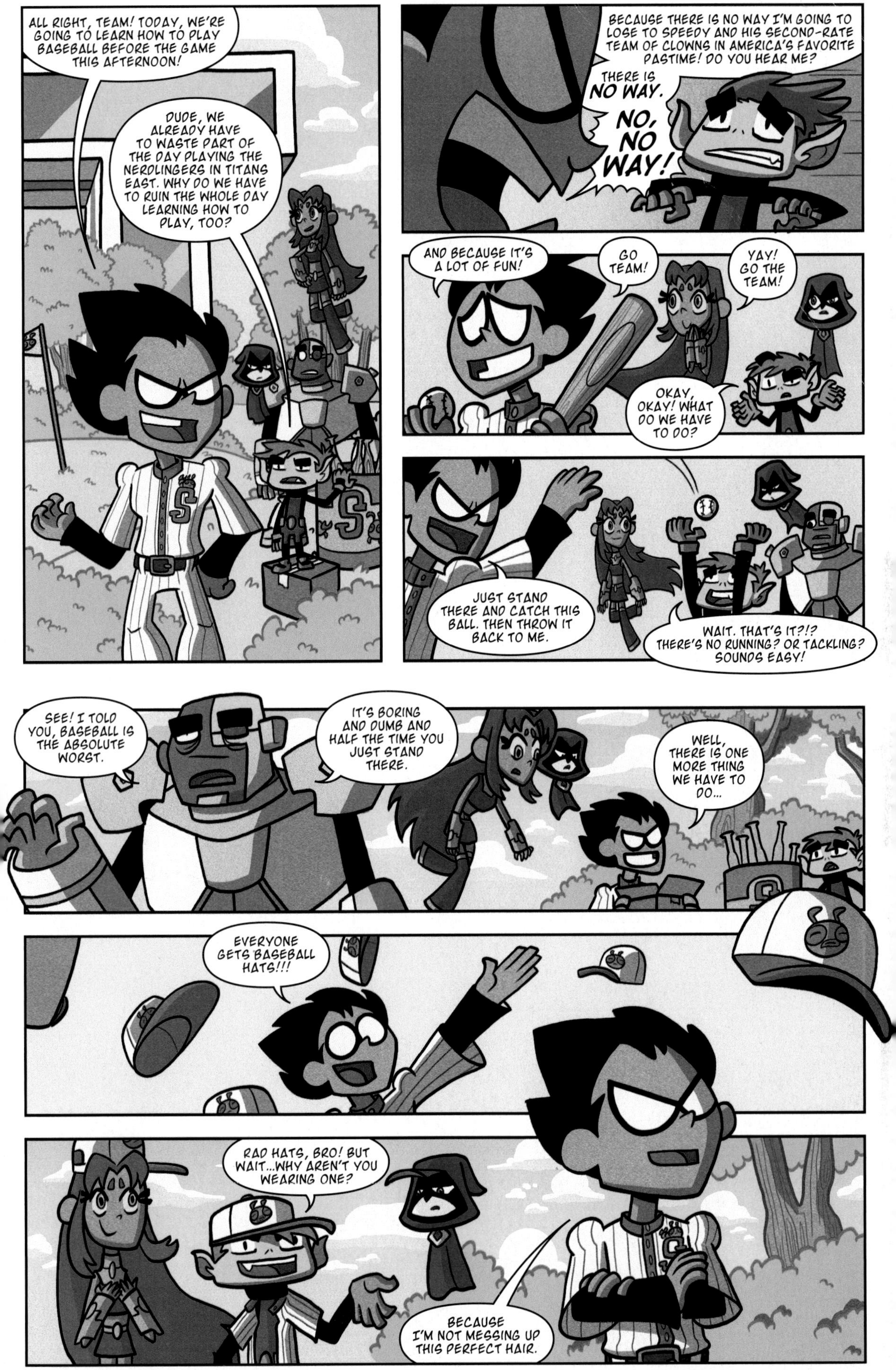
ALL RIGHT, TEAM! TODAY, WE'RE GOING TO LEARN HOW TO PLAY BASEBALL BEFORE THE GAME THIS AFTERNOON!
DUDE, WE ALREADY HAVE TO WASTE PART OF THE DAY PLAYING THE NERDLINGERS IN TITANS EAST. WHY DO WE HAVE TO RUIN THE WHOLE DAY LEARNING HOW TO PLAY, TOO?
BECAUSE THERE IS NO WAY I'M GOING TO LOSE TO SPEEDY AND HIS SECOND-RATE TEAM OF CLOWNS IN AMERICA'S FAVORITE PASTIME! DO YOU HEAR ME?
THERE IS NO WAY.
NO, NO WAY!
AND BECAUSE IT'S A LOT OF FUN!
GO TEAM!
YAY! GO THE TEAM!
OKAY, OKAY! WHAT DO WE HAVE TO DO?
JUST STAND THERE AND CATCH THIS BALL. THEN THROW IT BACK TO ME.
WAIT. THAT'S IT?!? THERE'S NO RUNNING? OR TACKLING? SOUNDS EASY!
SEE! I TOLD YOU, BASEBALL IS THE ABSOLUTE WORST.
IT'S BORING AND DUMB AND HALF THE TIME YOU JUST STAND THERE.
WELL, THERE IS ONE MORE THING WE HAVE TO DO...
EVERYONE GETS BASEBALL HATS!!!
RAD HATS, BRO! BUT WAIT...WHY AREN'T YOU WEARING ONE?
BECAUSE I'M NOT MESSING UP THIS PERFECT HAIR.

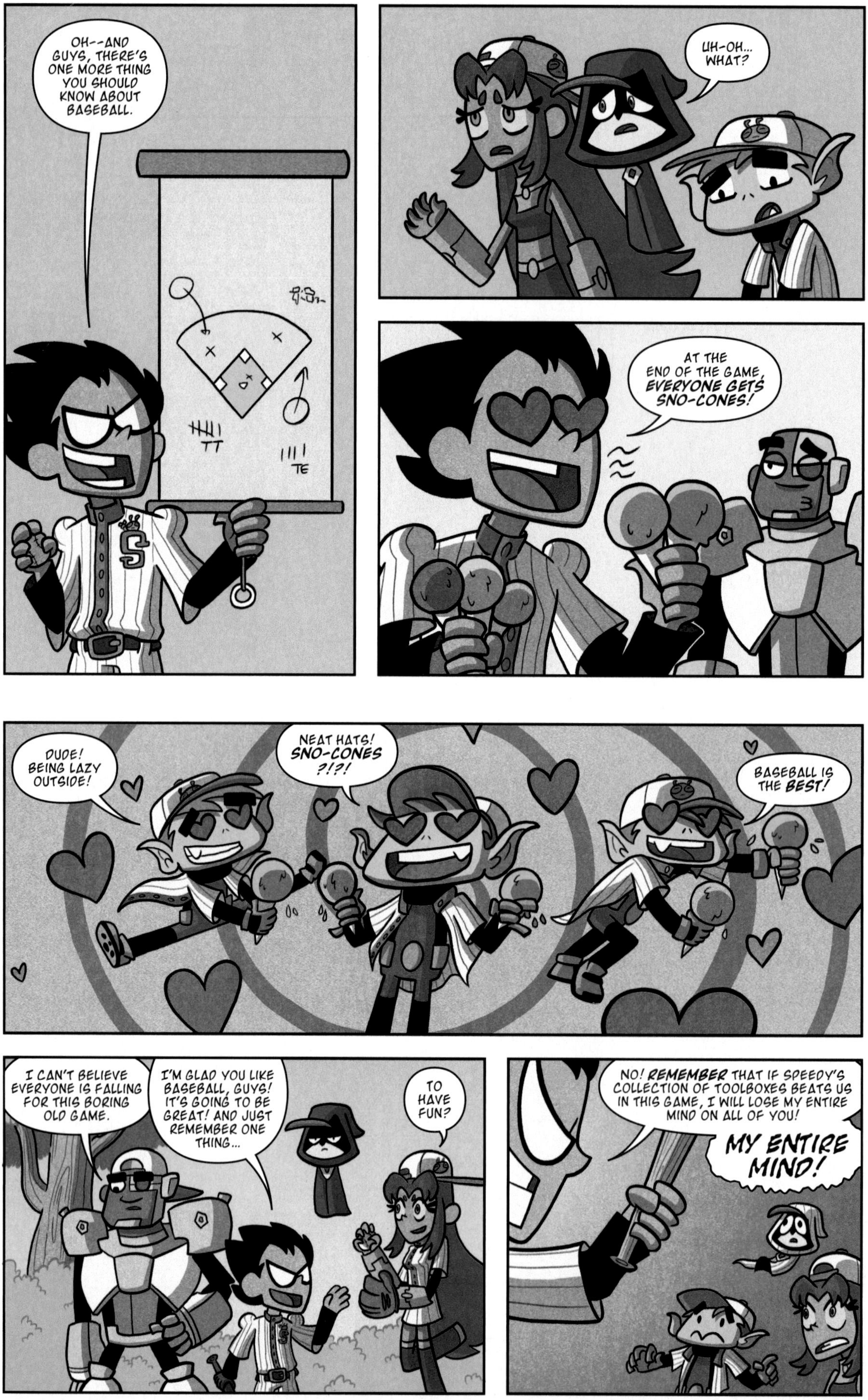
OH--AND GUYS, THERE'S ONE MORE THING YOU SHOULD KNOW ABOUT BASEBALL.
UH-OH... WHAT?
AT THE END OF THE GAME, EVERYONE GETS SNO-CONES!
DUDE! BEING LAZY OUTSIDE!
NEAT HATS! SNO-CONES ?!?!
BASEBALL IS THE BEST!
I CAN'T BELIEVE EVERYONE IS FALLING FOR THIS BORING OLD GAME.
I'M GLAD YOU LIKE BASEBALL, GUYS! IT'S GOING TO BE GREAT! AND JUST REMEMBER ONE THING...
TO HAVE FUN?
NO! REMEMBER THAT IF SPEEDY'S COLLECTION OF TOOLBOXES BEATS US IN THIS GAME, I WILL LOSE MY ENTIRE MIND ON ALL OF YOU!
MY ENTIRE MIND!

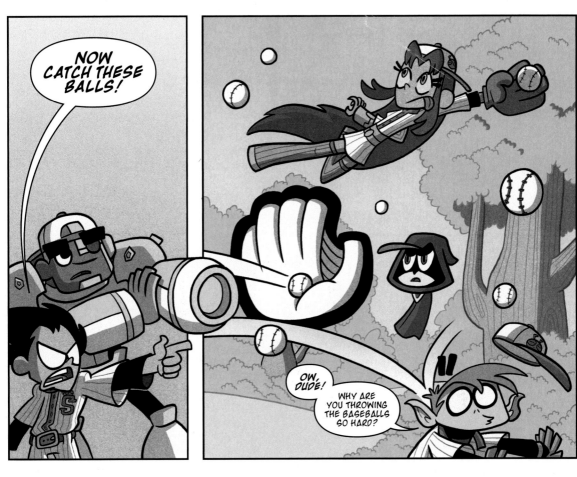

NOW CATCH THESE BALLS!

OW, DUDE! WHY ARE YOU THROWING THE BASEBALLS SO HARD?

OH, I'M SORRY, BEAST BOY. YOU THINK AQUALAD IS GOING TO PLAY EASY WITH YOU WHEN HE HAS A CHANCE TO KNOCK YOUR BLOCK OFF? DO YOU??!

N-NA... N-NO?!

NOW I'M GOING TO TEACH YOU HOW TO BAT IN THE MOST POWERFUL WAY POSSIBLE.

AHH, IS THIS BATTING SOMETHING THAT YOU LEARNED GROWING UP FROM THE BAT MAN?

UM...YEAH... KIND OF SOMETHING LIKE THAT.

STUPID BATTING PRACTICE! I CAN'T BELIEVE ROBIN SIGNED US UP FOR THIS GAME.

MAN, I HATE BASEBALL!

BUT WHY, CYBORG? BASEBALL IS THE BEST!

BuWAGHHH!

WHAT ARE YOU?

I'M DIAMOND DAN--THE SPIRIT OF BASEBALL! THE GREATEST GAME IN THE WORLD!

WHAT ARE YOU TALKING ABOUT, DIAMOND DAN? BASEBALL IS SO BORING! THERE'S NOT NEARLY AS MUCH ACTION AS FOOTBALL OR BASKETBALL.

BUT THAT'S WHERE YOU'RE WRONG, CYBORG!

BASEBALL HAS PLENTY OF ACTION!

FROM HITTING THE BALL!

TO STEALING A BASE! TO SLIDING INTO HOME...

I LOVE TO HIT THINGS!

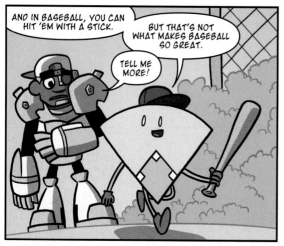

AND IN BASEBALL, YOU CAN HIT 'EM WITH A STICK.

BUT THAT'S NOT WHAT MAKES BASEBALL SO GREAT.

TELL ME MORE!

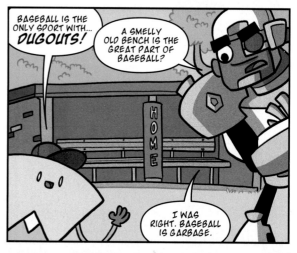

BASEBALL IS THE ONLY SPORT WITH... DUGOUTS!

A SMELLY OLD BENCH IS THE GREAT PART OF BASEBALL?

I WAS RIGHT. BASEBALL IS GARBAGE.

DON'T YOU GET IT, BUDDY? A DUGOUT BLOCKS THE REST OF THE WORLD FROM SEEING YOU! ANYTHING CAN HAPPEN IN THE DUGOUT!

WANT TO MAKE FUN OF THE OTHER TEAM? GO FOR IT! NO ONE CAN SEE YOU! GOT AN ITCHY BUTT? SCRATCH IT! IF THE CROWD CAN'T SEE YOU, THEY CAN'T JUDGE YOU!

HERE. HAVE SOME OF THESE PEANUTS...

THANKS, DIAMOND DAN, BUT WHAT DO I DO WITH THE SHELLS?

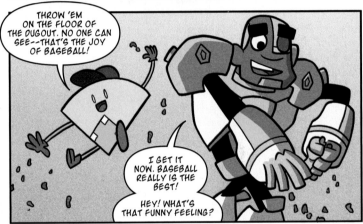

THROW 'EM ON THE FLOOR OF THE DUGOUT. NO ONE CAN SEE--THAT'S THE JOY OF BASEBALL!

I GET IT NOW. BASEBALL REALLY IS THE BEST!

HEY! WHAT'S THAT FUNNY FEELING?

CYBORG? ARE YOU OKAY?

WHAT'S GOING ON? WHERE'S DIAMOND DAN?

WHO'S DIAMOND DAN? ACTUALLY...CYBORG? YOU MAY BE HAVING SOME HEAD ISSUES.

BRO, I'M SO SORRY! I WOULD NEVER INTENTIONALLY HIT A BALL INTO YOUR HEAD!

ARE YOU OKAY, DUDE?

PLEASE BE OKAY.

OH, I'M BETTER THAN OKAY, BEAST BOY!

I FINALLY UNDERSTAND WHY BASEBALL IS SO GREAT--

-- AND I'M READY TO BEAT TITANS EAST!

AND IT'S ALL THANKS TO MY MAGIC TALKING DIAMOND BUDDY!

MAGIC TALKING DIAMOND? I DON'T THINK CYBORG REALLY GETS WHAT IS GOING ON.

SHH! SHHHH! WE NEED HIM IF WE HAVE ANY HOPE OF BEATING TITANS EAST!

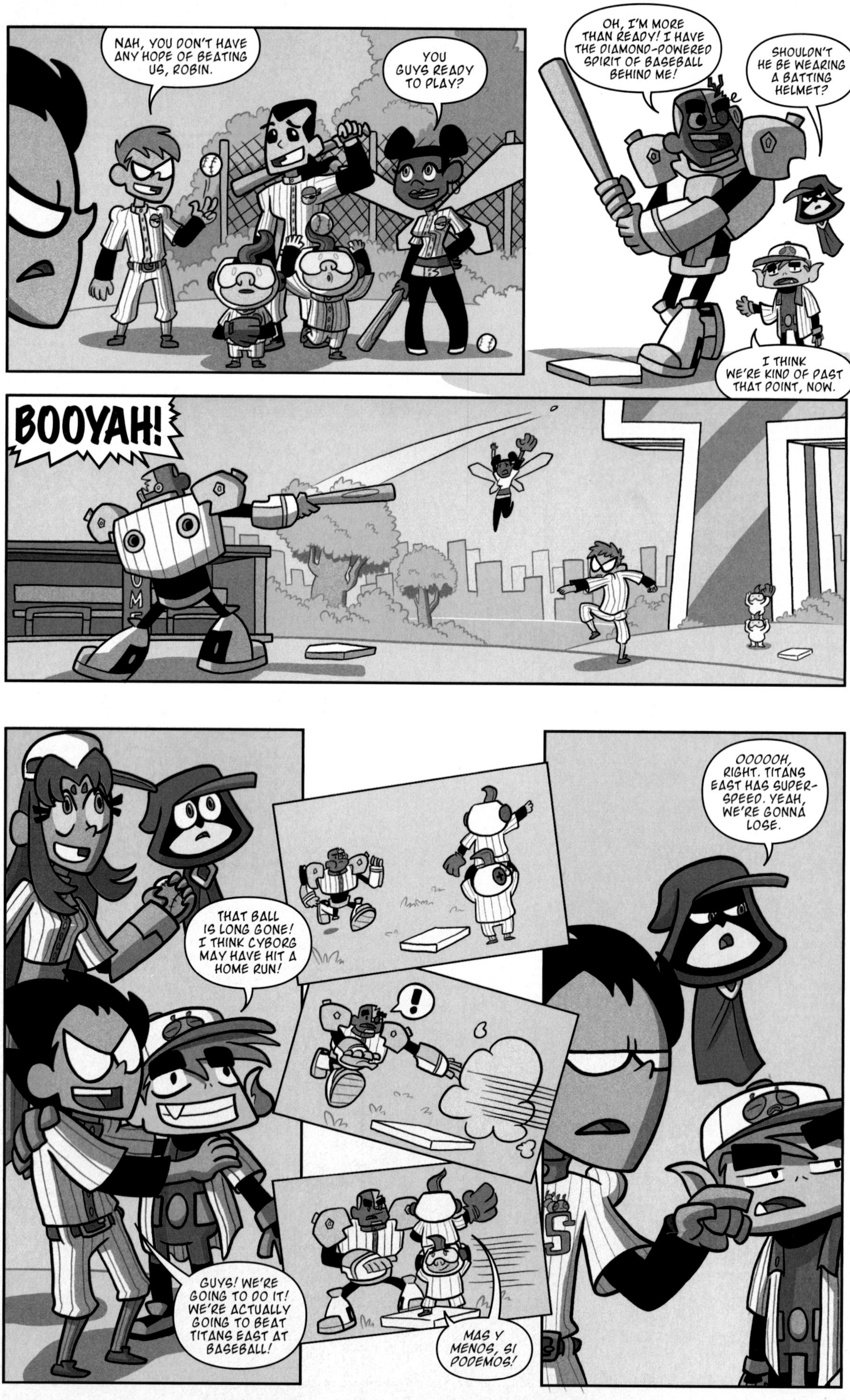
NAH, YOU DON'T HAVE ANY HOPE OF BEATING US, ROBIN.
YOU GUYS READY TO PLAY?
OH, I'M MORE THAN READY! I HAVE THE DIAMOND-POWERED SPIRIT OF BASEBALL BEHIND ME!
SHOULDN'T HE BE WEARING A BATTING HELMET?
I THINK WE'RE KIND OF PAST THAT POINT, NOW.
BOOYAH!
THAT BALL IS LONG GONE! I THINK CYBORG MAY HAVE HIT A HOME RUN!
GUYS! WE'RE GOING TO DO IT! WE'RE ACTUALLY GOING TO BEAT TITANS EAST AT BASEBALL!
!
MAS Y MENOS, SI PODEMOS!
OOOOOH, RIGHT. TITANS EAST HAS SUPER-SPEED. YEAH, WE'RE GONNA LOSE.

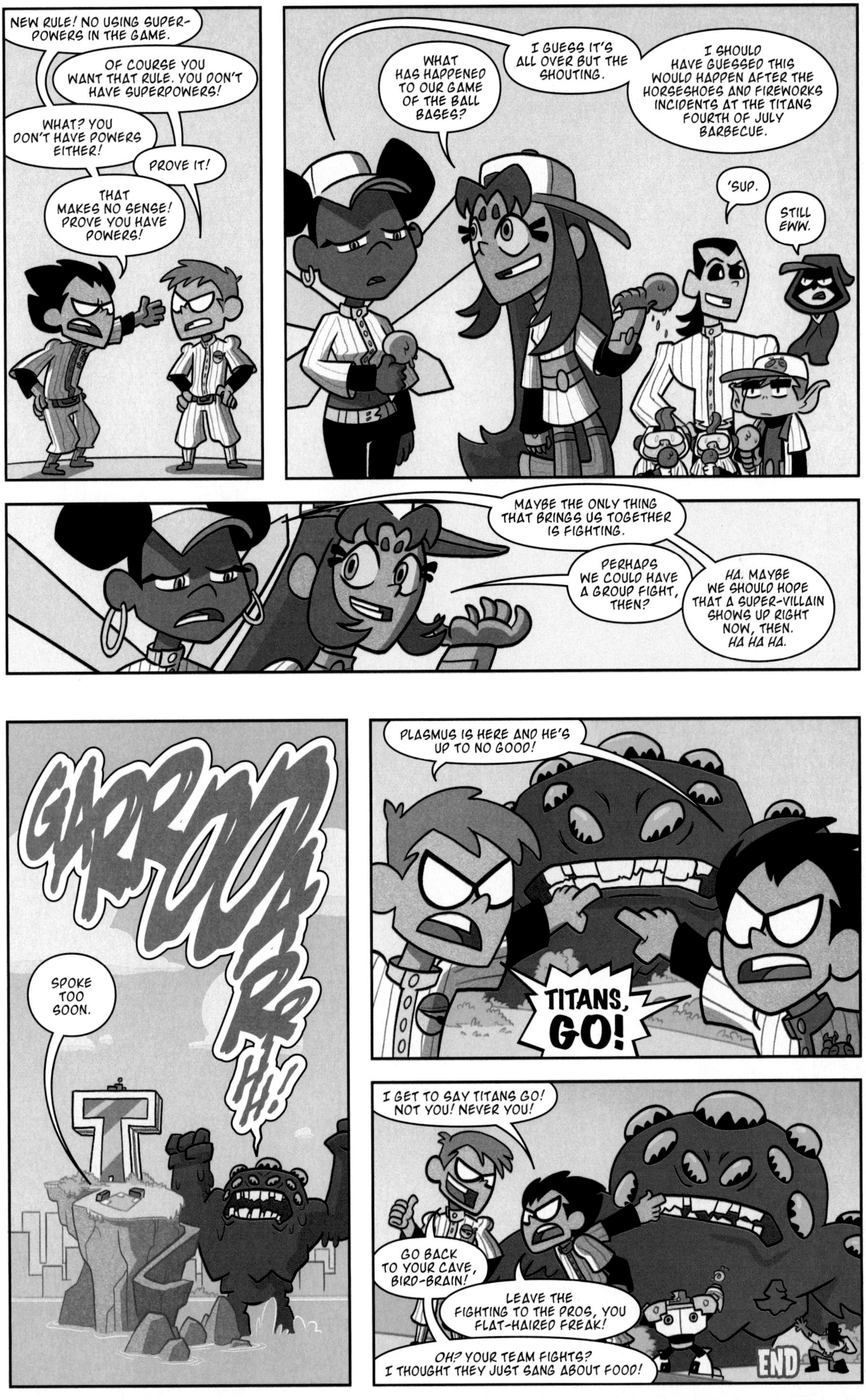
NEW RULE! NO USING SUPER-POWERS IN THE GAME.
OF COURSE YOU WANT THAT RULE. YOU DON'T HAVE SUPERPOWERS!
WHAT? YOU DON'T HAVE POWERS EITHER!
PROVE IT!
THAT MAKES NO SENSE! PROVE YOU HAVE POWERS!
WHAT HAS HAPPENED TO OUR GAME OF THE BALL BASES?
I GUESS IT'S ALL OVER BUT THE SHOUTING.
I SHOULD HAVE GUESSED THIS WOULD HAPPEN AFTER THE HORSESHOES AND FIREWORKS INCIDENTS AT THE TITANS FOURTH OF JULY BARBECUE.
'SUP.
STILL EWW.
MAYBE THE ONLY THING THAT BRINGS US TOGETHER IS FIGHTING.
PERHAPS WE COULD HAVE A GROUP FIGHT, THEN?
HA. MAYBE WE SHOULD HOPE THAT A SUPER-VILLAIN SHOWS UP RIGHT NOW, THEN. HA HA HA.
GARROOOARRHH!
SPOKE TOO SOON.
PLASMUS IS HERE AND HE'S UP TO NO GOOD!
TITANS, GO!
I GET TO SAY TITANS GO! NOT YOU! NEVER YOU!
GO BACK TO YOUR CAVE, BIRD-BRAIN!
LEAVE THE FIGHTING TO THE PROS, YOU FLAT-HAIRED FREAK!
OH? YOUR TEAM FIGHTS? I THOUGHT THEY JUST SANG ABOUT FOOD!
END

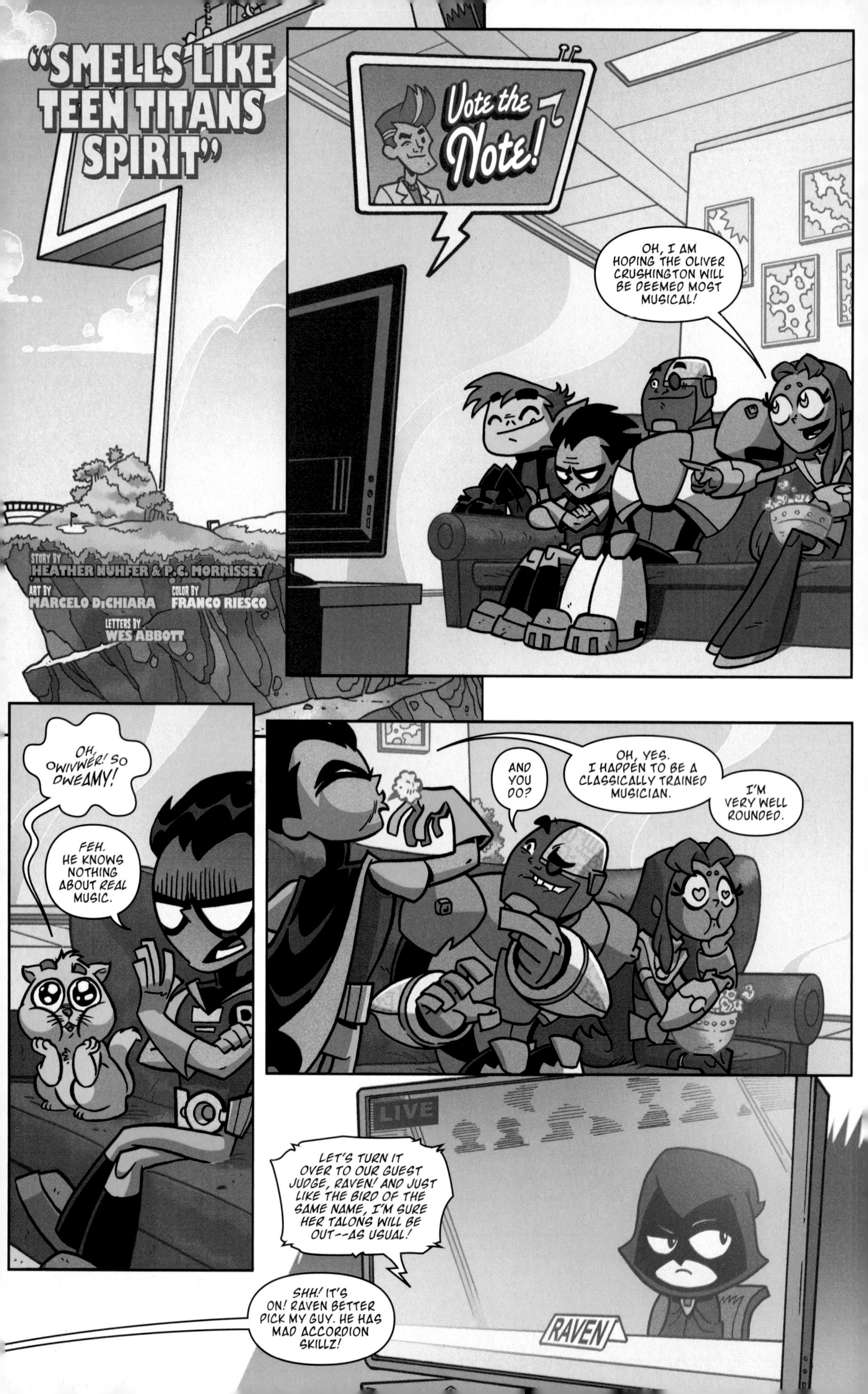
"SMELLS LIKE TEEN TITANS SPIRIT"
STORY BY HEATHER NUHFER & P.C. MORRISSEY
ART BY MARCELO DiCHIARA
COLOR BY FRANCO RIESCO
LETTERS BY WES ABBOTT
Vote the Note!
OH, I AM HOPING THE OLIVER CRUSHINGTON WILL BE DEEMED MOST MUSICAL!
OH, OWIVWER! SO DWEAMY!
FEH. HE KNOWS NOTHING ABOUT REAL MUSIC.
AND YOU DO?
OH, YES. I HAPPEN TO BE A CLASSICALLY TRAINED MUSICIAN.
I'M VERY WELL ROUNDED.
LIVE
LET'S TURN IT OVER TO OUR GUEST JUDGE, RAVEN! AND JUST LIKE THE BIRD OF THE SAME NAME, I'M SURE HER TALONS WILL BE OUT--AS USUAL!
SHH! IT'S ON! RAVEN BETTER PICK MY GUY. HE HAS MAD ACCORDION SKILLZ!
RAVEN

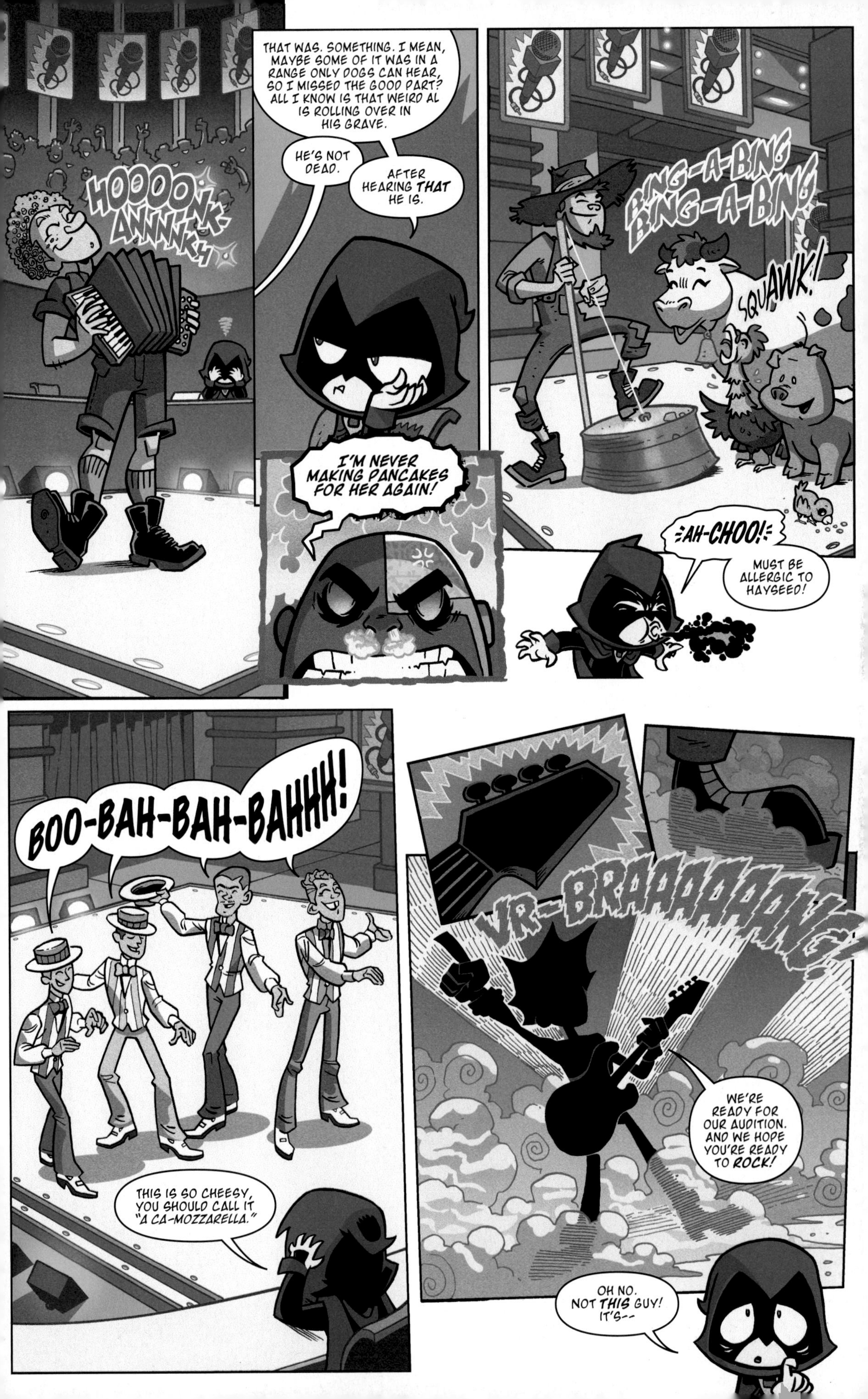
HOOOONK ANNNNKH
THAT WAS. SOMETHING. I MEAN, MAYBE SOME OF IT WAS IN A RANGE ONLY DOGS CAN HEAR, SO I MISSED THE GOOD PART? ALL I KNOW IS THAT WEIRD AL IS ROLLING OVER IN HIS GRAVE.
HE'S NOT DEAD.
AFTER HEARING THAT HE IS.
I'M NEVER MAKING PANCAKES FOR HER AGAIN!
BING-A-BING BING-A-BING
SQUAWK!
AH-CHOO!
MUST BE ALLERGIC TO HAYSEED!
BOO-BAH-BAH-BAHHH!
THIS IS SO CHEESY, YOU SHOULD CALL IT "A CA-MOZZARELLA."
VR-BRAAAAAANG!
WE'RE READY FOR OUR AUDITION. AND WE HOPE YOU'RE READY TO ROCK!
OH NO. NOT THIS GUY! IT'S--

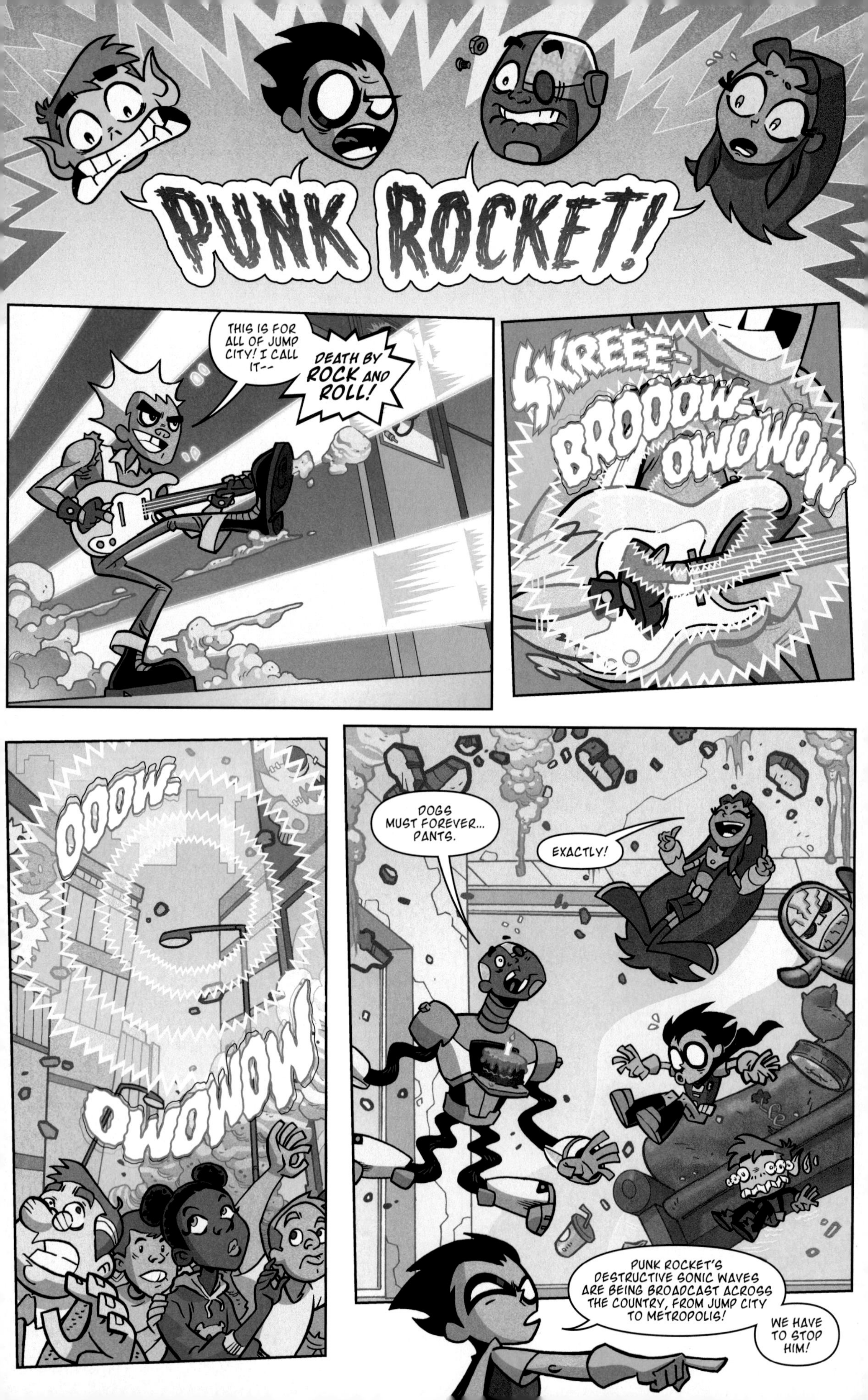
PUNK ROCKET!
THIS IS FOR ALL OF JUMP CITY! I CALL IT--
DEATH BY ROCK AND ROLL!
SKREEE-BROOOW-OWOWOW
OOOW-OWOWOW
DOGS MUST FOREVER... PANTS.
EXACTLY!
PUNK ROCKET'S DESTRUCTIVE SONIC WAVES ARE BEING BROADCAST ACROSS THE COUNTRY, FROM JUMP CITY TO METROPOLIS!
WE HAVE TO STOP HIM!

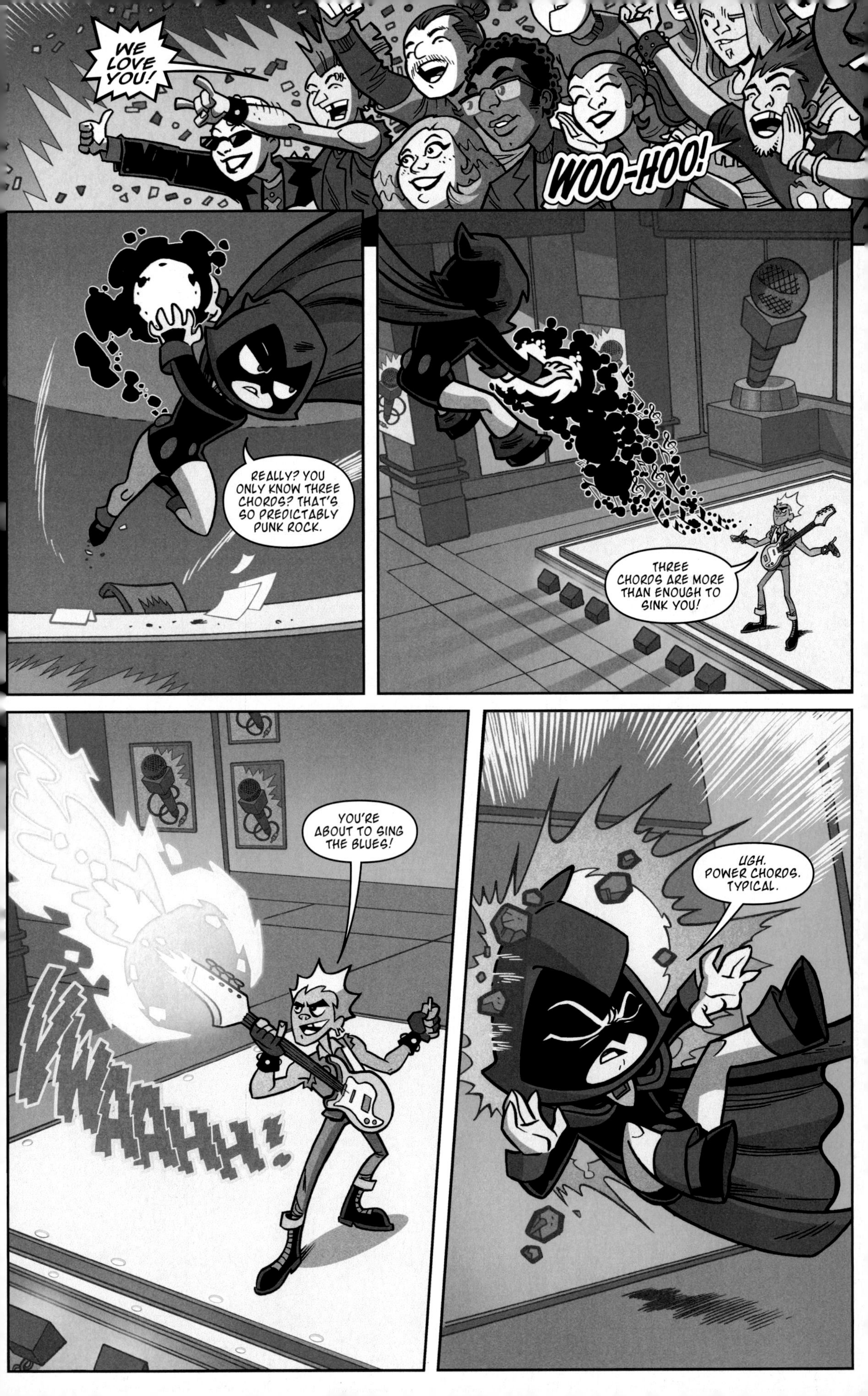
WE LOVE YOU!
WOO-HOO!
REALLY? YOU ONLY KNOW THREE CHORDS? THAT'S SO PREDICTABLY PUNK ROCK.
THREE CHORDS ARE MORE THAN ENOUGH TO SINK YOU!
YOU'RE ABOUT TO SING THE BLUES!
VWAAHH!
UGH. POWER CHORDS. TYPICAL.

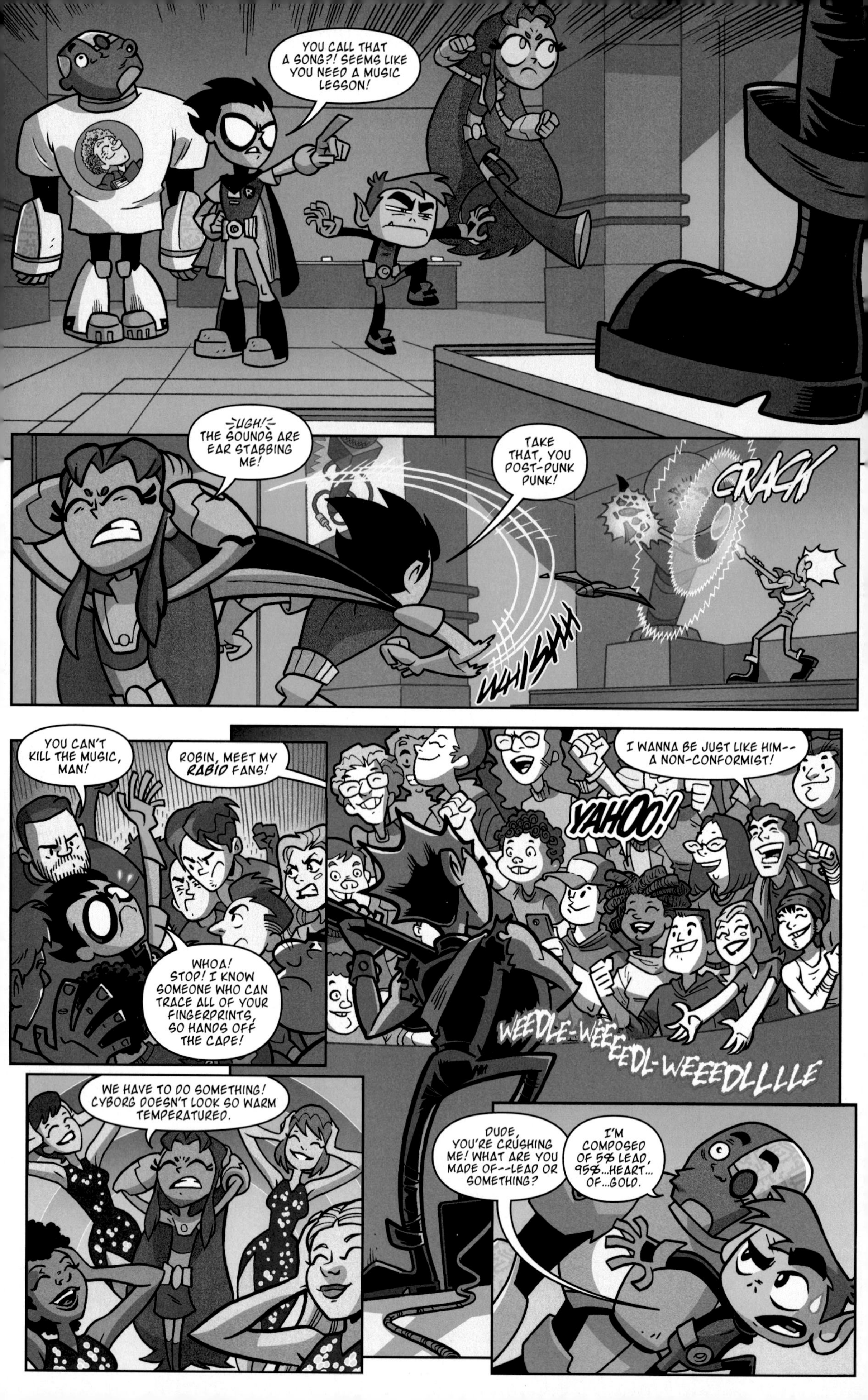

YOU CALL THAT A SONG?! SEEMS LIKE YOU NEED A MUSIC LESSON!
UGH! THE SOUNDS ARE EAR STABBING ME!
TAKE THAT, YOU POST-PUNK PUNK!
CRACK
WHISHH
YOU CAN'T KILL THE MUSIC, MAN!
ROBIN, MEET MY RABID FANS!
WHOA! STOP! I KNOW SOMEONE WHO CAN TRACE ALL OF YOUR FINGERPRINTS, SO HANDS OFF THE CAPE!
I WANNA BE JUST LIKE HIM--A NON-CONFORMIST!
YAHOO!
WEEDLE-WEEEEDL-WEEEDLLLLE
WE HAVE TO DO SOMETHING! CYBORG DOESN'T LOOK SO WARM TEMPERATURED.
DUDE, YOU'RE CRUSHING ME! WHAT ARE YOU MADE OF--LEAD OR SOMETHING?
I'M COMPOSED OF 5% LEAD, 95%...HEART... OF...GOLD.

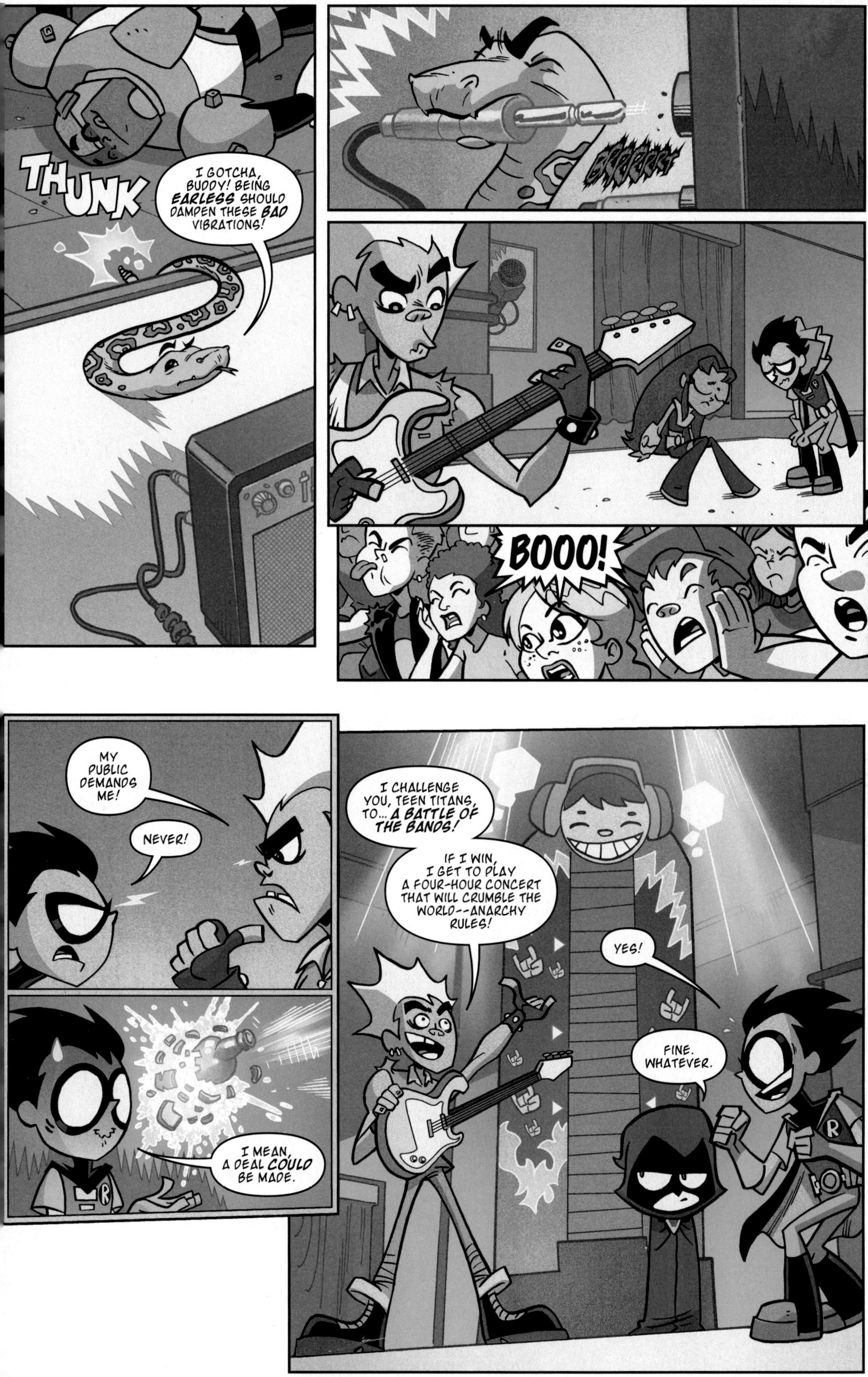
THUNK
I GOTCHA, BUDDY! BEING EARLESS SHOULD DAMPEN THESE BAD VIBRATIONS!
BRRRRT
BOOO!
MY PUBLIC DEMANDS ME!
NEVER!
I MEAN, A DEAL COULD BE MADE.
I CHALLENGE YOU, TEEN TITANS, TO... A BATTLE OF THE BANDS!
IF I WIN, I GET TO PLAY A FOUR-HOUR CONCERT THAT WILL CRUMBLE THE WORLD--ANARCHY RULES!
YES!
FINE. WHATEVER.

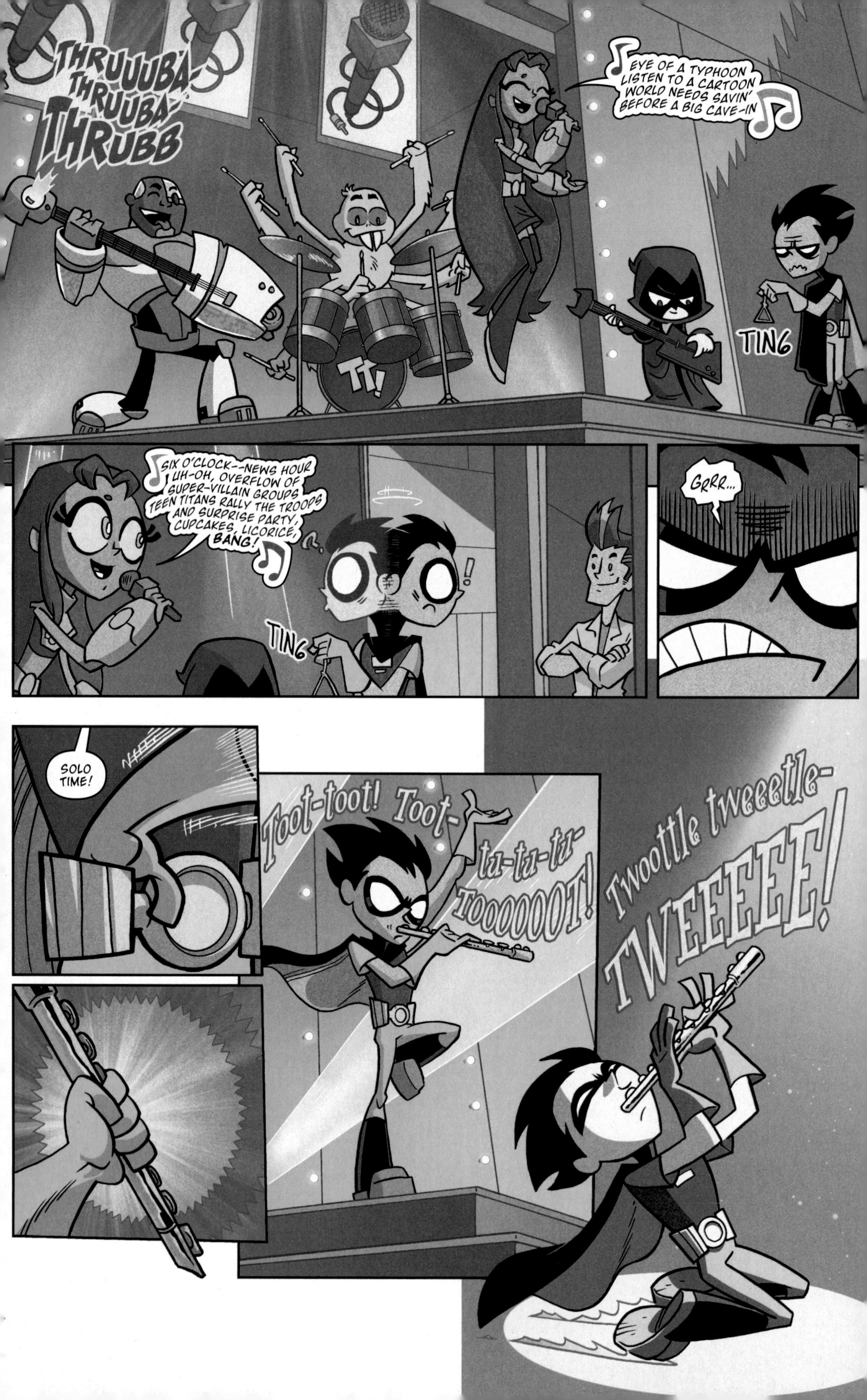
THRUUUBA-THRUUBA-THRUBB
EYE OF A TYPHOON LISTEN TO A CARTOON WORLD NEEDS SAVIN' BEFORE A BIG CAVE-IN
TING
SIX O'CLOCK--NEWS HOUR UH-OH, OVERFLOW OF SUPER-VILLAIN GROUPS TEEN TITANS RALLY THE TROOPS AND SURPRISE PARTY, CUPCAKES, LICORICE, BANG!
TING
GRRR...
SOLO TIME!
Toot-toot! Toot-ta-ta-ta-TOOOOOOT!
Twoottle tweeetle-TWEEEEE!

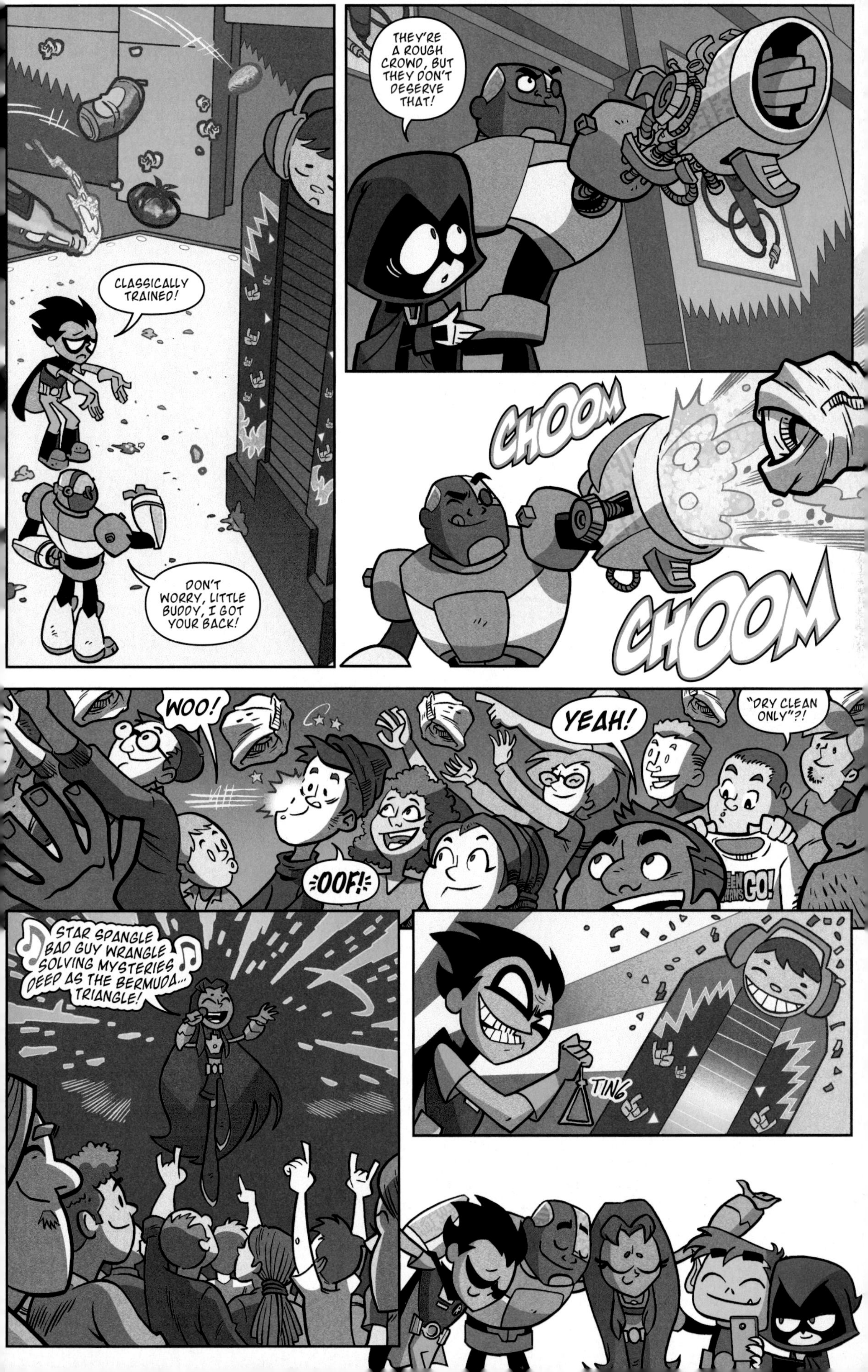
CLASSICALLY TRAINED!
DON'T WORRY, LITTLE BUDDY, I GOT YOUR BACK!
THEY'RE A ROUGH CROWD, BUT THEY DON'T DESERVE THAT!
CHOOM
CHOOM
WOO!
YEAH!
"DRY CLEAN ONLY"?!
OOF!
STAR SPANGLE BAD GUY WRANGLE SOLVING MYSTERIES DEEP AS THE BERMUDA... TRIANGLE!
TING

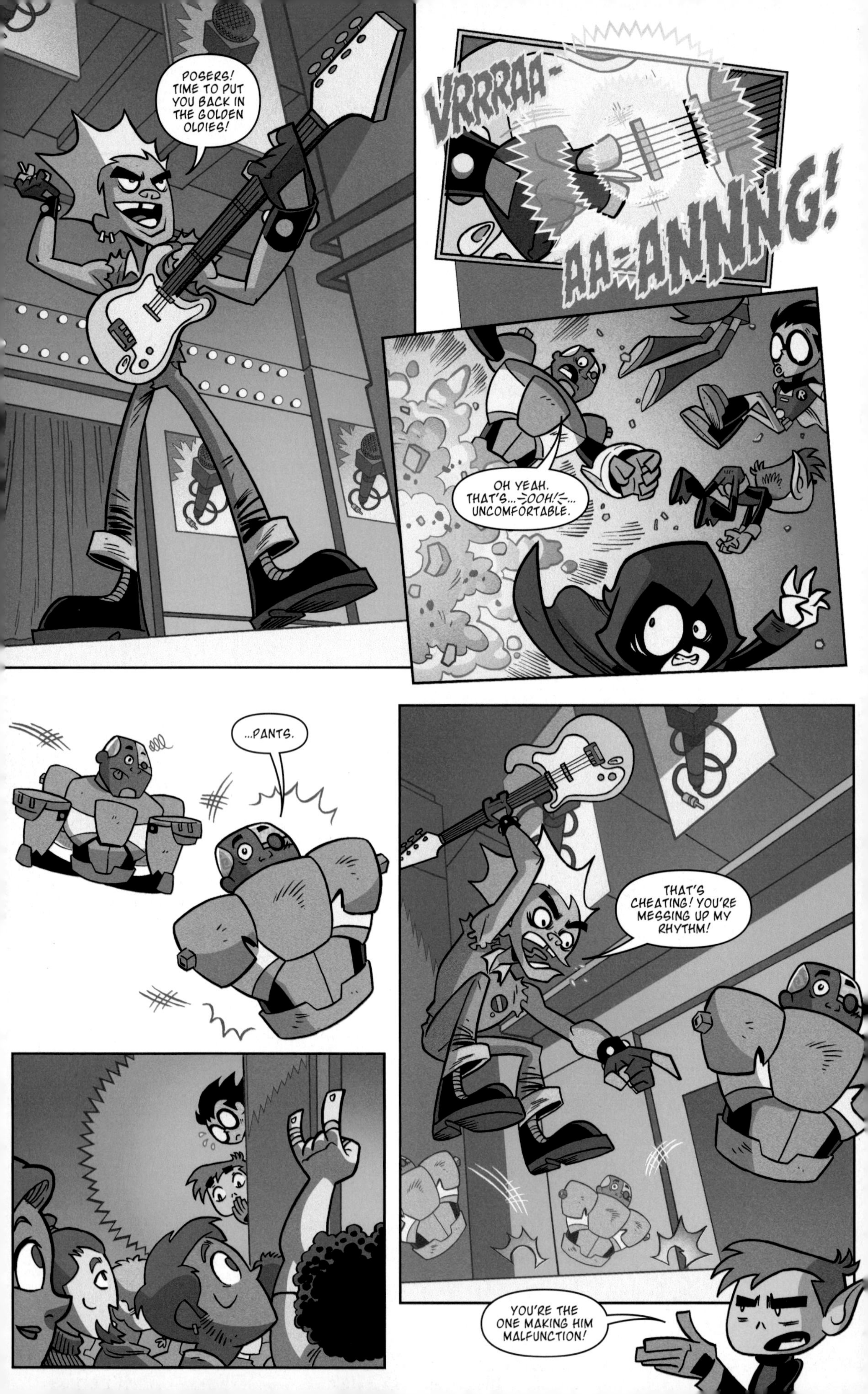
POSERS! TIME TO PUT YOU BACK IN THE GOLDEN OLDIES!
VRRRAA-
AA-ANNNG!
OH YEAH. THAT'S... OOH! ... UNCOMFORTABLE.
...PANTS.
THAT'S CHEATING! YOU'RE MESSING UP MY RHYTHM!
YOU'RE THE ONE MAKING HIM MALFUNCTION!

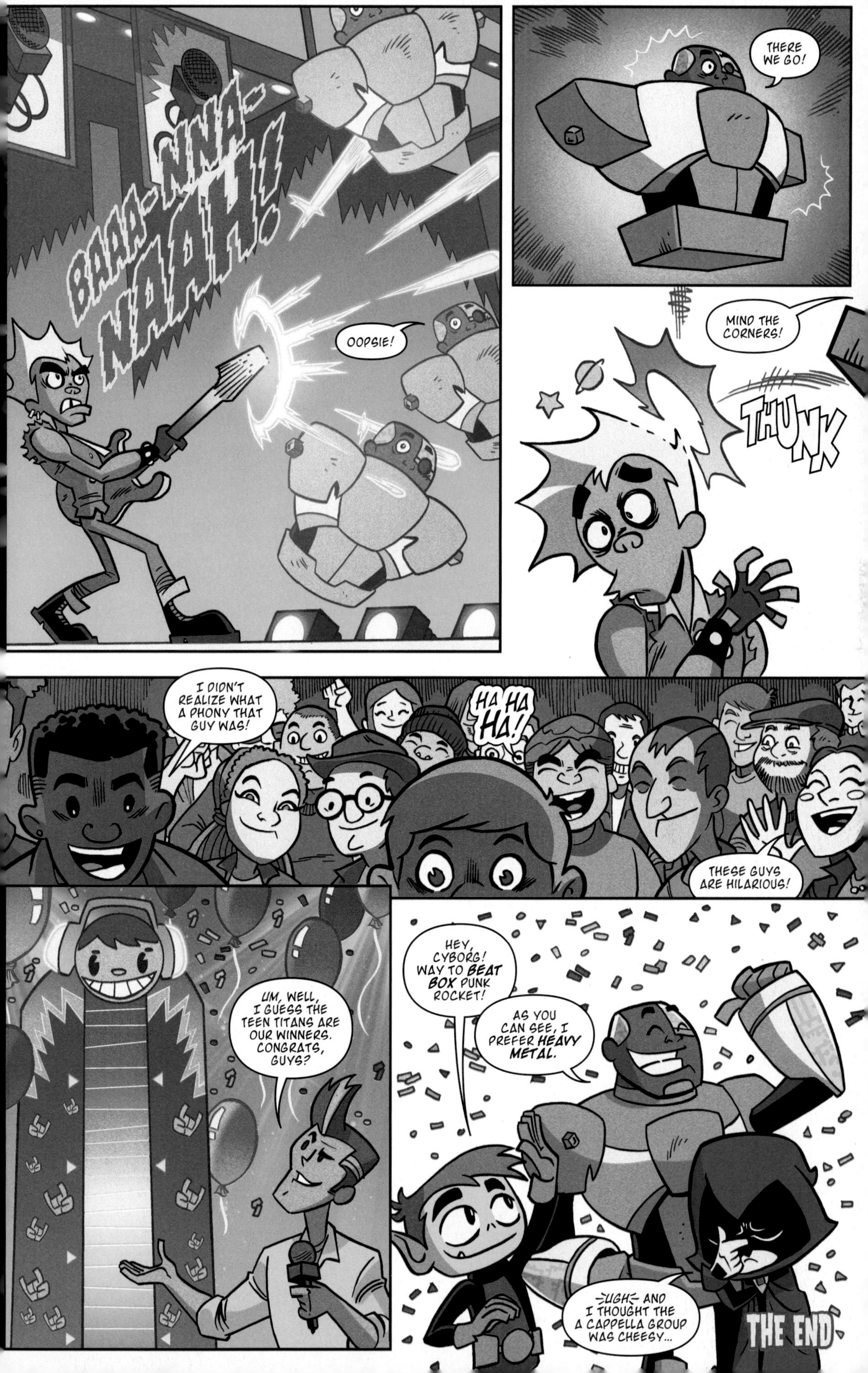
BAAA-NNA-NAAH!!
OOPSIE!
THERE WE GO!
MIND THE CORNERS!
THUNK
I DIDN'T REALIZE WHAT A PHONY THAT GUY WAS!
HA HA HA!
THESE GUYS ARE HILARIOUS!
UM, WELL, I GUESS THE TEEN TITANS ARE OUR WINNERS. CONGRATS, GUYS?
HEY, CYBORG! WAY TO BEAT BOX PUNK ROCKET!
AS YOU CAN SEE, I PREFER HEAVY METAL.
UGH AND I THOUGHT THE A CAPPELLA GROUP WAS CHEESY...
THE END

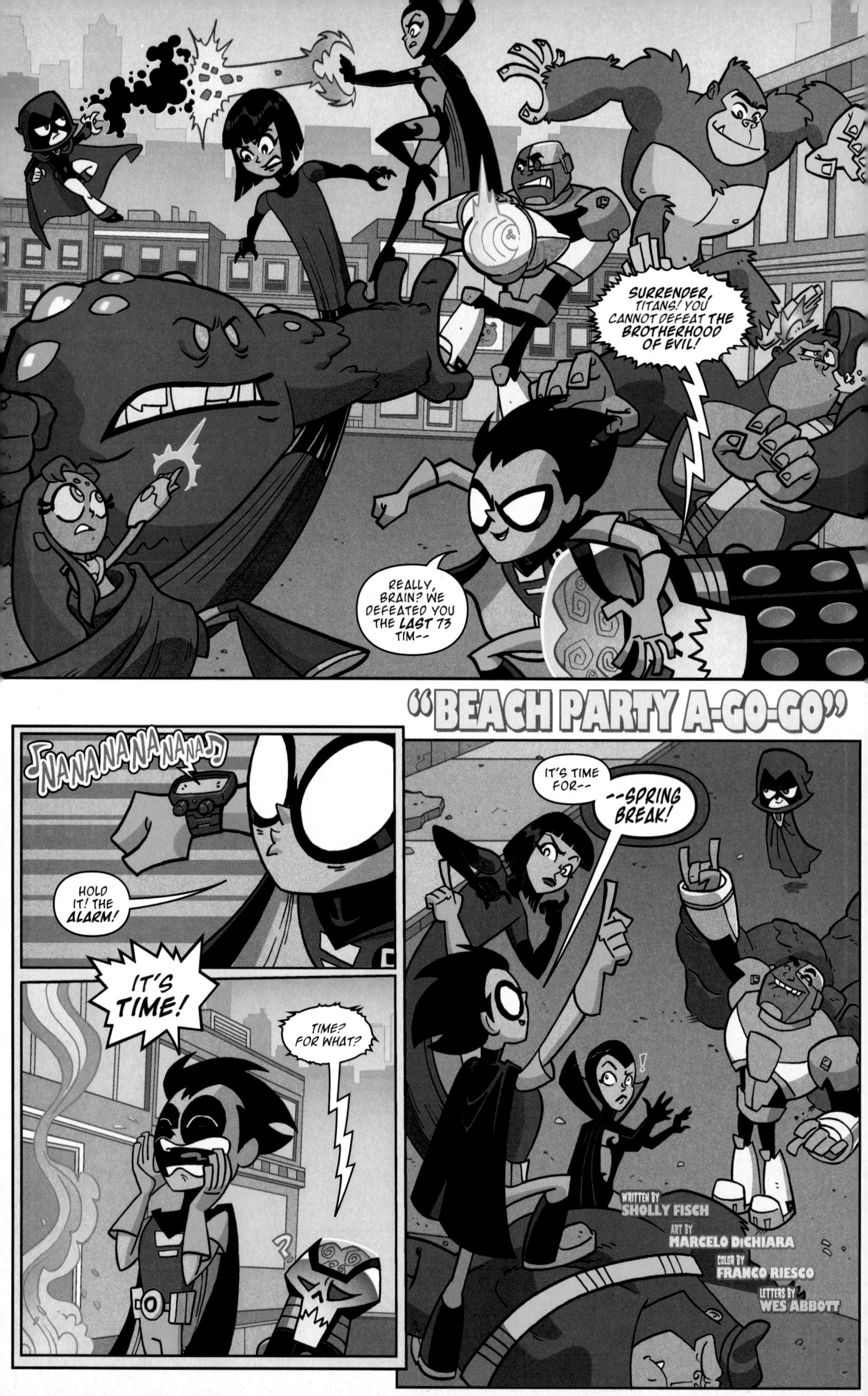
SURRENDER, TITANS! YOU CANNOT DEFEAT THE BROTHERHOOD OF EVIL!
REALLY, BRAIN? WE DEFEATED YOU THE LAST 73 TIM--
"BEACH PARTY A-GO-GO"
NA NA NA NA NA NA
HOLD IT! THE ALARM!
IT'S TIME!
TIME? FOR WHAT?
?
IT'S TIME FOR--
--SPRING BREAK!
!
WRITTEN BY SHOLLY FISCH
ART BY MARCELO DiCHIARA
COLOR BY FRANCO RIESCO
LETTERS BY WES ABBOTT

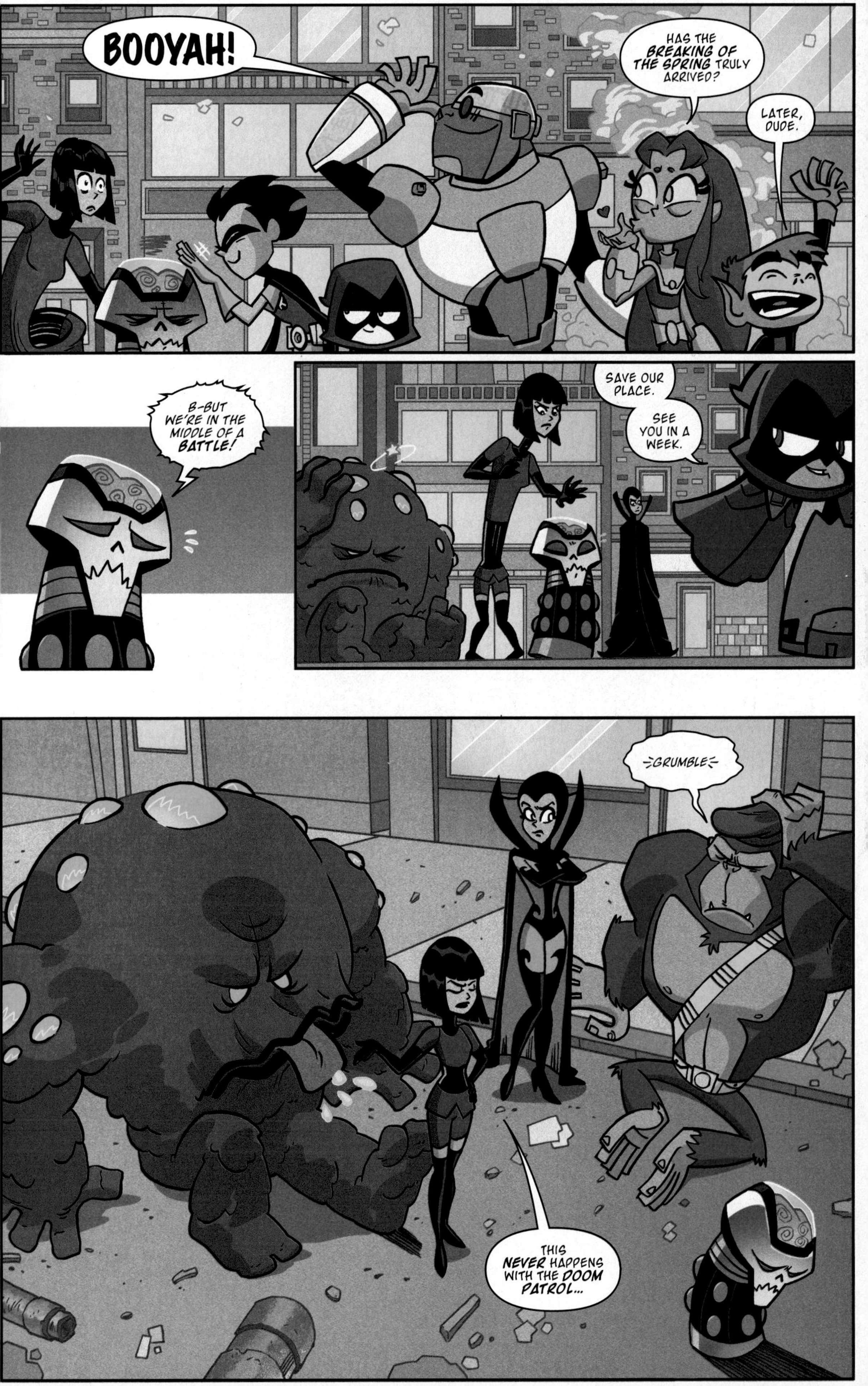
BOOYAH!
HAS THE BREAKING OF THE SPRING TRULY ARRIVED?
LATER, DUDE.
B-BUT WE'RE IN THE MIDDLE OF A BATTLE!
SAVE OUR PLACE.
SEE YOU IN A WEEK.
GRUMBLE
THIS NEVER HAPPENS WITH THE DOOM PATROL...

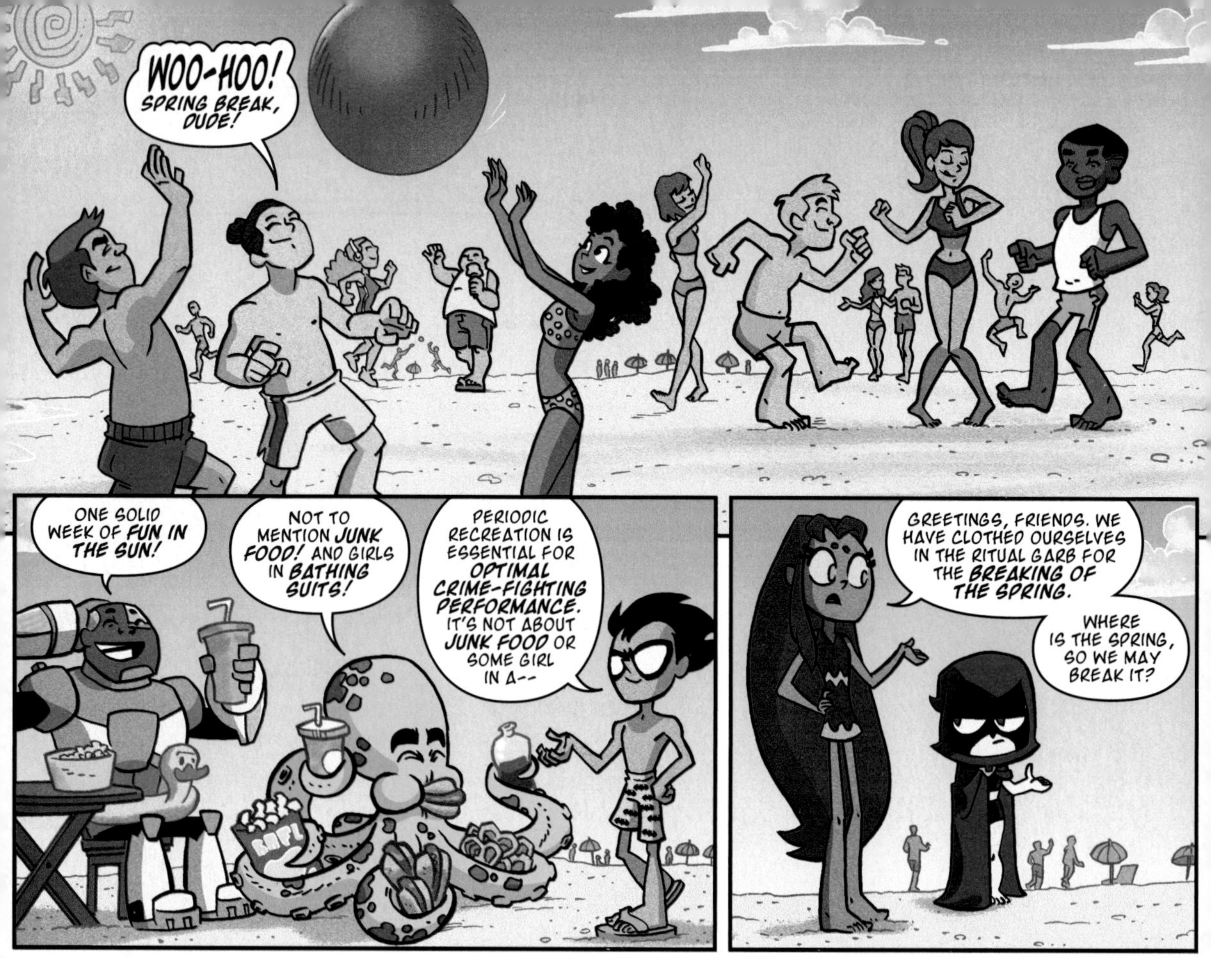
WOO-HOO! SPRING BREAK, DUDE!
ONE SOLID WEEK OF FUN IN THE SUN!
NOT TO MENTION JUNK FOOD! AND GIRLS IN BATHING SUITS!
PERIODIC RECREATION IS ESSENTIAL FOR OPTIMAL CRIME-FIGHTING PERFORMANCE. IT'S NOT ABOUT JUNK FOOD OR SOME GIRL IN A--
GREETINGS, FRIENDS. WE HAVE CLOTHED OURSELVES IN THE RITUAL GARB FOR THE BREAKING OF THE SPRING.
WHERE IS THE SPRING, SO WE MAY BREAK IT?

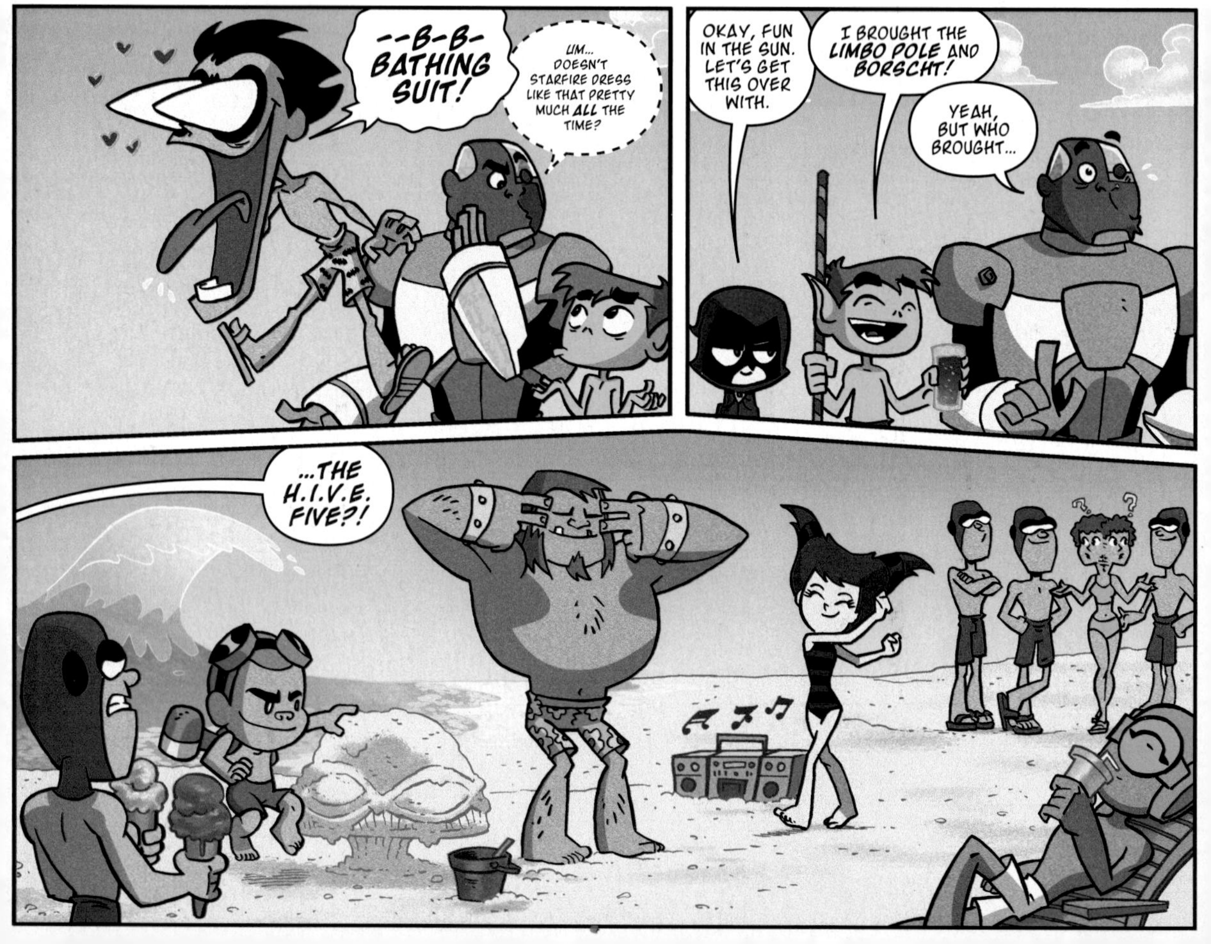
--B-B-BATHING SUIT!
UM... DOESN'T STARFIRE DRESS LIKE THAT PRETTY MUCH ALL THE TIME?
OKAY, FUN IN THE SUN. LET'S GET THIS OVER WITH.
I BROUGHT THE LIMBO POLE AND BORSCHT!
YEAH, BUT WHO BROUGHT...
...THE H.I.V.E. FIVE?!

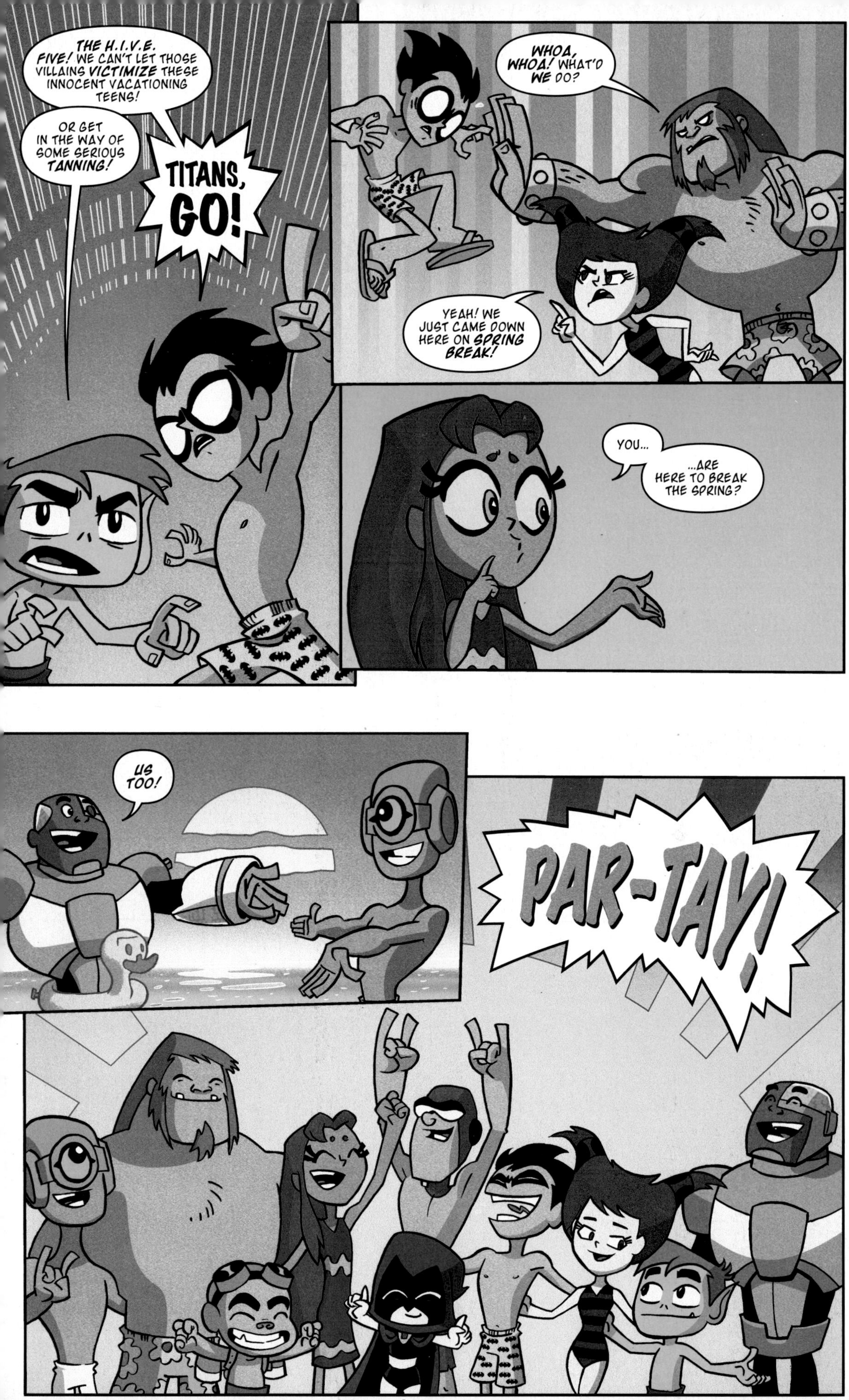
THE H.I.V.E. FIVE! WE CAN'T LET THOSE VILLAINS VICTIMIZE THESE INNOCENT VACATIONING TEENS!
OR GET IN THE WAY OF SOME SERIOUS TANNING!
TITANS, GO!
WHOA, WHOA! WHAT'D WE DO?
YEAH! WE JUST CAME DOWN HERE ON SPRING BREAK!
YOU...
...ARE HERE TO BREAK THE SPRING?
US TOO!
PAR-TAY!

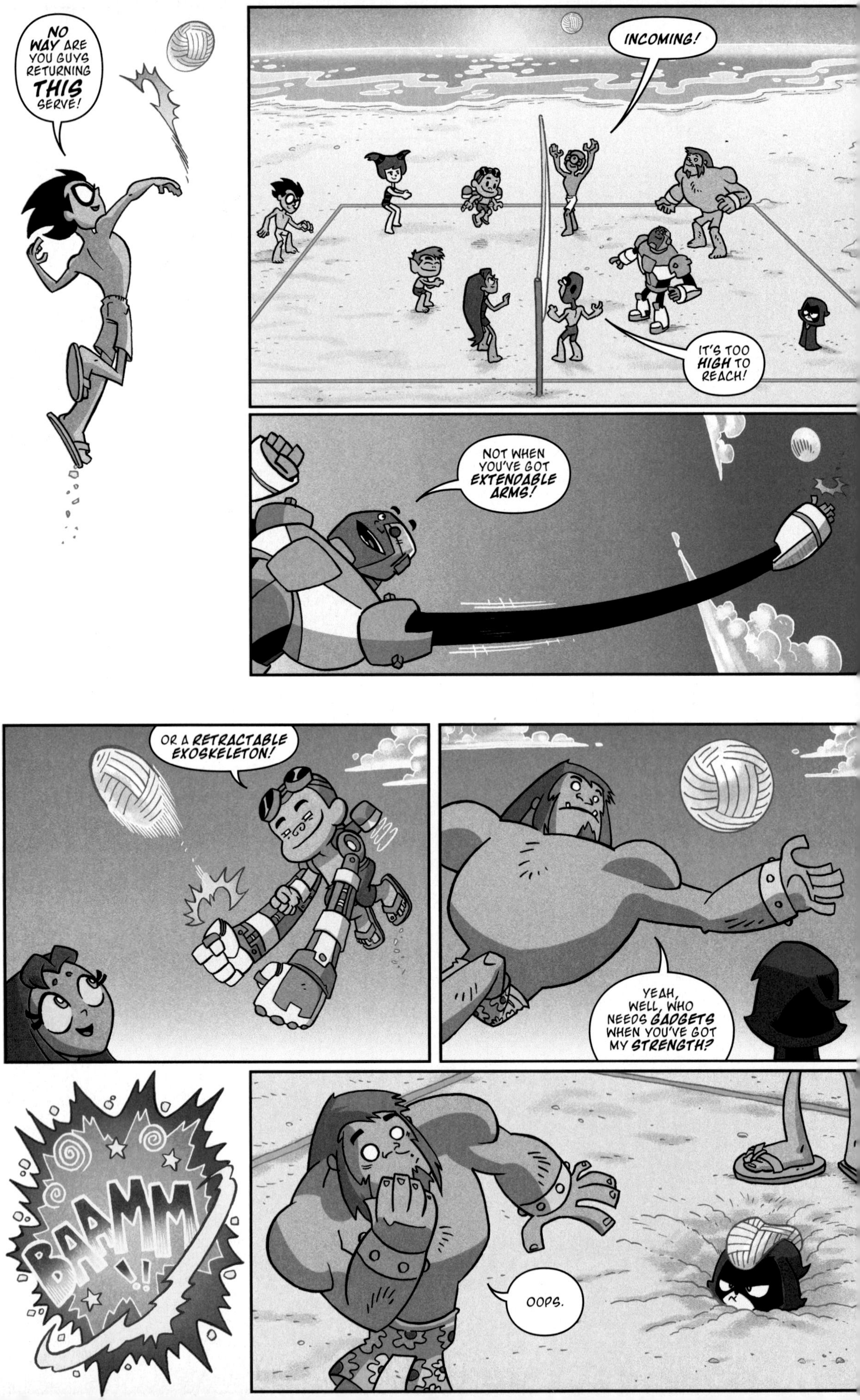
NO WAY ARE YOU GUYS RETURNING THIS SERVE!
INCOMING!
IT'S TOO HIGH TO REACH!
NOT WHEN YOU'VE GOT EXTENDABLE ARMS!
OR A RETRACTABLE EXOSKELETON!
YEAH, WELL, WHO NEEDS GADGETS WHEN YOU'VE GOT MY STRENGTH?
BAMM!!
OOPS.

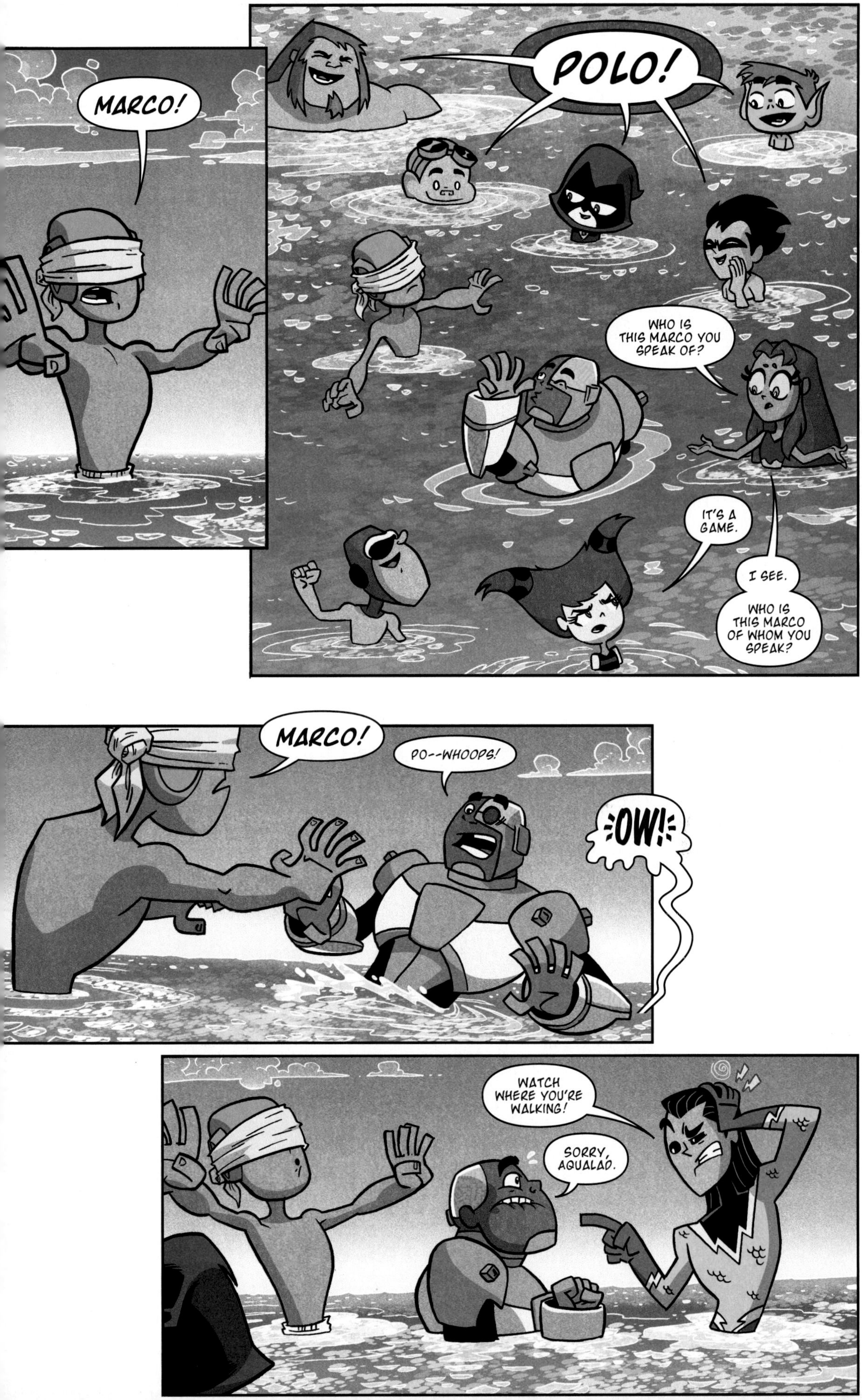
MARCO!
POLO!
WHO IS THIS MARCO YOU SPEAK OF?
IT'S A GAME.
I SEE.
WHO IS THIS MARCO OF WHOM YOU SPEAK?
MARCO!
PO--WHOOPS!
OW!
WATCH WHERE YOU'RE WALKING!
SORRY, AQUALAD.

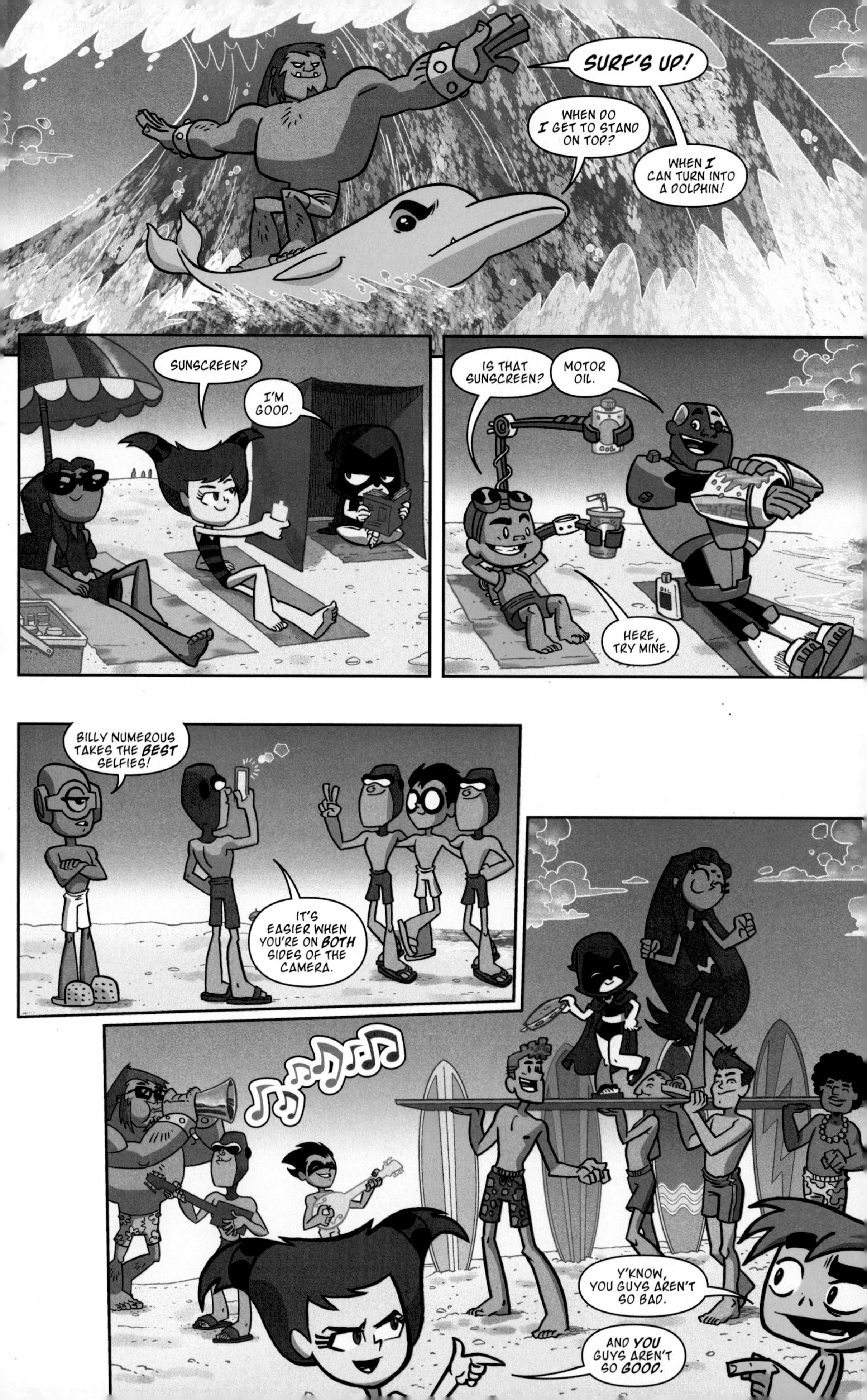
SURF'S UP!
WHEN DO I GET TO STAND ON TOP?
WHEN I CAN TURN INTO A DOLPHIN!
SUNSCREEN?
I'M GOOD.
IS THAT SUNSCREEN?
MOTOR OIL.
HERE, TRY MINE.
OIL
BILLY NUMEROUS TAKES THE BEST SELFIES!
IT'S EASIER WHEN YOU'RE ON BOTH SIDES OF THE CAMERA.
Y'KNOW, YOU GUYS AREN'T SO BAD.
AND YOU GUYS AREN'T SO GOOD.

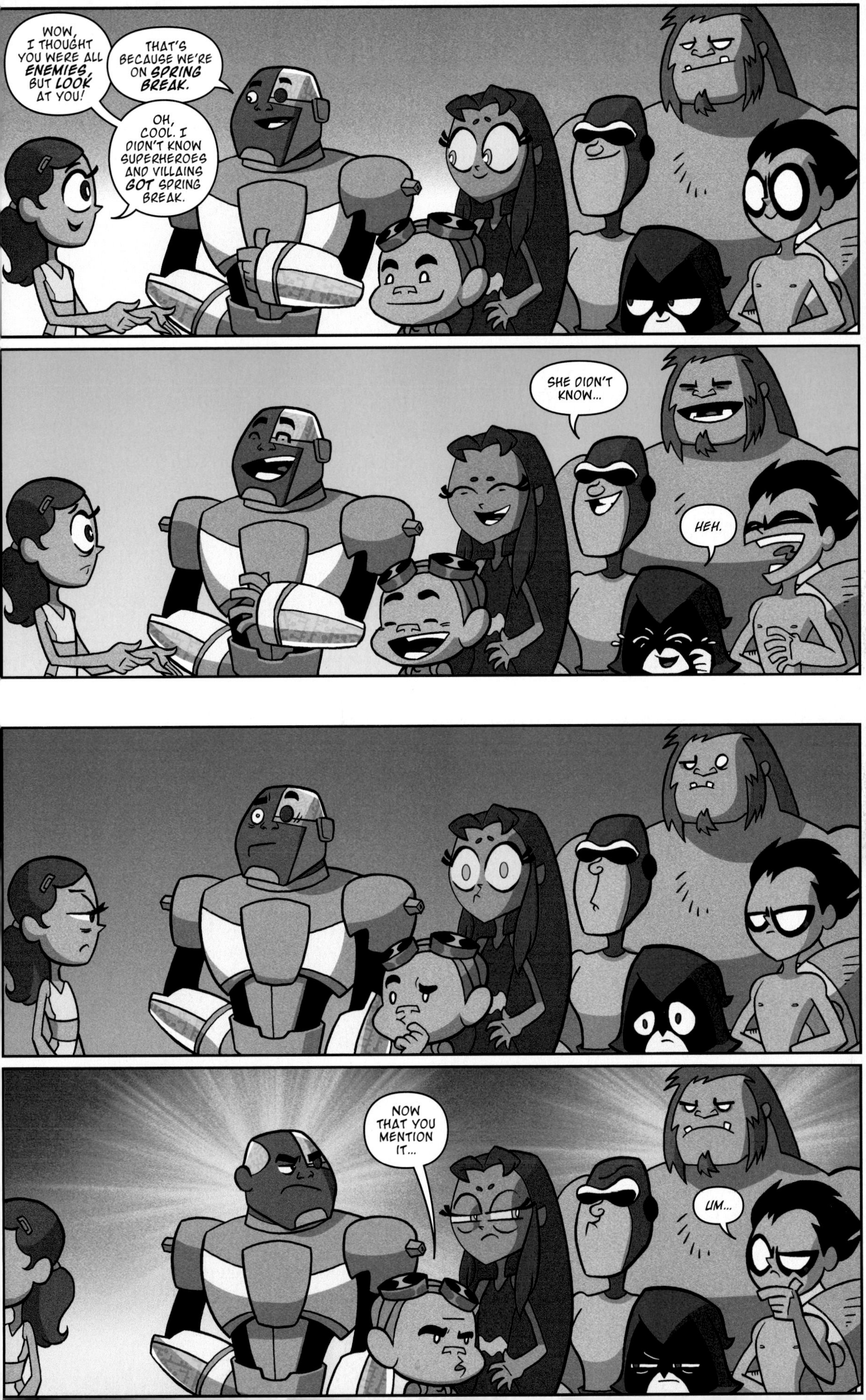
WOW, I THOUGHT YOU WERE ALL ENEMIES, BUT LOOK AT YOU!
THAT'S BECAUSE WE'RE ON SPRING BREAK.
OH, COOL. I DIDN'T KNOW SUPERHEROES AND VILLAINS GOT SPRING BREAK.
SHE DIDN'T KNOW...
HEH.
NOW THAT YOU MENTION IT...
UM...

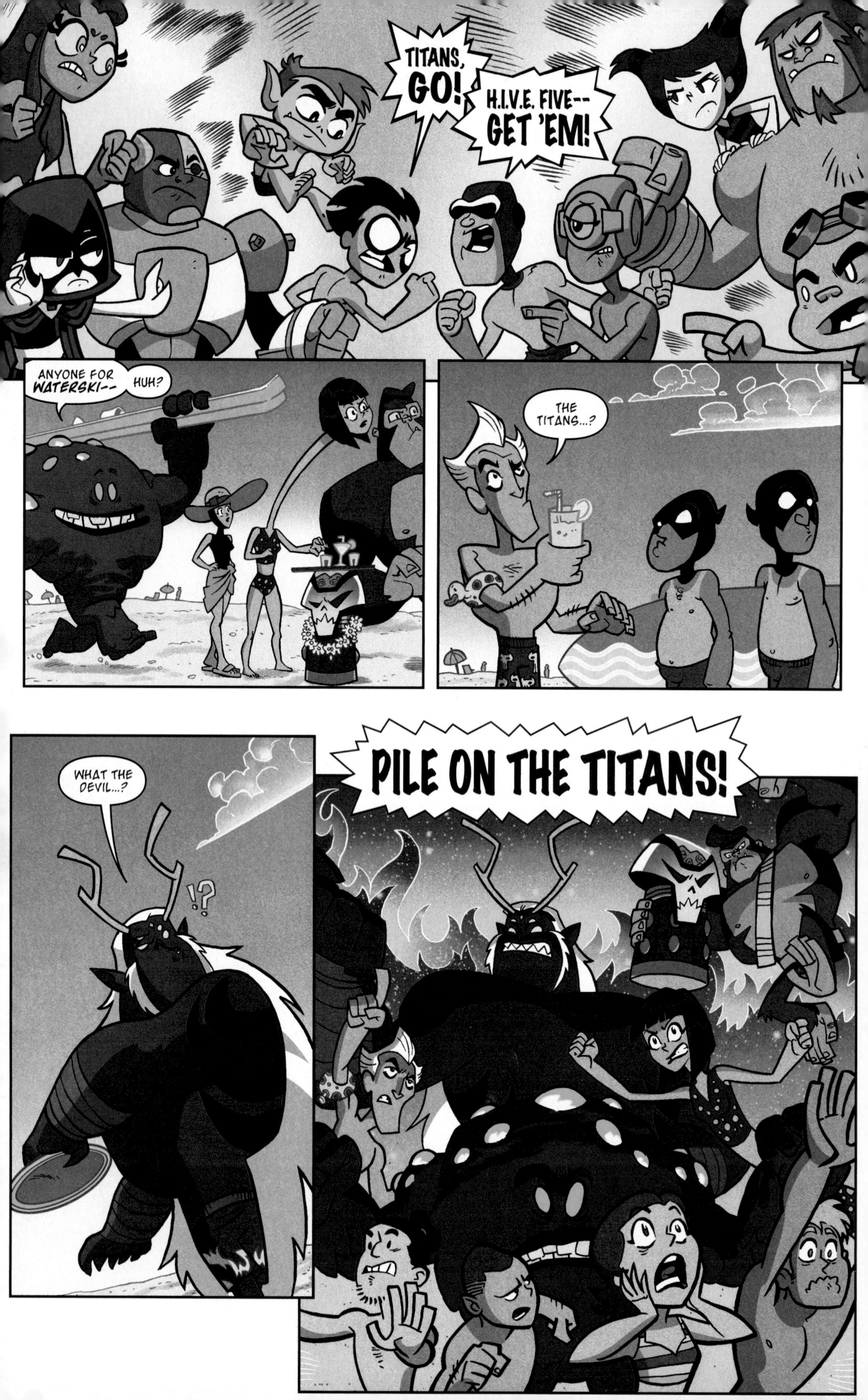

TITANS, GO!
H.I.V.E. FIVE-- GET 'EM!
ANYONE FOR WATERSKI--
HUH?
THE TITANS...?
WHAT THE DEVIL...?
!?
PILE ON THE TITANS!

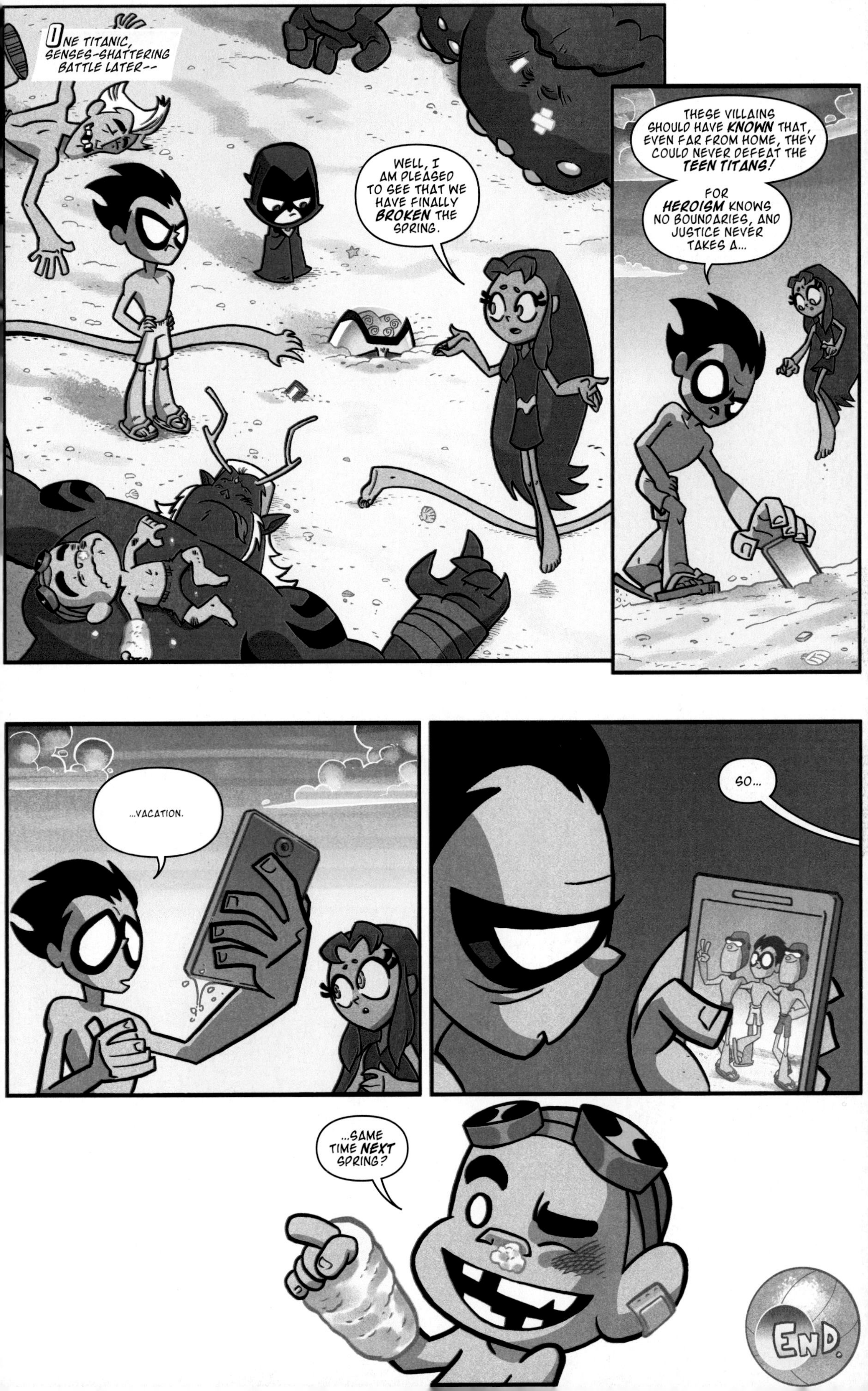
One titanic, senses-shattering battle later--
Well, I am pleased to see that we have finally broken the spring.
These villains should have known that, even far from home, they could never defeat the Teen Titans!
For heroism knows no boundaries, and justice never takes a...
...vacation.
So...
...same time next spring?
End.

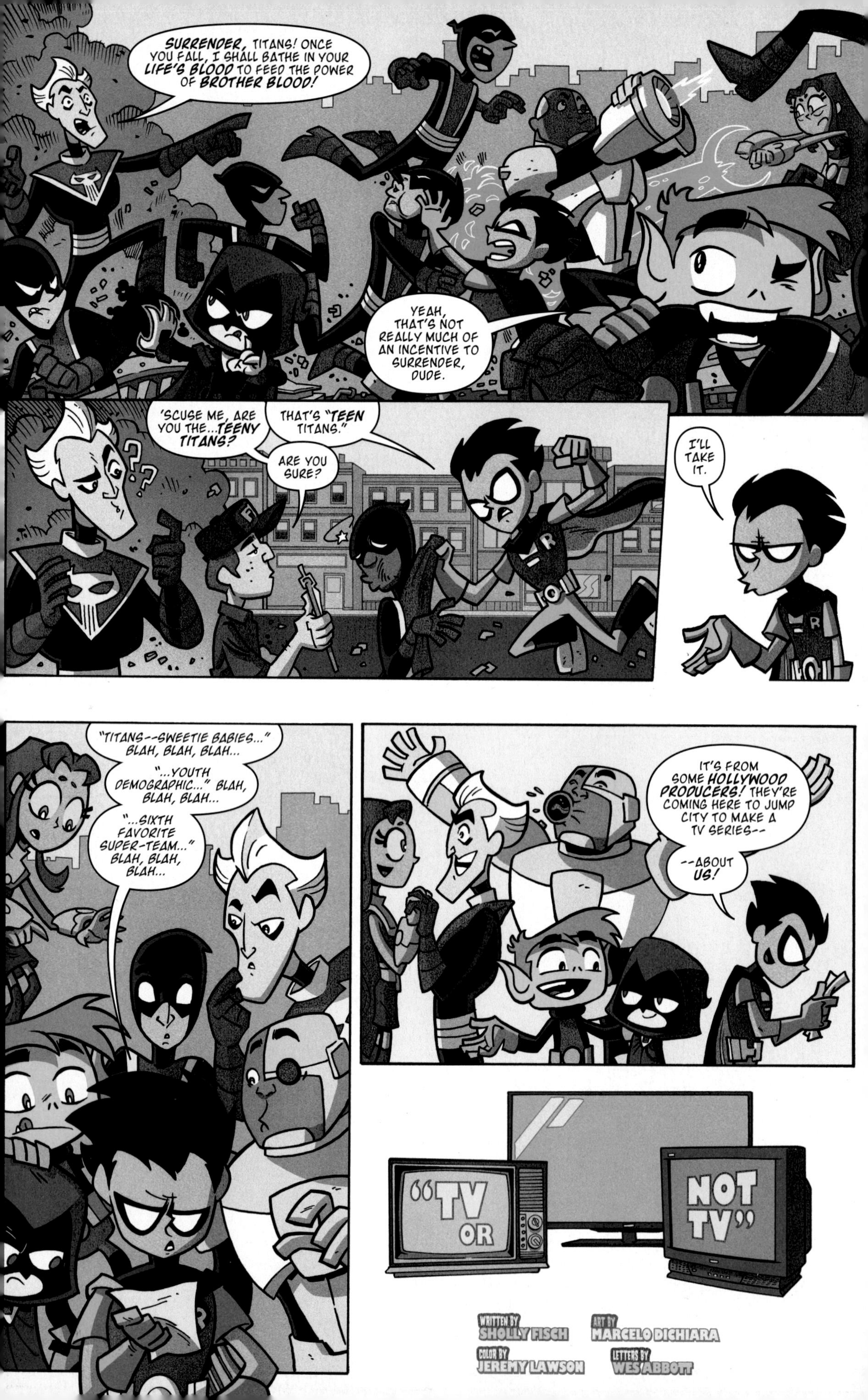
SURRENDER, TITANS! ONCE YOU FALL, I SHALL BATHE IN YOUR LIFE'S BLOOD TO FEED THE POWER OF BROTHER BLOOD!
YEAH, THAT'S NOT REALLY MUCH OF AN INCENTIVE TO SURRENDER, DUDE.
'SCUSE ME, ARE YOU THE...TEENY TITANS?
THAT'S "TEEN TITANS."
ARE YOU SURE?
I'LL TAKE IT.
"TITANS--SWEETIE BABIES..." BLAH, BLAH, BLAH...
"...YOUTH DEMOGRAPHIC..." BLAH, BLAH, BLAH...
"...SIXTH FAVORITE SUPER-TEAM..." BLAH, BLAH, BLAH...
IT'S FROM SOME HOLLYWOOD PRODUCERS! THEY'RE COMING HERE TO JUMP CITY TO MAKE A TV SERIES--
--ABOUT US!
"TV OR NOT TV"
WRITTEN BY SHOLLY FISCH
ART BY MARCELO DICHIARA
COLOR BY JEREMY LAWSON
LETTERS BY WES ABBOTT

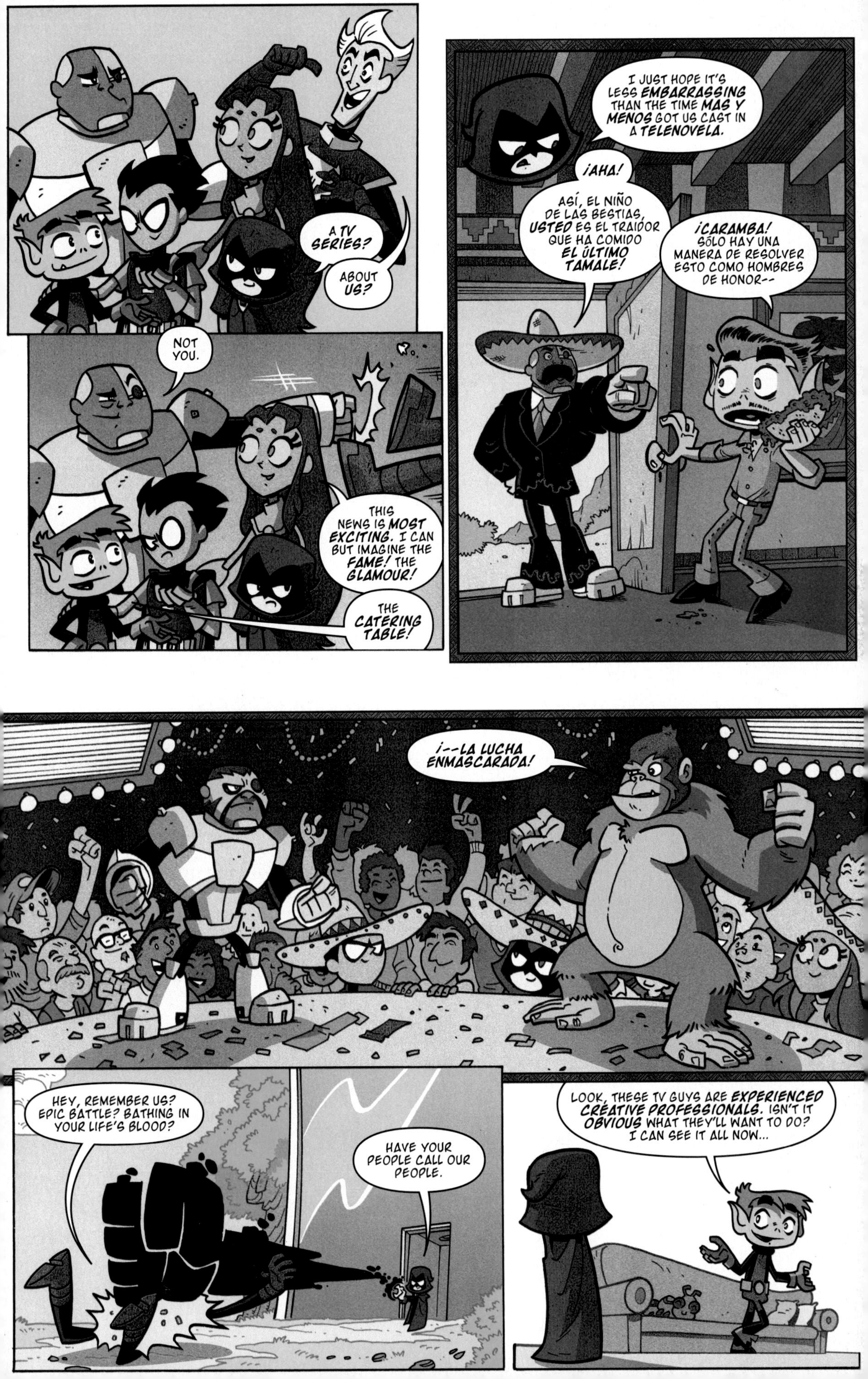

A TV SERIES?
ABOUT US?
NOT YOU.
THIS NEWS IS MOST EXCITING. I CAN BUT IMAGINE THE FAME! THE GLAMOUR!
THE CATERING TABLE!
I JUST HOPE IT'S LESS EMBARRASSING THAN THE TIME MAS Y MENOS GOT US CAST IN A TELENOVELA.
¡AHA!
ASÍ, EL NIÑO DE LAS BESTIAS, USTED ES EL TRAIDOR QUE HA COMIDO EL ÚLTIMO TAMALE!
¡CARAMBA! SÓLO HAY UNA MANERA DE RESOLVER ESTO COMO HOMBRES DE HONOR--
¡--LA LUCHA ENMASCARADA!
HEY, REMEMBER US? EPIC BATTLE? BATHING IN YOUR LIFE'S BLOOD?
HAVE YOUR PEOPLE CALL OUR PEOPLE.
LOOK, THESE TV GUYS ARE EXPERIENCED CREATIVE PROFESSIONALS. ISN'T IT OBVIOUS WHAT THEY'LL WANT TO DO? I CAN SEE IT ALL NOW...

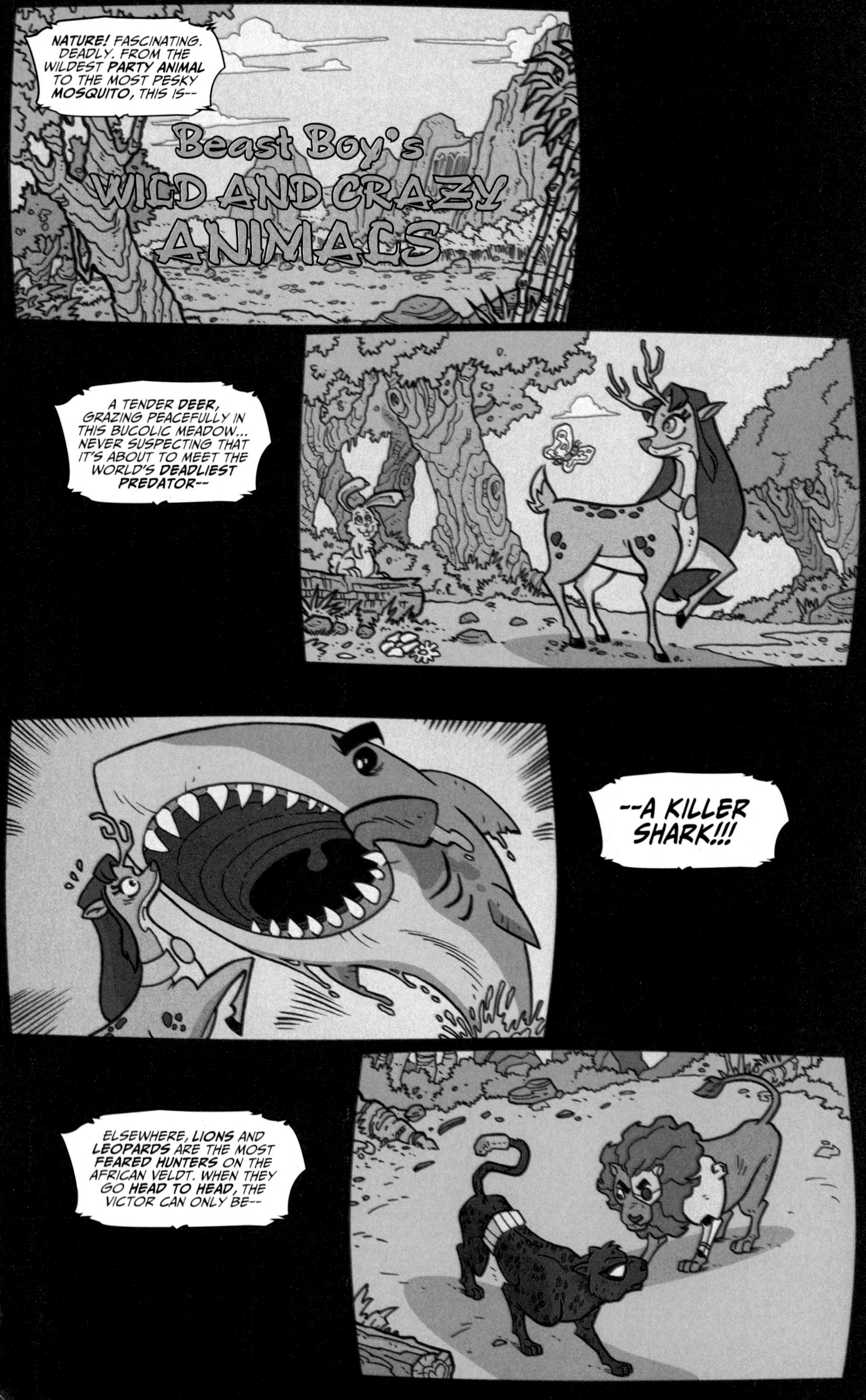
NATURE! FASCINATING. DEADLY. FROM THE WILDEST PARTY ANIMAL TO THE MOST PESKY MOSQUITO, THIS IS--
Beast Boy's
WILD AND CRAZY ANIMALS
A TENDER DEER, GRAZING PEACEFULLY IN THIS BUCOLIC MEADOW... NEVER SUSPECTING THAT IT'S ABOUT TO MEET THE WORLD'S DEADLIEST PREDATOR--
--A KILLER SHARK!!!
ELSEWHERE, LIONS AND LEOPARDS ARE THE MOST FEARED HUNTERS ON THE AFRICAN VELDT. WHEN THEY GO HEAD TO HEAD, THE VICTOR CAN ONLY BE--

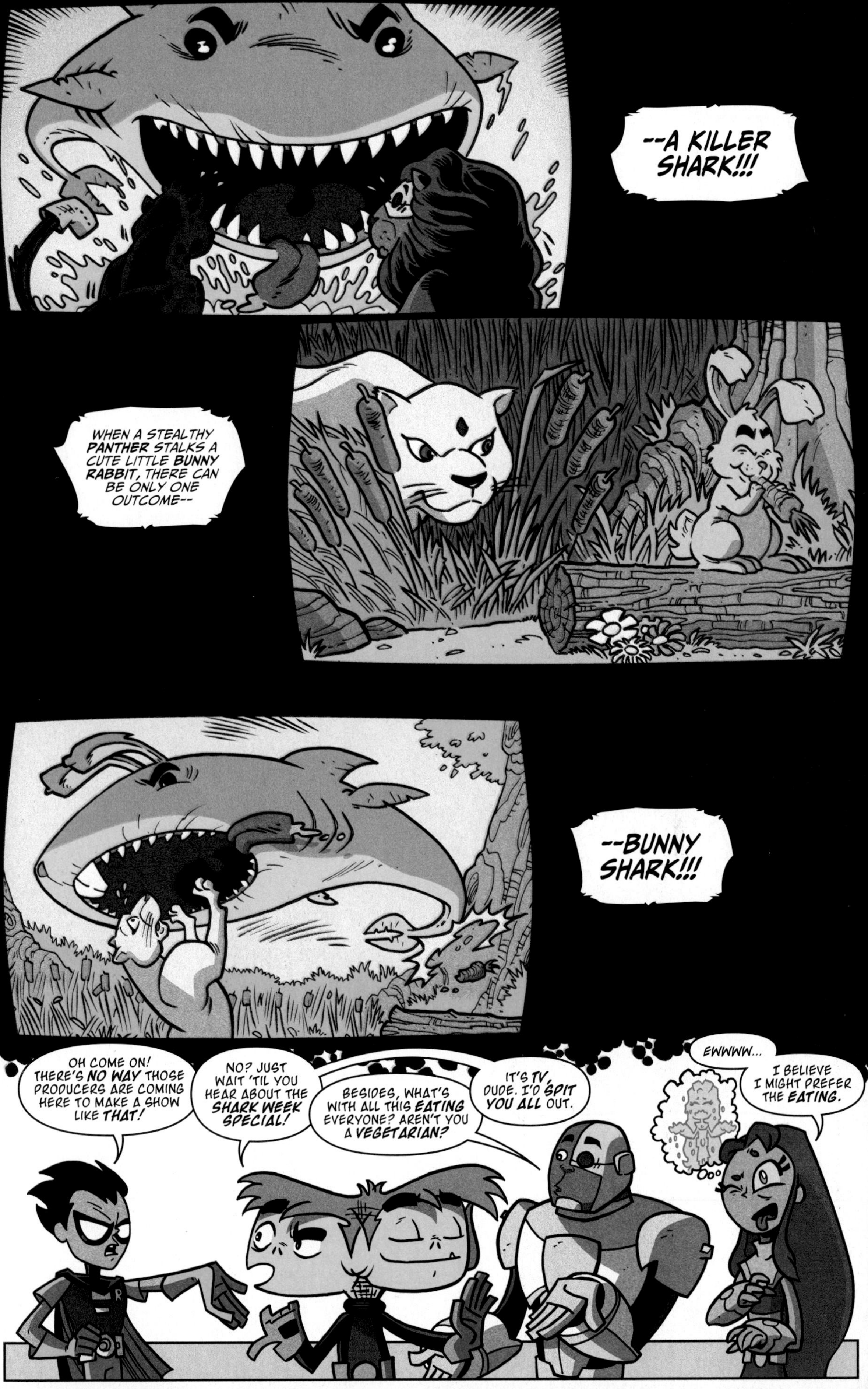
--A KILLER SHARK!!!
WHEN A STEALTHY PANTHER STALKS A CUTE LITTLE BUNNY RABBIT, THERE CAN BE ONLY ONE OUTCOME--
--BUNNY SHARK!!!
OH COME ON! THERE'S NO WAY THOSE PRODUCERS ARE COMING HERE TO MAKE A SHOW LIKE THAT!
NO? JUST WAIT 'TIL YOU HEAR ABOUT THE SHARK WEEK SPECIAL!
BESIDES, WHAT'S WITH ALL THIS EATING EVERYONE? AREN'T YOU A VEGETARIAN?
IT'S TV, DUDE. I'D SPIT YOU ALL OUT.
EWWWW...
I BELIEVE I MIGHT PREFER THE EATING.

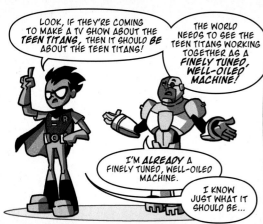

LOOK, IF THEY'RE COMING TO MAKE A TV SHOW ABOUT THE *TEEN TITANS*, THEN IT SHOULD *BE* ABOUT THE TEEN TITANS!

THE WORLD NEEDS TO SEE THE TEEN TITANS WORKING TOGETHER AS A *FINELY TUNED, WELL-OILED MACHINE!*

I'M *ALREADY* A *FINELY TUNED, WELL-OILED MACHINE.*

I KNOW JUST WHAT IT SHOULD BE...

*A*NOTHER PEACEFUL MORNING-- UNTIL AN *URGENT SUMMONS* COMES FROM THE HIDDEN MOUNTAIN HEADQUARTERS OF THE *TEEN TITANS!*

TEEN TITANS

ROBIN CALLING TEEN TITANS! ROBIN CALLING TEEN TITANS!

KID FLASH HERE!

AQUALAD'S IN THE SWIM!

AND WONDER GIRL'S MAKING THE SCENE!

WHAT'S UP, ROBIN BOBBIN?

HEADS UP, TITANS! SOME *UPTIGHT ALIENS* ARE INVADING THE EARTH FOR AN UNSTATED AND POORLY DEFINED REASON!

EVERYBODY *BEAT FEET* TO COORDINATES *ALPHA ALPHA SIGMA NINE*--ON THE TRIPLE!

*A*T ONCE, THE FOUR YOUNG HEROES RACE TO COORDINATES *ALPHA ALPHA SIGMA NINE!*

SUFFERIN' SHAD! A *GIANT ALIEN ROBOT!*

BUT AT LEAST HE'S GOT A *GROOVY BOW TIE!*

MERCIFUL MINERVA! I-- I CAN *HARDLY MOVE!*

BECAUSE YOU'RE *SCARED?*

NO, BECAUSE THE *ANIMATION* IN THIS SHOW IS SO *LIMITED!*

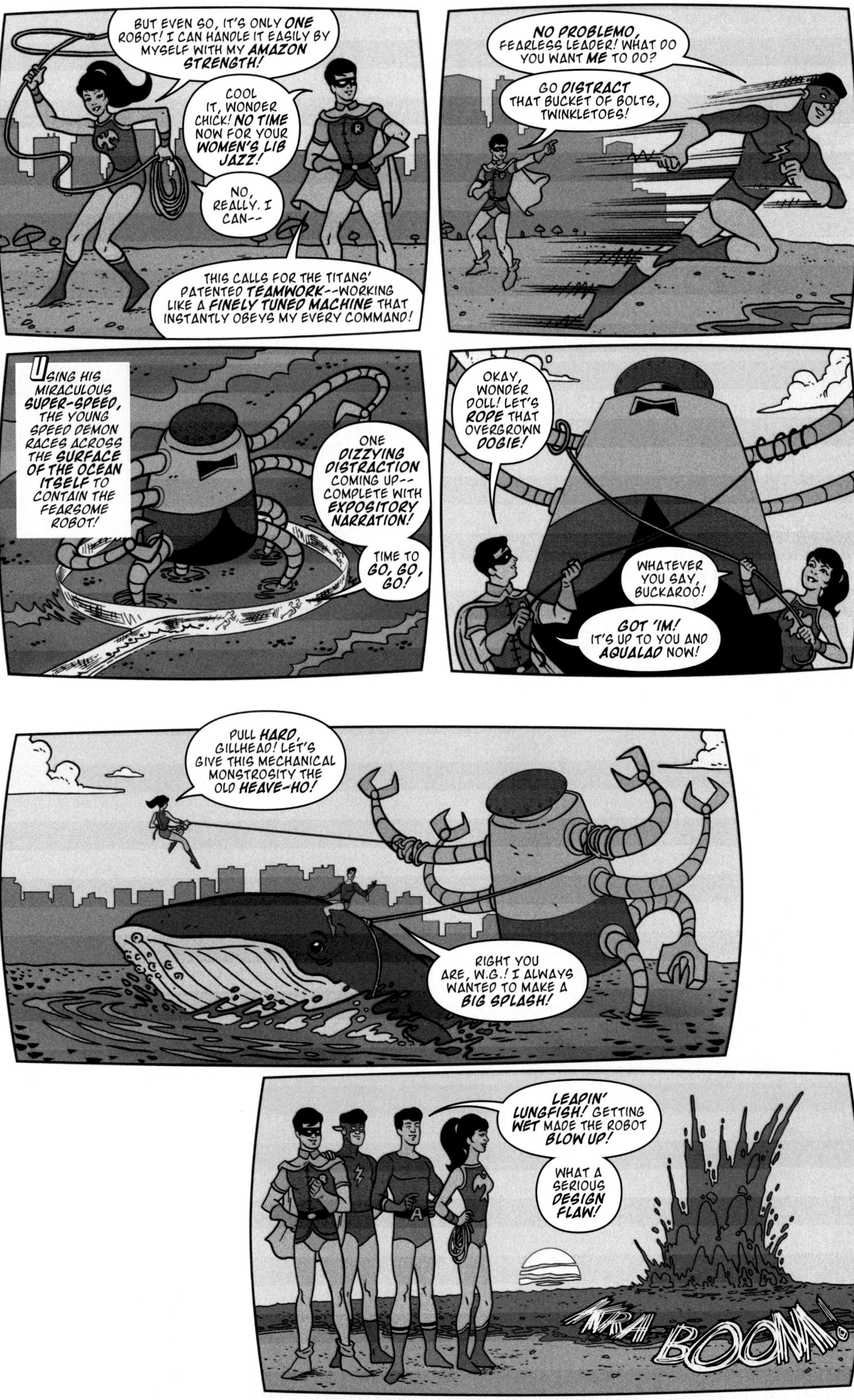

BUT EVEN SO, IT'S ONLY ONE ROBOT! I CAN HANDLE IT EASILY BY MYSELF WITH MY AMAZON STRENGTH!
COOL IT, WONDER CHICK! NO TIME NOW FOR YOUR WOMEN'S LIB JAZZ!
NO, REALLY. I CAN--
THIS CALLS FOR THE TITANS' PATENTED TEAMWORK--WORKING LIKE A FINELY TUNED MACHINE THAT INSTANTLY OBEYS MY EVERY COMMAND!
NO PROBLEMO, FEARLESS LEADER! WHAT DO YOU WANT ME TO DO?
GO DISTRACT THAT BUCKET OF BOLTS, TWINKLETOES!
USING HIS MIRACULOUS SUPER-SPEED, THE YOUNG SPEED DEMON RACES ACROSS THE SURFACE OF THE OCEAN ITSELF TO CONTAIN THE FEARSOME ROBOT!
ONE DIZZYING DISTRACTION COMING UP--COMPLETE WITH EXPOSITORY NARRATION!
TIME TO GO, GO, GO!
OKAY, WONDER DOLL! LET'S ROPE THAT OVERGROWN DOGIE!
WHATEVER YOU SAY, BUCKAROO!
GOT 'IM! IT'S UP TO YOU AND AQUALAD NOW!
PULL HARD, GILLHEAD! LET'S GIVE THIS MECHANICAL MONSTROSITY THE OLD HEAVE-HO!
RIGHT YOU ARE, W.G.! I ALWAYS WANTED TO MAKE A BIG SPLASH!
LEAPIN' LUNGFISH! GETTING WET MADE THE ROBOT BLOW UP!
WHAT A SERIOUS DESIGN FLAW!
KRA-BOOM!

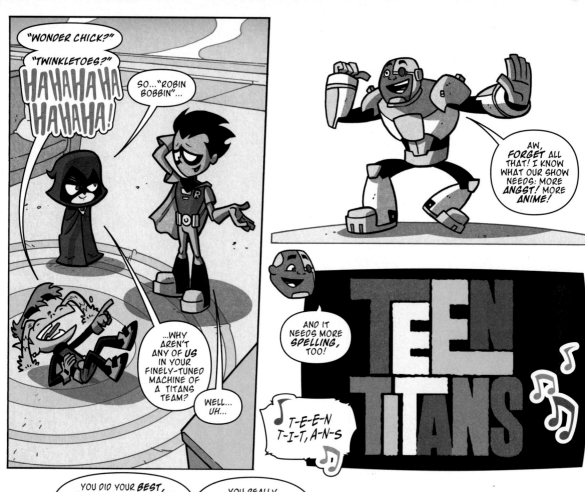

"WONDER CHICK?"

"TWINKLETOES?"

HAHAHAHA HAHAHA!

SO..."ROBIN BOBBIN"...

...WHY AREN'T ANY OF US IN YOUR FINELY-TUNED MACHINE OF A TITANS TEAM?

WELL... UH...

AW, FORGET ALL THAT! I KNOW WHAT OUR SHOW NEEDS: MORE ANGST! MORE ANIME!

AND IT NEEDS MORE SPELLING, TOO!

T-E-E-N T-I-T, A-N-S

TEEN TITANS

YOU DID YOUR BEST, TITANS. BUT EVEN YOUR BEST IS NOTHING COMPARED TO DEATHSTROKE, THE TERMINATOR!

YOU REALLY NEED TO MAKE UP YOUR MIND ABOUT YOUR CODE NAME, DUDE. IS IT "DEATHSTROKE" OR "TERMINATOR"?

IT GETS CONFUSING.

ARRGHH! I'D DO SOMETHING ABOUT THIS--IF I WEREN'T PARALYZED BY TEEN ANGST!

IF ONLY CYBORG WERE HERE! SURELY, A HERO OF HIS MAGNITUDE COULD RESCUE US ALL!

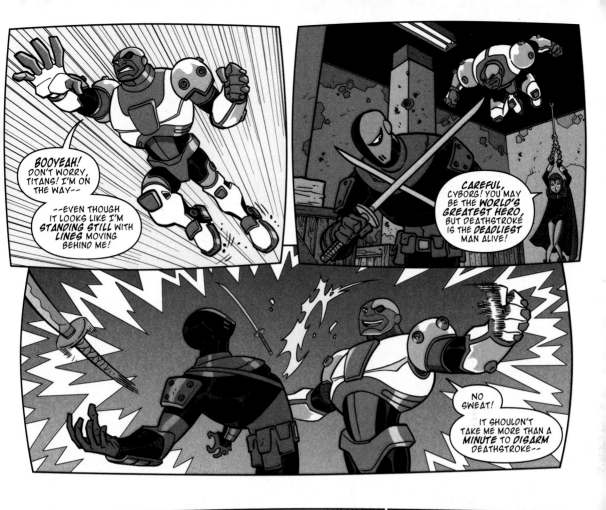

BOOYEAH! DON'T WORRY, TITANS! I'M ON THE WAY--

--EVEN THOUGH IT LOOKS LIKE I'M STANDING STILL WITH LINES MOVING BEHIND ME!

CAREFUL, CYBORG! YOU MAY BE THE WORLD'S GREATEST HERO, BUT DEATHSTROKE IS THE DEADLIEST MAN ALIVE!

NO SWEAT!

IT SHOULDN'T TAKE ME MORE THAN A MINUTE TO DISARM DEATHSTROKE--

--AND BEAT HIM IN HAND-TO-HAND COMBAT!

SEE? SEVENTEEN SECONDS.

NOW TO RESCUE ALL OF YOU-- AGAIN.

WE SURE ARE LUCKY TO BE YOUR SIDEKICKS, CYBORG.

BUT LOOK BEHIND YOU! IT'S--

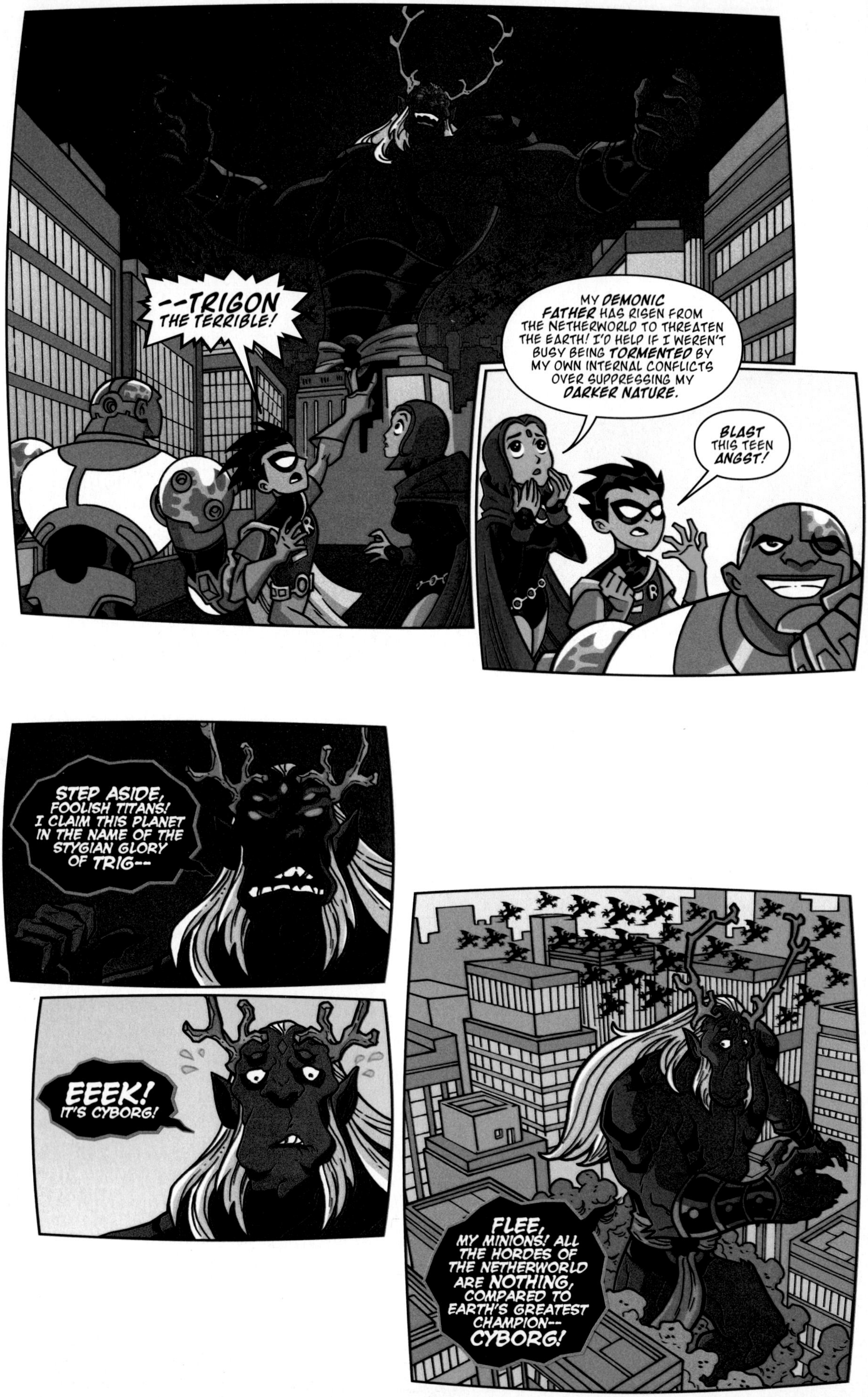
--TRIGON THE TERRIBLE!
MY DEMONIC FATHER HAS RISEN FROM THE NETHERWORLD TO THREATEN THE EARTH! I'D HELP IF I WEREN'T BUSY BEING TORMENTED BY MY OWN INTERNAL CONFLICTS OVER SUPPRESSING MY DARKER NATURE.
BLAST THIS TEEN ANGST!
STEP ASIDE, FOOLISH TITANS! I CLAIM THIS PLANET IN THE NAME OF THE STYGIAN GLORY OF TRIG--
EEEK! IT'S CYBORG!
FLEE, MY MINIONS! ALL THE HORDES OF THE NETHERWORLD ARE NOTHING, COMPARED TO EARTH'S GREATEST CHAMPION-- CYBORG!

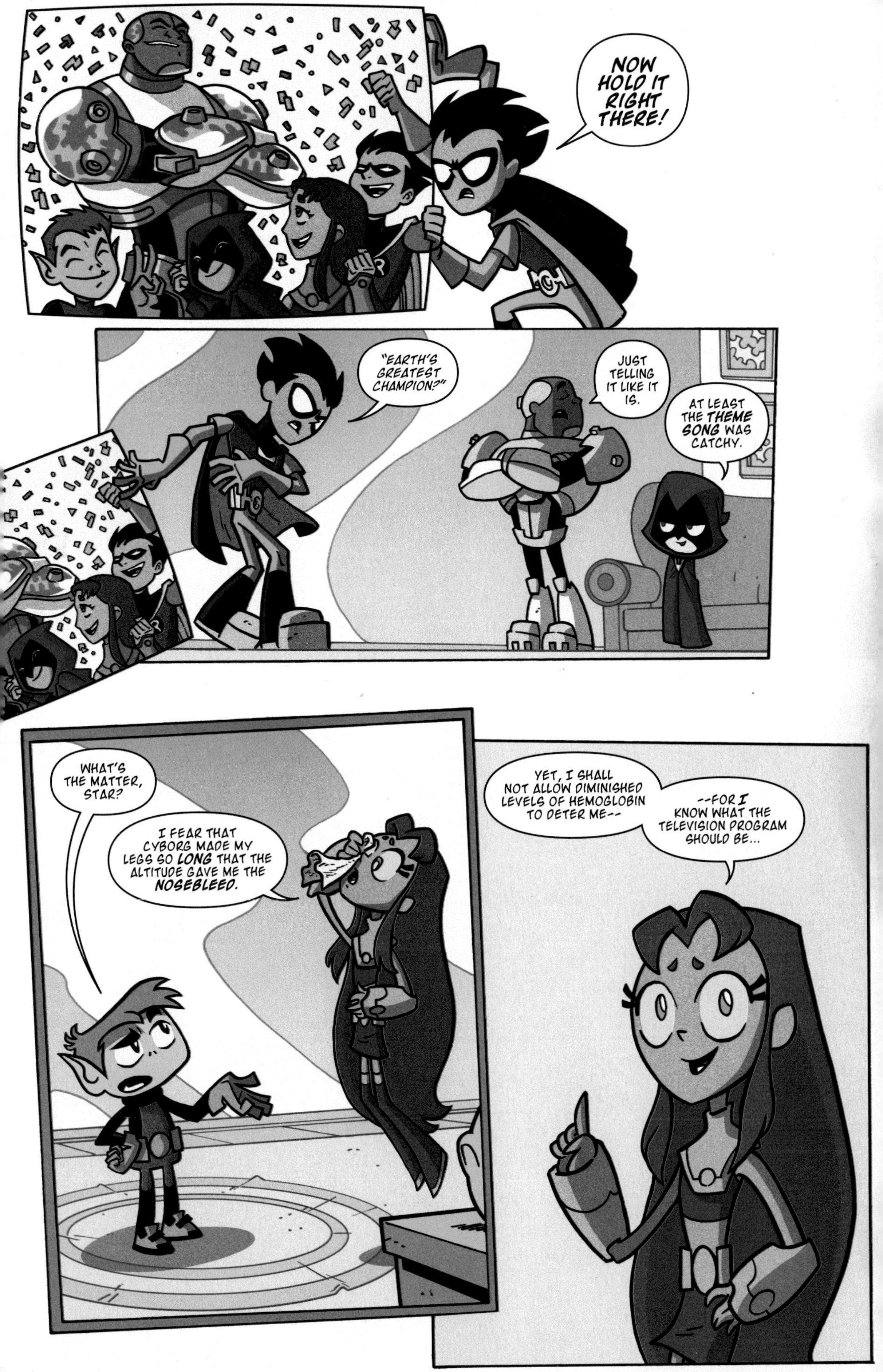
NOW HOLD IT RIGHT THERE!
"EARTH'S GREATEST CHAMPION?"
JUST TELLING IT LIKE IT IS.
AT LEAST THE THEME SONG WAS CATCHY.
WHAT'S THE MATTER, STAR?
I FEAR THAT CYBORG MADE MY LEGS SO LONG THAT THE ALTITUDE GAVE ME THE NOSEBLEED.
YET, I SHALL NOT ALLOW DIMINISHED LEVELS OF HEMOGLOBIN TO DETER ME--
--FOR I KNOW WHAT THE TELEVISION PROGRAM SHOULD BE...

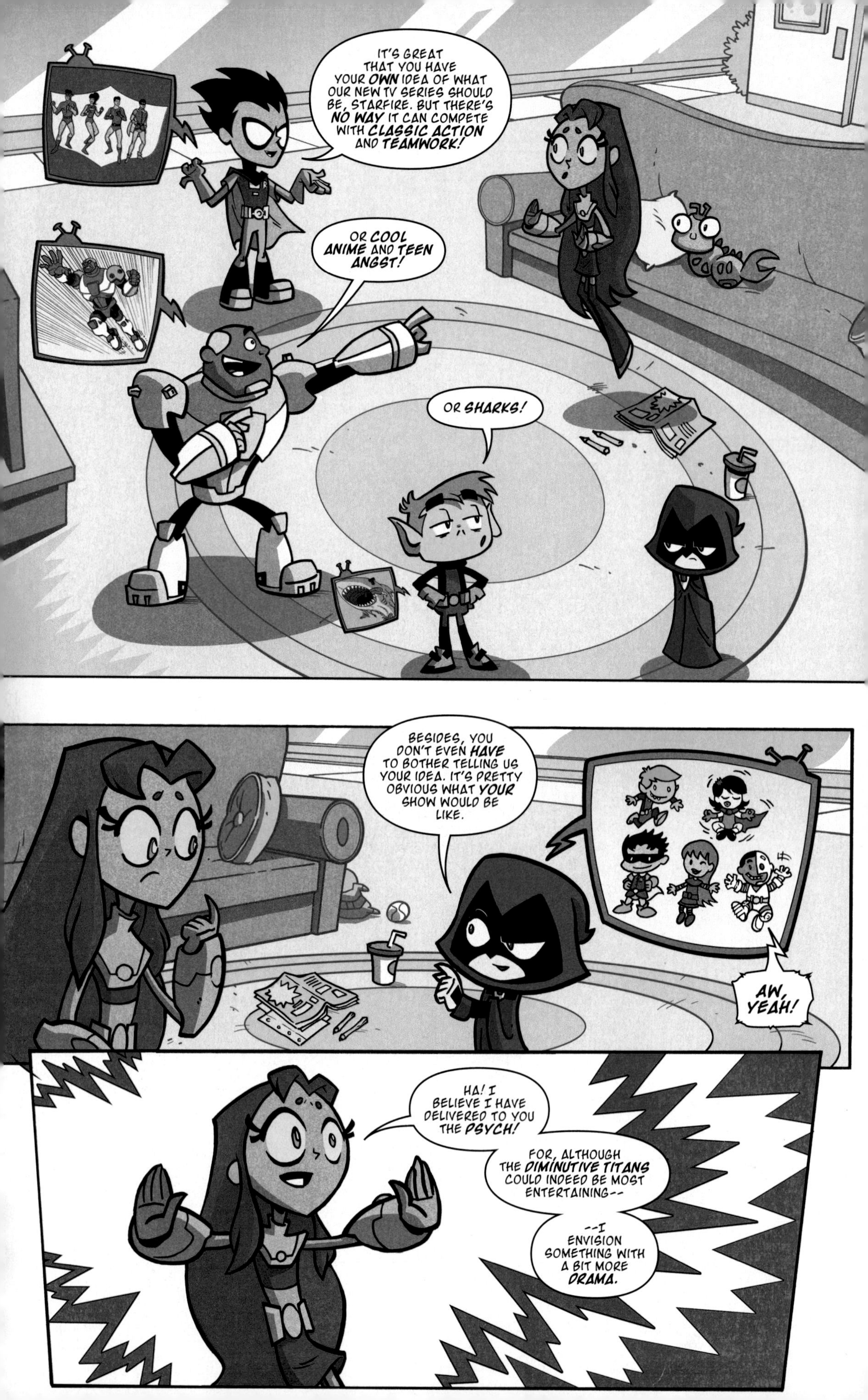
IT'S GREAT THAT YOU HAVE YOUR OWN IDEA OF WHAT OUR NEW TV SERIES SHOULD BE, STARFIRE. BUT THERE'S NO WAY IT CAN COMPETE WITH CLASSIC ACTION AND TEAMWORK!
OR COOL ANIME AND TEEN ANGST!
OR SHARKS!
BESIDES, YOU DON'T EVEN HAVE TO BOTHER TELLING US YOUR IDEA. IT'S PRETTY OBVIOUS WHAT YOUR SHOW WOULD BE LIKE.
AW, YEAH!
HA! I BELIEVE I HAVE DELIVERED TO YOU THE PSYCH!
FOR, ALTHOUGH THE DIMINUTIVE TITANS COULD INDEED BE MOST ENTERTAINING--
--I ENVISION SOMETHING WITH A BIT MORE DRAMA.

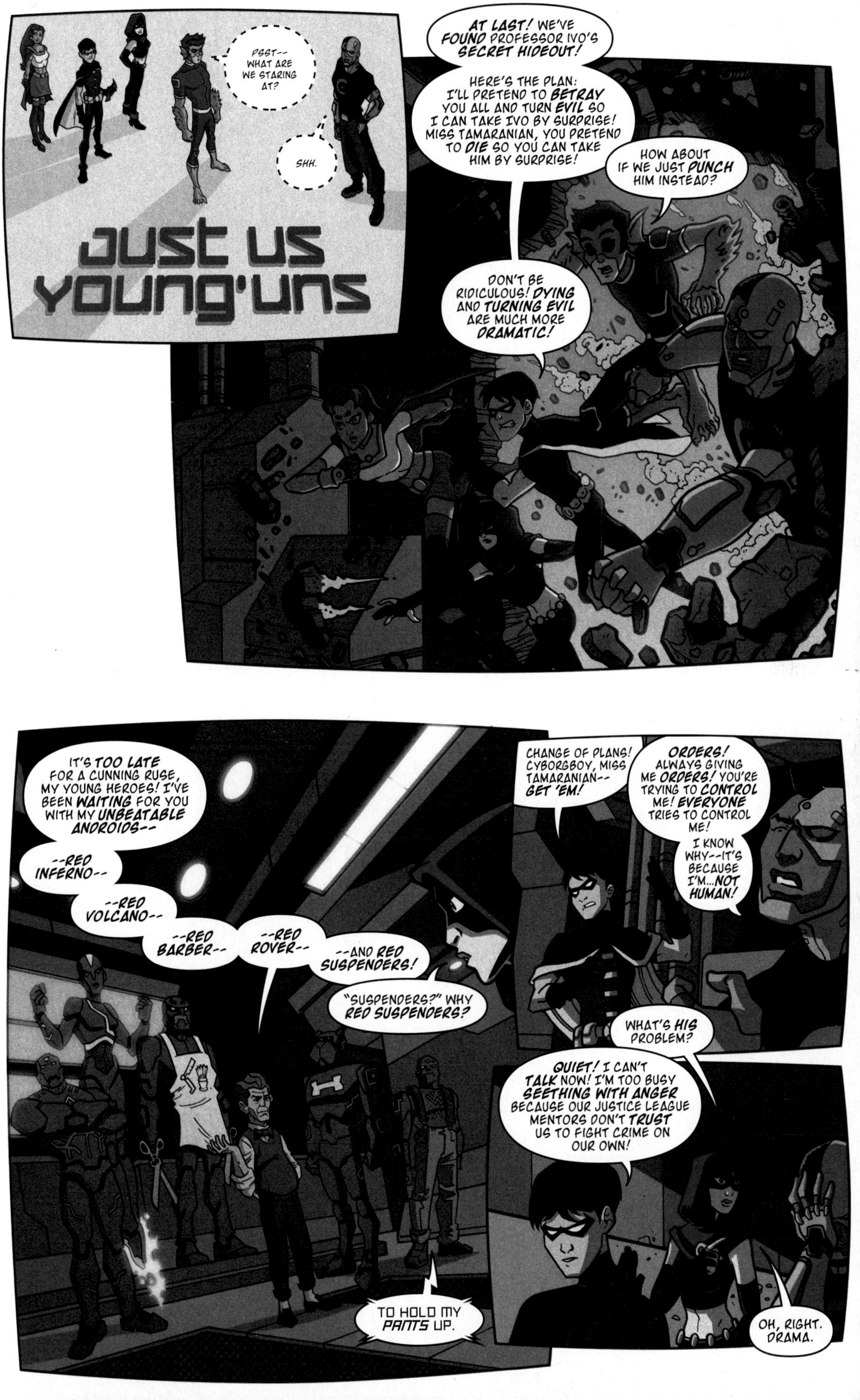
PSST--WHAT ARE WE STARING AT?
SHH.
JUST US YOUNG'UNS
AT LAST! WE'VE FOUND PROFESSOR IVO'S SECRET HIDEOUT!
HERE'S THE PLAN: I'LL PRETEND TO BETRAY YOU ALL AND TURN EVIL SO I CAN TAKE IVO BY SURPRISE! MISS TAMARANIAN, YOU PRETEND TO DIE SO YOU CAN TAKE HIM BY SURPRISE!
HOW ABOUT IF WE JUST PUNCH HIM INSTEAD?
DON'T BE RIDICULOUS! DYING AND TURNING EVIL ARE MUCH MORE DRAMATIC!
IT'S TOO LATE FOR A CUNNING RUSE, MY YOUNG HEROES! I'VE BEEN WAITING FOR YOU WITH MY UNBEATABLE ANDROIDS--
--RED INFERNO--
--RED VOLCANO--
--RED BARBER--
--RED ROVER--
--AND RED SUSPENDERS!
"SUSPENDERS?" WHY RED SUSPENDERS?
TO HOLD MY PANTS UP.
CHANGE OF PLANS! CYBORGBOY, MISS TAMARANIAN--GET 'EM!
ORDERS! ALWAYS GIVING ME ORDERS! YOU'RE TRYING TO CONTROL ME! EVERYONE TRIES TO CONTROL ME!
I KNOW WHY--IT'S BECAUSE I'M...NOT HUMAN!
WHAT'S HIS PROBLEM?
QUIET! I CAN'T TALK NOW! I'M TOO BUSY SEETHING WITH ANGER BECAUSE OUR JUSTICE LEAGUE MENTORS DON'T TRUST US TO FIGHT CRIME ON OUR OWN!
OH, RIGHT. DRAMA.

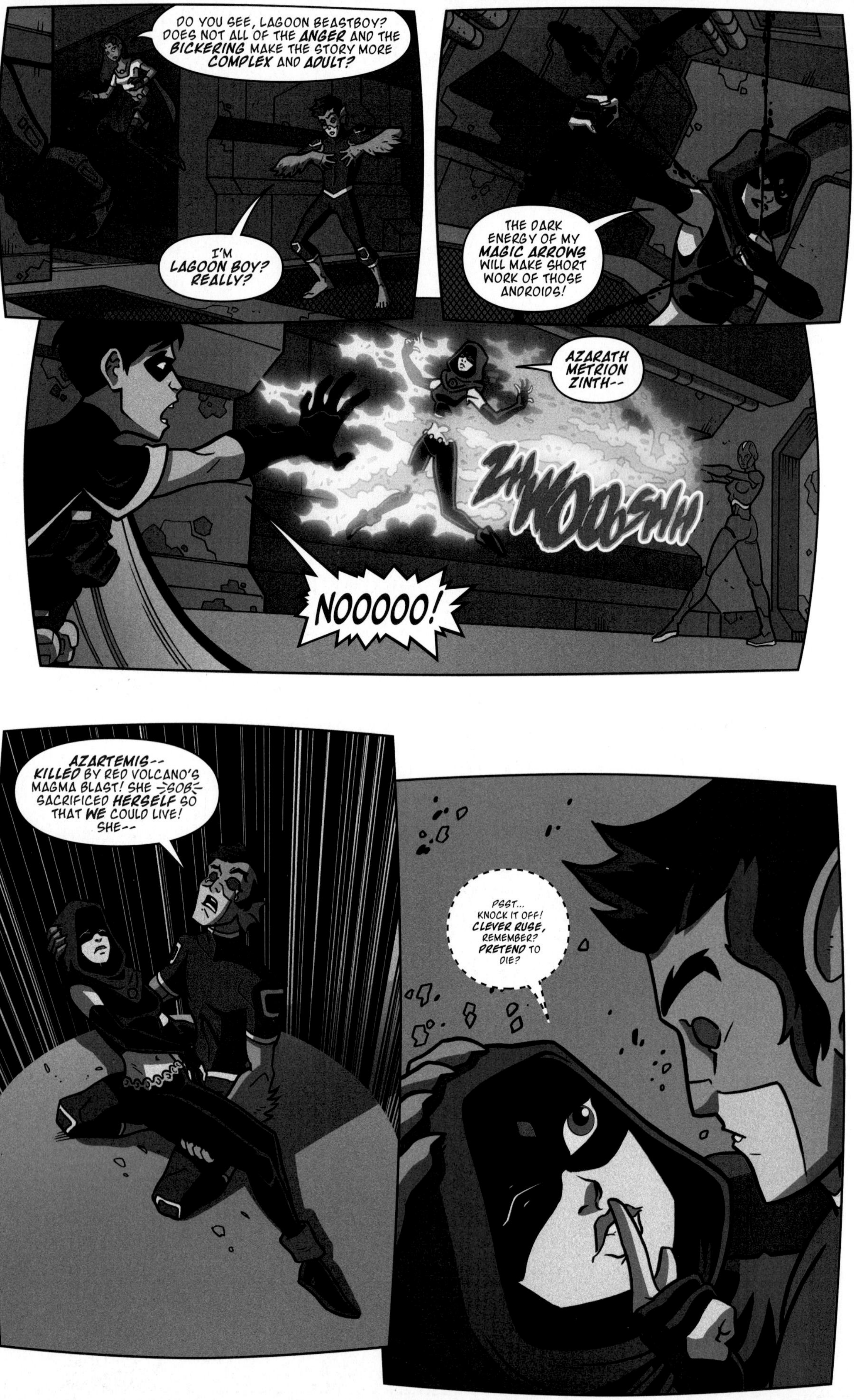
DO YOU SEE, LAGOON BEASTBOY? DOES NOT ALL OF THE ANGER AND THE BICKERING MAKE THE STORY MORE COMPLEX AND ADULT?
I'M LAGOON BOY? REALLY?
THE DARK ENERGY OF MY MAGIC ARROWS WILL MAKE SHORT WORK OF THOSE ANDROIDS!
AZARATH METRION ZINTH--
ZHWOOSHH
NOOOOO!
AZARTEMIS-- KILLED BY RED VOLCANO'S MAGMA BLAST! SHE -SOB- SACRIFICED HERSELF SO THAT WE COULD LIVE! SHE--
PSST... KNOCK IT OFF! CLEVER RUSE, REMEMBER? PRETEND TO DIE?

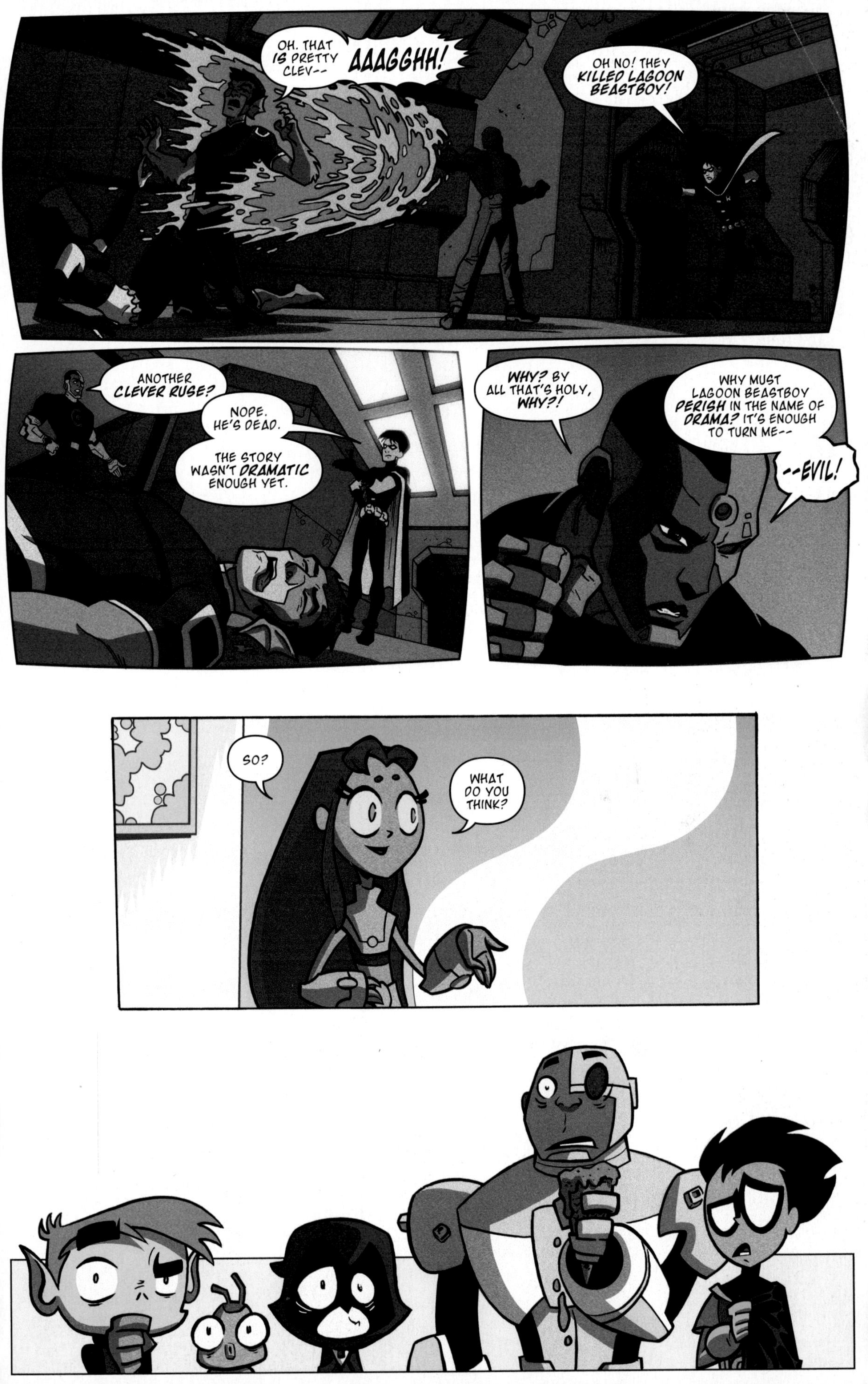

OH. THAT IS PRETTY CLEV--
AAAGGHH!
OH NO! THEY KILLED LAGOON BEASTBOY!
ANOTHER CLEVER RUSE?
NOPE. HE'S DEAD.
THE STORY WASN'T DRAMATIC ENOUGH YET.
WHY? BY ALL THAT'S HOLY, WHY?!
WHY MUST LAGOON BEASTBOY PERISH IN THE NAME OF DRAMA? IT'S ENOUGH TO TURN ME--
--EVIL!
SO?
WHAT DO YOU THINK?

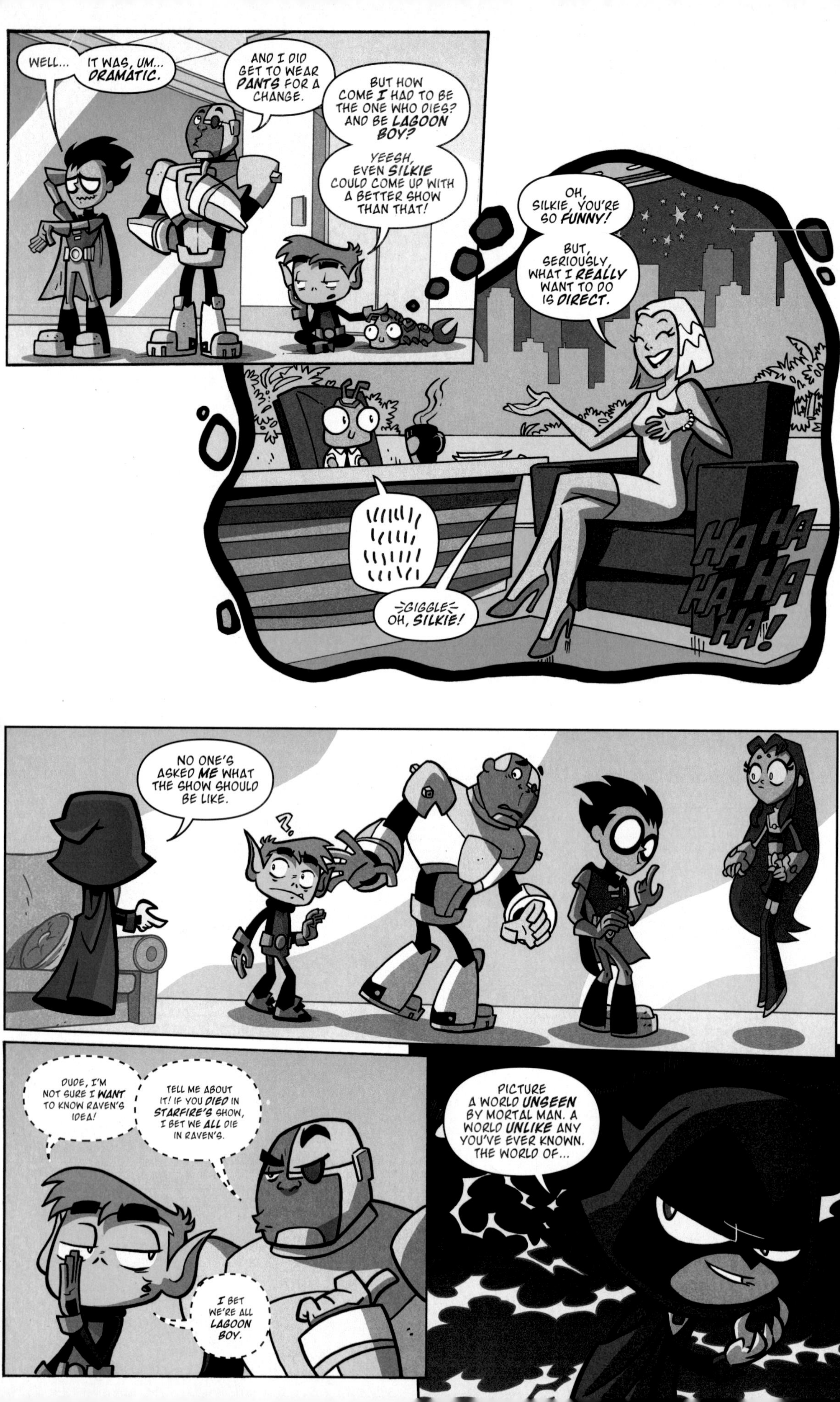

WELL...
IT WAS, UM... DRAMATIC.
AND I DID GET TO WEAR PANTS FOR A CHANGE.
BUT HOW COME I HAD TO BE THE ONE WHO DIES? AND BE LAGOON BOY?
YEESH, EVEN SILKIE COULD COME UP WITH A BETTER SHOW THAN THAT!
OH, SILKIE, YOU'RE SO FUNNY!
BUT, SERIOUSLY, WHAT I REALLY WANT TO DO IS DIRECT.
=GIGGLE= OH, SILKIE!
HA HA HA HA HA!
NO ONE'S ASKED ME WHAT THE SHOW SHOULD BE LIKE.
?
DUDE, I'M NOT SURE I WANT TO KNOW RAVEN'S IDEA!
TELL ME ABOUT IT! IF YOU DIED IN STARFIRE'S SHOW, I BET WE ALL DIE IN RAVEN'S.
I BET WE'RE ALL LAGOON BOY.
PICTURE A WORLD UNSEEN BY MORTAL MAN. A WORLD UNLIKE ANY YOU'VE EVER KNOWN. THE WORLD OF...

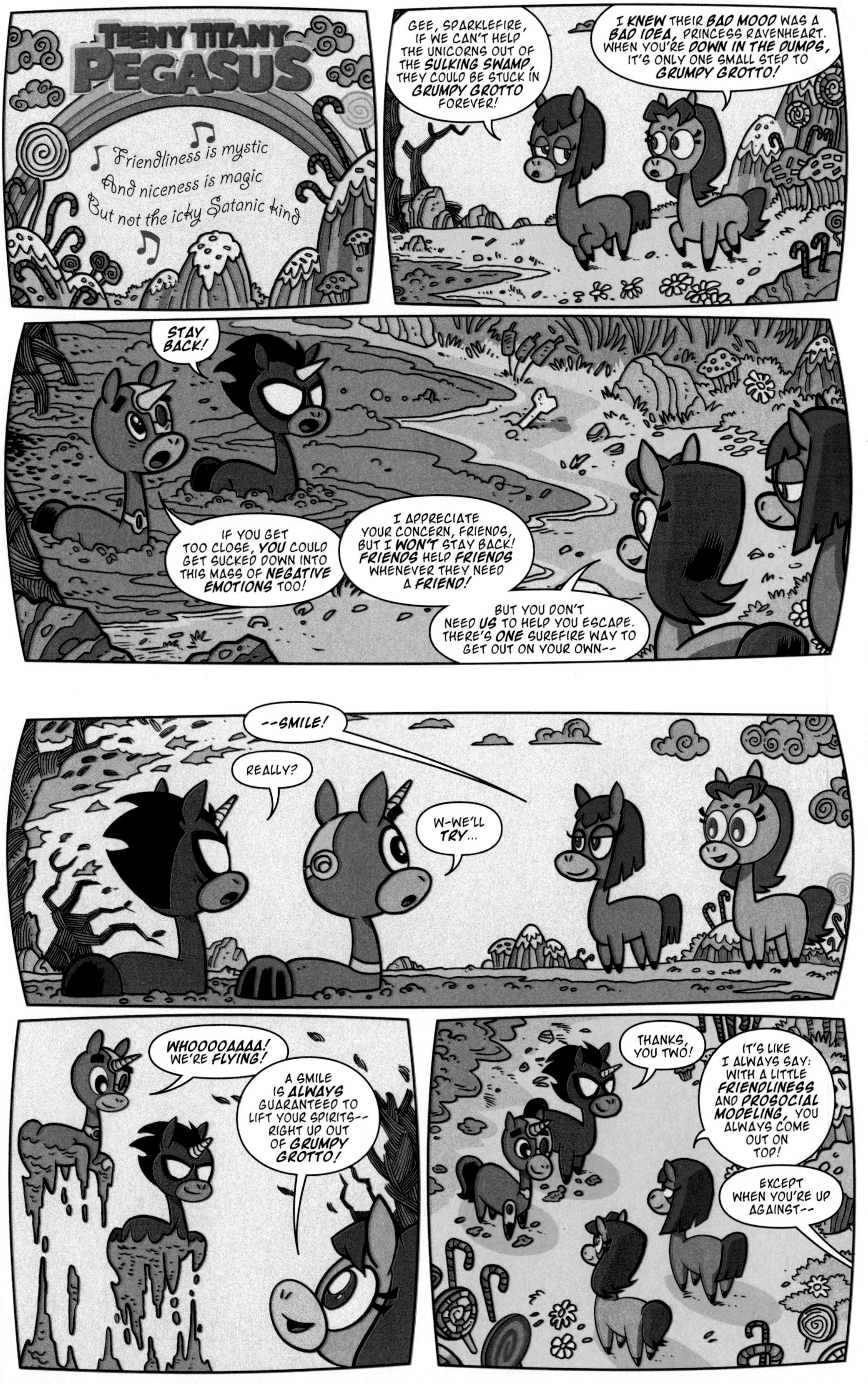

TEENY TITANY PEGASUS
Friendliness is mystic
And niceness is magic
But not the icky Satanic kind
GEE, SPARKLEFIRE, IF WE CAN'T HELP THE UNICORNS OUT OF THE SULKING SWAMP, THEY COULD BE STUCK IN GRUMPY GROTTO FOREVER!
I KNEW THEIR BAD MOOD WAS A BAD IDEA, PRINCESS RAVENHEART. WHEN YOU'RE DOWN IN THE DUMPS, IT'S ONLY ONE SMALL STEP TO GRUMPY GROTTO!
STAY BACK!
IF YOU GET TOO CLOSE, YOU COULD GET SUCKED DOWN INTO THIS MASS OF NEGATIVE EMOTIONS TOO!
I APPRECIATE YOUR CONCERN, FRIENDS, BUT I WON'T STAY BACK! FRIENDS HELP FRIENDS WHENEVER THEY NEED A FRIEND!
BUT YOU DON'T NEED US TO HELP YOU ESCAPE. THERE'S ONE SUREFIRE WAY TO GET OUT ON YOUR OWN--
--SMILE!
REALLY?
W-WE'LL TRY...
WHOOOOAAAA! WE'RE FLYING!
A SMILE IS ALWAYS GUARANTEED TO LIFT YOUR SPIRITS--RIGHT UP OUT OF GRUMPY GROTTO!
THANKS, YOU TWO!
IT'S LIKE I ALWAYS SAY: WITH A LITTLE FRIENDLINESS AND PROSOCIAL MODELING, YOU ALWAYS COME OUT ON TOP!
EXCEPT WHEN YOU'RE UP AGAINST--

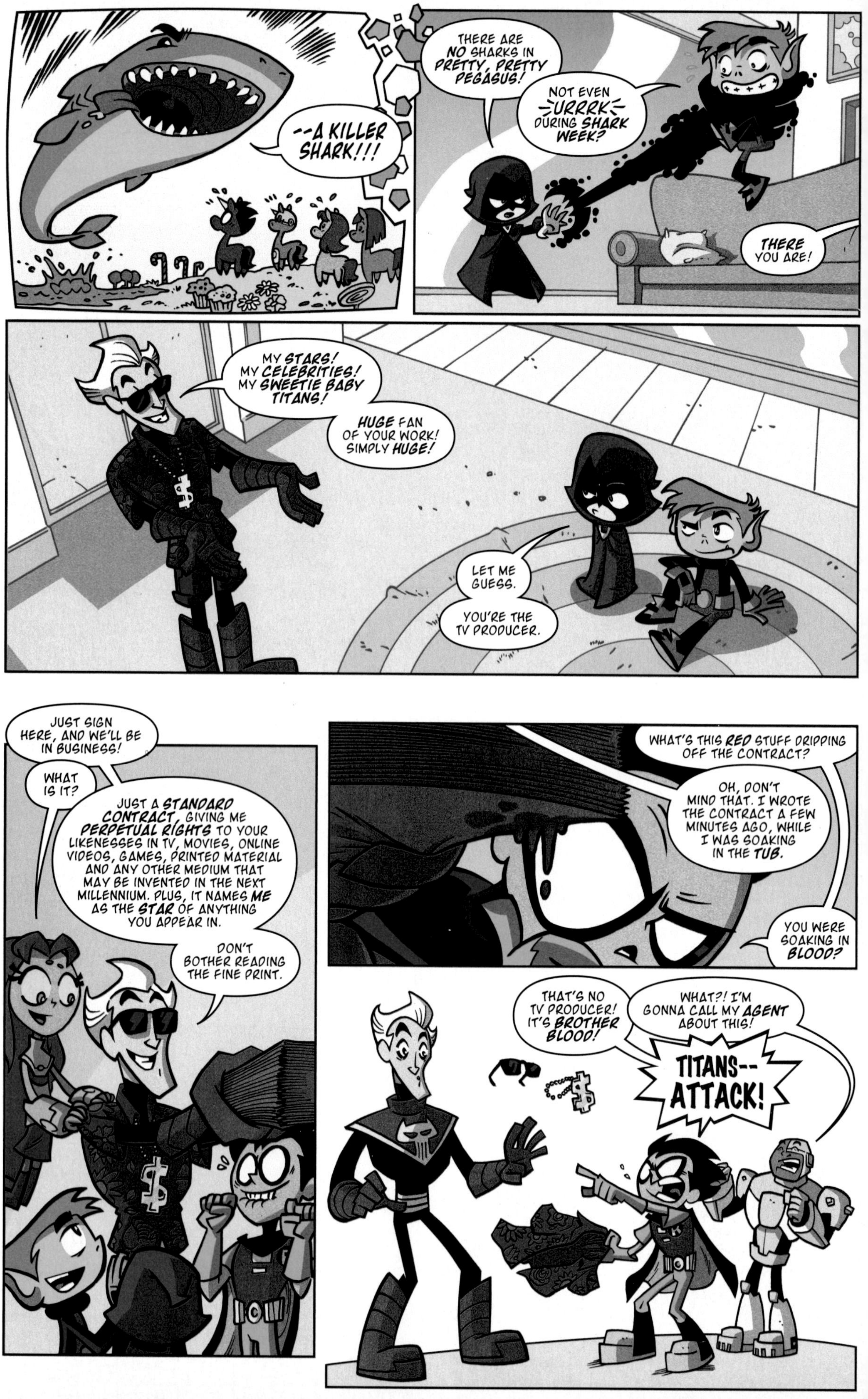
--A KILLER SHARK!!!
THERE ARE NO SHARKS IN PRETTY, PRETTY PEGASUS!
NOT EVEN URRRK DURING SHARK WEEK?
THERE YOU ARE!
MY STARS! MY CELEBRITIES! MY SWEETIE BABY TITANS!
HUGE FAN OF YOUR WORK! SIMPLY HUGE!
LET ME GUESS.
YOU'RE THE TV PRODUCER.
JUST SIGN HERE, AND WE'LL BE IN BUSINESS!
WHAT IS IT?
JUST A STANDARD CONTRACT, GIVING ME PERPETUAL RIGHTS TO YOUR LIKENESSES IN TV, MOVIES, ONLINE VIDEOS, GAMES, PRINTED MATERIAL AND ANY OTHER MEDIUM THAT MAY BE INVENTED IN THE NEXT MILLENNIUM. PLUS, IT NAMES ME AS THE STAR OF ANYTHING YOU APPEAR IN.
DON'T BOTHER READING THE FINE PRINT.
WHAT'S THIS RED STUFF DRIPPING OFF THE CONTRACT?
OH, DON'T MIND THAT. I WROTE THE CONTRACT A FEW MINUTES AGO, WHILE I WAS SOAKING IN THE TUB.
YOU WERE SOAKING IN BLOOD?
THAT'S NO TV PRODUCER! IT'S BROTHER BLOOD!
WHAT?! I'M GONNA CALL MY AGENT ABOUT THIS!
TITANS-- ATTACK!

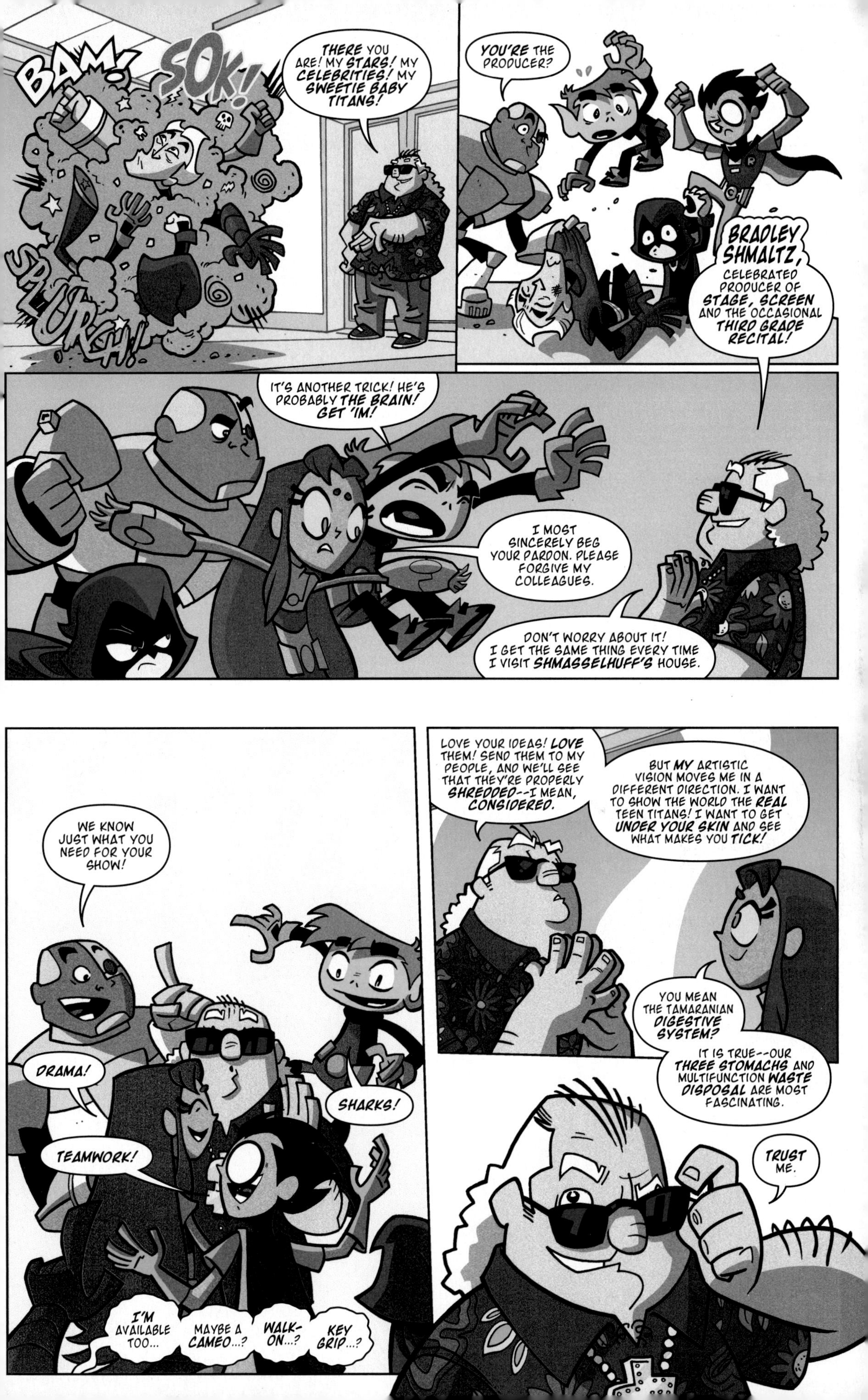
BAM!
SOK!
SPLURSH!
THERE YOU ARE! MY STARS! MY CELEBRITIES! MY SWEETIE BABY TITANS!
YOU'RE THE PRODUCER?
BRADLEY SHMALTZ, CELEBRATED PRODUCER OF STAGE, SCREEN AND THE OCCASIONAL THIRD GRADE RECITAL!
IT'S ANOTHER TRICK! HE'S PROBABLY THE BRAIN! GET 'IM!
I MOST SINCERELY BEG YOUR PARDON. PLEASE FORGIVE MY COLLEAGUES.
DON'T WORRY ABOUT IT! I GET THE SAME THING EVERY TIME I VISIT SHMASSELHUFF'S HOUSE.
WE KNOW JUST WHAT YOU NEED FOR YOUR SHOW!
DRAMA!
SHARKS!
TEAMWORK!
I'M AVAILABLE TOO...
MAYBE A CAMEO...?
WALK-ON...?
KEY GRIP...?
LOVE YOUR IDEAS! LOVE THEM! SEND THEM TO MY PEOPLE, AND WE'LL SEE THAT THEY'RE PROPERLY SHREDDED--I MEAN, CONSIDERED.
BUT MY ARTISTIC VISION MOVES ME IN A DIFFERENT DIRECTION. I WANT TO SHOW THE WORLD THE REAL TEEN TITANS! I WANT TO GET UNDER YOUR SKIN AND SEE WHAT MAKES YOU TICK!
YOU MEAN THE TAMARANIAN DIGESTIVE SYSTEM?
IT IS TRUE--OUR THREE STOMACHS AND MULTIFUNCTION WASTE DISPOSAL ARE MOST FASCINATING.
TRUST ME.

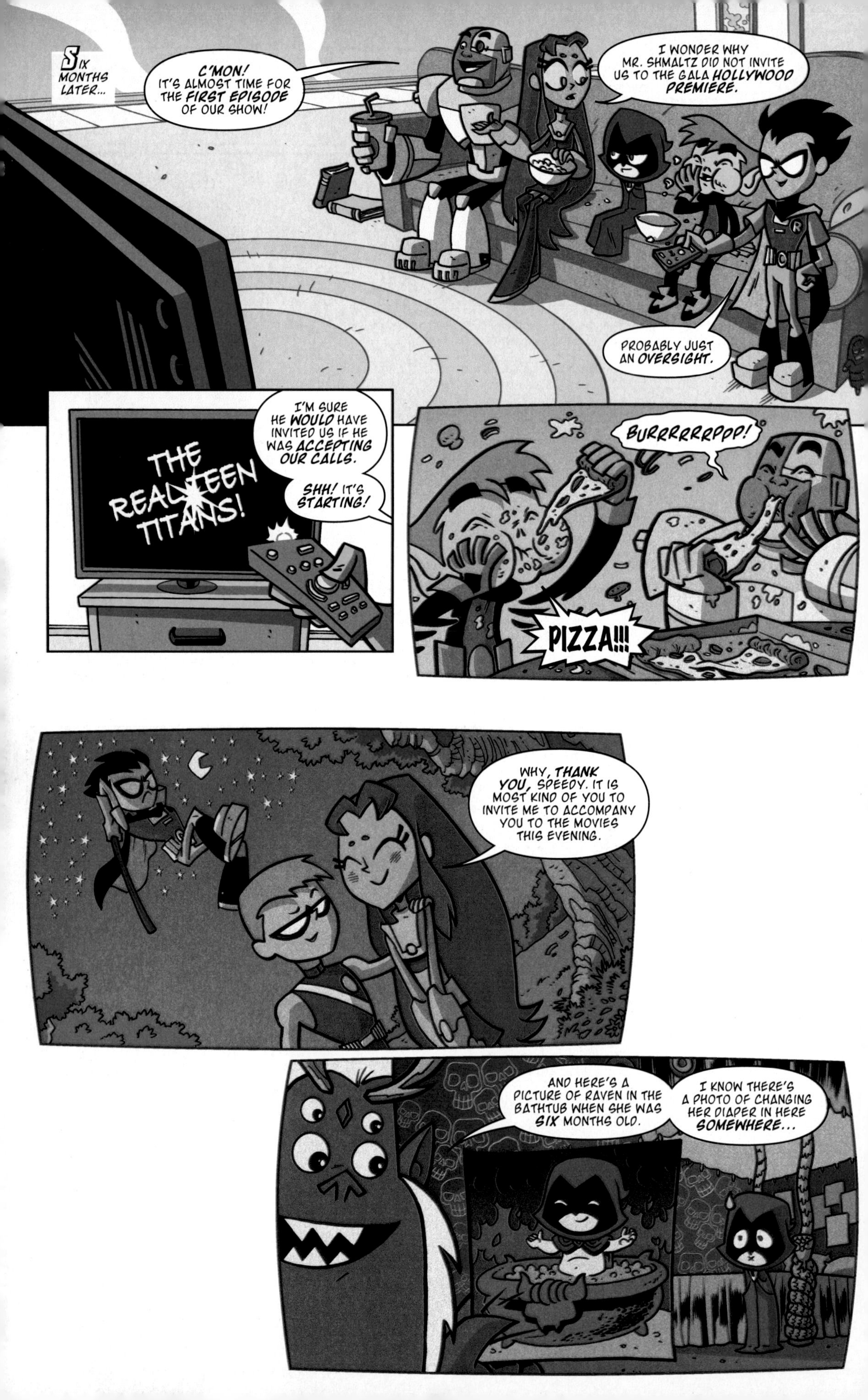
SIX MONTHS LATER...
C'MON! IT'S ALMOST TIME FOR THE FIRST EPISODE OF OUR SHOW!
I WONDER WHY MR. SHMALTZ DID NOT INVITE US TO THE GALA HOLLYWOOD PREMIERE.
PROBABLY JUST AN OVERSIGHT.
I'M SURE HE WOULD HAVE INVITED US IF HE WAS ACCEPTING OUR CALLS.
SHH! IT'S STARTING!
THE REAL TEEN TITANS!
BURRRRRRPPP!
PIZZA!!!
WHY, THANK YOU, SPEEDY. IT IS MOST KIND OF YOU TO INVITE ME TO ACCOMPANY YOU TO THE MOVIES THIS EVENING.
AND HERE'S A PICTURE OF RAVEN IN THE BATHTUB WHEN SHE WAS SIX MONTHS OLD.
I KNOW THERE'S A PHOTO OF CHANGING HER DIAPER IN HERE SOMEWHERE...

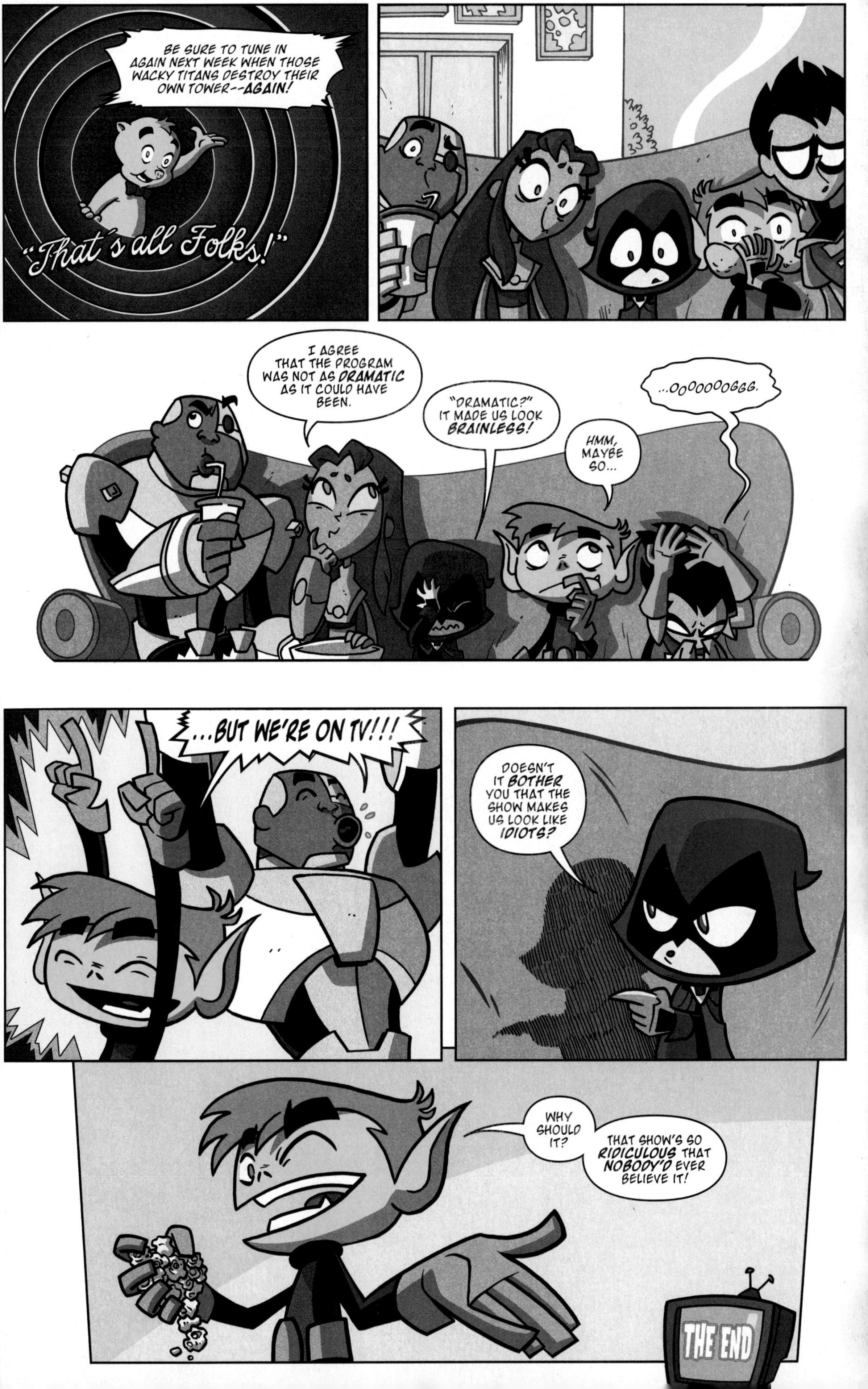
BE SURE TO TUNE IN AGAIN NEXT WEEK WHEN THOSE WACKY TITANS DESTROY THEIR OWN TOWER--AGAIN!
"That's all Folks!"
I AGREE THAT THE PROGRAM WAS NOT AS DRAMATIC AS IT COULD HAVE BEEN.
"DRAMATIC?" IT MADE US LOOK BRAINLESS!
HMM, MAYBE SO...
...OOOOOOOGGG.
...BUT WE'RE ON TV!!!
DOESN'T IT BOTHER YOU THAT THE SHOW MAKES US LOOK LIKE IDIOTS?
WHY SHOULD IT?
THAT SHOW'S SO RIDICULOUS THAT NOBODY'D EVER BELIEVE IT!
THE END

TEEN TITANS GO! #1 cover by Dan Hipp

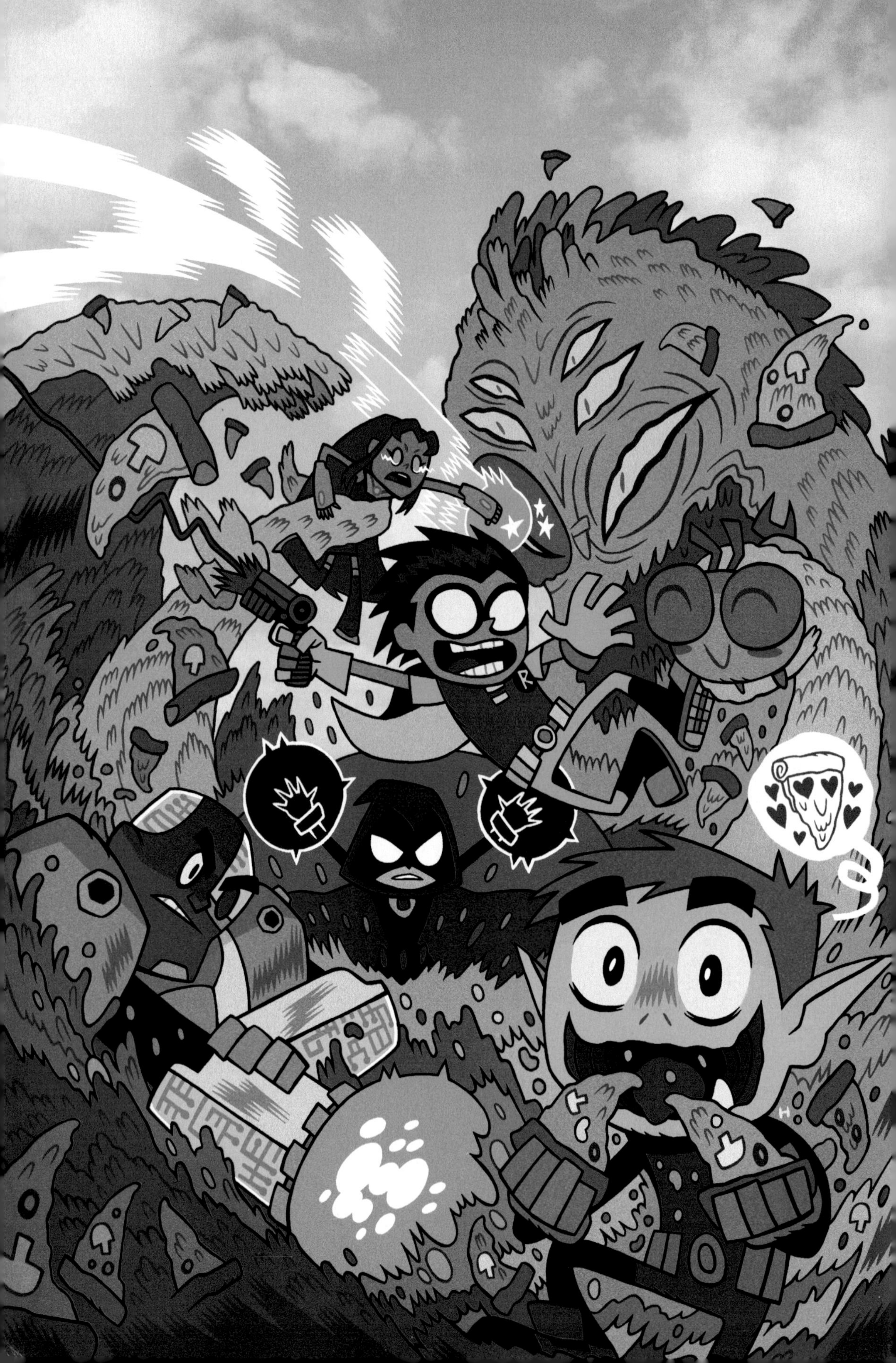

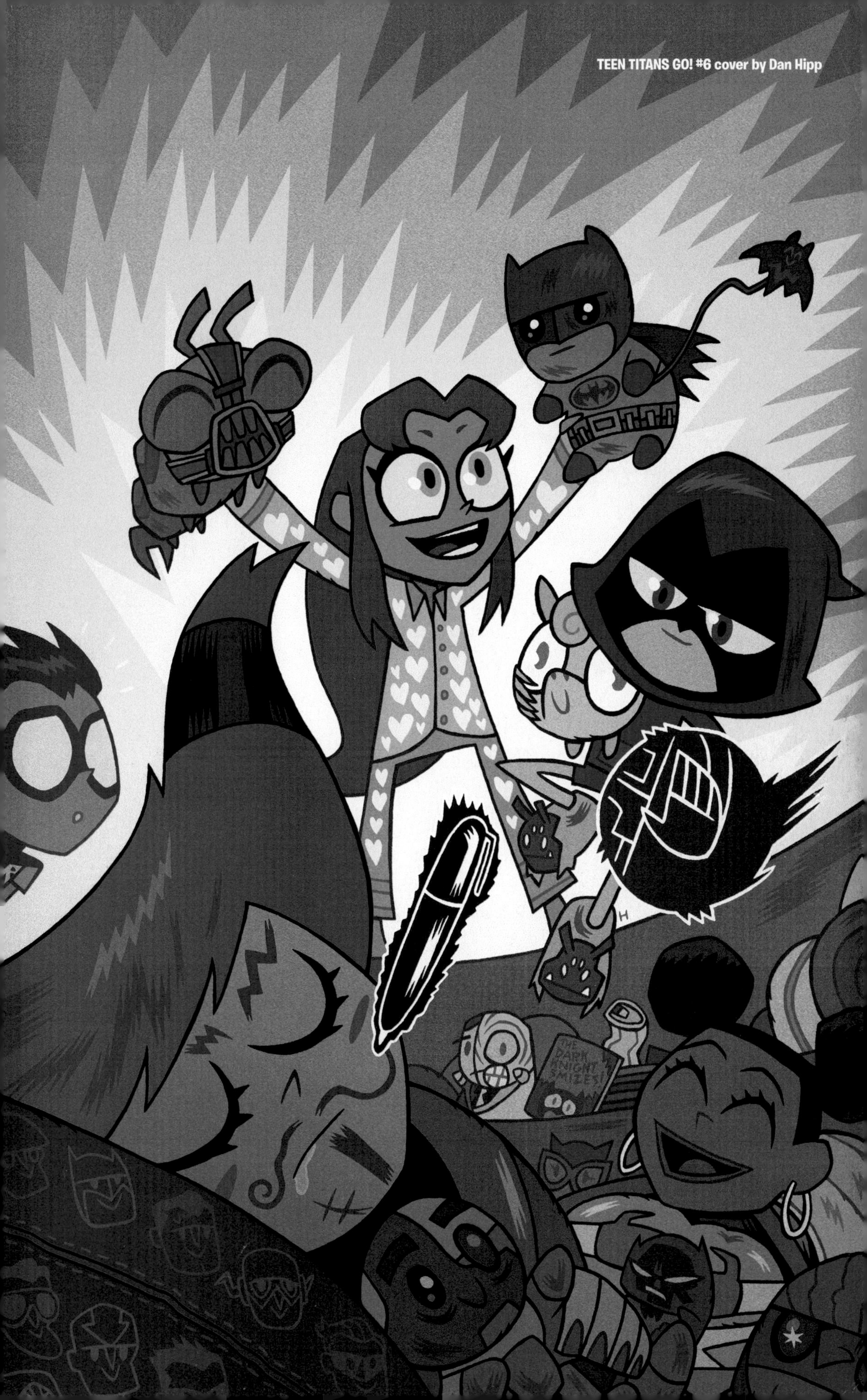
THE DARK KNIGHT SMIZES!

TEEN TITANS GO! #6 cover by Dan Hipp

TEEN TITANS GO! #11 cover by Dan Hipp

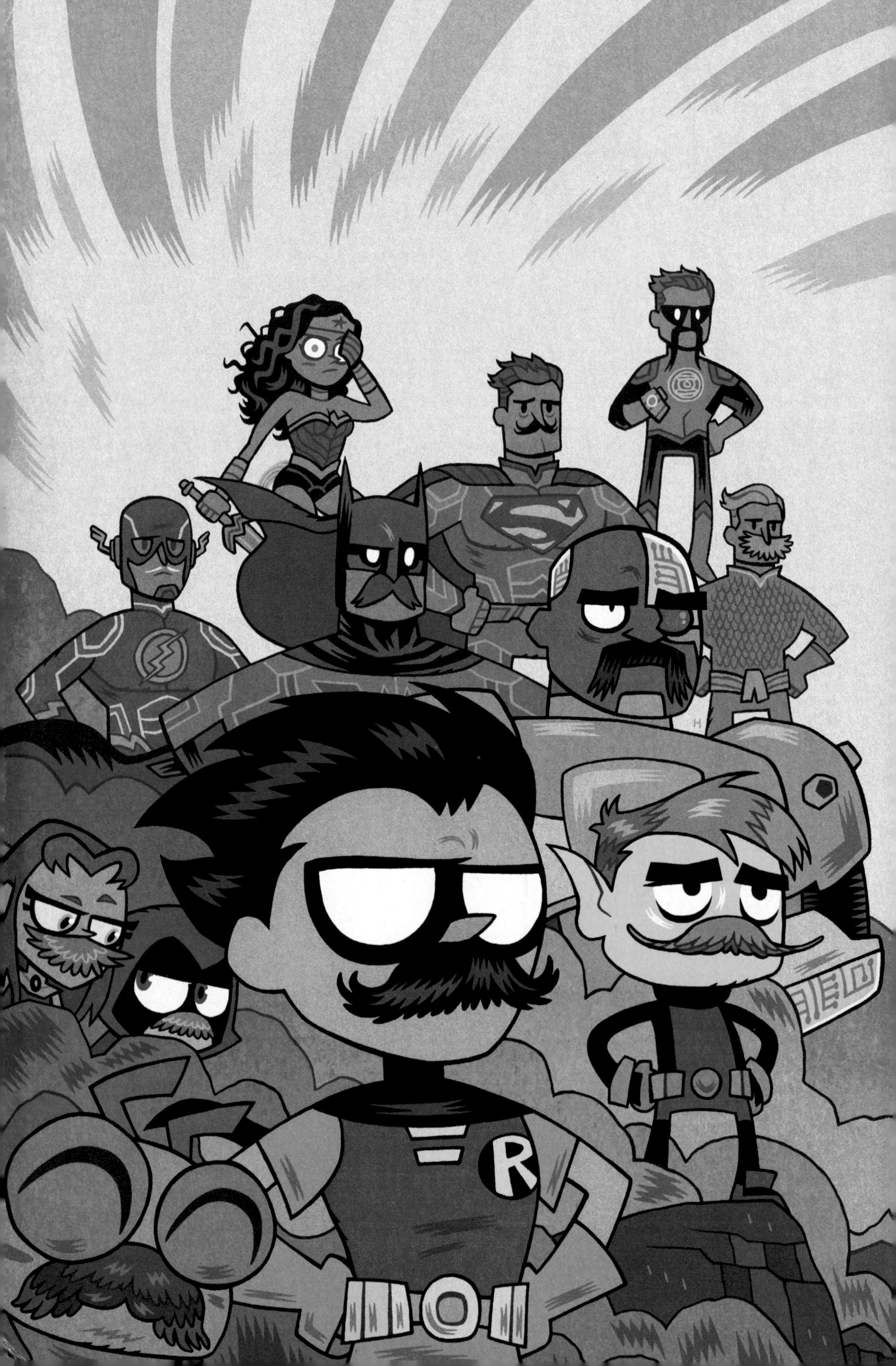
R

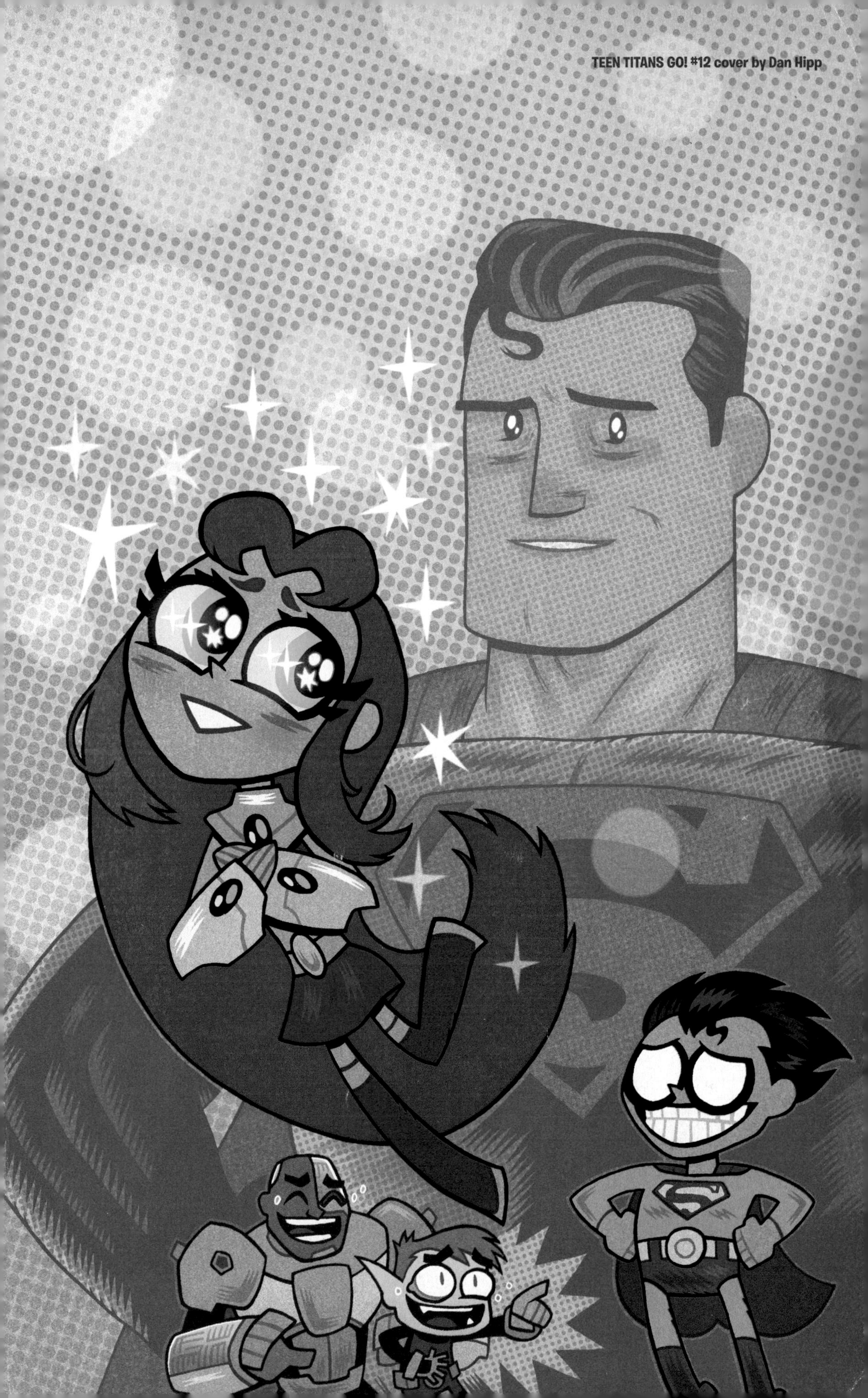

TEEN TITANS GO! #12 cover by Dan Hipp

TEEN TITANS GO! #14 cover by Dan Hipp

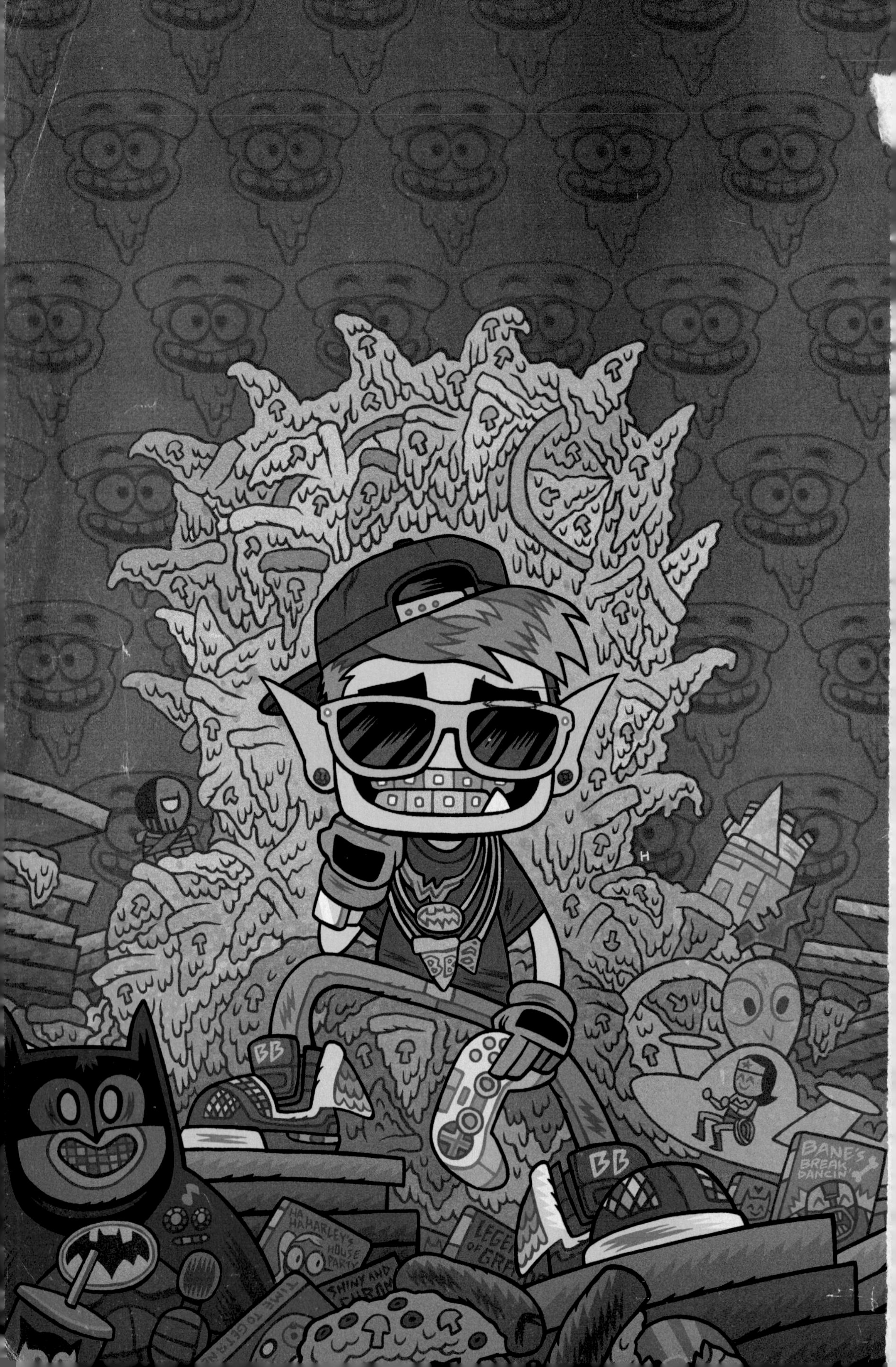
BB
BB
BB
HA HAHARLEY'S HOUSE PARTY
BANE'S BREAK DANCIN'